BREAKING
AND ENTERING

BREAKING
AND ENTERING

[A Novel]

Eileen Pollack

FOUR WAY BOOKS

TRIBECA

Please direct all inquiries to:

Editorial Office

Four Way Books

POB 535, Village Station

New York, NY 10014

www.fourwaybooks.com

Library of Congress Cataloging-in-Publication Data

Pollack, Eileen, 1956-

Breaking and entering : a novel / Eileen Pollack.

p. cm.

ISBN 978-1-935536-12-3 (acid-free paper)

1. Jewish families--Fiction. 2. Domestic fiction. I. Title.

PS3566.O4795B74 2012

813'.54--dc22

2010052238

This book is manufactured in the United States of America
and printed on acid-free paper.

Four Way Books is a not-for-profit literary press. We are grateful for the assistance we receive from
individual donors, public arts agencies, and private foundations.

This publication is made possible with public funds
from the National Endowment for the Arts

NATIONAL
ENDOWMENT
FOR THE ARTS

A great nation
deserves great art.

and from the New York State Council on the Arts, a state agency.

State of the Arts

NYSCA

Distributed by University Press of New England
One Court Street, Lebanon, NH 03766

We are a proud member of
the Council of Literary Magazines and Presses.

[clmp]

For Therese Stanton,

who has saved me so many times,

in so many ways

ONE

LOUISE'S AVALANCHE OF WOES HAD STARTED WHEN ONE OF her husband's clients, a computer engineer named Sophie Pang, managed to swallow enough of her rugby-playing housemate's painkillers to put an end to her own pain forever. Sophie's parents held Louise's husband responsible, although their anger at their daughter's insistence on living with her female "friend" rather than marrying the wealthy Chinese businessman they had picked out for her to marry was the true cause of the girl's depression.

They decided not to sue. But Richard blamed himself so unrelentingly for his client's death that Louise was afraid he would sue himself. Lots of therapists lost a client. But Richard couldn't accept his failure. To distract him from his misery, Louise left their daughter, Molly, with Louise's best friend, Imelda, and took Richard on a camping trip. But there in Colorado, priming their little stove, he accidentally set fire to the canopy of tinder-dry evergreens above their heads. As forest fires went, this one wasn't big. No one got hurt. The authorities let Richard off with a phenomenal fine, which he could cover because his father had insisted at their wedding that Richard buy something called an "umbrella liability policy," which Louise had pictured at the time as the enormous striped umbrella her father-in-law carried in his golf bag.

But after the case was settled, Richard wouldn't leave the house. He saw his older clients, but only if they drove out to the house to see him. He wouldn't spend time alone with Molly for fear he had become so accident prone he might inadvertently harm *her*. He refused to mow the lawn or use his electric saw. He wouldn't cook or light the grill. Most days, he barely got off the couch.

Louise missed the man she loved. Before he misjudged Sophie Pang's grief, before he set fire to those trees, her husband had moved through the world with an unpretentious confidence in the rightness of his diagnoses, the good will of strangers, his ability to operate nearly any machine, his talent in the kitchen, and his even greater talent in bed. After the fire, he couldn't trust anyone, least of all himself. Louise tried to get him help. She was a therapist. So was he. For a while, he saw a colleague who specialized in trauma. Then Richard muttered a perfunctory "This isn't doing any good" and stopped keeping his appointments. A psychiatrist friend prescribed the obvious medications, but Richard refused to take them. "Just what I need, to be even less clear-headed than

I am." Month after month, Louise waited for his confidence to come back. But it was like waiting for your wallet to be returned; the longer time went on, the less likely you were to recover it, and even if you did, something valuable would be missing.

For better or worse. Of course. But the worse wouldn't seem to end. She tried to convince Richard that no one was saying anything behind his back except that he was taking his client's suicide too much to heart and blaming himself too harshly for the fire. But he refused to spend *another fucking hour* listening to patients who believed their spouses owed them top-of-the-line BMWs or two-hundred-thousand-dollar kitchens. When he decided they had to move, Louise couldn't find the heart to argue. They were going under financially, and she was worried for Richard's health. He had a cousin in southwest Michigan, and this cousin had a friend who worked at the penitentiary in a city called Potawatomie and swore good jobs there were going begging. Richard's doctoral dissertation had been in forensic psych. With credentials like that, he could enter the system as a Psychologist P11 and rocket up from there.

And so she agreed to move. While their friends and neighbors cried and waved goodbye, she stood in their driveway strangely numb, as if she and Richard and Molly had been trapped beneath a landslide and her only hope of saving them was cutting off a limb. She didn't want to be disloyal. Besides, she still loved Richard. And she couldn't bear to think of Molly living in California while her father lived in Michigan.

"We'll be starting over, both of us," Richard said, and even though Louise wasn't sure why *she* needed to start over, she was determined to make the best of things. She would find new friends in Potawatomie. Molly would grow up in a place where kids rode their bikes to school and didn't judge each other by the cars their parents owned and it didn't take two struggling therapists every penny they earned and every minute of their attention not to fall so far behind in the expectations they had to meet and the distances they had to drive that they flew off the treadmill on which they were forever trotting and went careening into space.

But in the six months since they moved, Louise hasn't made a single friend, unless you count the construction workers who show up every morning and tease her about how much she and her husband overpaid for their house. She has sent applications to every junior high and high school within a hundred miles of their town, but until now she hasn't gotten a single interview. She had nearly lost hope when the director of special ed for the Potawatomie public schools called to say they had an opening. Louise was overjoyed. She was wildly overqualified for the job and figured she would be a shoo-in. She would meet people who liked to read. Music teachers. Artists. She just needed to give things time. Richard would get his courage back. Their marriage would regain its spark.

And so, on this dreary day in March, she has driven to Potawatomie, where she turns in the high school lot and parks in a spot marked VISITORS, hoping that the next time she comes here, she might park in the lot for STAFF. Bowing to the wheel, she offers the sort of prayer a person offers before an interview for a job that might save her life. She locks the van, then stands in the misty chill looking up at the building she hopes to work in. POTAWATOMIE HIGH SCHOOL, SOUTHWEST MICHIGAN FOOTBALL CHAMPIONS, 1990 – 91. It reminds her of the school she attended in upstate New York, a Gothic W.P.A. brick-and-mortar fortress, which, unlike her parents' house, seemed remarkably solid, not to mention that it was supervised by adults who, unlike her parents, seemed to have her best interests at heart.

She pushes open the metal doors, with their grid of wire diamonds embedded in the glass, and immediately she feels at home. She once read that dogs can sniff out the ingredients of a baking cake, and as remarkable as that feat seems, Louise is certain she can identify every separate smell in the corridor of a high school—the wet-sheep musk of drying sweaters, the boyish bravado of Brut and Old Spice, the zest of rotting gym socks, the hunger-inducing scent of cinnamon toast from home ec, and the cheerfully industrious tang of sawdust and oil from shop. She trots up the stairs and runs her fingers along the lockers. The gargantuan trophies in the display case are topped with brass-plated players almost large enough to be the real teenage boys who won them. *Please,* she prays, *let me get this job. Let me walk down these halls to my office and spend the morning listening to whatever students need me. Let me unfold my sandwich in the lunchroom and talk to the other grown-ups about whatever happened in the news the night before. Let me pick up my daughter from a decent school and take her home to an orderly, well-lit house. Let my husband come to bed and make love to me the way he used to.*

She ducks in the bathroom, and her throat immediately freezes from the dizzying stench of hairspray. (Could the girls in Potawatomie still be using hairspray?) Thankfully, no one else is there. In California, her fine skin and high cheekbones, blue eyes, and long blonde hair seemed nice but unremarkable. She isn't really young—she just turned thirty-nine, and whenever Molly draws her portrait, she sketches laugh-lines shooting like rays from her mother's eyes—yet here in Potawatomie everything about her seems flashy and too expensive, like a pair of too-new shoes.

She smoothes her hair and puts on lipstick, then goes out and finds the office, which she enters with a tentative but unnecessary knock. Behind the counter, the receptionist springs up, a small, frail older woman, so fair Louise can see the blue veins and pink capillaries branching beneath her skin. The mere act of greeting Louise ignites a rash across her chest.

"I have an appointment with Mrs. Moorehouse," Louise says. "The director of Special Education?"

"Mrs. Shapiro? Oh, yes. Mrs. Moorehouse asked if you could wait. There's been a little difficulty. One of our instructors, Mrs. Krauspe, sometimes has a bit of trouble controlling . . . Well, you know how it is with special ed." The receptionist flops open her hands to show how helpless everyone is when it comes to special ed. Around her wrist hangs a colorful ribbon stitched with letters Louise can't quite make out. "May I get you something hot to drink?"

Ordinarily, Louise wouldn't risk dribbling coffee on her blouse. But she slept so poorly the night before. "Yes, thank you," she says, "that would be wonderful."

While the receptionist—her nameplate reads BEVERLY BOOTH—fiddles with the coffee machine, Louise studies the photos taped to the wall above her desk, row after row of wallet-size graduation portraits, the kids' shaggy hair and sideburns indicating they are now Louise's age, if not older. Below the photos sits an impressive collection of Beanie Babies; Louise has counted sixty-four of the stuffed creatures when the receptionist hands her a mug printed with the motto HOME IS WHERE THE HEART IS and the picture of a mouse curled up in a heart-shaped candy box. "This is great," Louise says, although the coffee is watery and barely warm.

A trio of students tumble in. "Hey there, Mrs. B!" All three students—a girl and two boys—wear those same lettered bracelets, and Louise wonders if they belong to some club and Mrs. Booth serves as their advisor.

"Guess what we found?" The girl holds out a small stuffed rabbit.

"Ears the Bunny! I thought he wasn't due out for another week." Mrs. Booth wags a finger. "I've told you, you mustn't buy me gifts." But Louise can understand why they want to please her; it has something to do with the way happiness plays so clearly across her face. Louise wants to please her, too. "Just don't do it again," the receptionist warns, and the students make their promises and tumble out, after which Beverly Booth asks Louise if it's true that she comes from California. An image of her house in San Rafael and the mountain behind it, which Louise loves to climb with her friend Imelda, flashes through her mind, and her longing for all three—the house, the view, the friend—nearly makes her ill. "I wasn't born there," she explains. She grew up in a tiny town several hundred miles north of New York City, went to college at SUNY Binghamton, then got her master's in social work from Cornell. But yes, before moving to Potawatomie she lived in Marin County, just north of San Francisco.

Beverly Booth smiles ruefully. "My baby brother lives in San Francisco. He was one of those flower-power people who dropped out in the sixties. We didn't hear one solitary word from him for twenty-three years. Then out of the wild blue yonder he sends us a card. He runs a business there, he says. Something to do with balloons. But we haven't given up hope he'll move back home."

Louise stifles the urge to suggest that the brother might now consider San Francisco his home. How can she, when his absence still darkens his sister's eyes? It comes to her that Midwesterners resent California so much because California is the place their loved ones drift, the way, if you were to let go one of those balloons Beverly's brother sells, it would float to the clouds and vanish.

The receptionist forces herself to brighten. "Do you have any children? There's an ice-cream social every June. The older students set up booths to entertain the younger ones and raise money for the school. Your children would have a wonderful time, and you and your husband could get a head start on meeting all of us."

Louise hadn't wanted to move to Michigan. But how can she not be happy living in a town that still has ice-cream socials and warm-hearted women like Beverly Booth?

"And I *must* introduce you to our librarian." The woman claps her hands like a child. "Janet Cohen. Such a cultured, sweet person. You two will get along like fleas."

It dawns on Louise that Beverly Booth, like most people she has met in Michigan, assumes she is a Jew. She wants to say that her husband is the Shapiro, while she was born a Heinz, a name she was all too ready to relinquish, associated as it was with ketchup and her parents. But disabusing people of the notion that she's Jewish feels more like a betrayal here than it did in California.

The door opens, and Louise steps aside to allow the entrance of a thin, severe woman in a tailored gray suit.

"Oh, here's Mrs. Moorehouse now. Mrs. Moorehouse? This is Mrs. Shapiro. She's here for her interview. For the social worker's job?"

Having worked in schools on both coasts, Louise expects special ed directors to be untidy, warm, and round. But her interviewer is prim and ramrod straight, with close-cropped black hair and a small but glittering diamond cross around her neck.

"Do come in." She ushers Louise into an office so devoid of decoration it seems a symptom of some emotional anorexia. "Why don't we begin with where you did your training?"

Relieved, Louise recites the answers she prepared the night before. After a short discussion in which Mrs. Moorehouse verifies that Louise has indeed received the proper certification to work in Michigan—Louise takes this as a sign that the interview is going well—Mrs. Moorehouse lobs her a question that Louise is certain she can smash back for a winner. "We have a very diverse student body," Mrs. Moorehouse says. "Or rather, it's more diverse than most cities our size in Michigan. Because of the prison. You know about the prison, don't you?"

Louise does know; her husband works there. Many of the inmates are black or Hispanic men from Lansing and Detroit. Often, when these men get out, they stay in Potawatomie, which has led to the assumption that any black or Hispanic man living in Potawatomie has to be a criminal. According to Richard, most of the black and Hispanic families actually moved here to pick onions in the onion fields or work in the city's factories, which produce canned onion-rings and twine. Besides, most of the inmates at the prison are white.

But Louise doubts her interviewer wants to hear such facts. Instead, she launches into a description of the Asian and Latino kids she counseled in San Francisco and the poor white and Native American students with whom she did her training in northern New York. She tells Mrs. Moorehouse how especially proud she is of the way she handles "issues of sexuality."

Mrs. Moorehouse shifts in her chair. "I am afraid that is a very complicated question." She places two fingers to her necklace. "Coming from where you do—" Louise wonders if she means this in the sense of sixties slang—*I know where you're coming from*—then realizes she means the phrase literally. "Coming from where you do, you might make the wrong assumptions." She does something with her hands that reminds Louise of the rhyme about the steeple and the church. "Our students experience the same conflicts as the students you have encountered in other venues. But the

9

framework within which they view these same conflicts . . . One of our young ladies was absolutely *convinced* that a certain male teacher had sent his demons to possess her." She laughs crisply, although Louise isn't sure if she is laughing at the student or at any social worker who might try to disabuse the girl of such ideas. "And a student who comes to you tormented by gender-identification issues . . . you mustn't assume that he or she wants your assistance in *releasing* those desires."

Mrs. Moorehouse waits for Louise's response. Naturally, Louise knows she needs to respect her students' beliefs. But how could she not suggest to a teenage girl that her delight in a man's appearance isn't necessarily the Devil's tool?

"And teenage pregnancy . . . I am sure you are accustomed to offering a great many choices for a young woman to consider. But even to present such a possibility might instigate her parents' calling for your dismissal."

Clearly, Mrs. Moorehouse is giving Louise a chance to show she understands the restrictions under which she will be required to practice her profession. She is desperate for this job. But how can she lie to get it? "Of course," Louise says, "a social worker's role isn't to persuade a pregnant teenage girl to consider an abortion. The girl's wishes, and her parents' wishes—"

"Wishes! What have wishes to do with . . . If a woman is lucky enough to conceive a human life—" The phone rings. "Excuse me." She picks up the receiver. "Oh no. No! She didn't." She closes her eyes and rubs them, signaling a frustration that Louise guesses has much to do with Mrs. Krauspe. "I am afraid I am going to have to cut our meeting short. I do *so* hope you will find living in Potawatomie a pleasant change. We *will* be in touch."

She holds out her hand, which is as cool and dry as rope,

but Louise hates to let it go. Mrs. Moorehouse leads her back to the reception area and leaves Louise to the comforting ministrations of Beverly Booth.

Who guesses that the interview has not gone well. "Would you like another cup of coffee?"

Louise waves off the offer but can't bring herself to leave. "Do you mind if I ask what it says on your bracelet?"

"This?" The receptionist looks fondly at her wrist. "W. W. J. D. Just a friendly reminder to help me get through my day."

What would Jesus do. Her friends in California would have busted out laughing, but Louise feels like begging to join the club. Not that she believes in Jesus. Her parents raised her to think that people turn to God because they are too frightened or irrational to make their own decisions. And after thirteen years of marriage to a husband whose father and uncle barely escaped the Nazis, she can recite the entire litany of crimes committed in Jesus' name. Yet she can't help but think how convenient it would be to be able to resolve every conflict in her life by considering what a man who lived two thousand years earlier would or would not have done.

"Good luck, dear," Mrs. Booth says, at which Louise musters a smile and backs out in the hall.

Where a bell clamors and releases hundreds of shiny new adults who flutter and swarm around her. A mob of adolescent girls in choir uniforms come bursting around a corner. A ring of ninth-grade boys push an older boy against his locker until he throws up his hands and says, "Fuck you! I *said* I'm sorry!"

How could anyone not want to work in such a place? Even the kids who pretend they don't give a shit actually care so much—about failing a course or getting cut from a team or losing a parent's love—they will contemplate violence toward themselves rather than live with their disappointment. Louise has befriended students everyone assumed were headed for the gallows, and these same students later sent her cards to say they were going in the army or getting out of rehab or earning their G.E.D.s. Her friends pity her for scraping by on such pathetic pay. *You could do anything,* they insist, which yes, she supposes she could. But she would miss the kids too much.

She gazes wistfully at the last few stragglers. One punked-out girl has the most adorable prairie-dog face, with hair the color of the cherry hard-sauce you can get your cone dipped in at a Dairy Queen. The girl stands talking to an equally appealing boy with a tufted haircut that makes his head resemble a vegetable scrubber. Louise knows she ought to leave. It's a Friday afternoon, and Richard has grudgingly agreed to come home early and stay with Molly. Louise doesn't want to push her luck. But she has no desire to leave this building, which feels more welcoming and familiar than anywhere else in Michigan.

She ducks in the cafeteria, with its comforting stench of meatballs and marinara, ammonia, ice cream sandwiches, and warm, waxy milk. A custodian is sweeping up; crumpled napkins, pizza crusts, candy wrappers, and plastic straws bubble up ahead of his broom like foam before a boat. The doors at the far end burst open and a gang of boys chase each other in, weaving and feinting. Two of the boys are black, but they let the white kids take the lead.

"Hey, Korny!" This from the tallest boy, whose newly deepened voice rebounds from the walls and floor. "Yeah, I'm talking to you."

The custodian is a sad-looking man with slumped shoulders, thinning hair, and a face weighted by a heavy brown moustache that resembles a smaller version of the broom.

"What you said on that radio show of yours?" The boy motions to the black kids, who hang back by the bleachers. "We didn't like it, okay? They're our teammates. If they don't play, neither do we." He and the other white kids close in around the janitor. "We're not scared of you *or* your stupid friends." The boy grabs the rag from the janitor's pocket and snaps it against his face. From Louise's teenage years, which she spent working as a chambermaid at Imelda's parents' hotel, she knows exactly how sour a rag like that can smell. She wants to intervene, but what authority does she have? She assumes the janitor is the announcer for some sports show on which he has made derogatory remarks about the black kids. But the man is so badly outnumbered and so pitifully slow Louise finds it difficult not to take his side.

"Hey, Korny! Over here!" The boys, in a circle, taunt him. Louise waits for the janitor to raise his broom and fight his way out, or to threaten the whole crew with detention. But he makes no move to defend himself. Only when the boys toss his rag above his head in a game of janitor-in-the middle does he finally speak up.

"Give me that!" Such a resonant, commanding voice has no business coming from such a dumpy, downtrodden man. Even the boys seem startled, although surely they have heard the voice before.

The boy who holds the rag tosses it at the janitor's feet. "No hard feelings, right? We were just having a little fun. We're grateful to you, Mike, for keeping this place so clean."

The janitor snatches up the rag. Louise finds herself hoping he might come up with some rejoinder. Beneath the heavy moustache, his fleshy lips work. But he resumes pushing the broom in the same direction he was headed in before the boys came in. Louise presses her spine against the door to let the boys leave, then watches the janitor's back as he clears another swath of floor. When he reaches the far wall and arcs his broom toward her, he seems startled to discover that his disgrace has had a witness and shoots her such an intimidating stare she steps back in the hall.

Dazed, she wanders the school, not noticing much of anything until she finds herself in front of a display of Native American history. Someone has constructed a miniature Potawatomi village, complete with little Lego Indians and cardboard canoes. According to a report taped to the glass: *When the white man arrived, the Potawatomi were settled around the area now known as Green Bay, Wisconsin, but later came to dominate a region that extended to western Michigan, Indiana, and Illinois.* On the back of the display hangs a silhouette of the war chief Pontiac, whom Louise recognizes as the high school mascot. She is wondering if any Potawatomis still live in Michigan when a short, sallow woman with curly black hair comes up behind her. She reminds Louise of Molly, an impression made even more unsettling by the woman's being pregnant.

"Is something wrong? Is it the display? Or are you the mother who called about the book I gave your son?"

Oh no, Louise says, she isn't here to complain. She came to see Mrs. Moorehouse about a job, and the receptionist, Mrs. Booth, suggested she stop by the library and introduce herself.

The woman's face changes. "Beverly! Yes. She's very nice. Does that mean you'll be joining us on staff?"

Louise startles herself by bursting into tears. Then she feels obliged to tell the woman what happened in the interview.

The librarian pats her arm. "I shouldn't really say this, but you're probably better off. This is a difficult place for . . . people like us to work. I haven't given notice yet, but my husband just got a job in Ann Arbor, and I'll be working there part-time.

I guess I got tired of defending *Catcher in the Rye* and Judy Blume." She leans closer. "Three of the five biology teachers in this school are creationists, if that tells you anything."

Louise glances around to see if anyone is listening—she has never worked in a place where you needed to look over your shoulder before speaking to a colleague. "There was this janitor in the cafeteria? The students were ganging up on him." The account comes out jumbled, but the librarian seems to understand.

"Oh, yes, the custodian. That's Mike Korn. He has this awful radio show." A trio of teachers ambles by and the librarian waits until they have passed. "You could move to Ann Arbor. You could get a good job there."

The idea seems tempting. She and Molly could have a nice life in Ann Arbor. Richard could spend the week in Potawatomie and commute to Ann Arbor on weekends. But she hates the idea of Molly seeing her dad so rarely. And to be honest, she doesn't want to leave the house they bought in Stickney Springs, a quaint, quiet town a few miles east of Potawatomie. The house is a beautiful old Victorian, and she and Richard already have spent nearly sixty thousand dollars gutting and rebuilding it. She loves this house more than any house she has ever lived in, even their house in San Rafael. Besides, moving to Ann Arbor seems the coward's way out. She has lived most of her life in college towns—Ithaca first, then Berkeley. What kind of person can only survive in a college town? How can she consider herself too good to live in a working-class city like Potawatomie, coming as she does from Mule's Neck, New York, where her father earned his living renting rowboats and selling worms?

The librarian makes Louise promise she will visit her in Ann Arbor, where she will be working in the children's room of the main library. Then she pats her belly as if it's the reference book that holds all the information about her life. "Although at some point, you know, I'll be taking time off."

On the drive back to Stickney Springs, Louise considers setting up a private practice. But that would require furnishing an office, establishing ties to other therapists so they could refer their overflow to her, and then waiting months, if not years, for word to get around. Just thinking of all that work leaves her so exhausted she nearly closes her eyes.

Then she drives up and sees her house. She has wanted to live in a yellow house since she was Molly's age. In fact, this is the exact yellow house she always wished to live in. Daffodils line the front walk, their fronds extending up and out like a diva's arms, heads thrown back, exuberant, their frilly orange mouths trumpeting in song. The clapboards are a delicate shade of yellow paler than the daffs, with gingerbread along the eaves. She doesn't have the vocabulary to describe the structures atop the roof. Gables? Turrets? Dormers? (*Froufrou*, Richard calls it, although he loves the house as much as she does.) It's a beauty of a house. If not for missing Imelda and wishing Richard were better company, Louise might be content. She is lonely, that's all. They have no neighbors except Matt Banks and his mother, who live on the farm next door, and whoever owns the shabby bungalow down the road (having grown up in such a bungalow, Louise tends to associate it with eccentrics like her parents). A few yards beyond the bungalow rises the shabby wood steeple of the Joyful Noise Church and beyond that runs a gravel road marked WOLVERINE SPORTSMANS CLUB KEEP OUT.

None of this would have mattered if she could have gone inside their house and found Richard playing with their daughter, wrestling with her, tickling her, the way Molly has always loved. Instead, she finds Richard lying on the couch reading *Field and Stream*, an odd choice, given that he has never held a gun or caught a fish.

"Where's Molly?" she asks.

"Who? She's in the yard."

"She's outside by herself?" They never let her play alone in California. Not that she ever wanted to; Molly is the kind of child who prefers to stay in view. She is older now, and there's less traffic on Stickney Road. But it strikes Louise as odd that Richard, who until recently was so frightened for her safety that he didn't trust himself to watch her, now allows their daughter to play outside with no one watching her at all.

"That was before," Richard says. "After we moved here, I saw how much we'd been sheltering her. She doesn't know how to do anything for herself."

Louise goes to the window and is relieved to see Molly sitting on a stump reading a piece of paper. Still, she isn't about to let Richard off so easily. "Aren't you going to ask how the interview went?" Over his shoulder, she can see he is studying an ad in which two men stand in a stream up to their chests in rubber boots.

"Judging by your expression, I would say you blew it."

"You're blaming me?"

"You're not even trying to fit in here."

Not trying? She has just spent an entire afternoon ingratiating herself with people who believe that the only choice for a homosexual is to spend his life in the closet. She tells Richard what Janet Cohen said about the creationists. She tells him about the custodian who hosts a racist talk show.

"You think everyone in the Midwest is narrow-minded. But they could say the same about you."

"I do not think the entire Midwest—"

"What good is it being a social worker if you're only willing to work with people who are the same as you?"

She is so harried and exhausted this almost makes sense. "So it's okay that Molly's teachers are going to tell her that God created the universe in seven days?"

"Our daughter has a good mind. I don't think she'll have any trouble figuring out what to think about Creation. Which, by the way, took six days, not seven."

It seems too tiring to consider what their daughter might or might not make of the theory of evolution in a biology class she might or might not attend ten years down the road. All Louise knows is that she's starving, which means Molly is starving, too. She has no idea what they can eat. The kitchen is a shambles—the old appliances have been torn out and the new ones haven't yet arrived. This far from Potawatomie, you can't get a pizza delivered. So far, they've eaten most of their meals in restaurants, which, in this part of the state, means eating at Bill Knapp's, Elias Big Boy, Denny's, Ponderosa, and Old Country Buffet. Louise is sick of eating out, and she doesn't want to get in the van and drive back to Potawatomie. The mom-and-pop grocery store in Stickney Springs closed an hour ago. All they have in the house is a jar of peanut butter, a pack of saltines, a can of Spanish olives, and a pouch of Tang.

"I'll fix us something," she says, hoping Richard will come up with a better idea, which he doesn't. Smearing the peanut butter on the crackers and stirring the Tang in water takes only a few minutes. She sets this feast on paper plates on the upturned cardboard box they are using as a table. "Molly!" she calls. "Come in, sweetie! Dinner!"

And in Molly runs, waving the piece of paper she was reading on the stump. Despite her dark hair, she has translucent vanilla skin and the flat, triangular nose of a rabbit. Louise thinks she is adorable, but sometimes she gets the sense strangers don't share her opinion.

"Mom? People in our town think it's all right to kill a baby. Who could think *that*?"

The images on the paper are such a blur Louise can barely make them out. She only hopes Molly thinks the pictures show a tiny curled-up doll being extracted from a purse by a pair of kitchen tongs and, in the second photo, that same doll lying broken in the trash. Unfortunately, the words beneath the photos are all too clear: PEOPLE WHO THINK ITS ALL RIGHT TO KILL BABIES LIVE RIGHT HERE IN STICKNEY SPRINGS.

She asks Molly where she got the paper, and Molly says someone must have dropped a whole bunch of them because they're blowing around *everywhere*. Louise looks at the sheet again. At the bottom is a schedule for the April 1995 Easter week activities at the Joyful Noise Church.

She hands the sheet to Richard, who glances at it before placing it beside his plate. "Yeah. Not real subtle. But she could have found garbage like this in any city in America." He eats a few saltines. Finally, he sighs and says, "Molly, sweetheart, the people who wrote this paper are talking about some very grownup things. It's nothing a kid needs to worry about."

Molly doesn't usually let her questions go unanswered, but she must sense that the answer to this particular question isn't something she actually wants to know. "This is a very good dinner," she announces, licking peanut butter from her thumb.

To change the mood, Louise mentions that she is planning to paint Molly's room the next day, at which Molly claps and says, "Really? I get to sleep there? Can I pick the color?"

Louise tells her she has to wait until the paint is dry, but yes, in another day or two, Molly will be able to sleep in her very own room.

"I hope you're not hinting I should help paint it," Richard says.

Well, Louise thinks, what if she is? Since they moved to Michigan, he hasn't done a thing to help. And it isn't because he doesn't know how. Unlike Louise's father, whom she once needed to instruct on how to operate a pencil sharpener, Richard can take apart any appliance, wiggle this and tighten that, then put everything back together so it works. That's one thing she has always loved about him, how competent he is. But since moving to Stickney Springs, he has left all the repairs to her. And because Louise barely knows a regular screwdriver from a Phillips head, she has been forced to hire workers for every job, the house filling up with plumbers, masons, plasterers, electricians and their assistants at a sorcerer's apprentice rate. The previous owner wired the house himself and none of the work is up to code. The shiny maize-and-blue paint he used in the living room was intended for boats and cars and couldn't be painted over; every single wall needed to be re-plastered. The electrician took so long to finish the rewiring (even now, his assistant is futzing around with some minor task Louise doesn't understand) that the plasterers were delayed, which caused Louise to lose the painting crew. She could have waited another month until the painters were able to fit them in, but the renovations have dragged on so long she is impatient to get the job done and is painting the interior walls herself. "I *could* use some help," she tells Richard.

He flicks the cracker crumbs from his lap. "Do you want a husband or a handyman? Because I've never been quite sure. Would you have married me if I hadn't been so good with tools?"

They sit glaring at each other from either side of a

cardboard box set with paper plates. Everything seems so flimsy, one good kick could send the entire marriage flying. But where would she be then? She could take Molly back to California, but what would they do once they got there? On their camping trips, Richard is the one who reads the maps. Leaving him now would be like trying to find her way home with the sun going down, no compass or trail to follow . . . and no home at the other end.

He grabs the last saltine. "I'm going next door to talk to Matt. The steelheads are running, and he wants me to help him test out some new rods and reels before we head up north next weekend."

And then he is gone, leaving Louise to wonder what kind of fish steelheads are and whether he expects her to gut and clean the ones he brings home. Not that she doesn't know how. She must have cleaned hundreds of fish for her father's customers. But if Richard isn't going to help her paint Molly's room, Louise isn't going to help him gut and cook his stupid steelheads.

Molly sips her Tang. "What do you always do that makes Daddy so angry?"

And even though Louise knows Molly doesn't really mean the fight was her fault, the question she has asked, like the question of whether a person approves of killing babies, can't even be given voice without making the person who has been accused feel guilty of the crime.

The next morning, Louise tries to put her disastrous interview behind her. She will find something else she can do, some other position to apply for.

But first she is going to paint her daughter's room.

Up and down she rolls the roller, watching the irregularities smooth themselves to a shiny light-peach coat. A little after noon, Richard shuffles in and offers to paint the ceiling. Hiding her surprise, she hands him a roller and watches as he climbs the stepladder, arches his back, and starts rolling the ceiling white. She feels relief to the point of miracle. He doesn't seem afraid to climb the ladder. He doesn't seem to think he might accidentally commit some crime with that roller and can of paint.

But even a single drop of Shiny Cloud Nine White dripping in someone's eye can upset such an unstable peace. Richard bats at his face and curses, then lifts his shirt to wipe the paint, exposing the hairy V that runs along his belly and disappears inside his sweatpants. Molly is busy painting smiley faces on the switch plates Louise has given her to paint, so she uses this opportunity to run her tongue around the perimeter of her husband's navel.

Richard totters and drops his roller, which lands on the tarp with a sodden *thunk*. "What do you think you're doing?" He steps down to retrieve the roller and stands looking at her. "Would you have bestowed that particular favor if I hadn't just done a chore to earn it?"

The comment stuns her. She wasn't rewarding him for his paint job; she was celebrating his return to the living. "For your information, that qualifies as a completely gratuitous bit of belly kissing."

"Yeah, well, it took me by surprise." He seems ready to forgive her, but his pager chooses that moment to go off. He glances at the number and goes downstairs to use the only phone in the house that works.

"Is something bad happening?" Molly asks.

Louise slumps against the ladder. "Nothing's wrong, sugarplum. Someone at the prison just needs your dad."

Richard comes back. "One of the inmates is threatening to

kill himself. He says he'll only talk to me, and unless I come down there—"

"But nothing has happened yet?"

He shakes his head, and Louise asks about the weapon the guy is using—she has been through enough attempted suicides with her own clients to know that the weapon a person chooses reveals a great deal about his intentions, as well as his chances for survival.

Richard hammers the underside of his fist against the freshly painted wall. "A spoon. A sharpened spoon. I should have known. I should have known!"

"Sweetheart, with an entire prison full of seriously damaged men and only two psychologists—"

"Never mind, I need to go."

She reaches out and swipes a fleck of paint from his nappy, dark hair. He hasn't shaved that day and the stubble on his face is misted white.

He jerks back, tells her not to wait for him for dinner, pulls on a ripped Berkeley sweatshirt, and stomps out.

Louise fetches the roller and resumes rolling the ceiling white. Upset as she is, she offers silent thanks that the inmate isn't dead. The idea that Molly will get to sleep in this beautiful light-peach room cheers her and keeps her working. In their house in San Rafael, Molly lived in a walk-in closet. More than anything, this house convinced Louise that moving to Michigan needn't be the exile from Utopia everyone in California thought it was. After Richard accepted the job, she and Molly flew out to Potawatomie to help him look for a place to live. The real estate agent showed them a few promising choices. Then the three of them went for a drive and stumbled into Stickney Springs, which looked incredibly sweet, a real Midwestern town only a few miles from the prison. They walked along Main Street, with its cobbled walks and charming storefronts. An elderly woman in a velvet hat stopped to speak to Molly. The woman rummaged through her purse and found a mint and held it out to Molly, who looked to Louise for permission to accept it, and then popped it in her mouth. "Thank you," she said, at which the woman patted Molly's head and chirped, "What a pretty, well-brought-up child."

After that, they had gotten back in their rental car and driven a few miles out of town, where they passed a three-story Victorian with a for-sale sign on the lawn. Later, the agent told them the house was being offered for a lot more than it was worth. Louise held her breath, thinking, *How much is too much?* "One eighty-five!" the agent said. "They're asking one hundred and eighty-five thousand dollars for a house in Stickney Springs!" At which Louise and Richard burst out laughing. In Marin County, a house with four bedrooms and two full baths on one-and-a-half acres of land—if you could have found a house with that much land—would have sold for several million dollars. One hundred and eighty-five thousand dollars for a *house*? She and Richard laughed so hard that Molly pouted and reminded them it wasn't nice to laugh unless you shared the joke, at which Louise told her, "Oh, honey, it's only that Mommy and Daddy have found our new house."

Now, she rolls the last corner of the ceiling white, rerolls the section of wall marred by the half moons of Richard's fist, and tells Molly that after they clean up, the two of them will go out and get something good for dinner. Molly dots two tiny black eyes on the last of the switch plates and slashes on a blood-red smiling mouth. "How can you kill yourself?" Molly asks. "Doesn't it hurt too much?"

Startled, Louise says, "Yes, that's why almost nobody ever does it." She doesn't know what else to say, so she simply hugs Molly to her chest and holds her.

Molly pushes her away. "I always forget Daddy's people are crazy." She holds out the switch plate, which leers in a way that unsettles Louise.

"That's beautiful, pumpkin, we'll put those up tomorrow." She takes the paintbrush from Molly's hand, then ferries the dripping rollers and trays and paint cans to the basement, where she rinses everything in the sink and puts the equipment on a shelf. Her arms and shoulders ache, but it's the comforting kind of pain that reminds you that you've painted your daughter's room.

Afterward, she goes back upstairs and helps Molly scrub the paint from beneath her nails, then she brushes her daughter's hair and wipes her face. Holding her own soapy arms beneath the faucet, Louise finds herself transfixed by the sight of her own blue-veined wrists. She has often counseled students who say they no longer wish to live. But neither do they want to die. They only wish to be free of the flesh that houses their souls, the bodies that make them vulnerable to other people's scorn, visible, a target, an attractor for indifference, repulsion, guilt, and shame. They wish to be pure spirit, slipping here and there without the weight of responsibility. Free of all that mass, that cumbersome *existence*, they might yet soar aloft and fulfill the expectations of parents, teachers, friends, or their own amorphous dreams.

Louise loves her life too much ever to think of ending it. But a few minutes later, standing on the porch and fumbling to lock the door, she finds herself wishing her marriage might simply *end*. A person can get so tired of trying to hold everything together she feels the urge to just let go. She wouldn't actively seek divorce, any more than her students would place pistols in their mouths. But this house contains her marriage, and just for an instant, she wishes it might burn down. Has she left the stove on? No. The house doesn't even *have* a stove. The iron? No, she and Richard have been living here six months and they haven't yet unpacked it. Maybe the workmen who installed the furnace earlier that day misconnected the valves, and even now lethal fumes might be seeping through the basement. The roof will bulge, then burst, a pregnant, swollen pod releasing its inhabitants to drift on the wind until they settle to the muddy earth to sink their roots elsewhere.

What a horrifying idea. She lays her palm to the heavy door beside the stained-glass rosette the way a woman overcome with tenderness might lay her palm to a lover's chest. No one knows this house as intimately as Louise knows it. No one else appreciates the way sunlight scatters through this window and glazes the hardwood floor, or the satisfaction of turning the corner from the stairs and being greeted by the alcove, with its perfectly positioned pie-safe and the ceramic pot she and Richard stole in revenge for their mistreatment at a bed and breakfast in Sausalito years before. Only Louise knows which length of molding she reattached with superglue instead of nails and the exact degree of force needed to turn the key to lock this door.

"Mom?" Molly looks up from where she squats. "Did you know that two infinities still make the same infinity?" She uses a twig to poke a worm. The dirt gives off the fusty smell Louise associates with her father's bait shop. "I mean, one infinity plus one infinity is still infinity."

The teachers at Molly's preschool in California scolded Louise for pushing her too hard, when the truth is Louise could barely keep up. Molly taught herself to multiply while sitting on the toilet, staring at the tiles. "Mom," she said, "did you know two threes are six? And three threes are nine?" All Louise had done was provide the terms—"multiply," "times," "divide"—and Molly used this information to put on a "multiply show" at school. Louise doesn't want to think what the teachers in Stickney Springs might make of a child of six asking if they understand the nature of infinity. There is no kindergarten in Stickney Springs, and Molly won't be starting first grade until the fall. Louise and Richard haven't yet looked for daycare. But if Louise manages to find a job, they will need to hire someone to watch her. There is the Little Lambs Nursery down the road. But even if Louise hadn't read that awful mimeographed sheet, she would have been leery of leaving her daughter at a church whose congregants worship the Lord with cymbals, fifes, and drums and a shrill white-people kind of gospel so raucous it sets your teeth on edge from half a mile away.

"There might be a god," Molly announces, cupping her hand above the worm. "But he doesn't need to be a *God*. He doesn't need to be able to do *everything*."

Louise guesses what her daughter must be thinking. "You're right," she says. "And there might be another god above *that* god. And that god wouldn't know if there was another god above him. And if the chain kept going long enough, you might eventually reach a god who did have all the power. A god who was a God."

Molly pops up so impulsively she nearly hits her mother's jaw. Using two twigs, she chopsticks the worm to safety in the grass, blows it a good-luck kiss, then grabs her mother by the hand and skips them toward the van.

"Alley-oop," Louise says, swinging Molly up and in and buckling her across the chest with a padded device designed to make a seatbelt fit such an undersized passenger. She climbs in the driver's seat, adjusts the mirrors, then backs out carefully, exulting in her competence, the child of ineffectual parents who nonetheless has grown up to take proper care of her own daughter.

"So." Molly clicks the beverage holder in and out. "Are we going out for fast food or slow food?"

Without Richard, Louise has no hope of surviving the wait for a meal at an ordinary restaurant. Not that Molly gets rowdy. She just asks so many questions that by the time the entrée arrives Louise is too worn out to eat it. So fast food it is. But there are no fast-food restaurants in Stickney Springs. The town boasts only one eating establishment, a steakhouse called the Busy Bee, and the Bee is no place to take a child, especially a child who doesn't eat meat.

They pass the neighbors' farm—a modest white Colonial with a weathered barn and a stubby abandoned silo that reminds Louise of a former boyfriend's penis. The owner, Dolores Banks, is standing on the porch, straining to change the flag. She is a stout, motherly woman with a sagging face and a cloud of sparse gray hair; with the flag above her head, she looks like Lady Liberty leading a mob of citizens to storm the Bastille. Louise has known Dolores for six months but still can't decide if she likes her. On their second night in the house, Dolores rang the bell and entered the kitchen with an armload of fresh corn and a jar of sour-cherry preserves. Louise thanked her and asked how long she had lived in Stickney Springs. Without answering, Dolores stacked the corn on the counter, set the preserves on the sill, and then reached up and pressed a button in her throat. "All. My. Born. Days," she croaked in an uninflected metallic voice. She hit the button again. "Voice. Box. Thyroid. Cancer."

Louise felt an inch tall for thinking the woman was cold when the truth was she couldn't speak unless her hands were free. Dolores is as conservative as a person gets. Her sentiments are so predictable the button in her throat might have controlled a tape. Whenever Bill Clinton's name comes up, she hits her button and sputters, "That. Sinner. Will. Get.

His. Comeuppance. In. Hell." But she seems a good neighbor. And you can't predict when you might need to run next door and ask for help.

"Hello!" Louise calls out now. "Dolores!"

Dolores slides the flagpole in its holder, then, hands free, hits her button. Whatever she announces comes out sounding like the garbled airport plea for Mr. Indecipherable to pick up a phone. Realizing she hasn't been understood, she gestures to the glittery red-and-purple egg on the banner, then to Molly, then back to the egg. Folding her paws beneath her chin, she mimes a rabbit hopping.

"Oh! Peter Rabbit!" Louise shouts, at which Dolores nods enthusiastically.

Despite living on a farm, the Bankses aren't farmers. Farming no longer pays, as Matt often complains, grumbling about the sorts of government regulations that Richard and Louise secretly approve of. Instead of raising crops for food, the Bankses sell holidays: pumpkins on Halloween, turkeys for Thanksgiving, wreaths and trees at Christmas. For most of March, they have been offering newly hatched chicks, adorable lop-eared bunnies, and a dazzling array of irises. "Our biggest moneymaker is fireworks on the Fourth," Matt once confided. "Not that everything we sell is strictly approved by Uncle Sam. But *you* won't tell him, will you." His wink of assumed complicity had given Louise a start—she'd had a classmate in seventh grade who'd lost a finger to a rocket.

If she lives here long enough, she will time the year by the flags the Bankses fly—the Pilgrim hat and blunderbuss for Thanksgiving, Rudolph's glowing nose, the shamrock on St. Pat's, and this gaudy egg for Easter. The Bankses like hanging out flags so much, she wonders if she might convince them to expand their repertoire to include a menorah on Chanukah and a lamb's shank for Passover, which is coming up in two weeks (if Richard expects her to put on a Seder, he'd better help). Not that there would be much of a market for Jewish paraphernalia in Stickney Springs. As far as Louise can tell, Richard is the only Jew in town, and the few Jews who live in Potawatomie drive to Ann Arbor to fulfill their religious needs. Besides, for a mercantile people, Jews buy almost nothing for any holiday except Chanukah or Passover, and the Bankses can't very well grow dreidels or gefilte fish.

She taps the horn in farewell. Dolores blows Molly a kiss.

"Mom?" Molly asks. "Mrs. Banks said that Easter is about Jesus Christ dying then coming back to life. Do Christians really think a dead person can come back to life?"

It occurs to Louise that if she has to live in a place where people talk about Jesus so much, she will either kill herself or convert. "I don't know, sugar. They believe *Jesus* came back to life. And since Jesus brought other people back to life, I guess they believe ordinary people can come back, too."

"But Jews think you die and that's it?"

Louise knows even less about what Jews believe than what Christians believe. But yes, she says, as far as she can tell, Jews don't believe in resurrection.

Molly starts to bring up something else, then folds her hands and faces front. They drive through Stickney Springs, which is lovely at this hour, wreathed in an Edward Hopperish yellow light. They pass Nicholson's Five-and-Dime, the Seven Sisters Bakery, the upholstery store, the appliance store, the newsstand and tobacconist, and the professional building in which a descendant of the town's founder, Charles Stickney, practices law. They drive past the elementary school Molly will attend come fall. The schoolyard is empty, but Molly presses her face to the glass as if imagining children climbing the jungle gym and swinging on the swings.

A mile out of town, Louise merges onto a two-lane highway

surrounded by flat brown fields and scrubby wind-bent trees. The landscape isn't unattractive. It just doesn't lift your heart the way the mountains and coast of California lift them. Michigan resembles upstate New York, but with all the hills smoothed out, as if an over-zealous housewife had shaken out the quilt so no one could guess what she and her husband had done in bed the night before. What Louise can't understand is why every Michigander she meets seems determined that she acknowledge an allure that doesn't exist. "At least we don't get earthquakes," the cashier at Kroger said when she saw Louise's California license. "Or those mudslides, we don't get those." Well, Louise thought, what about tornadoes? In only six months, she and Molly already have lived through two horrible, heavy days when the sky went a sickly green, a queasy stillness hit, and Dolores hurried over to make sure they understood that they needed to hunker down in the cellar until the tornado threat had passed. "You should see the lake," the guy at the paint store told her. Lake Michigan was "just like Cape Cod," although he admitted that he had never *been* to Cape Cod, and Louise didn't bother to remark how suspicious she was of places that people felt obliged to claim were exactly like someplace else.

They pass the sign that reads POTAWATOMIE, MICHIGAN, POP. 57,000, A FINE PLACE TO LIVE, and despite the self-righteousness of the claim, Louise is forced to agree that Potawatomie does have its charms. Only these aren't the charms the city boosters try to boost. She isn't taken in by the one historic block that has been refurbished with fake gaslights, red-white-and-blue trash receptacles, an ice cream shoppe, a struggling health-food store, a souvenir kiosk, and a renovated movie theater, which, oddly, for as long as they have been living there, has been showing *Dr. Strangelove*. What Louise likes about Potawatomie are the parts that time forgot—the seedy luncheonettes, the Hemingway Arms Hotel, the shop that sells prostheses, or maybe it sells socks, you can't be sure from the amputated legs in the display. In Potawatomie, you can't always tell what a store sells by looking at the front. Once, Louise stepped inside a hushed establishment with Grecian urns to either side of the door expecting to find antiques, but three elderly ladies looked up from their magazines and fluttered their fingers to the bullet-shaped dryers on their heads.

If anything, Louise feels more comfortable in Potawatomie than she felt in San Francisco. This dreary, neglected city in southwest Michigan reminds her of the dreary, neglected cities near where she grew up in upstate New York—Syracuse, Troy, Albany, Schenectady, all those senile giants of the Empire State's industrial youth. California had been too stimulating. She once saw a play in which a Russian count proclaimed that he preferred living in Siberia because his emotions were a harp that vibrated to the faintest wind and the storms in Moscow wore him out, and Louise knows what that Russian meant. Even the soppy gray Michigan weather—a person felt as if the entire expanse of Lake Michigan, a few miles to the west, was floating above her head—can't keep her internal harp from humming.

She and Molly drive past the imposing brick barricade that hides the prison. Every time she sees this wall, with its rolls of barbed wire along the top and the towers at either end, each with a revolving spotlight that casts an aura of surveillance across the town, she understands why her husband would want to work here. He wants to be kept an eye on. He wants to be punished. If he causes another death, the victim won't be a talented engineer with her entire life to lose.

She pulls in at the McDonald's—if a McDonald's can look old-fashioned, this one does, all red and yellow brick, although the owners have added a glassed-in playground around the back—then takes Molly by the hand and leads her in. When they reach the register, Louise stands blinking up at the menu. "I'll take a fish fillet," she tells the girl. Knowing better than to think that Molly will eat a Happy Meal, she orders a vanilla shake and fries in a deluded attempt to get some calcium and vitamins into a daughter who won't eat anything that's ever been alive.

The order takes forever to come, and by the time she has added ketchup and straws to their tray, Molly is gone. After a panicked minute, Louise finds her swinging back and forth in a seat attached to a table in the play area around the back. The playground cheers Louise. Toddlers stagger joyously toward the tunnels and vanish inside like messages sucked up pneumatic tubes. The slides are as tall as houses, smooth orange-and-purple tubes curving and intersecting in spirals so complex Louise can't help but feel jealous, as she has found herself envying the hands-on museums, Omnimax theaters, video arcades, and theme parks that a child in the nineties gets to visit. Molly doesn't care about the playground any more than she cares about the food or the little toys that come with the meals. She only likes coming to McDonald's to meet the kids who do care. When Louise thinks about how much Molly misses her friends in California, a fist squeezes her heart. Molly has met a few girls her age in Stickney Springs, but Louise's requests that their mothers bring them to the house to play have been greeted with polite apologies. She doubts this is Molly's fault. Molly is wispy and a little odd, but kids tend to like her. She is kind. She never pushes or hits. Best of all, she invents games for the other kids to play, spinning out stories whose plots concern wounded birds and animals that Molly and her friends nurse back to health. No, her daughter's stigma is that she has moved here from a state most Michiganders associate with acid trips, love-ins, and homosexuals. And Louise is beginning to suspect that parents in Stickney Springs only let their children play with children whose families they know from church.

Studiously, Molly squeezes a mound of ketchup on the tray, dips in a French fry, and licks off the ketchup. "Where does plastic come from?" she asks.

"Plastic?" What does Louise know about plastic, except that its manufacture has something to do with oil. But how can a substance so colorful and solid be made from oil? "I'm sorry," she admits, "Mommy doesn't know."

Upset by her mother's uncharacteristic reluctance to offer a hypothesis, Molly sets the potato on the tray and hops off toward the playground, only to be stopped by a sign that reads CHILDREN MUST BE THREE YEARS OLD TO ENTER. Louise needs a moment to figure out the problem. Molly still takes the world at face value. The space between the intended and the accidental where humor is born hasn't yet opened in her mind. According to this sign, only children who are *exactly* three years old are entitled to play on this playground. Children as old as twelve can be seen crawling through the tubes, but Molly isn't one to disregard a prohibition.

"It's okay, sweetie," Louise tells her. "The sign means that you have to be *at least* three years old."

Molly frowns as if she believes the sign either should be corrected immediately or obeyed for what it says. What a highly developed superego a child of six can have! But Louise gives her a little shove, and this dislodges Molly from her adherence to the strict grammatical logic of the sign. She runs off to the section meant for the youngest kids and wriggles inside a tube. Sighing, Louise goes back to their table, unwraps her fish sandwich, peels back the bun, and stares furiously at the patty of limp whitish *stuff*, wondering why she isn't sitting with Imelda at their favorite restaurant in Monterey, eating a sandwich made of some aquatic creature she can identify.

At the nearest table, a family gets up and leaves. Since they haven't bothered to bus their trash, the next customers, a father and two young girls, need to clear the mess. The man is tall and loose jointed. When he sits in the chair beside her, Louise can see that he has an earring hole but no earring. His two fair-haired daughters, each a little older than Molly, wear identical yellow skirts with bumblebees across the front. While Louise sucks her diet Coke, they pry the lids from their salads and gobble every wisp of greenery, every cheese shred, every cucumber slice and crouton, stopping only to sip their milk—real milk, not the fake dairy shake she ordered for Molly. They blot their mouths with napkins and ask if they can be excused.

"What's this?" Their father holds up a packet of dressing. "You promised you would eat everything I set in front of you."

"Oh, Daddy! You're such a crazy lunatic!"

"Crazy lunatic, am I?" He hooks one daughter in each elbow and blows noisy kisses against their cheeks. He has longish fair hair that Louise guesses would feel soft, unlike Richard's hair, which is wiry. Green eyes. A thin crooked nose. A solemn pocked face. Louise knows from working with so many teenagers that men who were scarred by acne in their youth often don't realize how handsome they've grown up to be. At least, this man doesn't appear to. He forks a translucent tomato to his lips, and, turning to Louise, smiles an expectant smile, as if she might start a conversation.

"I'm stuck, Mom! Come unstick me!"

Louise glances around the playground.

"Help me, Mom! Come help me!"

Reluctantly, she walks over to the play structure, and,

when Molly calls again, kicks off her pumps and hoists herself up a crisscross of knotted ropes like something dangling from a pirate ship. At the top, she squeezes inside a tube nearly too small to admit a grownup. Static pricks her arms. She can't navigate by sight, and Molly's cries reverberate against the walls in such a chaotic way Louise can't pinpoint their source. On she crawls, sweating, until she comes upon her daughter crying hotly at the top of a slide that corkscrews into nothingness. "It's okay, sweetie, we'll crawl back down." But Molly refuses to retrace the trail that has gotten her where she is. Rather than argue, Louise scissors her legs around her daughter, leans back, and pushes off. They go plummeting through the dark, Molly's screams vibrating against Louise's chest until they shoot into a cage of colored balls, Molly laughing now, delighted, tossing balls at her mother's head, and Louise looks up to see the girls' father frowning down at both of them. She crawls to the exit, struggling to emerge gracefully, which isn't possible. Slipping on her shoes, she hobbles back to join the man where he stands waving up at his girls, who have conquered the structure's peak.

"They're beautiful," she says, "and very well-behaved," hating herself because, though the compliments are true, she is using such smarmy praise to please their father. "I've never seen a child eat a salad at a McDonald's."

He studies her, deciding if she can be trusted. "They keep kosher. I'm not Jewish, but their mother is." He stops, and she can see he isn't happy with his answer. "I'm a minister. My name is Ames Wye."

Louise doubts she could be friends with a minister. Still, he isn't stiff or standoffish. "Are you . . . What sort of church do you run?"

He looks up through the glass roof at the indigo sky above

them, and Louise follows his gaze, feeling suddenly as if they are floating inside a fish tank, hovering among the colorful castles and plastic weeds. "Sometimes I think the church runs me," he says, then turns to her, his eyes so green she wishes paint came in that color; she would feel very much at peace surrounded by that particular shade of green. "Around here, most people don't even consider a Unitarian church to be a church."

"You're Unitarian?" Richard finds Unitarians colorless and prim, but they offer agnostics like Louise the possibility of believing in God without relinquishing their common sense. She knows quite a few Unitarians in California, so meeting this minister is like moving to a foreign country and running into a fellow expatriate who, if not from the United States, at least comes from Canada. She uses this opportunity to confide that in addition to her regular job in Berkeley, she used to volunteer for an AIDS organization staffed by Unitarians.

"Really?" Ames says. Because of the prison, there is an unusually high incidence of H.I.V. in Potawatomie, and he has helped to organize an AIDS coalition and set up a safe house where people with the disease can live. He also runs a group that is trying to prevent the city's right-wing Christians from banning the teaching of evolution in the schools. Louise starts to say she would be very interested in joining such a coalition, but Ames keeps glancing at his watch. "We're supposed to meet the girls' mother," he explains. Not "my wife," "the girls' mother." He stands and clears their table. His hands are bony and long. Looking at a man's hands used to be the way she gauged if she wanted him to touch her, but since marrying Richard, she hasn't looked at anyone else's hands. Then again, Richard hasn't touched her in months. And this minister's hands are so expressive she can't force herself to look away.

To forestall his departure, she asks if he happens to know a good daycare center in Potawatomie. "Did your daughters go somewhere you could recommend?"

He stares at her. "That's quite a coincidence. When our daughters were small, my wife started a daycare co-op. I don't mean to get personal, but are you and your daughter Jewish?"

"Her father is. I'm not." She hopes he will acknowledge this bond, that each of them is married to a Jew, but he is writing on a napkin. *All Faiths Daycare. 50 Spruce Street.*

"More like *no* faiths," Ames says, giving his head a shake. "It's nothing fancy. A dozen kids, two rooms, a teacher and an aide. But it might be what you're looking for." He points to the top of the play structure, where, miraculously, Molly stands between his daughters, all three of them as radiant as adventurers setting off to find new lands.

"Molly!" Louise cries. "Look at you! How did you get up there?" She waves frantically at her daughter, as if the ship might sail without her. "Happy Easter!" she blurts out, not yet understanding why she would utter such a phrase, unless it's because she feels buoyed by her new belief that even if the dead can't be made to rise, a fresh, green beginning might be granted anyone.

When they get home the house is cold. The last thing Louise wanted for her daughter was to live in a house that felt uncared-for, as her own parents' house used to feel. Yet here it is, a house that is beautiful on the outside but unwelcoming on the inside. The exposed lathes, dangling wires, and wraithlike outlines of the absent appliances make the place gloomy as a morgue. Not to mention that the air smells rancid. The electrician's assistant, a rubbery-faced young man named Rod who wears his hair in a mullet and has vaguely unfocused eyes, insists on bringing his dog to work. The animal is one of those heavy-haunched, shovel-jawed beasts no one in his right mind would want as a pet. Not only might the dog remove Molly's head with a dainty bite, Louise keeps finding yellow stains in the kitchen. The new plaster and paint will cover the dog's transgressions, but Louise will always be aware there is dog pee underneath. She has asked the electrician's assistant repeatedly if he could please leave his pet home. Yeah, well, Rod said, the dog got neurotic—he used that word, *neurotic*, as if the brute were a cowering, cringing pup—if he was left alone too long. Rottweilers just had a bad rep. Smack was gentle as a poodle and would never do his business—Rod used that phrase, *do his business*—anywhere except outdoors. Whoever left those puddles, it wasn't Smack.

Louise didn't appreciate the implication that her daughter was less well housetrained than a dog, but she agreed that Rod could bring his pet to work if he locked the animal in the basement. Now, sniffing the sour air, she wishes she had forbidden the dog to come at all. Molly is using a wire coat-hanger to coax dust balls from the nook where the refrigerator used to be. Goosebumps prickle Louise's arms, but Molly never feels the cold. Louise considers telling her to wait outside. What if the smell is gas? It's one thing to wistfully imagine your house blowing up; it's another thing for the house actually to explode—with your daughter inside. Louise trots downstairs to see if anything is amiss. And there sits her husband, cross-legged before the furnace, the manual by his side and a box of Ohio Blue Tip matches on his lap. Her heart sinks; he must have been sitting there a long time, getting up the nerve to strike a match.

She walks up behind him and strokes his hair. "I'll call the furnace guys tomorrow. They'll send someone right away."

"I did this a million times in Ithaca. But now I just can't seem to—"

Tears well up in her eyes. She feels terrible for Richard. Of course she does. But she also feels terrible for herself.

The doorbell rings. "I'll be right back," she says, relieved of the need to watch her husband suffer. She assumes their caller must be Dolores Banks. Who else would be ringing their bell this late on a Saturday? She hurries past Molly, who is poking her dust balls with her hanger and chatting to them like pets. But as Louise nears the door, she can see through the glass that their visitor isn't Dolores Banks, but her hulking son, Matt.

He touches the visor of his plaid wool cap. "Evening, Mrs. S."

"Hello, Matt." She has told him over and over to call her Louise, but he seems incapable of addressing an older married woman by her first name. "You must have come about the plate." A few days earlier, Dolores brought over a gooey cake stuffed with apples from their orchard. Louise tells Matt she'll run and get the dish the strudel came on.

He removes his hat, causing his hair to spring up in little points. Louise is tempted to reach out and smooth these down, but her arm wouldn't stretch that far. Matt is six feet five inches tall, with shoulders so broad he needs to angle sideways to get through their door. Not long after Louise and Richard moved in, he took them into his barn and showed them his barbells, the old-fashioned kind an Olympic weightlifter from the Soviet Union might have used, describing in detail which exercises shaped which muscles, holding out a limb or exposing a stretch of torso to be admired. He always wears clothes designed to show off his superhero's physique. Tonight, despite the cold, he has on a black leather vest with nothing underneath and a pair of tight black jeans.

"Didn't come about the plate. When my ex ran off, she left the dinnerware. I got enough plates to run a china shop."

Louise can't help but laugh at the idea of bullish Matt Banks managing a china shop. Why can't she admit she likes him? His smile is guilelessly disarming. Behind those oversized tinted aviator glasses, his eyes are a trustworthy blue. "The furnace went out, and Richard . . ." She doesn't want to appear disloyal. "It's some newfangled model." *Newfangled*? "He can't figure out how to light the pilot."

"Happy to help," Matt says. And truly, he does seem happy to help, as he seemed happy to help Louise change a tire on the van, and happy to help her set a ladder against the eaves and scoop leaf-soup from the gutters. Why should it matter if some farmer in Michigan is confirmed in his belief that Californians are unable to change their tires and Jews are inept and soft? Because surely there is that. Matt attributes everything about Richard to his religion. Like all apocalyptic Christians, he considers the conversion of the Jews to be essential to the completion of the epic in which he and his coreligionists are the stars. But he also admires Jews for fearing the Lord Jehovah. If anything, Louise envies the attention Matt bestows on Richard. "I once knew a Jewish fella," he always starts, before launching into a story that has nothing to do with anything except that a Jew figures in the telling. Twice since their arrival, Matt has found it apropos to joke: "I don't know why people go on about you Jews controlling all the money when we have all the Bankses!"

Now he huffs across the kitchen—for such a well-built man, he is unable to cross a kitchen floor without getting out of breath—and pats Molly on the head. "Hello there, Miss Molly. How about if you come over to the farm this Sunday and join us in just about the biggest most exciting egg-hunt you have ever seen?"

From that angle, with his massive chest and face, he must strike Molly as a stony, fantastic monster, but she keeps tending her herd of dust balls. "Jews don't celebrate Easter," Molly says.

"I happen to know that. You may think I don't know anything about Jewish people, but I do. And there is nothing in that Old Testament of yours about Jews not eating jellybeans. Don't you think old Moses himself enjoyed a few jellybeans now and then?"

Actually, Richard has told Louise that jellybeans aren't kosher. The prohibition has something to do with gelatin, which is made from ground pigs' knuckles, a fact that makes Louise not want to eat them either.

"And can you tell me why a nice little Jewish girl shouldn't be allowed to find colored eggs in the grass? Or chase a bunny? Because that's what we do. Every child in Stickney Springs turns out for the Bankses' Easter Eggs-travaganza. We let loose one of our bunnies, and all the children chase it, and if a child catches that bunny, why, she gets to keep it."

For a moment, Louise sees everyone in Stickney Springs chasing a terrified Molly. Then the scene changes and she sees Molly skipping through a field carrying a basket of colored eggs. If she and Richard refuse to attend any celebration in Stickney Springs that smacks of Christianity, they will never leave the house. "Sweetheart," she says, "there's no reason you should miss this." *You're Mommy's daughter, too. I went on plenty of Easter egg hunts when I was your age.* Except that she never did. As a child, Louise had wanted nothing more than to be driven to town for the annual egg-hunt sponsored by St. Mary's Church. She adored the sight and smell of the Christmas tree Imelda's mother put up in the lobby of their motel and begged to be permitted to attend her schoolmates' baptisms and confirmations. And even though Louise can't bring herself to believe in the existence of a god who cups his hand above her head, the way Molly cupped her hand above that worm, she very much *wants* to be convinced. "Thanks for the invitation," she tells Matt. "Let us know if there's anything we can do to help."

"Good! We'll expect to see you there." He finds the basement door and uses the beams above the stairwell to ease himself down. Louise follows him a few steps and then watches as he slaps Richard on the back. "So what's the problem, good buddy?" He drops to his knees as heavily as a gut-shot buffalo, then crawls toward the furnace, lowering his head and peering above the tops of his aviator frames. His vest hangs open to expose the dark tangles beneath his arms, the brutal jungle of his chest. Louise settles on the bottom step and closes her eyes. There definitely is an acrid odor in the basement. Maybe Rod's dog did his business in some corner. Or the furnace truly is malfunctioning. She has read that natural gas emits no smell until the gas company adds a chemical scent so customers can detect a leak. Too bad scientists haven't found a way to add a scent to warn of other dangers—a friend's cancer, a husband's impending breakdown.

The men's murmur of consultation lulls Louise into a dreamy doze. How can a weight-lifting farmer be so out of shape while Richard, who rarely leaves his desk, remains as lithe as the day they met? It had been brutally hot that afternoon, and Louise had allowed her housemates to persuade her to leave off reading her adolescent-psych homework and accompany them to the reservoir that was the accepted place to skinny dip in Ithaca—illegally, she had been told, although the cops didn't seem to care. The reservoir was glorious that time of year, a verdant leafy gorge surrounded by granite walls from which drunk guys liked to jump. The day she met Richard, a beefy guy did a belly flop from the cliff and landed with such a resonant *thwap* that everyone was sure he would drown. When the guy finally surfaced, his face and chest tomato-red, he staggered to the shore and raised one scarlet arm, at which everybody clapped and cheered.

Louise stripped off her T-shirt and cutoffs and took a dip in the frigid stream. Then she stretched out on the heated rocks to take a nap. A noisy commotion woke her. Rain, she thought. A storm. But when she opened her eyes, the sky was cloudless. The Ithaca police, in their ridiculously heavy uniforms, were blowing whistles and waving nightsticks and shouting for everyone to *halt where you are*.

Louise darted through the woods. But when the trail petered out, she thought better than to bushwhack naked through a clump of trees overgrown with poison ivy. She crouched behind a rock, aware of nothing more than her own ragged gasps, until she heard someone panting along the trail. A cop? No. Whoever it was sounded too light on his feet to be a cop.

The young man who galloped into the clearing was agile as a deer. He was Jewish, Louise guessed, and not only because his penis was circumcised. He was beautiful in a particularly Jewish way, with glistening copper skin, shiny black curls, and yes, a Jewish nose, bumpy and a little long, but it made him seem alert, like some sinewy, virile mammal with an intelligent sense of smell.

He stopped where the trail ran out. "Mind if I join you?" he asked, although her hiding place obviously left much to be desired. "Can you believe the cops have nothing better to do than chase a bunch of kids whose only crime is swimming naked?" He held out his hand. "Richard Shapiro. From East Versailles. It's a little town near Rocky Glen." Their palms touched, and the effect seemed a coupling of their naked selves. "I've got to get back to campus for an exam. You don't need your clothes, do you?"

This puzzled her. How could she walk around campus naked?

He ran his palm down his hairy, wet chest. "No, I mean, do you care about the clothes you left at the reservoir? I've got some gym stuff in my car. It's kind of gross, but it's better than nothing. I could give you a lift back to campus."

Sure, she said, thank you. She didn't care about her clothes. All she had been carrying in her pockets was a bookmark. But how could they get back to his car without running into the cops?

"You can trust me," he promised and led them back the way they had come.

"Are you crazy?" she asked, then decided she had no choice but to let whatever happened happen. In the meantime, she enjoyed watching his well-knit legs carry him down the path.

"Here." He showed her a turnoff she must have missed the first time and indicated that Louise should take the lead. She tried not to be self-conscious, knowing he must be studying her ass as intently as she had studied his. When they reached the road, they needed to walk a few yards along the shoulder, but, mercifully, no cars drove past.

"What about your car key?"

He reached beneath the fender of his Dodge Dart and plucked out one of those magnetic key-holders Louise had meant to buy her parents, who locked themselves out of their ancient Chevrolet with astonishing regularity. He opened the trunk and pulled out a carnelian gym bag with the university crest on one side, removed two pairs of shorts, each of which he sniffed, giving the fresher-smelling pair to Louise, along with a T-shirt that read YOU CAN TELL A CORNELL GIRL BY THE MUSCLES IN HER THIGHS, an allusion to the climb most freshmen girls needed to make to get from their dorms to their classes.

Louise laughed and asked if he was always so well-prepared.

"The Shapiro family motto—" He raised one slender palm.

"Everything in its place. Also: If something's worth doing . . . And: Don't put off until tomorrow . . ."

"Not to mention: Keep an extra pair of gym shorts in the trunk in case you and some naked girl get busted."

"Yes. Definitely. That was on the list, too." He held open the door and Louise slid in. The Dart was old, but so neat and well maintained it might have come off a showroom floor. When they pulled up to her apartment, Richard leaned across her lap, opened the glove box, and took out a pad and a pen. "Here's my address. Whenever you feel like dropping off the clothes, that would be great."

She got out and watched the Dart drive off. Why hadn't he asked her out? Hadn't he liked what he had seen? What if she stopped by to return his clothes and he wasn't there? After they started dating, Richard explained that it had struck him as cheap to ask out a girl who'd had the misfortune to be trembling naked behind a rock when some guy she didn't know ran down a trail to evade the cops. But they might never have *started* dating—as Louise feared, he wasn't home when she returned his gym clothes—if not for the much remarked-upon coincidence that, a week later, each of them happened to attend a lecture by the psychologist Thomas Szasz. All through that talk, in which Szasz propounded his peculiar notion that madness doesn't exist, Louise stared at the student a few seats over, trying to figure out what to say to help him recognize her with her clothes on. She missed most of Szasz's lecture, not that she considered that a loss. How could anyone pretend madness didn't exist?

The lecture ended, and before she could think better of it, she had gone up to Richard and said, "Hi, I'm Louise Heinz, the woman from the reservoir? I just wanted to thank you again for saving my ass." The joke hit them both and they broke out laughing.

"Uh," Richard said, "do you want a cup of coffee?" and she followed him up the aisle, relieved that she liked the way he looked in khakis nearly as much as she liked him with nothing on.

They settled in threadbare armchairs in the hippie cafe across the quad from the auditorium. "Just don't tell me you agree with that ridiculous lecture," Richard said, and that was that for both of them. They dated, had sex, and fell in love. Louise finished her master's degree in social work and found a job at a middle school not far from Ithaca while Richard completed his doctorate in forensic psych. He insisted they move to Berkeley, where he had always dreamed of living. He ran a facility for troubled teens, and, to pay the rent, saw a few private clients. Those early years in Berkeley had been the happiest of Louise's life. She had been crazy for him, hadn't she? And not just because he managed their lives so well. She liked the way her husband looked. He looks the same way now. If anything, his face is more intriguing. Why does she no longer enjoy his touch? Because he seems weak? A woman doesn't want to sense something wounded in a man. If the alpha wolf begins to limp, the female shakes off his advances.

No. That's ridiculous. She and Richard aren't wolves. He might look as handsome as the day they met, but he doesn't make love the way he used to. He has become tentative and restrained. *May I put my lips here? May I lay my hands there?* He touches her as if he might set fire to her hair.

She opens her eyes. Matt is on his feet, slapping his hands to remove the grit. "Isn't anything wrong with this furnace," he says, then swaggers around the basement, stopping to inspect a valve. "If that doesn't beat all. Someone turned off the gas!" He reaches up and yanks a lever. "There. That ought to do it."

Of course. When the kitchen guys took out the old

appliances, they must have shut off the gas. "Matt," she says, "how can we ever repay you?"

He shrugs. "Sure would have been a waste of money to get a repairman out here just so he could tell you you had the gas switched off."

The furnace swooshes on and Richard jumps. Not that Louise blames him. The sound of anything catching fire spooks them both.

"Okay," Matt says, "now *that's* taken care of, the real reason I came over here was to invite the little girl to the egg-hunt and you two to the Tax Blast."

"Tax Blast?" Richard echoes.

Matt mimes lifting a rifle. "It's a little get-together to show the government how we feel about paying taxes. We hold it every year on or about April 15."

Louise feels a jolt of panic. "I don't think we can come. We're always behind with our taxes," a statement that isn't true; Richard never fails to mail in their forms on time.

"Oh, Tax Blast has nothing to do with getting your taxes done. We meet at the Sportsman's Club. Tap a few kegs. Fire up the grill. Eat some weenies and potato salad. Then we tack a bunch of 1040s to the trees and use them for target practice."

Louise tells herself it's no more unsettling to think of their neighbors here in Michigan refusing to pay their taxes to support a government they deem too leftist than their friends in California sending back blank forms to protest their government's expenditures on right-wing dictatorships. But their friends in San Francisco don't tack their tax forms to trees and shoot them. That's all we need, she thinks, to bring Molly to a party where people get baked and fire guns. "We're not really comfortable around firearms," she tells Matt, hating how self-righteous she sounds.

Up go two heavily knuckled fists. "That's because you haven't been around them enough!"

But that's not true. Everyone Louise knew growing up owned a gun. What scared her was the havoc guns could cause in the hands of the chaotic people allowed to use them. Her classmates' parents had gotten drunk and beaten up their kids with frightening regularity. A boy in her class, despondent over his inability to control his father's brutality toward his mother, stole one of his neighbor's rifles, shot his father, and then shot himself.

Then there were the weekend warriors from Manhattan. Stockbrokers from New York drove up to the Adirondacks, chugged a few beers, then went out and shot anything that moved. No one got upset when they hit each other, but at least once a year they hit someone's dog or child. One time, Louise and Imelda had been sitting in Louise's back yard comparing notes about a boy they liked when a bullet buried itself in a branch an inch above Imelda's head. The hunter begged them not to tell, and to Louise's enduring regret, they hadn't. Children could be so protective of adults it made her weep.

"I can understand the way you feel, Mrs. S. But when the trouble hits the fan and everyone from Chicago and Detroit comes swarming out here looking for food, you're going to want to hold on to what's yours."

She glances at Richard. In the old days, he would have told Matt that if someone dropped an atomic bomb on Chicago or Detroit, he and Louise would gladly have shared what food they had. "Thanks for the invitation," her husband says. "I just might take you up on it."

"Good!" Matt says. "Party's next Saturday. Bring a covered dish to pass. If you don't know how to shoot, we'll loan you a gun and teach you. We figure when the trouble comes, the more people on our side, the better chance we have." He hoists his bulk back up to the kitchen. Molly is nowhere to be seen, but she has left her wire hanger poking from an outlet. The knowledge of what might have happened if that socket had been hooked up nearly knocks Louise to the floor. Richard's distraction over his client's suicide led him to start that fire, which led them to move to Michigan, which led them to be yammering in the basement while Molly jammed a hanger in an outlet. A child's being smart doesn't mean you don't need to watch her. Maybe you need to watch the brightest kids the most.

"Here." Louise hands Matt the cake plate. Richard walks him to the door, then surprises Louise by accompanying Matt outside. She stands in the foyer, listening to the men talk about smelt. "I've got to warn you," Matt tells Richard. "The first time you go smelting, the deal is, you've got to put one of those suckers in your mouth and bite off its head while it's still alive." She hears the two men laugh and an unreasoning anger sweeps over her. Why doesn't she have anyone out here to talk to? Once a week, she calls Imelda and entertains her with descriptions of the football-patterned wallpaper the previous owners used in the upstairs bathroom or the closet light for which the previous owner apparently forgot to install an on-off switch. But that isn't nearly the same as laughing over sushi at their weekly gabfests in Oakland. Besides, the doctors have discovered a lump in Imelda's remaining breast. She is scheduled for a biopsy the following week. Louise hardly has the right to complain about her right-wing neighbors, or, for that matter, anything else.

She wipes her eyes and climbs the stairs. Molly is lying on the floor re-reading the last Mad-Lib book she and Louise filled in together. To think she might have electrocuted herself! How can any parent let her child out of her sight? Then again, Louise's own parents left her on her own from the time she was younger than Molly, and all she had suffered was a broken toe, which she had gotten from stubbing it on a rock.

"Molly, sweetheart, you mustn't ever, ever stick anything metal into an electric outlet." She strokes Molly's hair, picking out a sticky pill of Play-Doh. "You could get a terrible shock."

"Remember this one?" Molly holds out the book. "This is my favorite." She reads the nonsense poem aloud: "'Three blind noses. See how they skydive. They all went after the petunia's wife, who pooped off their belly buttons with a leafy knife. Did you ever sneeze such a salami in your life as a zillion ugly mice.'" She keeps reading Mad-Libs aloud and giggling while Louise runs water for her bubble bath; when the tub is full, Molly climbs in and blows the foam at her mother, laughing until she hiccups. Is it possible that this will-o'-wisp of a child, opalescent and frail as the bubbles that surround her, belongs to the same species as Matt Banks?

"Time for a hair wash," Louise sings, and with her hand between Molly's shoulders tips her backward. Molly's curls repel the suds and Louise needs to work the shampoo in. It is one of the many responsibilities of motherhood she loves. When Louise was Molly's age, her parents left her hygiene to her. As a form of protest, she refused to wash her hair, and even though she knows a child's susceptibility to lice has nothing to do with how dirty her hair might be, she still blames her parents for the infestation she eventually picked up. Her teacher must have noticed her clawing at her scalp, because she sent Louise home with a note that said she wouldn't be allowed back unless she submitted to an inspection and no more nits were found. Louise dreaded showing the note to her parents, who would say it was no one's business what was living in their daughter's hair. In tears of shame, she asked Imelda's mother to help. After picking nits for hours,

Mrs. Robertson massaged mayonnaise into Louise's scalp to smother the remaining lice. The next day, she wrote a note attesting that Louise was now symptom-free and should be admitted back to class. The shame and relief come back to her every time she washes her daughter's hair.

She uses a cup to rinse out the soap. "That's it, sweetie, clean as a whistle."

Molly hops out, dripping, and Louise encloses her still-warm muffin of a daughter in a fluffy yellow towel. She carries her to the futon in the guest room, turns back the Little Mermaid quilt, and drops Molly on the mattress.

Molly rolls over and lies facedown. "Are you sure it isn't wrong for me to go on that egg-hunt?" she asks in a muffled voice.

Louise lowers herself to the futon and curls around her daughter, inhaling the cotton-candy sweetness of Mr. Bubble and Pooh Shampoo. "Sure it's all right. It isn't as if anyone is asking you to worship some god you don't believe in." And what if someone did? What if someone were to hold a gun to Molly's head and demand she renounce her faith? Wouldn't Louise want her to say *I'll worship whomever you want me to worship. I'll bow down to whatever stupid idol you want me to bow down to.* What kind of principle demands you let some fanatic take your life? If Richard had asked Louise to convert, she would have converted. So why is it wrong to convert from fear but not from love?

Besides, Molly isn't technically a Jew. Only the child of a Jewish mother is a Jew. Richard had asked Louise if she minded raising Molly Jewish anyway. His father had narrowly escaped the Holocaust and, as Richard's mother put it, letting the religion die would be like letting Hitler win. So Louise had told Richard yes. Her own parents' *laissez faire* approach to child rearing hadn't left her independent and welcoming of anarchy, as they had hoped it would; all it had accomplished was to leave her feeling unprotected and abandoned.

"How come no one made a big deal about Easter in California?" Molly asks. "Nobody in California cared that Dad and I were Jews."

Louise tries to explain that a lot more Jews live in San Francisco than in Potawatomie and that Christians in California tend to be more liberal than Christians in the Midwest, but she keeps getting sidetracked by Molly's questions. "What's a liberal?" Molly asks. "Why aren't there more Jews in Michigan?" At some point, the questions stop coming and Louise realizes Molly is asleep. She tucks her in and kisses her, then goes to her own room and gets undressed and lies beneath the covers, listening for Richard's steps. These days, he speaks to her so rarely she can locate him only by the floorboards' sigh or the toilet's flush. It's like living with a ghost. If she asks about his job, he says, "I'm getting used to it." How can she not be curious about what goes on inside a prison? How can she not want to know what it feels like to sit alone with a man who has fed his wife's body through a wood chipper or drowned his infant son?

She hears him shuffling around the living room. Some nights, even now that their room has been re-plastered, he sleeps on the couch downstairs.

Go to him, she thinks. But she hates the possibility that she might be rebuffed. *What would Jesus do?* The refrain keeps running through her head, but no obvious answer comes, and when Richard finally climbs the stairs, she simply trusts to instinct and reaches out and caresses his face until he moans and moves toward her. He lifts off her shirt and begins sucking at her breasts. Usually, when he does this, she feels an electric thrill. But as tentative as he has been since the fire, he is now that aggressive. His movements have a hysterical quality, like the overexertion of a long-distance runner who starts out at a sprint and will soon tire and give up.

Which is exactly what happens. Richard stops before she comes and collapses with his head between her legs. She lies there with her hand on the back of his head, staring at the ceiling and blinking back tears, and if anyone were to ask her right then what could be sadder than a man lying with his head between his wife's legs while she stares at the ceiling, crying, Louise would answer, *Nothing. Not a thing could be sadder.* But a few hours later, she will be forced to revise that judgment. In fact, the saddest thing is to fall asleep after a failed attempt at lovemaking, only to awaken to the rocking of your marriage bed and your husband's stifled gasps as he masturbates by your side.

In thirteen years of marriage, Louise has never been to church, so she can't very well get up the morning after their dispiriting attempt at making love and tell Richard she is going to Potawatomie to attend a service. She might as well say he has driven her to a nunnery.

Luckily, Richard and Molly are still asleep. She pulls on a filmy spring shift, as if dressing for a season might make it come sooner, then puts on her coat and slips outside. The sky is such a dense quicksilver gray she almost expects to see an inverted image of herself above her head. There is nothing she needs to do and nowhere she needs to be, a condition that unsettles her. As a child, she found Sundays to be intolerable. Her parents didn't own a television set. Imelda was the only other girl for miles, and she needed to help her mother check out the guests at the family's motel. Attending church took on a mystical significance, as if, should Louise ever get inside, she would be part of a holy family as lovingly maintained as the figures in the crèche on the Town Hall lawn.

A few times, when she got older, she went to church alone. But sitting in a pew with no one on either side made her feel even more abandoned. In college in the seventies, no one went to church. The only student she knew who attended religious services was Richard, and he attended synagogue only out of guilt because his father had survived the Nazis.

But Richard hasn't shown much interest in anything Jewish since arriving in Stickney Springs. Passover is coming up, but he has ignored Louise's entreaties that they drive to Ann Arbor and stock up on kosher-for-Passover food. It's as if, when they moved to Michigan, he forgot to bring his faith, or, like their iron, hasn't bothered to unpack it.

She drives to Potawatomie and asks directions to the Unitarian Church. The first three people she stops don't know. The fourth, a blue-haired old lady in a colorful crocheted shawl, whispers how to get there, as if Louise has asked her about a cult. The houses around the church are shabbier versions of Louise and Richard's Victorian in Stickney Springs. Later, Louise will learn that in the early 1940s, a judge's widow left her house to the city's still-churchless congregation of Unitarians. In those days, the Protestant middle class lived on these tree-lined streets. But they have since moved farther west, and the church is now surrounded by black and Hispanic families who attend the Catholic and Baptist churches in the center of Potawatomie, where the factories and prison stand.

A small marquee beside the parking lot announces that this is the FIRST UNIVERSALIST-UNITARIAN CHURCH, and below that runs a quote: "I wish to live deep and suck out all the marrow of life. —H.D. Thoreau." Services have already started, which leads Louise to hope that the minister will be too busy to notice her come in. Then again, the church is so small she has nowhere to hide.

Just inside the door hang notices about hunger relief

in Potawatomie, a request for volunteers to staff the AIDS Coalition, and a reminder for everyone to sign up to build a house for Habitat for Humanity. The sanctuary resembles someone's parlor; the folding metal chairs are occupied by a dozen hunched women in shapeless frocks and their pale, gangly husbands in short-sleeve shirts and cardigans. Two overweight shaggy men sit in the front row holding hands. In San Francisco, it was hardly radical to be a Unitarian, but here in Potawatomie it requires a certain courage to attend a church where Christ isn't considered divine and posters ask for help in running a safe house for people with H.I.V. and two men sit in the front row holding hands.

Louise slips into a chair at the back of the room. The sanctuary's white walls are relieved only by a stained-glass "window" made from bits of translucent colored paper pasted on a cardboard square. A stage runs along the front, with an urn of pussy willows, a lectern, and a tall iron candlestick holding a single large beeswax candle. Ames sits beside the urn staring over his congregation's heads. He wears a collarless linen shirt with an embroidered stole that resembles a longer, skinnier version of the *tallis* Richard wears to synagogue. Louise's heart flickers when she sees him. That's all she can think—her heart flickers the way the candle on that candlestick flickers whenever the back door opens and someone lets in a draft. Ames's long bony hands are folded on his lap. He seems lonely and cut off, although this might be because the chairs on either side of him sit empty.

A slender woman with lanky platinum hair and long legs encased in silver trousers—she reminds Louise of a pair of scissors—walks to the stage and thanks the mustachioed man at the piano for providing that day's musical accompaniment. She announces a hymn, and everyone stands to sing it. Louise finds the page and sings along: *Now the green blade riseth from the buried grain. Wheat that in dark earth many days has lain. Love lives again, that with the dead has been. Love is come again like wheat that springeth green.*

The pianist hammers the final chords on his jangly, jarring upright, and Ames stands and trades places with the woman at the lectern. He rubs his chin and squints. "The theme of today's service is rebirth. But before we get to the rebirth part, we should probably do the birth part. I know that Marge and Alan Greene want us to rejoice with them in the recent appearance of their daughter, Mary Caitlin. Alan called this morning to say that mother and daughter are resting peacefully and they send their best to everyone."

A murmur of genuine pleasure rises from the parishioners. Ames looks around the room. "I see we have some visitors here today, if they would care to introduce themselves."

Louise feels her face flush. Does he do this every Sunday, or has he singled her out? Behind her a chair squeaks, and she swivels to see a woman in a pink silk blouse stand and smooth her skirt. "I just moved here from Ohio," the woman says nervously, "and my friend Jocelyn here—" She glances down at her friend, who smiles around and waves, at which Louise realizes that the section in which she sits is populated entirely by single women. "My friend Jocelyn here has been a member at this church for, what now, a year? And she told me I would like the way you Unitarians don't talk about people committing sins and being damned. And she said I would like the minister. Which, so far, I do." The woman sits. Her friend jabs her, and she jumps back up. "My name is Irene Charmanian. Like the toilet tissue, but with an extra 'ian.'"

A second member of the minister's cheerleading section introduces herself, followed by a man in a muskrat-brown toupee who is sitting near the front. In a chirpy singsong the congregation welcomes each newcomer. *Welcome, Irene.*

Welcome, Nancy. Welcome, Alexander. All the while, Ames keeps rearranging his stole, as if it were a live animal that refuses to lie still. Finally, he emerges from behind his lectern.

"Most Unitarians don't make much of a fuss about Christ's rising on Easter morning," he reminds his congregation. "As Unitarians, most of us don't even make that much of a fuss about Christ." This gets a gentle laugh. "But I want to start today's sermon by considering what it means when someone uses the word *passion*. What it means for someone to say 'Christ's passion on Golgotha,' or 'Christ's passion on the cross.'"

Once he hits his stride—literally, he begins pacing across the stage—he is a very impressive speaker. He consults no notes, which gives the impression that he is taking his cue from God. Because of his Boston accent—he says "gahden" instead of "garden" and "dahk, dahk path ahead" instead of "dark, dark path"—Louise keeps thinking of Jack Kennedy responding to questions from the press, making up jokes as he goes along.

She misses a good bit of what comes next, then tunes in again when Ames defines passion as a desire that can never attain its object. As such, it is a condition that requires suffering. "We don't say that a person *enjoys* a passion, do we? We say that a person *endures* a passion. He *suffers* a passion. Passion is a love for something unattainable. Love that brings the lover pain. What could be healthy about love like that? No one wants to suffer. Better an easy, companionable relationship with a partner who is available. Better an easy, companionable relationship with a god who doesn't make demands. A god who doesn't even demand that you believe he exists."

Ames becomes so engrossed in his speech that he passes too near the candlestick, and the wake from his stole causes the candle to tilt. "Yet even with everything I have said against it, doesn't passion have a lot to recommend it? Doesn't a passion for anything pump up the volume on your life? Even if you can't attain it, doesn't the passion give your life energy and definition? Didn't the ecstasy that Christ experienced on the cross, the ecstasy of knowing God, of forgiving his tormentors, help him transcend his pain?"

The members of the congregation shift in their seats, although Louise guesses that Ames has misconstrued the reason for their distress. "I know, I know. Most of us today aren't comfortable with the mere notion of suffering. We take a more levelheaded approach to love and work and politics. What's the point of wanting something that can't exist? The perfect love. The perfect job. The leader who won't betray us. The god who answers all our prayers." Finally, to everyone's relief, he rights the candle, after which he stands studying his waxy fingertips before wiping them on his stole. "And yet," he goes on, "without passion, aren't we too timid? Doesn't life lack, well, vibrancy? Enthusiasm?" He looks out across the congregation. "Interesting word, *enthusiasm*. Does anyone know its derivation?" He doesn't wait for a response. "It means 'possessed by the gods.' When was the last time anyone in this room felt *possessed* by anything? Why is it that only people who inhabit the extreme end of the spectrum don't feel ashamed to be enthusiastic about their faith?"

This time, he looks around as if he truly expects someone to raise a hand. Louise tries not to show how much this question troubles her. She has always wanted to feel secure. Yet she also longs for passion. This isn't a promising recipe, she knows. She is like one of those firefighters who lights illicit fires only to put them out.

She gets so lost in trying to answer Ames's question that she almost misses what comes next. *Dionysus*, Ames says, then launches into an improvised retelling of Dionysus's young manhood, his gambols with the nymphs, his discovery of how to brew wine.

"What does he want us to do," a voice behind Louise whispers, "get drunk and hold an orgy?"

"If he's officiating, count me in."

"With that wife of his, he must be desperate. What do you expect?"

Abruptly, Ames finishes and takes his seat. As far as Louise can tell, he has offered no moral. Probably, Unitarians don't believe in morals. The woman who looks like a pair of scissors reminds everyone that doughnuts will be served following the final hymn. Louise considers sneaking out. If she stays, Ames might come down the aisle and see her. But if she darts out now, she will be even more conspicuous.

They sing the final hymn and close their books. There is only one door, and Ames plants himself beside it. Louise sees no choice but to get in line. There are wet marks beneath his arms. Up close, the stole looks wrinkled. She hadn't noticed this before, but his ears are pointy, like Mr. Spock's.

He has shaken the hand of everyone who has passed before him, but when he sees Louise, he steps back and lets his hand drop. She wasn't sure he would remember her, and she certainly didn't expect that her appearance would disconcert him, but apparently it does.

Someone bumps up behind her. "The AIDS Coalition," Ames says hurriedly to Louise. "Didn't you say you want to help?"

A man in green plaid golf pants jostles Louise aside. "So, Rev, with all that stuff about Dionysus, I was kind of hoping there would be a nice merlot to go with the doughnuts."

Ames makes a gesture to indicate to Louise how sorry he is that they won't have a chance to speak. The conspiratorial way he looks at her makes her feel lightheaded. *With that wife of his, he must be desperate.* She has no notion of what to do, and so, when he turns to offer a rejoinder to the man in plaid pants, she takes the opportunity to slip away.

Outside, the clouds have lifted. The air smells pleasantly of mud and smoke. The women who were sitting behind Louise in church now stand beside her van, puffing cigarettes.

"He couldn't get away with talking about Dionysus if he wasn't so damn good-looking," one of the women says.

Louise climbs in her van and inches past them. A yellow haze hovers above their heads. In the mirror she can see Irene Charmanian lift her arms and shimmy like a flamenco dancer, or like a woman in the throes of passion, or maybe she is only stomping her foot to put out her cigarette.

TWO

HE HANGS HIS STOLE BEHIND THE DOOR. WITHOUT IT, AMES feels clumsy and inarticulate, like Superman without his cape. He has never been sure what Natalie intended when she stitched the colored whorls and wisps. God's spirit, or His breath? But every time he remembers his young wife with the fabric across her knees, plying her needle across an old-fashioned wooden hoop, he feels such a furious longing for their past that he puts his face against the fabric, as if the smell might transport him back to that first year of their marriage.

But the odor of the stole is stale. When did he last take it to the cleaner's? Will those waxy finger-marks come out? He hates the idea of explaining to the young woman at Wenzeler's that no, this isn't a scarf or shawl. He will need to admit he is a minister, at which she will stammer and blush, and he will need to say something slightly risqué to prove he isn't the prissy strict-constructionist most of his colleagues are.

He straightens the notepad on his desk, then peeks out the office door. Everyone has given up and left, including the new woman, the one with the name like toilet tissue, and her friend, Ellen Benson, who once confided to Ames that his congregation admires him for staying with his wife but hardly expects him to live like a monk.

Outside, the gravel crunches beneath his shoes. Earlier, he glimpsed the sun, but it has since gone back behind the clouds; the weather in this part of Michigan could break a person's heart. His Escort rasps and heaves, a sound that reminds him of his mother coughing in the night. Even now, the memory brings a scratchy terror to his throat; as a boy, Ames felt torn between going in to see if he could help her and dreading what he would find if he did.

He pumps the gas and the engine catches. Why on earth did he tell his congregation about Dionysus? He doesn't consider it *preaching* if the minister reads his sermon from neatly typed sheets, but allowing room for inspiration leaves the door open to whatever repressed garbage is crammed in a person's soul. What does he know about Dionysus, except what he remembers from an undergraduate production of *The Bacchae*, during which he was so stoned he barely remembered his lines?

He turns on the radio. Click and Clack, the Tappet Brothers, laugh uproariously about a guy who thinks he can get another hundred thousand miles out of his Volkswagen van. "Face the facts, fella," one of the brothers says. "The sixties are dead, and so is this van of yours." The other brother brays so loudly Ames switches down the volume. Do the brothers laugh that raucously in real life, or is their laughter a radio trick they turn on and off? Years before, in Cambridge, Ames lived around the corner from the Good News Garage, where Tom and Ray used to work. He took his MG in for repairs a few times but can't recall if he heard either brother laugh. Why has it taken him so long to catch the Christian connotations of the name? Is this radio show a clandestine way of spreading the faith? The brothers bray again. Do they go on the radio without a script? How do they keep from saying stupid things? All that nonsense about passion in daily life . . . He had intended to inspire his congregation to bring more than grudging obligation to their worship of God and their service to the community. Instead, he delivered a sermon so blatantly self-revealing he might as well have confessed that he hasn't had sex in weeks.

He cracks the Escort's window to blow away his own acrid stink. What no one ever tells you about preaching is how much it makes you sweat. The spring air wafts in, a scent like mentholated shaving cream. Sunday is the only day a person in this town can smell anything besides frying onions. The windshield is spattered with yellow pollen-fluff. He turns on the wipers, but that only makes a bigger mess. A wasp buzzes weakly against the glass. Should he kill it, or flick the wasp outside? It upsets him that he has the nerve to do neither.

Right on Hoover, right on Oak, then a third right on Grand. The tight pink phallic buds on the maples make Ames's crotch tingle, an effect intensified by the sight of his neighbor, Mrs. Keeler—in his mind, he calls her Mrs. *Kneeler*—down on all fours, her not-insignificant rump sheathed in some stretchy lilac material as she grubs among her plants. Another neighbor, a man whose martial ardor and secrecy have led

Ames to suspect he belongs to the CIA, pushes a mower across his lawn, although the grass isn't long enough to need a clipping. The man is always outside performing some task that doesn't require doing, as if he needs an excuse to spy on his neighbors.

Ames's mother would say that the lower classes think all they need to do to pass for members of the upper class is to plant flowers and mow their lawns. She has been to Potawatomie only once, to celebrate Bec's third birthday, and as they drove in from the airport she asked Ames if he and Natalie intended to get one of those bathtub Marys, although none of his neighbors actually have such a statue. *How thoroughly drab and unremarkable*, his mother sniffed, not realizing that this is exactly what her son likes about the place. It's like being in a witness-protection program; he has never lost his fear that the terrible person he was in his twenties might someday try to find him, and that arrogant, shallow shit would never think to look for him in a neighborhood such as this. This fear about the past plagues him more strongly some days than others, and today is such a day. First there was the sermon about Dionysus, then that pretty blonde woman from California showing up at his church.

The Escort rattles down the long, curving drive to his garage. He parks to the side, to give Natalie's Volvo room. The girls' playhouse has blown over again. He had intended to build them a real wooden playhouse, but when the clerk at Home Depot showed him the plans and materials he would need, Ames bought a ready-made plastic house instead.

He kneels and tips it upright. Toys spill out the door— plastic teacups, a plastic hamburger on a bun, a plate of plastic fried eggs with plastic strips of bacon and plastic sausages. Natalie has gone so overboard in keeping kosher he's surprised she hasn't prohibited their daughters from serving plastic bacon to their dolls. The sausages look like turds, but he presses one to his lips, as he often does with his daughters' toys, and finds himself thanking God that he is the father of two daughters who hold tea-parties for their dolls and that he didn't end up the man he started out to be, a man who saw no reason to be alive other than to sleep with as many women as he could and waste his family's modest fortune on expensive cars and spur-of-the-moment trips to South America to purchase drugs. Not for the first time, he thanks God for this very gratitude, the startling sense of awe that is the only religious impulse that justified his calling to become a minister.

It's a feeling that first struck him years ago, while he was stumbling across the bridge from Cambridge to Beacon Hill. One of his plays had been performed the evening before, and he had passed the hours since the performance in a blur of hashish, booze, and women. He was halfway across the bridge when a jet lifted off from Logan and sheared the sun, and something about that jet, lit from behind by God's eternal spotlight, shook him with the understanding that none of what he saw had come about by chance—not the silvery thrilling jet, not the grimy train rumbling up from the tunnel beside the bridge, not the universities or research centers scattered across the city, not the very earth on which he stood, spinning as it was about that magnificent yellow sun. At that, Ames surprised himself by slipping to his knees amid the gull droppings and smashed bottles on the footpath and offering thanks to a God he hadn't known he believed in. Then he doubled back to Harvard Yard, where he sobered up at the Mug 'N Muffin, picked up an application to the Divinity School, filled it out at Widener, and turned it in before the awe could fade, which, so far, it hasn't.

He unlocks his back door, praying that his daughters might

be playing in the basement playroom, which—*thank you, God*—they are. Ann is stringing colored beads to make the lizard-shaped keychains that have become a fad in the past few months. Bec sits hunched over the small wooden desk he picked up at a church auction, sketching a very realistic duck rising from a pond. He bends and kisses her hair, which smells like vanilla frosting.

"That's terrific, Beccums. That duck looks as if it's flying right off the page."

Bec wrinkles her nose, which has a trough down the middle that her mother is afraid might mar her beauty, although Ames knows this is precisely the sort of imperfection a grown man might fall in love with. "I don't have the wings right. They're twice as big as they should be." She scowls and uses her teeth to tear a thumbnail.

Ann runs over and thrusts a sheet of paper in his face. "Look at mine. Bec does it the easy way. She draws things she can see. I make mine up." The drawing shows a stick-figure man standing beside a barber pole with a scarf around his neck—or maybe that's a stole—lifting his arms before a flock of bowling-pin-shaped birds that also are wearing scarves. DADDY AND THE PENGWINS, the title reads.

"That's wonderful, Anna-banana." He hugs his younger daughter, resisting the urge to correct her spelling or ask what she means by showing him preaching to a congregation of penguins at the North Pole.

"Why does Becca's duck have more than two wings?" Ann asks slyly.

"It only has two." Bec doesn't raise her face. "That's the way you show the wings are moving."

"They don't look moving to me. They look like the duck has a lot of wings. Dad, doesn't Becca's duck look like it has a lot of wings?"

"At least it isn't wearing a scarf. Dad, would you please inform Ann that real penguins don't wear scarves?"

Ann sticks out her tongue, but Bec can't see because she has lowered her head to the page. How different his daughters are; you would scarcely believe they're sisters. Nor does he see much evidence of his or Natalie's personality in either girl. Why do Christians consider it a miracle that God created man from clay, but not that a child's personality can develop gesture by gesture, joke by joke, and wound by wound from a string of nucleic acids?

Ann returns to stringing beads, Bec continues drawing, and Ames stands looking at them both. With all the women he has ever loved, he has never been so smitten that he couldn't take his gaze from a lover's face, as he can't stop staring at his daughters. It's all he can do not to keep touching them. As a boy, his mother once surprised him with his fingers in her cold cream jar and slapped it away, no doubt fearing that the next step would be for her sensitive, slender son to dress in her fancy underclothes. But really, Ames had only been tempted by the sight of that fresh, smooth cream, which is how he feels now about his daughters' skin.

"Will you take us to the movies?" Bec asks. "They're showing *Beauty and the Beast*."

"Would you, Dad? Everyone says it's good. There's this talking teapot, and a candlestick that—"

"Mother said *she* would take us," Bec adds gravely, "but she won't let us buy anything good to eat."

He resists the urge to capitalize on his wife's religious fanaticism to trump her place in his daughters' hearts.

Bec crumples her drawing. "She said to tell you to come up to the attic. She said to tell you you had some messages."

He kisses each girl, sucking in their flowery scents. Then he climbs the stairs to the living room, heavily, as if he were a boy trying to delay a scolding from his mother. Everything is in its place, the magazines fanned out attractively on the coffee table, the pillows perfectly plumped and placed on either end of the sofa. Even with the sun so weak, the room is suffused with light. For his own sake, he wouldn't care if he lived in a cardboard box. But for his daughters' sakes, he loves living in this house—the stability it represents, his success at not having subjected them to the childhood he had been subjected to, not shipping them off to boarding school or sending them bouncing around the country like packages whose labels have been scribbled out and replaced by NO SUCH PERSON AT THIS ADDRESS.

He only wishes Natalie hadn't insisted on furnishing their living room with antiques, most of which she scrounged from his grandfather's house up north and his mother's vacation home in Maine. Every time he opens a drawer he is afraid he might discover one of his grandfather's awful magazines, or a diary in which some long-deceased Puritan Wye describes putting a heretic to death.

He detours to the kitchen; he never eats before he preaches, so by the time he gets home he's starved. He prefers the kitchen to the living room since everything here is new. If only Natalie hadn't bought two sets of dishes, one for dairy and one for meat, and two sets of silverware. He finds it difficult to remember which set is which and so suffers a mild anxiety that he might inadvertently cause his wife to be tainted or damned.

He eats cornflakes from the box and chugs milk from the container. There is a message on the message pad—a request for a visit from an elderly shut-in named Priscilla Walker, whose father founded American Rope and Twine. If Priscilla Walker had been poor, Ames would have visited her that afternoon. But the idea that she is dangling a bequest in return for his attentions makes him feel soiled. Instead of returning her call, he goes in to take a shower.

He and Natalie haven't yet been reduced to sleeping in separate rooms, but every time he sees their bed he stops to calculate how long it's been since she's had her period and might make love to him again. By what bizarre twist of fate has he come to be living with a woman who observes the Jewish rituals of female purity? He balls his shirt and tosses it toward the hamper. When it hits the floor, he leaves it where it is as a protest against his wife's sexual withholding.

In the shower, he soaps the warm, hairy hollow beneath each arm and, without knowing exactly how, daydreams himself into a state of arousal. Retracing his train of fantasy, he becomes aware of the image of a naked woman splayed on her back in a cage of colored balls. The woman from McDonald's. The woman at his church.

He washes his hair, towels off, and then stands deciding if he might relax and put on jeans. No, he really ought to visit Priscilla Walker. It isn't fair to penalize her just because she is rich. He puts back on his good trousers, takes a fresh shirt from the wardrobe, then goes upstairs to see his wife.

The steps to the attic are so steep Ames feels as if he is climbing to a tree house. Natalie finished the room herself, which means that she paid minimal attention to comfort or aesthetics. The attic is very hot in summer and bitterly cold in winter, but Natalie doesn't care. She is a woman of extremes. She went from ignoring her mother's Jewish ancestry to observing the religion as ferociously as a Pharisee simply because she accompanied Ames to Israel for a two-week conference on Jewish-Christian-Muslim cooperation.

He stands and watches her work, the nape of her neck as bare and tense as a celery stalk. In a fit of obedience to the Jewish precept that no stranger should be seduced by a married woman's hair, Natalie shaved her head. She has since regretted doing it and is letting the reddish fluff grow back, but Ames can't help but wonder if his wife's religious mania is a form of mental illness. Then again, how can a minister suggest that someone's spiritual ardor might be a matter for therapeutic intervention? A fit of mania that came on so suddenly and blossomed to such extravagant proportions in such a short time might vanish as rapidly as it came. They *do* still have sex. There is only that two-week interval of abstinence every month. And Ames has to admit that he finds something beautiful in his wife driving to Ann Arbor to immerse herself in a ritual bath before driving home and presenting herself, thus purified, to him.

He comes up noisily behind her, but Natalie doesn't turn her head. She is sitting broomstick-straight to see inside the computer she is attempting to fix. As an undergraduate at Brown, she double-majored in political science and engineering; now, she uses her technical facility to install additional memory in their neighbors' P.C.s or fix whatever glitches are interfering with their spreadsheets. Maybe if she had pursued a real career instead of cobbling together part-time jobs—repairing computers, helping to run the preschool—she wouldn't have so much energy to pour into her religion.

Ames runs his palm up her neck and kisses her silky head. He wants her to lift her face to meet his mouth. He wants her to ask how services went and console him for his dissatisfaction. Then again, if she still paid him that much attention, he wouldn't have felt compelled to deliver such an inappropriate sermon. As often happens, he entertains the image of a woman bringing him bread and wine and rubbing lotion on his feet. It's the scene from *Jesus Christ Superstar* in which Jesus is attended by Mary Magdalene, and not only is Ames ashamed of equating himself with Christ or expecting any woman to bathe his feet, he knows it's pathetic for a minister to derive his religious inspiration from a Broadway show.

"Hello, dear." Natalie pats his cheek but doesn't turn and kiss him. Doesn't she miss the way they used to sit for hours and explore each other's mouths? He wants to unscrew her bony skull and yank out whatever circuits are in there and replace them with the chip that holds her memories of their earliest years together. "I told the girls you would take them to the movies, but you ought to pay a call on Mrs. Walker first." She lifts out a circuit board, lays it on a cloth, and picks up a second chip that looks identical to the first. "And there's a perfectly awful message on the machine. I was in the shower and missed the call. I don't *ever* want to hear anything like that again. Really, what if the girls had heard?" She wipes her hands on a special rag that whisks away the static. "I left a turkey sandwich in the fridge. Enjoy your bread while you can. Passover is coming up."

He pats her arm. It's only a turkey sandwich, but it is a kind of offering. "I'll make sure whatever it is doesn't happen again," he assures her, then starts back down the stairs. He will need to call Howie Drucker and tell him to save his tasteless gay jokes for when they see each other in person. Really, what kind of barely disguised hostility toward Natalie would cause Howie to leave such messages? And he will need to warn Howie that the woman from California might call to volunteer for the coalition. What's her name, Laura? Lois? Some ordinary, mousy name that doesn't do her justice.

Back in the kitchen, he finds the turkey sandwich and eats it standing up. He was wrong to use the coalition as an excuse to chat up a pretty woman. But he felt flustered seeing her in his church. Sometimes he thinks he left the East Coast precisely to get away from temptations like this. Unlike most Midwesterners, this Lara or Louise doesn't seem embarrassed by her beauty. She wears her hair long most Midwestern women cut their hair the minute they get married, a ritual as exacting as the Orthodox Jewish law Natalie has obeyed. And there's something lost about her. That's the hardest thing for him to resist, the sense that a woman grew up as neglected as he did.

He puts the plate from the turkey sandwich in the meat sink—at least he *thinks* it's the meat sink—and takes a pint of Ben and Jerry's from the freezer. There's no such thing as a small affair. At least not for him. And he isn't about to harm his daughters. Scientifically speaking, a parent's willingness to die for his child is Nature's way of protecting that parent's DNA. But Ames has a theory that a human being's drive to protect his genes is God's way of creating a species capable of feeling the kind of miraculously altruistic love that Ames feels for Bec and Anne.

The answering machine catches his eye. Whatever joke Howie left this time has to be a doozie. Looking around to make sure Bec and Ann aren't within earshot, Ames presses the button.

What he hears first is a recording of someone singing "Dixie," and then the same singer belting out a chorus of "The Battle Hymn of the Republic." The singer is Elvis, which would make sense, given that Howie is one of the King's biggest fans, but the voice that follows isn't Howie's, and it certainly isn't saying anything Howie would ever say.

"You traitor. You're polluting the race with AIDS. The day is coming when you and your Commie fag friends will be hanging from the trees. Take this as a neighborly warning and have a nice day."

By the time the message stops, Ames is vibrating with rage. He isn't frightened for himself. After centuries of being the oppressors, the Wyes have finally weighed in on the side of the oppressed, and messages like this are part of their atonement. Nor is he afraid for Natalie. If anyone can take care of herself, it's Natalie. He is worried for their daughters. Even if the moron who left this message isn't evil enough to hurt a pair of innocent little girls, there are kids at school whose parents share this moron's beliefs. Natalie might have been able to start her own daycare center, but she can't very well start her own middle school and senior high.

Ames looks out the window and sees that Mr. CIA is using an edger to trim his walk. *A neighborly warning*, the voice had said. Irrationally, Ames blames Natalie for refusing to accept invitations from the other women on the block because she and the girls can't eat non-kosher food. But he knows that the real reason for the threat isn't Natalie's conversion to Judaism but rather his own work in the community. What he blames Natalie for has little to do with religion. He removes a bowl from the cabinet and a spoon from the drawer and spoons ice cream in the bowl, chiding himself because a better man than he wouldn't derive such petty pleasure from knowing that the bowl and spoon are meant for meat.

THREE

AS IT TURNS OUT, LOUISE DOESN'T NEED TO LIE ABOUT GOING to church. Richard never asks. The minute she gets home, he shoots out the door to buy fishing supplies with Matt, while Molly and Louise spend the afternoon decorating Molly's room. Later, all three go out for pizza. Louise and Richard speak with extra fervor to their daughter, as if to keep from noticing they have nothing to say to each other. After they all get home, Louise tucks in Molly for her first night in her new bed. By the time she and Molly have finished the ritual, Richard is asleep on the couch.

This should worry Louise. But if he is sleeping on the

couch, they can't suffer a repetition of the last time they tried to make love.

In truth, the days are harder than the nights. Even as a child, Louise hated long stretches of unplanned time. To get through the formless summer afternoons, she had invented things to do. First, she would untie one of her father's rickety rowboats and row the lake's circumference, hoping to get in shape for the rowing team at the Ivy League college she was desperate to attend, although later she found out that "rowing" had little to do with the sorts of boats her father rented. After that, she used a long-handled net to fish golf balls from the shallows that bordered the public course; for every dozen balls, the Korean vet who ran the driving range paid Louise a dime. Finally, she tied up at the Lenape Lake Motel and let herself in the back way to the snack bar, where Imelda's mother was scraping crusted hamburger meat from the grill or shpritzing bleach on the tables. Imelda would come down from cleaning her last motel room, and she and Louise would sit at the counter and talk to Mrs. Robertson, who was the kind of mother whose own daughter didn't mind listening to her advice. *The trick in junior high is not doing anything cruel to anyone, even if they would do that exact same thing to you.* And: *You can smoke marijuana, but don't try any drug that requires a needle, a prescription, or a nose.*

When Louise won a scholarship to SUNY Binghamton but didn't get a penny from Cornell, Mrs. R consoled her by saying that if Louise did well at Binghamton, she could apply to Cornell for graduate school, which was exactly what happened. To help Louise earn tuition, Mrs. R had paid her to help Imelda clean the motel rooms. Louise offered to work for free, but Mrs. R wouldn't hear of it. Louise was eighteen before she realized why Imelda's father so rarely came down from his room, and why, when he did, he could barely navigate the stairs. But Imelda and Louise had turned out fine. Louise got her M.S.W. from Cornell and married Richard; Imelda studied math at Santa Cruz, joined the faculty at Berkeley, and married a composer who lived in Oakland. Louise is not the sort of therapist who craves seeing her name in print, but if she were, she would write an article about the fact that a kid with messed-up parents needs only one responsible adult to turn out fine. The reason she became a child psychologist was to give kids from fucked-up families what Mrs. R had given her. And to help them forgive the parents who had fucked them up.

Because you couldn't go on hating them forever, or pressuring them to change. Louise spent years employing both tactics, until she accepted how ill her parents were. *I'm in a boat*, she had told her therapist, an irreverent Jamaican woman named Vivienne, who had asked her to describe her most persistent image of her parents. *There's a big hole in the bottom of the boat and water is gushing in. My parents are on the shore. I stand up and shout and wave. But all they do is walk away.* Vivienne had offered Louise a box of tissues and said in that gentle lilt: *Well, dear, that's a lot of nonsense, isn't it. You like dreaming this little dream of yours because it allows you to sit in that boat feeling sorry for your own poor self, without stopping to admit that your parents could not save you because they did not know how to swim.*

At which Louise cried harder. Of course they couldn't swim! No one had ever taught them! They probably hoped they would fuck her up less by leaving her to her own devices than by trying to raise her. *Come on, girl*, Vivienne chanted. *Are you going to sit forever in that sinking boat just to prove how insufficient those poor people were? Are you going to go down with that ship and drown?*

Eventually, thanks to Vivienne, Louise had reached the

point where she could take Molly to Mule's Neck to see her parents, although this was mostly from a desire to show off her daughter to Imelda's mother. Molly loved fishing with Louise's father and touring her mother's studio; the first time they visited, Molly told Louise that Grandma Ellen had painted some really pretty paintings of the lake, and Louise agreed, although she had always found her mother's art blurry and sentimental. *We're Utopians*, her mother had once told her, which, when Louise looked it up, confirmed her suspicion that her parents lived in a dream world.

They had met at a socialist camp in the Adirondacks, where Louise's mother ran the arts and crafts program and her father was the director of athletics. Even then, he had hated regulations—Louise imagined him allowing the boys and girls to make up the rules to whatever games they played. This aversion to authority intensified in World War II until he refused to salute an officer, let alone get off the landing raft and join his ever-diminishing battalion to take another island from the Japanese. He would have been court-martialed, except that he was so tongue-tied and diffident his superiors thought he was shell-shocked and sent him to a hospital, where he was left to lie in peace until the war ended.

Which was when Louise's mother saved him. She had written him letters throughout the war, and after he was discharged she welcomed him home and married him. He used his G.I. loan to buy the rowboat concession on Friendship Lake. Camp Brotherhood closed in the fifties, when no one would risk sending a child to a Commie camp, but Louise's father had gotten by selling bait and renting boats to the summer tourists and supplying beer and jerky to the local men who drilled holes in the ice and sat drinking beside their tip-ups throughout the winter. Her parents weren't socialists so much as anarchists. They despised any form of government, which made their politics overlap with the Bankses' in that uncanny way the far left and far right have of circling around and meeting.

As for Louise, she would rather live with too many rules than too few, too much on her to-do list than too few items, and this makes it a struggle to pass the next few formless days, when she has nothing to do but play with Molly. In fact, she reaches a morning when she is able to force herself out of bed only because she hears a dog barking in the kitchen. Hurrying downstairs, she finds Molly on the floor rolling a pink Spauldene for Rod's hideous dog to fetch. Molly's being in her pajamas makes her seem even more defenseless. Although Louise has to admit the dog doesn't seem the least bit vicious. He crouches before Molly, so puppyishly eager to play that he clearly doesn't understand how ferociously big he is. But an agreement is an agreement. "Basement," she orders Rod, who narrows his eyes as if she were ordering *him* to the basement.

"Yeah," he says. "Right." He slips two fingers beneath the dog's studded collar and drags him toward the door.

"Can we get a dog?" Molly begs. "I promise I'll take care of it."

"We'll talk about that later," Louise announces with the formulaic gruffness required by this particular parental script.

"But, Mom—"

"Eat your breakfast." She sets a glass of milk and an untoasted Pop Tart on the new kitchen table. Then, while Molly sulks and refuses to eat, she leans against a wall and closes her eyes. Nothing is really wrong, except that she has moved halfway across the country to a town where she can't make any friends and has little hope of practicing her profession. It isn't as if she is naturally depressed. Her anxiety has a cause. If it persists, she can find a therapist in Potawatomie. That way, at least she will have someone to talk to once a week.

When she opens her eyes, Rod is standing so close that Louise can smell his cologne, a bitter, coppery scent, like the powder in a cap gun. She has the eerie sense he was about to stroke her neck. Is he on drugs? Is that it?

"Don't worry about Smack," Rod tells her. "I made him a nice little doggie bed out of a pile of rags downstairs. He knows I'm in the house so he won't feel too alone. He had a rough puppyhood, you know? And that left him with, what do you call them, abandonment issues."

Yes, well, Louise has abandonment issues, too, but you don't see her peeing on the floor. And those "rags" are the family's dirty clothes, waiting for the new washer to be delivered. Who *is* this kid? And really, he is a kid. Eighteen, maybe nineteen. Except for the wispy roach—with Rod hovering so close, she can count the individual hairs on his chin—he doesn't need to shave.

The phone rings, and the caller identifies herself as Beverly Booth. Louise needs a moment to remember that Beverly Booth is the secretary at the high school. It seems that Mrs. Krauspe, the special-ed teacher, lost her temper and struck a child. This student was a favorite of Ms. Leesome, the social worker, who in any event had been due to leave in June. And when Ms. Leesome tried to reason with Mrs. Krauspe . . .

The tale Beverly Booth relates is so intricate that all Louise can make out is that Mrs. Krauspe has been fired, and Ms. Leesome has resigned, and Mr. Barnes, the school psychologist, is due to go on disability for early-onset Alzheimer's, which will leave twelve hundred students without a special-education teacher, a social worker, or a psychologist. Because Louise is experienced in all three fields, they need her to fill in right away. "Could you come this afternoon?" Beverly asks breathlessly.

Louise's first thought is that there is in fact a God, and

He is showing her His approval for visiting His church. Her second thought is that she has nowhere to leave Molly. That clutchy panic strikes, the disquiet that comes over you when you realize you have moved thousands of miles from anyone required by blood or history to mind your child. She doesn't know anyone but Dolores Banks. And the Bankses own guns.

But what else can she do? Dolores adores Molly. The Bankses probably keep their guns locked up. Dolores is no more of a threat today than she was last week, when she brought over that soggy apple-cake, or all the times Louise has taken Molly to the farm to cuddle the chicks or milk the cow.

Louise finds the Bankses' number and is relieved when Dolores says that yes, she will be delighted to play with Molly. "I. Could. Watch. Her. Every. Day." Dolores's mechanical voice seems less disconcerting when it's coming from a phone than from a live human being. But the proposition is still alarming.

"That's very kind of you," Louise says, "but I only need someone to watch her this one afternoon." She hangs up and helps Molly get dressed. The delivery men show up, and it takes them forever to hook up the new appliances, but finally everything is in its place. She tips the men, then packs a few toys and snacks for Molly.

What she hasn't counted on is Molly's tirade about being left with Dolores Banks. "I won't go. You can't make me." Molly twists in the car seat. The belt across her chest creates the impression of an animal on a leash. "I don't want to. The Bankses make me scared."

This surprises Louise. She would have thought Dolores is the sort of grandmotherly figure any child would love. "I wouldn't leave you with anyone I don't trust," she assures Molly. "She's knitting you that sweater you like, the one with the frog on the front. The Bankses are just a little different from our friends in California. There's that button on her throat. But it isn't Mrs. Banks' fault she got sick." She squeezes Molly's knee, that bony, bare nubbin Louise rubs to produce good luck. "I have this new job and there's nowhere else for you to stay. You would be doing me a big, big favor. Okay, sweetie? Help me out just this once."

Thankfully, Dolores looks particularly benevolent this afternoon. She wears a flowered pink apron and a dress with a lacy collar that conceals her throat. Her hair floats like a meager but clean corona above her scalp. This is the first time since they moved in that Louise has been inside the Bankses' house. Most of the rooms are dark and old fashioned, but someone has sponge-painted the kitchen a cheery blue. The walls are papered with country plaid, and the windows have been hung with rice-paper shades printed with colorful butterflies.

A timer buzzes, and Dolores pours a pot of boiling water down the sink. She motions toward a rack of eggs cooling on the counter. "I. Need. A. Helper." She hoists Molly to a stool. "I. Have. A. Grand. Child. But. Her. Mother. Had. No. Use. For. Living. On. A. Farm. It. Isn't. Easter. If. You. Don't. Have. A. Child. To. Color. Eggs. With."

This is the longest speech Louise has heard Dolores utter. She knew Matt used to be married, but she had no idea he has a child. Poor Dolores. Her daughter-in-law ran off with her only grandchild. No wonder she can't get enough of seeing Molly.

Dolores goes to a closet and produces a colorful apron, which she slips over Molly's head. She winks and tells Louise not to worry about a thing, just go out and "show her best colors," as if Louise were an Easter egg herself.

Relieved, she kisses Molly and heads out through the mudroom, where she stops to belt her coat against another gray Michigan day and notices the calendar beside the door. *Militia Babes 1995*, the title reads, with a venomous snake that warns DON'T TREAD ON ME. The April babe wears a bulletproof vest—like Matt, she doesn't seem to believe in wearing a shirt beneath her vest. Miss May is draped in a bearskin cape; the animal's snarling head rests on her arm, while she draws a lethal-looking bow. Miss June wears a bridal gown pulled low to expose her cleavage. Her tongue curls up to lick the frosting from her lip as she brandishes a small machine gun, squinting playfully at the camera as if she intends to blow away the photographer, or at least shoot the buttons off his fly.

Louise tries to be fair. Most of the babes are middle-aged women and look sexy in ways commercial models don't. Not one is completely nude, and the effect is oddly good-natured, as if their boyfriends and husbands are standing offstage, proud to show off their wives' and girlfriends' skill with weapons. The slogans beneath the photos seem no more subversive than the Declaration of Independence. "As it becomes increasingly obvious that the Constitution of the State of Michigan and the Constitution of the United States are being ignored, violated, and trampled on, we find it necessary to establish the Potawatomie County Militia. . . ." Bizarrely, the calendar shows an ecumenical respect for holidays. The box for April 15 is crowded with a memo that Passover falls that day, a sloppily drawn bull's-eye, and the hand-inked announcement "Tax Blast!"

This last reminder gives Louise pause. Judging by the calendar and the poster, Matt belongs to something called the Michigan Militia. The only militia Louise has ever heard of is the one that fought the British. Do Matt and his buddies think the Russians might invade? Hasn't anyone told them the Cold War is over? She considers going back for Molly, but how would she account for her change of heart? And who will watch Molly while she works?

Louise hurries to the van, backs out without looking, and gets a jarring honk from an S.U.V. She pulls over to catch her breath and sits there on the shoulder across the street from the bungalow that is the only other residence on this stretch of Stickney Road. The yard shimmers with crystal balls, whirligigs, and chimes. As if the inhabitant of the bungalow has sensed Louise's presence, the door opens and out she comes, a gawky woman in orange overalls who sees Louise and flaps one arm in a graceless wave. Louise waves back, and then makes a mental note to bake a batch of cookies and take them over the next afternoon.

With a much lighter heart, she drives to Potawatomie. Just the possibility of this commute becoming a daily habit makes her giddy with relief. When Beverly Booth sees Louise come in, she flings up her hands and says, "I'm so glad all this worked out!"

Mrs. Moorehouse emerges from her office. "It's very good of you to come in. We're extremely shorthanded. But I have to be frank: this is a temporary position. We make no guarantee about a permanent job come fall. For now, you will be working under my supervision. And I think we can get by with your services three days a week."

It has been years since Louise worked under anyone's supervision. And it seems absurd that she will be expected to perform the work of three people in less than forty hours a week. But she is in no position to argue. Mrs. Moorehouse leads her up three flights to what will be her office. "I'm afraid it's very hot up here," she apologizes as Louise follows her down a corridor that resounds with shouts and thuds from the gym below. Mrs. Moorehouse unlocks a door with E. LEESOME painted across the window. Heat has warped the floorboards, and the desk and two chairs tilt on the waves. A pipe runs behind the desk. Someone—Ms. Leesome?—has picked at the duct tape that surrounds the pipe, and a fluffy white substance Louise hopes isn't asbestos puffs from the wound. She thinks of requesting that the janitor patch the pipe, but she is afraid Mrs. Moorehouse will send the man Louise saw cleaning the cafeteria.

A dented file cabinet leans against a wall. Mrs. Moorehouse pulls out a drawer to show Louise it's empty. "I'm afraid Miss Leesome didn't keep files. If any of her clients show up, you'll just have to improvise. What I am most concerned with is that we keep up with the spring assessments and special placements for the fall. I'll speak to the school psychologist and try to get his recommendations." She fingers the diamond cross around her neck. "The poor man. On bad days, he barely remembers his name."

After she has left, Louise walks around touching each piece of furniture in an attempt to make it hers. An inspirational poster of a kitten dangling from a rope is tacked to the corkboard. She takes it down, but a grotesque penis with hairy testicles is markered underneath, so she tacks it back up.

She sits behind the desk, the surface of which is absurdly stained with coffee rings. There seems to be no intercom or phone. What if a student threatens her? In Ithaca, a mother once flew into a rage at Louise's interference in her right to beat her daughter and smashed a lamp against the wall.

She checks her watch—2:45. She probably won't get many drop-ins, although she has gotten most of her clients that way in the past. And teachers send referrals. Of course, none of the teachers in Potawatomie know a thing about her. It will take months, if not years, to develop their trust.

She searches her desk, hoping to find an appointment book. Among the paper clips, tissues, and yellowing letterhead she finds a calcified hot pot, a tattered copy of *Clan of the Cave*

Bear, a paperback edition of the Bible, and a canister of mace. She uses one of the tissues to swab the sweat from between her breasts, then tries without success to open a window. She is looking out at a gym class that consists of boys throwing dodgeballs at each other when a broad-shouldered girl with white-blonde hair comes in. *My first student*, Louise thinks, and needs to restrain herself from appearing too eager.

"That's a pretty dress," the girl says. "I'll bet you didn't get it around this dump."

They chat about the fashion options in southwest Michigan before the girl settles on the edge of Louise's desk and introduces herself as Melody Hasbrouck. If her surname is any indication, her father runs the fish store in Potawatomie.

"I thought Erika—Ms. Leesome?—might be here packing up her stuff. She had a hot pot, you know? She used to make me a cup of cocoa and we'd sit around and talk." Melody motions to the poster. "If you haven't looked under there, I'd really advise you not to."

Louise laughs. "I thought it might make for some interesting conversations."

The girl snickers. "I don't suppose Mrs. Moorehouse told you what happened. Why Erika left, I mean."

Louise makes a noncommittal noise.

"She got in a fight with Mrs. Krauspe. Mrs. Krauspe blew her cool and started whaling on this black kid. And Erika tried to stop Mrs. Krauspe, and Mrs. Krauspe called Erika this really bad name, because Erika is engaged to this black guy at the prison? Erika met him when she was running a Bible study thing out there. And Mrs. Krauspe got fired. And Erika quit. Her fiancé gets out next month, and they're planning on going somewhere no one knows them. Some missionary thing? In India, you know, or Africa?"

Clearly, Christians lead complicated lives; it's just that

their lives are complicated in ways that aren't yet familiar to Louise.

"Okay," Melody says. "Enough about Mrs. Krauspe. Let's talk about me."

Although Melody has worked with Ms. Leesome for some time, Louise doesn't have much catching up to do. ("No offense," Melody says, "but Erika spent most of our sessions talking about herself.") Her parents are getting a divorce. It isn't bad enough they throw scenes at the fish store; Melody's older sister is a single mother with schizophrenia and an infant she can't take care of. To get away from all this uproar, Melody is hoping Louise can persuade her parents to let her live with her best friend, Jen.

As often happens when she listens to a student, Louise is filled with gratitude that her own childhood wasn't nearly as bad as she thinks it was. She suggests Melody tell her parents she wants to stay with Jen for a week or two, until things calm down, rather than inflame the situation by insisting she wants to live with Jen forever. Then Louise digs around in the desk and pulls out the crusted hot pot. "I'll find a cord for this thing and bring in some cocoa. Stop by whenever you want to talk." Melody jumps up from the desk and reaches out to hug her. Ordinarily, Louise is wary about touching students, but this time she can't resist.

Ms. Leesome, it turns out, does have some appointments. Two more students stop by—an anxious perfectionist who is headed for anorexia if she doesn't shake her need to please her parents, and a boy whose buck teeth and stutter make him a target for older thugs. Neither student seems particularly religious. Neither strikes Louise as all that different from the kids she knew in Berkeley.

Then a third student comes in—tall, wearing the usual jeans, a black T-shirt advertising a tourist attraction called the

Mystery Spot, and a gray hoodie with POTAWATOMIE STATE PRISON stamped across the chest, identical to the hoodie Louise's husband now wears when lounging around their house. The boy introduces himself as Parker Rosenkrantz, shakes Louise's hand—she isn't used to students shaking her hand—and sprawls in the empty chair, less from disrespect than the fact that his legs are too long to form right angles to the floor. With his basketball player's build and clean-cut blond good looks, he could have been popular and cruel, but he has the sweet demeanor Louise has come to associate with kids who are content to be themselves and let others do the same. He studies Louise and then utters a cryptic, "You aren't Ms. Leesome," which Louise at first interprets as disappointment that the social worker he has come to visit no longer works there, and then reinterprets to mean that he has been waiting until the former social left so he could try out a new one. The boy turns and stares out the window, whistling a shapeless tune that strikes Louise as a melodic imitation of a person thinking. Then he stops whistling and says, "No use beating around the bush. My dad is a total dick. Nothing anyone says or does is going to change one iota about the man. The thing is . . ." He tents his fingers across his thighs and drums them in an intricately rhythmic way. "The thing is, I have this quartet."

Of course, Louise thinks. A musician. Parker has the detached, distracted air of every student musician she has ever known, whether a precociously gifted violinist, a conga drummer, the bass player in a heavy metal band, or an aspiring operatic tenor; he gives the impression of someone whose exterior is a cork-paneled practice room within which he can play his instrument without disturbing anyone else, at any hour.

"We've got some gigs coming up in Detroit," Parker

explains, "but my dad won't let me go anywhere near Detroit. Part of it is, you know, Detroit is Detroit. The other part is, the guys in the quartet are black. My dad works at the prison. Let's just say he doesn't have the highest opinion of black people. Of course, when you look at the population he needs to deal with . . . This one black prisoner? My dad was walking past his cell, and the prisoner hit him with some . . . excrement. So it's not as if I don't cut my dad some slack. And one of the guys in this band, his father *did* serve some time. But the other guys, their parents work at the twine factory. And one of them, his dad is a guard at the prison, too."

Parker presents an exceedingly calm demeanor. But Louise can't help but note those fingers drumming against his legs, or Parker's habit of rubbing at his eyebrow. His features are so regular it has taken her this long to figure out why his face seems off-kilter—the eyebrow on the right is nearly missing.

"My dad, he's not very big on making distinctions. He hates black people. Period. He hates Detroit. Period. And he hates jazz—big time. Because it's black people music. I told him how Elvis—my dad is this total Elvis freak, which is how I got the name Parker, as in Colonel Tom, although I tell people I'm named after *Charlie* Parker, which is really cool, because, you know, I play the sax? Anyway, I tell my dad how Elvis's music is really black-people music, and he just goes apeshit. My dad, you cross him about anything to do with Elvis and it gets very, very scary."

Parker has made it through this entire explanation without taking a breath, a skill she imagines he developed playing the saxophone. But now he pauses, inhales, tries to compose his thoughts.

"I have this scholarship to this music school in Chicago. I was planning to move there after graduation. But I don't want to wait that long. I thought maybe I could take my G.E.D."

Louise congratulates Parker on his scholarship, commiserates with him on having a parent who doesn't acknowledge his talents and his right to decide what he wants to do with his own life, then asks if his father has ever hit him. The boy rubs his eyebrow and says sure, whose father *hasn't* hit his kid? But not since sixth grade. It's hard to explain, Parker says, but even if you're not afraid of getting hit, you don't want to mess with the man. You just *don't*.

Later, Louise will wish she had encouraged Parker to run away. Instead, she does what any social worker in her position would do: she tries to get him to make the best of a bad situation. "In my day," she jokes, "it was the kids who liked Elvis and their parents who put up a fuss," at which Parker looks out the window again and whistles a tune that seems a polite way of humoring a grownup who thinks she has any idea of what he's going through. "If your father likes Elvis," Louise tries again, "he can't be *that* bad."

Parker turns back and looks at her through those beautiful, thick, long lashes. "Actually," he says, "you have no idea just how bad the dude *can* be."

No, Louise says, she probably doesn't. But she tells Parker that staying for his finals will be a lot simpler than taking his G.E.D. Will another few months really hurt that much? Doesn't he want to stay and graduate with his class?

Sure, Parker says. What kid would want to miss the last few months of his senior year?

Well then, Louise says, his best choice would be to forgo the club dates in Detroit, finish his degree, then take the scholarship and move to Chicago, find a part-time job, and wean himself from any dependence on the man.

Parker pushes back from the desk and stands. With the boy towering above her, she gets a better sense of how physically imposing his father must be to account for Parker's fear. He supposes she's right, Parker admits. He appreciates her advice. He shakes her hand again, turns to go, then stops and asks, "Where did you move here from, New York?" When she tells him California, he rubs his eyebrow and says, "Geez, why would anyone do that." It isn't a question, and Louise doesn't feel obliged to answer, but Parker seems to guess that Louise didn't make the decision voluntarily. "I feel worse for you than I do for me. No matter what happens, I'm getting out of this shit hole pretty soon. My sentence is nearly up. But you, you just moved here. It's like you just got in for life."

Louise is stunned by this show of sympathy from a student. She is afraid she might start to cry, and even more afraid that if she does, Parker will attempt to comfort her. But by the time she has managed to croak out an unconvincing, "Thanks, I'll be fine," he has taken his leave and gone.

Another few minutes pass. She looks around her office one final time, locks the door, and goes downstairs. The air has a delicious scent she can't identify. Then she remembers: the onion-ring factory. Most of the faculty and staff have gone home, but a few women stand trading end-of-the-day gossip. An older man, perhaps Mr. Barnes, the school psychologist, wanders the lot looking for his car.

She hears someone say, "Excuse me!" and turns to see Janet Cohen trotting up. "You got the job! Linda, wasn't it?"

"Louise."

She taps her belly, as if to chide the baby as the cause of her forgetfulness. Louise tells her not to worry—most people seem to have trouble remembering her name. (Imelda used to tease her that it sounded like a laxative. *Take one tablet of Lou-ease and stay regular for a month.* When they started seventh grade, Imelda took to calling her Lulabelle. ("I'm going to miss you, Lulabelle," she had said as they tearfully hugged goodbye after their farewell lunch at Chez Panisse.) "I know the students are going to love you," Janet says. "I only hope the parents give you less grief than they gave me."

Louise finds her van and drives home, reminding herself to show appreciation to whatever god or Fate has rewarded her with this job. She will use the newly delivered stove to make Richard's favorite meal and serve it on their brand-new kitchen table. She will do as many Mad-Libs as Molly wants her to do.

After parking the van in the Bankses' drive, she forces herself to pass the Militia Babes calendar without looking at the pictures. "Hello, hello!" she cries, trying for a musical warble but coming out with the desperate plea of a woman lost in the woods.

"In. Here!" Dolores's voice crackles as if it's coming from an obsolete P.A. system. When Louise walks in, she sees Molly with her arms above her head in an attitude of surrender. Dolores lifts off the smock and ruffles Molly's curls. The kitchen is redolent with the sulfury smell of boiled eggs, the counters cluttered with cups of dye, thin-tipped brushes, sponges, and a collection of Easter stencils.

"Mom!" Molly leaps off the stool and runs into Louise so hard she nearly knocks her down. "I thought you were *never* coming back."

Louse can't imagine why Molly says this—she isn't a minute later than she promised. She goes over to the counter and exclaims at what a lot of eggs Molly has painted. And then, because she is afraid Molly might find such praise too glib, she looks more closely at the eggs. But all Louise can see—and she chooses not to comment on this observation— is that her precocious, determined daughter has painted every egg not only with a smiley face and a design appropriate to Easter, but also with a small, bright Jewish star.

That night, after Molly goes to bed, Louise tells Richard about her summons from Beverly Booth, her encounter with Bess Moorehouse, and her sessions with her students. He seems so genuinely pleased that she omits any reference to the calendar on the Bankses' porch and exaggerates her optimism about getting hired full-time in the fall. She even tells him that driving home that day she had the strangest idea that she might end up happier here than she had been in California.

"Really?" He goes over to the newly installed stove and puts the kettle on for tea. "That's how I feel at the prison."

This stuns her. He isn't miserable?

"Why would you think I'm miserable?"

Can a person be unaware of his own depression? "For one thing, you never talk." *For another thing, you never want to make love.*

"That's only when I'm on the outside. In the prison I feel . . ."

He shows no sign of finishing his sentence, so Louise ventures, "You feel protected?"

"No," Richard says. "I feel free."

Free? In the prison he feels freer than he does at home? The kettle shrieks, and Richard takes it from the burner and tips it to pour out the water without anchoring the lid, which tumbles on the cup and breaks it. He curses and drops the pot, stumbling out of reach of the scalding water, then stands whipping his fingers back and forth and staring helplessly at the mess.

Louise pretends she hasn't seen. "I was talking to someone at McDonald's the other day." Already it feels duplicitous to refer to Ames as *someone.* "I might do some volunteer work.

There's an AIDS coalition in Potawatomie. With the prison here, the incidence of H.I.V. is higher." Since her job at the high school will only be part time, volunteering seems the perfect way to fill her spare hours. She will make like-minded friends and establish connections to the social-work community.

Richard looks up from where he squats, mopping the floor with a towel they use to dry the dishes, an infraction of housekeeping rules for which he once would have chided *her*. "Have you given any thought to what to do with Molly?"

She still has the number of All Faiths Daycare. But what if she doesn't get hired in the fall? The drive twice a day to Potawatomie would be very inconvenient. Dolores can look after Molly. But Molly already has said she doesn't want to stay at the Bankses' farm.

Richard tosses the towel in the sink, then shambles over and kisses her. It is a dry kiss. A cool kiss. More like the minimum payment on a credit-card balance than a serious effort to pay off the principal. Still, it is their first kiss of any kind since that fiasco making love, and she asks if he wants to go upstairs.

"It's too early," he says, leaving her to wonder if he is turning down her proposition or merely delaying its acceptance.

Hopefully, she climbs the steps and puts on her best nightgown. She leaves the door ajar. But Richard never comes, and she falls asleep and dreams that the electrician's assistant, Rod, has received a vision that Jesus Christ is buried inside the walls of their house. The dream should be upsetting—it's like something out of Poe. But this treasure hunt for Jesus, this notion that of all the possible houses in the world, Jesus should have chosen to be entombed in hers, strikes Louise as thrilling. She and Rod pull down the freshly plastered walls without finding a single bone. *The basement*, Rod suggests. *Let's dig up the basement.* The suggestion is so compelling that even as morning comes and Richard's departure wakes her, she is tempted to go down and check.

Instead, she pulls on her robe and goes down to find Molly. Jesus might not be entombed inside their house, but Louise is excited about her plan to go over and meet the woman in the bungalow. She hasn't thought to buy eggs, so the cookie plan is out, but she and Molly go outside to cut some jonquils, which they arrange in an old-fashioned milk jug Louise finds beneath the sink.

The sun has come out and the earth smells fresh. Leaves have leafed and blooms have bloomed and wildflowers have burst out along the road. What kind of talent does it take to enjoy life in California? Here, it requires spunk. You need to make it through all the crappy winter months to qualify for a day like this.

"It's not so bad here," she says to Molly. "You might almost say it's pretty."

Molly stomps the gravel. "You're just saying that. This place isn't anywhere near as pretty as the place we used to live. Daddy works in a *prison*. I miss the blueberry bagels you used to buy and the peaches at the farmers' market. I miss my friends. *A lot.* I don't have one single friend here except Smack the dog. In California, you went to work and then you picked me up and you made this *huge* fuss over me. Now, we're together all the time and you *never* make a fuss."

Louise sets the bottle in the dirt and puts her hands on Molly's arms. If she were a different kind of mother, she might try to convince her daughter that everything is fine. But if there is one lesson she has learned as a social worker, it's that denying reality is the easiest way to make a child lose, well, her sense of reality. You might as well slap a kid in the face, and then say, *What do you mean? What slap?*

"You're right. Potawatomie is the pits. But we already bought this house. Dad promised he would work at the prison, and grownups have to spend a year or two making good on their promise to do a job or they'll never get a new one. So we're trying to make the best of things. I'm not sure about the blueberry bagels, but I think if we wait until the end of summer, we might find some fresh peaches here in Michigan."

Molly sneezes. Great, Louise thinks, she's allergic to the flowers. "If we still don't like it," Molly asks, "can we go back to California?"

"Maybe," Louise says. "But I can't make any promises. Every family has to go through a really bad time so they can look back and say, *Hey, everybody, remember that really bad time we went through?* It's called a bonding experience. It's what makes a family feel like a family. And this hasn't been long enough or bad enough to qualify. So let's give it our very best, and if that doesn't work—"

Molly pulls away, and in that fussy old-lady voice she picked up from Richard's mother, she says: "You and I both know we're never going back."

Sobered, Louise takes the bottle of jonquils in one hand and Molly's hand in her other hand and resumes walking down the road.

"Ouch," Molly says. "You're holding my hand too tight." She yanks it away and rubs it. "I'm only a kid. You shouldn't take everything I say so serious."

Molly is in the kind of mood in which she will oppose any idea Louise proposes, especially the idea of visiting some stranger in a run-down house. But the bungalow charms them both. With its shimmering whirligigs and tinkling chimes, it seems to be enclosed in a bubble of beneficence. Standing there, you half expect a hand to lift you up and shake you and cause a flurry of glittery flakes to swirl.

Molly jumps up and down. "It looks like the house the Keebler elves live in!"

"Why not ring the bell?" Louise suggests.

Molly prepares to do just that, but she is stopped by a card that reads PLEASE BRING BIRDS AROUND BACK. Molly glances around the porch. "I don't see any birds."

"It means *if* you have a bird."

"Oh. I guess we don't."

Birdless, they set off around the house, picking their way among discarded washtubs, buckets, and spools of chicken wire. In a cage large enough to hold Molly, a raggedy hawk hops on one leg, shaking its single wing like a disgruntled pirate. In a second cage, a magnificent snowy owl turns to face Louise with a bored, ruffled visage and a blank space where one of its eyes should have been. The birds remind her of the homeless men she and Richard used to feed at the soup kitchen in Berkeley, vagrants kept alive only by their numb surprise that anyone has deemed them worthy of a meal.

Louise nudges open the screen door and calls out, "Is anyone home?"

"Hallooooo!" cries an overly cheerful voice. "Halloo, halloo, come in!"

Molly giggles. "Whoever it is sounds like Piglet. Or Pooh."

"Be with you in a spinute!"

"A 'spinute'? Mom, she said a 'spinute.' What's a 'spinute'?" Molly is still hopping up and down. "Do you think she's going to be mad that we brought flowers instead of birds?"

Louise pinches off a jonquil. "Look at the canary. Fly away, little canary!" She tosses it in the air, but the "canary" falls to earth and lies there until Molly plucks it up and pets it.

"Poor little bird." She carries the flower inside, stroking it as if it really were a bird. The house is so dimly lit that

Louise needs a while to realize they are standing in a kitchen whose every surface holds a cage. Nearest the refrigerator, a dozen small bright birds flit from perch to perch like a crazy perpetual-motion machine. There are pigeons, cardinals, mourning doves, blue jays, crows, and robins—the commonest flying vermin, although their being in cages makes them seem beautiful and rare. The odor is loamy and moist, like the smell beneath a bridge. But it isn't that unpleasant.

A woman steps in from the living room. She has the most powerful legs of any woman Louise has ever seen, the calf muscles made even more prominent by the thick, strappy sandals and striped wool socks she wears. She has large unblinking eyes and shiny dark hair cut severely across her brow and drawn back in a braid. In her bibbed denim shorts, all elbows and protruding knees, she reminds Louise of Olive Oyl on steroids.

"Here you go." The woman hands Molly something wrapped in a towel, then pulls a plastic bag from her overalls, removes a furry lump, pries open the beak of whatever is in the towel, and forces the lump down its throat. "There. You did that fine."

"Was that a mouse you fed it?" Molly asks. "Was that a hawk?

"Turkey vulture. Rat."

The woman carries the vulture out and returns with another bird, which she instructs Molly to hold while she threads a tube down its throat and pumps in a mixture of mealy worms, cherries, and peanut butter.

"That was, like, totally weird," Molly says in the Valley Girl voice she absorbed from a favorite babysitter and still uses to express amazement. "It was, like, I could feel the bird's stomach fill up!"

The woman returns the bird to its cage and comes back

wiping her hands on her overalls. "So where's your little winglet? What's the smatter with the little smatterling?"

Louise wonders if her neighbor suffers from a neurological disorder. You can sense her hesitation before she pecks at the storehouse of vocabulary in her head and comes up with a choice that is off by a single letter—*worm* instead of *word*.

Louise holds out the jonquils, one of which is now a pathetically beheaded stem.

"Juleps!" the woman says. "I love juleps. The first sign of spring." She puts the flowers beside a cage and introduces herself as Em—not as in Emily or Emma, but as in the thirteenth letter of the alphabet. "It stands for this much longer name a shaman in Lansing gave me, but no one can pronounce it." She used to be a mail carrier in Stickney Springs, she tells Louise, but she had some kind of accident, and now she spends her days—and most of her disability check—caring for injured birds. "I used to cover a lot of territory. I saw a hurt bird and picked it up. It's like any other hobby. The collection just accumulates." She lifts her arms. "Folks go out in the back yard and find an injured robin, or a jay flies against the window, and if it's only adults, they generally let it die. But if there are kids present, the kids say, 'Mom, Dad, we have got to save this bird!' So the parents call the humane society, and the society tells them to bring it here."

She shows Louise and Molly the little hospital in the bathroom, complete with bandages, splints, and amoxicillin. In the basement, they see two battered playpens containing two battered swans, one without a foot, the other missing half its beak. "Motorboats," Em says angrily. "Just don't try to pet them. Swans can be nasty," a fact Louise knows well, having grown up on a lake. A chicken bobbles past their feet. Beside the washing machine stands a vat of writhing mealy worms and a freezer that turns out to be full of mice in Ziploc bags.

"You look like a girl who wouldn't mind slicing some frozen mice," Em says to Molly, and Molly admits she wouldn't. "And you're going to be careful with the knife and not slice your hand?" Again, Molly nods.

"Could I sell her to you?" Louise jokes.

"I *could* use an apprentice."

"I always forget with that apprentice thing who pays whom."

Em shakes her head in a funny twitch, as if shaking off mites. "I need a helper. But I also need money. I have a lot of beaks to feed."

Louise is desperate to find someone to take care of Molly. But she knows nothing about this woman. Early in her life she developed an intuition for judging strangers, and she likes to think this skill has only improved with her years as a social worker. But the minute she crossed the border into Michigan, her intuition went on the fritz. Her instinct says she ought to leave Molly with Dolores Banks. But from the way Molly is looking up at her now, she knows that her daughter much prefers to stay with Em.

"Are you reliable?" Louise asks.

Em flaps her arms. "Who's more reliable than a mailman?"

Louise glances around the basement. Clearly, Molly wouldn't be bored. She would learn something about animals, not to mention first-aid skills and compassion. Em is showing Molly an injured jay, so Louise climbs back upstairs and pokes around the house. Em's bedroom is remarkably unremarkable. A UNICEF calendar hangs on the wall. Three well-tended plants soak up sunshine along the sill. The only aberration is some sort of shrine on the bureau. Louise goes back in the kitchen, with the birds, and when Em and Molly join her there, she asks Em, "Are you a Buddhist?"

"Buddha, Vishnu . . . I might as well tell you I pray to Al Capone, for all the names would mean to you. Let's just say

I'm a little bit of a pagan. A little Wiccan. You have a problem with that? I'm a witch, but I'm a good witch."

Louise stands there trying to decide if she would rather have a witch take care of her daughter or a grandmotherly Christian farm wife whose son belongs to a nutty far-right militia that believes in shooting at their IRS forms.

"So it's all sedated?" Em asks.

"Sedated?"

Em slaps her cheek. "Head injury. I used to, you know, do my rounds on foot. I was putting mail in somebody's box and some idiot rounded the corner too fast on a Kawasaki. Could have been worse. Did something nasty to my back. Knocked a screw loose in the old noggin. Nothing that would interfere with my taking care of a child. Most people around here wouldn't even notice the difference. They're head injured without the head injury, if you know what I mean." She jots down the number of a former supervisor at the post office who will vouch for her. "So," Em asks hopefully, "is it settled?"

Louise hesitates, then surprises herself by saying it's fine with her if it's fine with Em. How can it hurt Molly to spend a few afternoons a week with a woman who mispronounces some words? Louise names a wage that is two dollars less per hour than what she would have paid in California, and Em whistles and says, "You would pay me that much to watch her, *and* I get a helper?"

"Apprentice," Louise corrects her.

Molly tugs Em's arm. "Are you really a witch? Can you fly? Can you teach *me* how to fly?"

"You can just forget the broomstick business," Em says sternly. "The only time you'll be using a broom in this house is to sweep up after the chickens." She taps Molly in the middle of her forehead. "Astral projection. That's how witches get where they want to go."

Louise forces herself to smile, hoping that all she's done is give Molly a chance to satisfy her instinct for helping wounded creatures while freeing her mind from a literal adherence to the gravity of facts. As for what Richard will say when she tells him the more aberrant details about their daughter's new daycare provider, the answer is: She won't.

A few days after she arranges with Em to look after Molly, Louise calls the Unitarian Church in Potawatomie and asks the secretary when and where the AIDS Coalition meets.

Why, lucky you! the woman says. The coalition's monthly meeting is only two days away. "I'm sure they'll take good care of you," the secretary adds in a whisper. "I hope those new drugs work."

And so, on her next free afternoon, Louise drives downtown and parks perpendicular to the curb, which is how all the cars in Potawatomie get parked, like horses at a trough, and enters the door beside the now-as-always-empty health food store. Upstairs, the coalition's headquarters turn out to be two dreary cardboard-paneled rooms. There aren't even posters on the walls. "We had a bunch printed up," explains the overweight woman who hands Louise a name tag, "but we figured other people need to know about condoms more than we do."

Still, she feels at home. The other volunteers look scruffier than their counterparts in California would have been, but they are recognizable members of the same species. A large, rumpled man with a lopsided Fu Manchu moustache comes over and holds out his hand, forgetting that it already holds a cracker heaped with cheese spread. "Jack Lovecraft," he says, and Louise recognizes him as one of the men who were holding hands in Ames's church. "And this is my partner, Howie Drucker." He introduces an equally large and sloppy man who, together with Jack, dispels the stereotype that all gay men are fit and stylish. Howie and Jack program the accounting system for Michigan String and Twine, which makes them seem like distorted Midwest versions of the Silicon Valley hotshots who used to be Louise's neighbors in California. "Did you hear the joke about the gay programmer who splurges on a cruise?" Howie asks. But when she tells him that after living in or near San Francisco for twelve years, she has heard every gay joke known to humankind, he looks so disappointed she lets him tell it anyway.

Each volunteer seems to represent a category of people Louise knew in California. There is a lesbian masseuse named Loretta Paterson, a Jewish social worker named Myrna Cott, an African-American lawyer named Ira Blackstone, a graceful Quaker activist named Mary Walz, and regal Eduardo Hwa, who is half Hispanic and half Chinese. The difference is that in San Francisco almost everyone was like Louise, with barely a *minyan* of conservative straight white Republicans, and in Potawatomie, it's the other way around.

After snacks and tea, the four new members sit on the floor among the old hands and relate why they want to join the coalition. Louise has led so many similar sessions that she needs to force herself to sit patiently through this one, starting with an activity in which everyone is required to pass around a stuffed bear and admit his or her least admissible fears about AIDS, followed by an extended period of role-playing, during which the more experienced volunteers pretend to be people living with AIDS, grumbling to their "buddies" about how hard it is to sit around dying all day while everyone else is out working or playing golf. Louise has little trouble "listening noncritically" and "setting limits." But when the time comes to sign up for a team, she is so weary of the very notion of "buddying," so exhausted by the vocabulary of "suffering" and "sharing," that instead of signing up to staff the AIDS hotline or drive clients to their medical appointments, she chooses the team that cleans apartments. The directness and humility of getting down on her knees to scrub a bathroom floor appeals to her just then. And when Jack Lovecraft informs her that the leader of the house-cleaning team is the Reverend Ames Wye ("He's a very dynamic man, you'll like him, everybody does"), she can't help but think that God is playing matchmaker.

Which apparently He is. When her phone rings a few nights later, Louise guesses it might be Ames. "I would like to speak to Louise Shapiro," the caller intones in a Boston twang so pronounced she thinks he might ask her to consider what she can do for her country instead of what her country can do for her.

"This is Louise," she says, although normally she would say, "It's me." Ames introduces himself as Reverend Wye from the AIDS Coalition and relates the address of the apartment they will be cleaning. Louise doubts he realizes he's speaking to the woman from the ball cage at McDonald's. But he will know her when he sees her.

And the next day, when Ames greets her on the porch of the building in which the coalition rents rooms for clients who can't afford to rent their own places or whose landlords have thrown them out, he does seem startled. "Yes, hello, I remember you. You came to services the other day." But he seems no happier to see Louise than he would have been to see anyone who helped him clean.

You're not so great, she thinks. And really, he isn't any handsomer than Richard. His pocked skin is, well, pocked, and he stands with his fingers splayed around his hips in an effeminate stance that makes him seem spoiled. He fumbles with the key, glancing around furtively, as if what they're doing is illegal.

"I don't mean to frighten you," he says, "but there are people in this town who, if they had any idea where this place was, would try to burn it down."

The explanation seems melodramatic, but the lock gives and they go in, and Louise lets the subject drop. They climb the dingy stairs and Ames lets them into the apartment. "We have two hours," he tells her. "One of the volunteers took the tenant to visit his sister in Battle Creek." He opens a closet and pulls out a mop. Then he goes back to his car and brings up an ancient upright Hoover. Louise gets out a dust cloth and sets to work.

Unfortunately, the very bareness of the apartment amplifies every beat of her heart, every vibration that passes between them. She is so exquisitely aware of Ames's presence—now he is swabbing the bathroom floor; now he is spraying Windex on the mirror in the hall—she decides that any two strangers who are left alone to clean an apartment eventually will be drawn to kiss.

Finally, they take a break. Ames sets his bucket on the kitchen floor, pulls out a chair from the dinette set, sits on it backward, and asks Louise what brought her to Potawatomie. She relates a compressed version of those events, at which Ames loosens up and tells her something of himself—how he grew up north of Boston, the descendant of a Puritan minister who took part in the witch trials but regretted it later; how the members of his family always have been much given to excess and regret; how he was kidnapped from his prep school and abandoned in Las Vegas by his compulsive-gambler father, and then rescued by his father's father, with whom Ames lived for a year in Chicago until he was brought back home by his alcoholic mother, who alternately petted and ignored him until he left for Yale. In the seventies and early eighties, he dabbled as a playwright with an avant-garde theater troupe in a converted garage in Cambridge. Then he felt a calling as a minister, long after it was fashionable to go in for such a thing, got his divinity degree from Harvard, received his credentials as a minister, did a stint running a community-development cooperative in east Detroit, was hired and ordained by a church in Indiana, and finally ended up here, leading a small congregation of unimpassioned Unitarians, doing what he can to keep the good fight alive.

Louise wants to ask what he means by "a calling." Did he simply feel compelled to choose the ministry as a career? Or does he think he heard God commanding him to serve? And if the latter, what did God's voice sound like? But she is afraid Ames might think she doubts his rationality. "Are you ever sorry you became a minister?" she asks instead.

He lets out a tortured sigh and stands. "I have quite a few regrets, but becoming a minister isn't one of them."

She might have found the courage to ask what aspects of his life he *does* regret, but he picks up his bucket and sets it in the sink. "Excuse me," he says, leaning across Louise to turn on the tap. As the bucket fills, he unbuttons one cuff and rolls it to reveal a narrow wrist haloed in a flexible gold watchband. Without thinking, she reaches out to touch his arm. But he jerks the bucket from the sink. Water sloshes to the linoleum.

"Damn," he says. Then: "I'm sorry, I don't usually—"

He stops, and Louise wonders, don't usually what? Swear? Disclose personal information about yourself? She shuts the tap, amazed at how close she has come to humiliating herself. There is one bedroom left to clean and she hurries off to clean it. The apartment is done in no time. Ames lugs the Hoover down the stairs. "I'll call you," he says. "I mean, when there's another apartment for us to clean."

Louise asks when that might be.

"Let's see . . . there are four of us on the team, and five

or six apartments. Most of the tenants do the lighter tasks themselves." He looks away and coughs. "When one of the tenants dies, we help pack up his things. If any relatives come to claim them, we carry the boxes to the car. If not, we donate everything to the Kiwanis. It tears you up, how many of our tenants don't have anyone come claim their things."

Louise nods. It's always amazed her that a person's family can allow him to die alone.

"We'd better go now," Ames warns her. "It isn't a good idea to allow members of the community to find out where these safe houses are." Pushing the Hoover awkwardly before him, he walks her to the van. "Goodbye," he says. He takes a hesitant step toward her and leans down just a bit, but he merely shakes her hand and leaves.

She drives back to Stickney Springs, wondering if she should feel guilty for being attracted to a man to whom she isn't married, or proud that she hasn't acted on that attraction. It's amazing how skillfully a person can rationalize her disloyalty to her spouse: she is allowed to indulge her feelings because a man like Ames Wye could never be interested in a woman like her; her husband has been acting so badly that he deserves it if she flirts.

She stops at Em's house to get Molly, who is annoyed to see her mother. "I still have all these mealy worms to grind." She frowns and puts her hand on one hip like an overburdened housewife. "Then I have to hose out the raptors' cages," at which Em assures her that "tomorrow is another play" and sends her home.

Back at the house, Louise whips up fajitas from a box— so this is who buys fajitas in a box!—and over chips and salsa tells Richard that she and "another volunteer" cleaned an apartment that day for the AIDS Coalition, which leads to a discussion of the incidence of AIDS at the prison and what few measures the administration is taking to prevent its spread. The new dishwasher came with a ruptured hose, so Louise washes the dishes by hand while Richard dries. Their proximity in that humid, soapy cloud, passing warm, slick dishes, leads Louise to think she wouldn't mind kissing him. She never follows through with this intention, but she feels confident that she will. And her hubris does her in. She is so certain of her ability to withstand her desire for Ames that she neglects to sandbag her heart against the deluge she knows is coming.

Then again, she isn't yet aware how much distance can open up between a husband and a wife in only one week. She has known for quite a while that a fault line lies hidden in their marriage. But she hadn't thought the pressure could build sufficiently to shift such heavy plates.

April 15 is coming, and, in the end, that's all it takes to cleave a yawning gulf between them. Richard notes the approaching deadline and goes through the motions of getting ready. Louise watches as he knifes open the boxes marked FINANCIAL DOCUMENTS, collects the proper forms, sharpens a handful of pencils, and collates the year's receipts. But he can't bring himself to start. He kicks the desk and swears, not caring if Molly hears.

"I'm sick of it," he tells Louise. "Every year, I fill out these stupid forms. Every year, I think if I put even one wrong number in a box, they'll haul me off to jail. If my calculations show I owe a hundred dollars, I kick in a hundred and five, and I *still* worry. A person's life shouldn't be a business. A man should have better things to do than put numbers in little boxes and worry about getting sent to jail."

After he storms out—at least storming is better than shuffling—Louise tiptoes in the den and finds their envelope from the I.R.S. To Richard, doing taxes is a chore. He has told

Louise how, just after his eighteenth birthday, his father took him in his inner sanctum and introduced him to the mysteries of *gross adjusted income*, *itemized deductions*, and *capital gains*. But Louise's parents refused to pay their taxes. Thankfully, the IRS never deemed it worthwhile to send an agent to collect the pittance they owed. But her parents' refusal to do what the government required filled Louise with dread. What if they got sent to prison? What would happen to *her*? Did her parents ever consider that?

She sits at Richard's desk and studies the instructions. Each year, she thinks, millions of Americans are given an exam that requires honesty and intelligence. They complete their forms and mail in their checks, and the government somehow transforms this bounty into highways, schools, medical labs, and soldiers. How can anarchists like her parents or right-wingers like Matt and Dolores Banks think they can accomplish any of this on their own?

And so Louise happily spends that week working on their taxes. And even though she wakes that Saturday morning knowing she has only a few more hours to get the job done, she isn't particularly mad or stressed. For a long period of her life, she wanted to be taken care of. But now that she's nearing forty, it's high time she learned to take care of herself.

What annoys her is that Richard insists on going to the Tax Blast. "Sorry, but I don't have any 1040s I can spare." She points to the crumpled forms beneath the desk. "And you'll need to find someone to stay with Molly."

Richard grunts his assent. Dolores will be at the Tax Blast, but Em agrees to sit for Molly for the day. He bakes a tuna-noodle casserole and tops it with a can of the crunchy fried onion rings for which their hometown is famous.

"Where's Daddy going?" Molly asks. "Why can't I go with him?"

Her father, Louise explains, is going to the Sportsman's Club on the other side of the Bankses' farm. The people at the club will be using guns and drinking beer, which is why Molly will need to be at Em's.

"Is *Daddy* using a gun?"

Louise holds her tongue. She needs to finish the taxes. The post office in Potawatomie is staying open an hour later than usual as a courtesy to local filers—it's probably so rare for anyone in this part of the state to file his taxes that the government wants to reward the law-abiding few—and she tells Molly she'll pick her up on her way back from town.

"Oh, all right," Molly says. "Only, I'm going to be worrying the whole day that Daddy might get shot."

Louise worries about this, too. Every so often, she is startled from her calculations by the dull pop of gunshots. Once, the house is shaken by a ferocious blast, and she goes out on the porch to find a curlicue of smoke hanging above the Sportsman's Club. Early fireworks? A homemade rocket? Satisfied that neither possibility poses much threat to Molly, she goes back inside and shuts the door.

And who can tell how or why, she enters a state that can only be described as the Zen of Doing Taxes. Concepts that have been obscure the entire week snap into focus, and Louise realizes that just as a good therapist can see the shape of a client's life from a few salient facts and fantasies, an accountant can comprehend the arc of a family's life from the lines on its 1040 form. Here are Richard's newer and lower salary at the prison, her own long months without a job, the sale of their old house in California for a ridiculously high profit, the acquisition of their new house here at a laughably lower price, and the drop in their charitable contributions as their puny misfortunes distracted them from helping those in more dire need. Richard complained that a man's life was not a business. But filing your taxes seems to have less to do with keeping track of profits and expenditures than the sort of accounting you might be called on to perform in Heaven.

She drives to Potawatomie and joins a line of hollow-eyed people copying their forms on the quarter-a-page machine at the library, then hurries to the post office and joins a similar group waiting to reach the window, a position she achieves at 1:15, at which she thanks the clerk for not shutting down at 1:00, as her counterpart in California would have done. Afterward, she stops at Em's to get Molly.

"One of the swans got better!" Molly flaps her arms in excitement, or in imitation of the swan. "We took her to the pond. You should have seen how happy she was to be with the other swans."

Another explosion goes off.

"Those jerks," Em says. "They keep scaring my poor birdies."

"It's true, Mom." Molly wrinkles her nose. "Did you hear that really big boom? The birds went *bonkers*."

Even now, the birds seem more twittery than usual. "It's not bad enough Matt and his idiot friends play with guns," Em says, "they've got to set off bombs."

Bombs?

According to Em, Matt and his militia friends like blowing up plastic milk-jugs filled with the type of chemicals you can find around any farm. Sometimes, they pack barrels with ammonium nitrate, which makes an even bigger ruckus.

Later, Louise will marvel that she wasn't more alarmed by this information. But she and Richard have invested too much in making this new life work. She tells herself that blowing up barrels of manure demonstrates nothing about Matt except an instinctual male need to blow things up. How can she believe that Matt and his friends pose a danger to her or Molly when her own husband is at the party where those explosions are going off?

Molly tugs her sleeve. "Em did this thing with cards. She said I'm going to have a lot of . . ." She turns to Em for prompting. "A lot of *upheavals*. But they'll make me a better person. She saw a fire in my future."

Louise holds the same opinion of fortune telling that most rational people do: she can't imagine a pack of cards revealing anything about anyone else's future but is eager to hear what they reveal about her own. The fire Em has glimpsed in Molly's future obviously is a reference to the fire in Richard's past. But Louise is still impressed. She hasn't told Em about Molly's father setting fire to those trees.

"I hope you don't mind," Em says. "Most of our neighbors think Tarot is Satan's gift, but I thought, because you're Jewish"—it comes out sounding like *Jew-witch*—"you might be more open-minded."

Weary of correcting everyone as to her religious affiliation, Louise tells Em she doesn't object to anyone telling Molly's fortune, as long as it doesn't upset her.

"You mean that?" Em says. "I don't suppose I could interest you in coming to a coven." She blinks a long slow blink. "We don't sit around stirring cauldrons or sacrificing babies or anything like that. Sometimes there's a little spell-casting. But real witches never cast a spell that has an evil invent."

As with fortune telling, Louise is dubious about the efficacy of casting spells, yet anxious to try it. "I don't think I'm cut out to be a witch, but it might be fun to watch a meeting."

Em smiles a crinkly smile that indicates she takes Louise's inability even to say the word *coven* as a sign she has little future as a witch. But Em seems to appreciate her neighbor's tolerance.

On the way home, Molly skips ahead a few yards, and then waits for her mother to catch up. "Em can talk to birds," she says. "She understands what they want. She can kind of read their minds."

Who is Louise to dismiss the possibility that a person who spends nearly all her time with birds can guess what they might be thinking? Maybe Americans in the Heartland have never been quite as down-to-earth as the national myths might indicate. Unless you consider it down-to-earth to fill barrels with manure and explode them for fun.

Richard doesn't get home until after dark. Breath beery, cheeks flushed, he is intoxicated to a degree Louise has never seen him.

"You should have been there." He fires an invisible pistol at the clock—*ptew, ptew.* "I won third prize in the beginner's pin-shoot."

"Pins? I thought they shot their tax forms."

He makes a face to indicate she is not only ignorant but judgmental. "The place is called a sportsman's club for a reason. They line up bowling pins and you shoot them and get a score." He holds out a jar of what looks like severed fingers. "You can't imagine how satisfying it feels to hit your target. And you cannot believe how much these guys know about surviving in the wild. There's this one guy, Floyd Goodman. You wouldn't catch Floyd messing around with some wimpy high-tech stove." He hands Louise the jar. "Pickled okra. We can try them with dinner."

"That depends on whether they're kosher for Passover or not."

His eyes grow fuzzy. "It's tonight? Since when does Seder fall on Tax Day?"

This is such a stunning non sequitur that Louise worries for his sanity. She has reminded him twice about the date. He has never been as observant as his parents, but he always takes time off from work and does whatever a Jew is supposed to do on a given holiday.

"Never mind," he says. "Life is too short. We *were* slaves in Egypt. *Now* we're free men."

Something about his blithely tossing away five thousand years of his people's heritage irritates her. "Do you actually believe these Nazis will let you join their club?"

He turns on her, as furious as any man whose wife considers it her prerogative to squelch his latest hobby or make fun of his friends. "Since when does being patriotic make someone a Nazi? My parents fled Europe. No other country would let them in. Why does being Jewish mean you have to be such a damn *pussy* about everything? Scared of taking one false step. You haven't even met these guys. Floyd *wants* Jews to join his outfit. Anyone, women, blacks, homosexuals, as long as the person believes America is worth defending. Heck, Floyd might be part Jewish himself. That's what he said. One of his ancestors might have been a Jew. *Goodman*, right? We know half a dozen Jewish Goodmans." He crosses his arms. "If you can hang around with that brain-damaged witch, I can hang around with Matt and Floyd."

If he hadn't already lost their daughter's sympathy, he loses it now. Molly goes up to her room and slams the door. Richard doesn't seem to notice. Just as well—this way, Molly doesn't hear her father say that Matt is helping him pick out a gun. Richard is planning to attend the Bankses' Easter party the next day. Some of the guys from the Tax Blast will be there with their kids. Richard, Floyd, and Matt might go over to the Sportsman's Club and test out some possibilities.

To keep from pointing out the obvious contradiction in firing guns on Easter, Louise refrains from saying anything, although Richard guesses what she must be thinking. "People change," he says, at which she also refrains from saying that not every change a person makes is admirable.

Richard's parents call to wish them a happy holiday.

"You talk to them," he whispers.

"He ran out to get more matzos," Louise lies to her mother-in-law. "It's like living in the wilderness. I found this one box at the Kroger in Potawatomie, but the matzo in it was so stale it sort of bent. It must have been left over from last year. Anyway, we need more than one box to get through all seven days. Next year, I'll drive to Ann Arbor to stock up." On and on she goes, placating Richard's parents, praying Molly won't hear her lie. She considers sharing with her accountant father-in-law her recently acquired enthusiasm for doing taxes. But she would need to reveal why Richard wasn't the one filling out their forms, and that would frighten her in-laws so badly that they would be on the next plane.

"Mom?" Molly has come downstairs. Usually, Louise puts her on to talk to her grandparents. This time, she motions for Molly to wait, then gets off the phone by pretending the gefilte fish is drying out. "Where did Daddy go?" Molly asks. "Why aren't we having a Seder?"

Louise gets down on her knees, as if the truth can only be passed on eye-to-eye. "Things are kind of mixed up, sweetie. You remember how I told you that Daddy was upset about that patient killing herself? Well, he's *still* upset. And we've been so busy with the house I forgot to shop for Passover. If you want, we can find the Haggadahs and hold our own little Seder. And maybe when Dad gets back—"

Molly shakes her head. "Seders go too long. I just like hunting for the *afikomen*." Louise is so relieved at not needing to lead a Seder that she offers to hide a graham cracker and reward Molly if she finds it before she goes to bed, which Molly manages to accomplish—not a difficult feat, considering that Louise has hidden the cracker on her pillow.

She kisses Molly goodnight and gets in her own pajamas, doubting she will get much sleep, pursued as she is by images of her husband standing against a tree with an apple on his head. *Sure, we need more Jews*, a shadowy Floyd Goodman scoffs. *Seems the old members never make it through more than a few rounds of target practice.*

But she not only falls asleep, she dreams the most powerful and satisfying dream of her life. A nuclear explosion goes off, the mushroom cloud billowing yellow to the west, over the Bankses' farm, although Louise could swear Detroit was the city that got attacked. Then the dream shifts to California, where Molly and her friends are gathered in the Shapiros' front yard. All their parents have been wiped out. Richard is dead, or maybe he's only missing, so the responsibility falls to Louise to lead the children to Vancouver, where the radiation hasn't yet reached. None of them have shoes or food, but they set out on an unpaved country road, and, despite the loved ones each of them has lost, Louise experiences the most wonderful relief, because she hasn't the slightest doubt that what she's doing is worthwhile. Having grown up on her own, she feels eminently qualified to keep a dozen homeless kids happy for however many miles they will walk to Canada. Her occasional glimpse of Ames, who appears from behind trees and rocks, lifting his palm and nodding at how far they have come, reinforces her sense of peace.

With all the psychology courses Louise has taken, she gives a lot of credence to her dreams. In some ways, they have always been the most unambiguous aspect of her existence. Before she met Richard, nothing put her off as much about a man as waking beside him and hearing his gruff avowal that he didn't remember any dreams from the night before, or noticing his boredom as she described hers. The first time she slept with Richard, they spent until noon discussing each other's dreams. It was like having four people in the bed— Richard and his unconscious, Louise and her unconscious, all four of them getting emotionally naked, stroking this and kissing that. In Richard's most common dream, he was required to carry out some impossible task, such as fixing the wiring in his parents' house while blindfolded. Often, he could fly, although only with great effort and never when anyone else could see. Most of Louise's dreams involved surviving in situations in which her lack of the needed skills made survival unlikely. She wants to tell Richard about the relief she felt leading Molly and her friends to Canada. But an odd delicacy prevents her from revealing what she's dreamed, if only because she would need to omit the part about the minister behind the trees.

When she gets out of bed that Easter morning, the clarity of her dream about the nuclear explosion gives way to the moral ambiguity she has been suffering since they moved here. The Bankses' Easter Egg-stravaganza is set for noon, and Molly plays happily around the house until it's time for them to walk over to the farm. They find Dolores in a pink sweatshirt with an Easter Bunny appliqué on the front and a pair of fuzzy rabbit-ears on an elastic band around her head. She stands behind a table collecting an admission fee of five dollars a child and selling home-baked pies, Easter hams, rabbit-shaped sugar cookies, daffodil bouquets, and rock-garden dishes of paperwhites and narcissi. A pie costs twelve dollars. The lop-eared bunnies cost ten dollars without a cage and fifteen dollars with. A homemade doughnut and a glass of lemonade sell for a dollar fifty. How can Louise fault her neighbors for trying to stay afloat when so many other farmers have gone under? How can she look down on them for providing an old-fashioned Easter for the kids of Stickney Springs?

At two, Matt leads the children to the barn and shows them how to climb the ladder to the loft, where one by one they grab a knotted rope and swing over a pile of hay and let go. Molly tentatively climbs the ladder, closes her eyes, and pushes off. She swings screeching across the barn before dropping like an apple into the fragrant hay, only to emerge wide-eyed and grinning, hay poking from her curls and the armbands of her dress.

"She's a cutie," Matt assures Louise, so how can she help but like him, even if he adds, "Anyone ever say how much she looks like a little bunny?"

After each child has taken a few turns, Matt leads them to the field where his mother has hidden the painted eggs. Both Bankses help the littlest ones toddle around with baskets and find at least a few. So what if Louise's husband is the only non-Christian? The Shapiros are the wealthiest folks in town, the rich Californians who bought the old McKnight place and spent a bundle to fix it up. The other guests are just regular Americans. The fathers lead their toddlers to the bushes, pull down their elastic-waisted pants, and shake the boys' peanut-sized dicks before tucking these back inside their tight white cotton shorts. And the mothers, like mothers anywhere, comfort children who are sobbing bitterly because they haven't found enough eggs. No one makes a comment about Molly's Jewish stars. Maybe no one notices. Why does Louise assume she will never fit in here? Because none of these people play tennis or go on retreats to ashrams in Telluride or Vail? Because the clothes they wear come from Target instead of catalogues that feature silk-and-yak-wool garments modeled by men and women who sport the rugged glamour of Robert Redford or Susan Sarandon as they sail boats or ride thoroughbreds?

She comes across Richard and his friends behind the barn. They seem genuinely absorbed in what Richard has to say. One of the men asks Richard if he thinks the government could implant a computer chip in a person's teeth and send orders to control his thoughts.

"Well, Floyd," she hears Richard say, "any dentist could implant a radio in your teeth. But you would have to *let* him do it. And even then, the best the radio could do would be to drive you crazy with commercials. It could *suggest* you do something, but why would you do it if you didn't want to? Just because some shmuck tells you to go out and buy a Hyundai, doesn't mean you do."

The men nod, and it becomes clear to Louise that in Richard they have found an expert on all things Californian, on the way New Yorkers think, and on what science, medicine, and Jews are capable—or not capable—of doing. She dawdles a little way off and eavesdrops. Most of the conversation revolves around the best kind of hunting boots a man can buy. There are jokes about Janet Reno. Someone mumbles something about "that Jewish professor at Harvard" who defends all the biggest crooks and is now defending O. J. Simpson.

Louise waits for Richard to object, but he laughs wryly, as if the man has made a joke. Richard stands with his fingers in his pockets, thumbs angled toward his crotch, a posture Louise has never seen him take. It's clear he doesn't want to acknowledge her, but she enters the circle anyway. Instantly, the men stand straighter. Their attention falls away from Richard. Grudgingly, he inclines his head in her direction and says, "This is my wife, Louise."

The man to Richard's right is tall and well built, with a rectangular face and clear, sad eyes. "Happy Easter there,

Louise." He has a scar beneath his chin, as if someone pressed there with a knife. "Aren't you the pretty one." He hums a few bars of "California Girls."

"This is Floyd," Richard tells her sullenly.

Floyd's ears stick out, and there is something too glossy about his moustache, but the overall effect is appealing. Louise hears herself say that Richard talks about him all the time.

"Does he now?" Floyd grins at Richard like a high school athlete who has just learned that the smartest girl in class has a crush on him. "I wish I could return the compliment. I've asked Rich time and again about his missus. But all he'll say is you've got some sort of job at the high school." He winks. "Next to being a full-time mom, teaching school is just about the noblest thing a woman can do."

Louise doesn't bother to explain that she is a social worker, not a teacher. Richard wants her to leave, and what point could she make by staying? She wishes the men a happy Easter, then loiters long enough to hear Floyd suggest they all "mosey over" to the Sportsman's Club. Matt goes in the house and comes out with three rifles, which the men hand around and discuss. They walk off down a path that must be a back way to the club, and for a second time she wonders why no one sees the contradiction in shooting guns on Easter. What surprises her is just how much she cares that it is Easter. Somehow, she finds herself deeply moved by the image of a slender, half-naked man being taken down from a cross and cradled in his mother's arms, wept over, washed, then buried in a cave. She is even more moved by the idea of this same young man appearing a few days later to his grieving mother and bereft apostles, walking among them, laying his hand on this one's arm, promising that one to return if the disciple keeps his faith. Even Molly could appreciate the universal symbolism of the grass and leaves reappearing every spring, all that budding and rebirth.

Looking around, she sees that she and Dolores are the only female mammals on the farm that aren't pregnant, and she finds herself overcome with the sacred, eternal promise of sex and resurrection. Until recently, Christianity struck Louise as silly, with its insistence that a man can be a god and a virgin might bear a child. Now, the religion strikes her as useful. Christians are more concerned than Jews with temptations such as lust. If adultery becomes a preoccupation in your life, what you need is Christianity.

That she can imagine joining Ames's church frightens her. What's the old adage—beware of any enterprise that requires new clothes? How much more wary should one be of an enterprise that requires a new religion? Yet her willingness to join his church makes her feel flexible and generous, instead of rigid and ungiving, as she has lately felt with Richard. A phrase from Ames's sermon—*we celebrate the young god rising*—keeps running through her head. Is there too much religion in this world, or not enough? Maybe she *is* a snob. Why shouldn't she follow Richard to the Sportsman's Club and take up shooting? It might be fun to make a bomb. Or pose for next year's calendar.

Still, she can't help but panic at the sight of everyone gathering around Dolores as she sets a cage on the ground and prepares to spring the door. The parents' exhortations—*Grab it quick, Dylan! Go on and get that bunny, Clint!*—and the children's lack of care as to where they grab the animal make Louise think they might chase anything or anyone with equal zeal. An older girl snatches the frenzied creature and lifts it by the ears, but the rabbit kicks so furiously she lets it go. Louise is glad to see the rabbit zigzag among the Christmas trees and escape behind the barn. When her disappointed daughter, hair matted to her scalp like the pelt of a Russian lamb, says she wishes she had a pet because the other girls might come over to the house to play with it, Louise offers to *buy* her a rabbit. The Shapiros do not need to catch their pets. A rabbit does not require the same attention as a dog.

"Really?" Molly skips up and down in that torrent of delight every parent hopes she can induce in her child. "You would really let me have one?"

Louise leads her to the pens where the last few rabbits huddle, and she isn't the least surprised when Molly points to an oatmeal-colored runt curled in a quivering ball smaller than a fist.

"That. One. Might. Not. Be. Healthy," Dolores says. "Why. Don't. You. Pick. That. Bigger. White. One."

But Molly insists on the runt. Shaking her head, Dolores scoops up the trembling mass of fur and pops it in a cage. Louise hands her a twenty and tells her to keep the change, which Dolores insists on returning. "What. Do. You. Intend. To. Name. It?" Dolores asks, and when Molly refuses to answer, Dolores suggests Peter, Bugs, and Hoppy, at which Molly looks up and says, "Hey, Mom, doesn't he look like the matzo balls Grandma Nan cooks for Seder? And see, it's a good name because he's as much a Passover rabbit as an Easter one."

"What's. That?" Dolores puts her hand to her ear as if she has trouble hearing as well as talking.

"Matzo Ball," Louise repeats. "She decided to name it Matzo Ball."

"Mazza. What?"

"Matzo Ball. It's a sort of Jewish dumpling."

Dolores shakes her head and turns away, carrying the cage in which the remaining rabbits crouch. *Got to have their own dumplings. Can't just eat the kind regular people eat.*

Did Dolores really say what Louise thinks she heard? But

how could Dolores have pushed the button in her throat if she was carrying the cage? Maybe, like a mother who intercepts her neighbors' conversation on a baby monitor, Louise has been granted the illicit privilege of reading Dolores Banks' poorly hidden thoughts. Or maybe, as Richard has suggested, she simply is getting paranoid.

The Wednesday after the Bankses' Easter party, Louise has the day off—there's plenty to do, but Bess Moorehouse seems to think if Louise isn't allowed to work full-time, she won't get ideas about the job being hers. Molly could have played around the house, but she prefers Em's company to Louise's, so Louise walks her to the bungalow, and then considers how to spend the day. All the major remodeling projects are complete, so there is nothing left to do but unpack the last boxes in which their belongings have been stored for so many months.

Which is how, on the morning of April 19, 1995, Louise finds herself in the crawl space above the eaves, labeling boxes of winter clothes and boots and finding spaces for Molly's high chair and crib, which they ought to have sold at their yard sale in California but brought to Michigan because Louise still harbored the hope that Richard would recover from his slump and want a second child. The electrician's assistant, Rod, is installing a fan at the other end of the attic so something called ice dams won't form that coming winter. Even if Louise hadn't been absorbed in her memories of Molly's babyhood, she would have considered it classist or anti-male to entertain the fear that a repairman might molest her. So she is doubly startled when Rod suddenly appears beside her and clutches at her breast. Terror makes her stupid. She can't accept that she is being fondled by the same young man she has been kind enough to allow to keep his dog in her basement.

Then she swings around and slaps him, catching him on his windpipe, which, judging by his strangled yelp, probably was more effective than slapping him on the cheek.

"I thought you liked me." He nurses his neck. "The guys said you and your husband, you know, aren't getting along that well."

If she screams, Dolores or Matt might hear. But the farmhouse is a football field away.

"I don't have to *make* my girlfriends kiss me. It's just . . . the guys said you liked me. And women from California—"

"I'm leaving the house," Louise says. "If you're not gone by the time I get back, I'll have you fired. And if I ever, *ever* see your face again, I'll call the cops and press charges." She crosses the attic with a falsely brave demeanor and walks down the stairs without glancing back to see if Rod is following. She unlocks the front door, gets in the van, and drives off.

And that's where she is when she hears the news. She is driving to Potawatomie, not because she has any reason to drive there, but because she has nowhere else to go. Living in Stickney Springs isn't like living in California, where a drive in any direction brings you to a mountain or a beach or a quaint café. She has no idea what she will do in Potawatomie except stop in the health food store and buy yet another bag of chocolate-covered cherries, then go upstairs and see if Howie or Jack is sitting at the desk waiting for the hotline to ring.

She switches on the radio and hears about a bomb going off in Oklahoma City. Preliminary estimates put more than a thousand people at the site. The building also housed a daycare center. No one can be sure how many toddlers have been killed.

She reaches the prison, thinks of going in, demanding to see her husband and asking him to please make everything all right, but instead gets back on the highway and continues driving north. She feels like the captain of a submarine that had been patrolling some remote Arctic sea when her homeland was destroyed.

When she reaches Grand Rapids, she turns around and starts back. Somehow, the van ends up outside the high school. She watches a pair of seniors smoke a joint, then goes inside and walks up to her office. Everything is as she left it—the Turkish rug she and Richard bought for their first apartment, which wasn't much bigger than this office; the Matisse poster she brought in to cover the penis on the corkboard; and the brilliant red bromeliad blooming beautifully in the heat. She sits behind the desk, picking insulation from the pipe. After a while, she closes the office and starts back down the stairs—just as Bess Moorehouse is coming up.

"This isn't . . . What is this, Wednesday? You needn't come in on Wednesdays. I hope you aren't thinking . . ."

Louise feels as if she is about to get detention. "I was just driving around, and I didn't know where else to go." They stand on opposite ends of the same step. A student runs up between them. When the student is out of sight, Bess stiffly throws out her arms and pulls Louise toward her like a French general clasping some poor hero to his chest. The entire encounter lasts a fraction of a second. By the time she has trotted up the stairs, Louise wonders if any of it really happened.

Finally, she drives back home. She is hungry and low on gas and wants to see pictures of the wreckage, the firemen and nurses rushing to help the wounded, the woman whose only hope is to allow the paramedics to amputate her leg, not because she enjoys seeing such upsetting sights but because she hopes the actual images of the carnage might replace the even more horrifying images in her mind.

Rod's van is gone, thank God. Cautiously, she nudges open her front door, grabs the phone in case Rod is still lurking inside and she needs to summon the police, and then searches all the rooms; although she smells the lingering presence of his cologne and his dog, she finds no trace of Rod. She locks the doors and bolts them, then stretches out on the couch and gives herself over to the news. She feels guilty about deriving a perverse excitement from what she sees, but how can people *not* be obsessed with tragedies that destroy so many lives, or even lesser disturbances like the Clarence Thomas hearings or O.J.'s eternal trial? If TV could provide a backward glimpse of the Revolutionary War or Lincoln's assassination, who wouldn't tune in? Everyone wants to add a chapter to the national narrative, preferably about a relative or a friend who has gotten caught up in the terror but escaped unscathed. She doesn't know a soul in Oklahoma City. But even as she lies on the green brocade sofa she and Richard lugged from Ithaca to Berkeley and from Berkeley to San Rafael and from San Rafael to Stickney Springs, she suspects that the dread she has felt hanging over her in Michigan is connected to the fear that is descending on everybody now.

She picks up the phone and calls Imelda, but Imelda's husband, Andrew, tells her Imelda is at the hospital getting another opinion on her biopsy. "It's one of those better-safe-than-sorry deals. Except that being safe here means removing my wife's second breast." He starts crying and Louise tries to comfort him, but all she can come up with are the usual clichés. *Imelda is such a fighter. Maybe the tests are wrong.* Obviously, neither Imelda nor her husband is paying much attention to the tragedy in Oklahoma. Louise promises to call back later, then hangs up and has a good long cry— for Imelda and Andrew, for the injured and the dead. By the fifth time she has seen the footage of the fireman cradling the bloody body of a girl whose first birthday was only the day before, she can't put off the desire to hold her daughter.

Em knows nothing about the bombing. How could she, with no TV? Hurriedly, Louise whispers a synopsis of the day's events.

"Why did you come so early?" Molly pouts.

"I missed you," Louise says. "I wanted to give my huggle-bug a hug."

Clearly, in Molly's mind, this does not justify her mother's taking her home. She squirms from Louise's arms, and when they get back to the house, she mopes. Somehow, Louise manages to keep from turning on the TV. How can she expose a six-year-old to the truth that adults might blow up a preschool? She and Molly play Life, although Louise would prefer Candyland, which doesn't even pretend to introduce a child to reality, as if nothing worse might happen to a person than a tree falling on an uninsured house or the stock market crashing.

"I want a pink peg," Molly insists when she lands on the marriage square. "I want to marry Em," which might have made Louise jealous if she hadn't had more important things to think about.

Molly rolls a five and retires to Millionaire Acres, the first time she has ever beaten her mother at a game, and this puts her in a better mood. Richard comes home. By covert winks and shushes, they agree to wait until Molly is in bed to discuss the news, which, it turns out, Richard caught on the radio at lunch and analyzed with the other prison psychologist, a man named Ron Lowenstine, who, like Richard, assumes Arab terrorists are responsible.

But why Oklahoma City? How would an Arab even know where Oklahoma *is*?

Well, Richard says, he just hopes Louise isn't buying those

lies about the bomb being planted by a militia group. Would a patriot attack his own government? Would a guy who sees himself as a defender of family values kill a child?

She sees no point in arguing. If, before the Tax Blast, Richard had seemed a shell of his former self, now a complete stranger inhabits her husband's skin.

Besides, the need to argue is rendered moot the first time Louise sees a photo of the man who is now accused of driving the rental truck full of fertilizer into that office building. She hadn't realized she knew what Satan looked like, but here he is—that lean, sharp face, those icy eyes, that infuriatingly smug expression indicating that only *he* knows the truth, a truth so absolute it justifies the deaths of however many innocents.

What drives her crazy is Richard's refusal to acknowledge that Timothy McVeigh is connected to the same militia as Matt and Floyd. Within days, every newspaper and TV station in America is running exposés of the right-wing fringe to which Timothy McVeigh belongs, the militia nuts, the extremists who believe the United States is being taken over by a Communist-Zionist conspiracy poised to destroy the ordinary citizen's right to bear arms, worship the Christian God, and raise his children the way he wants. According to the papers, McVeigh was aided by an accomplice who lives on a farm in Michigan, where the two men practiced building and exploding ammonium-nitrate bombs. McVeigh attended one or more meetings of the Michigan Militia—*Newsweek* goes so far as to run one of the tamer photos from the calendar that's hanging even now on the Bankses' porch! The same issue quotes Floyd Goodman, who denies that Timothy McVeigh ever belonged to his chapter of the militia and claims no one in his group would be so misguided as to avenge the government's wrongs by killing kids.

But Floyd can't deny that a militia member named Mike Korn, a custodian at the high school in Potawatomie, spends an hour each week spewing hate across the airwaves as "Michigan Mike, the Voice of the Militia." Since the bombing, Korn has publicly professed that McVeigh is the scapegoat in a plot to frame the militias and divert attention from a plan to round up all the decent, God-fearing citizens and herd them into concentration camps. Louise has read that the FBI have taken Korn in for questioning, pronounced him a malicious windbag, and let him go. She sees footage on the news—not only the local stations, but CBS and NBC—of the small mob that has gathered around Korn's house in Potawatomie, half the people calling for him to come out and let them hang him, the other half holding up signs to the effect that the government has set him up. When the station shows Korn leaving his house, Louise loses her breath. She isn't at all surprised that Mike Korn is the janitor she saw sweeping the cafeteria the day of her interview. He clearly is a man whose simmering rage would seek an outlet through a medium that allows him to vent his hate without being held accountable. But seeing him on the news amplifies her fears to a national level.

After the segment airs, their friends on both coasts call to make sure she and Richard are all right. Until now, Louise has resisted the urge to regale them with stories about the Bankses and the Tax Blast. But her misgivings about working in the same school as Mike Korn prove to be overpowering. Imelda, in particular, insists on hearing about all her fears.

"Are you sure?" Louise asks. "This seems pretty trivial compared to what you've been through. Do you want me to fly out there and cheer you up?"

"It's the other way around," Imelda says. "I keep thinking, 'What's losing a breast compared to losing what all those poor people in Oklahoma City lost?'"

So, at Imelda's urging, Louise tells her everything about Mike Korn and the militia nuts. Richard, who overhears the conversation, dismisses her worries on the grounds that she is scaring herself so she will have good stories to tell their friends.

And that's it. That's all it takes for Louise to go ballistic. "Doesn't it bother you that your wife has to work in the same building with that creep? Your pals from the Tax Blast, don't you think they listen to Mike Korn's show? They probably sat next to McVeigh at those militia meetings. Did you ask Matt if he knows the bastard? Did you? Did you even think to ask?"

Unbelievably, Richard rolls his eyes like an adolescent boy whose mother is nattering about fears he considers groundless. "Just because Matt owns a militia calendar, that makes him guilty? He probably bought it for the babes. More likely, he takes it in the bathroom and jerks off to the guns. Even if he does belong to a militia, that doesn't mean he bears responsibility for the actions of some crackpot who attended one or two meetings. Anyone can attend a meeting. *I* could attend a meeting."

For days after that, she manages to avoid running into Matt. Having tried to give her neighbors—and everyone else in Stickney Springs—the benefit of the doubt, she feels doubly betrayed by the revelation that the militia to which Matt belongs is connected to the bombing. She learns all she needs to know about Matt's position from Richard: Matt insists the explosion was a plot by the FBI to make the militias look bad. Apparently, you can tell from the date: April 19 was the same date the British attacked the American irregulars at Lexington, the same date the Germans burned the Warsaw Ghetto, and the same date the Feds blew up the Branch Davidians and raided Ruby Ridge.

"So what?" Louise asks Richard. "Imelda's father's birthday

is April 19. Is *he* part of the conspiracy? As for the Warsaw Ghetto, do you mind telling me how that fits in? No matter what Floyd Goodman might tell the press, those militia guys hate the Jews. He and his gun-crazy friends are on the *Germans'* side. Aren't they, Richard? Have you read the militia literature the papers have been running? Matt and his pals are on the side of the guys who *burned down* the Warsaw Ghetto."

How could she be the one presenting this evidence of anti-Semitism to her Jewish husband? She never would admit this, but at some level she married him because marrying a Jew was a sign of tolerance and rebellion without the problematic fuss of marrying someone black. It was fine to be married to a Jew in California, where, as a neighbor of theirs once put it, "We don't have religions, we have cuisines." But she has ended up living in a place where it's no small matter to be married to a Jew, since, if you share his name, you're taken for one yourself.

"You're a Jew," Louise reminds Richard. "And we're living in a town with a bunch of guys who apparently have no compunctions about murdering little kids even if they *aren't* Jews. If that doesn't worry you—"

But it doesn't. Richard's refusal to share her fears reminds her of the inability of the heroine in a horror movie to get anyone to believe that a man-eating monster has slopped up from the swamp. But even in those movies, the heroine eventually convinced her husband she was right. Didn't she? Didn't she finally make him see the monsters were not only real, they were just outside their door?

FOUR

WHENEVER RICHARD DRIVES BEHIND THE WALL, HE FEELS invisible. Safe. Not like someone hiding. More like Clark Kent slipping into his phone booth. Louise might make fun of Matt Banks for seeing himself as a superhero, but every man, from the most timid to the most aggressive, harbored that vision of himself, the only difference being that before Richard moved to Michigan, most of his friends had been sophisticated enough to keep such daydreams to themselves.

He turns his crappy old Corolla into the lot reserved for officers and employees and pulls in an unmarked space next to a row of bold, blue-lettered signs: LIEUTENANT,

CAPTAIN, SUPERINTENDENT, DPTY SUPERINTENDENT. If everything goes as planned, in another few months he will be parking in the space reserved for DIRECTOR OF PSYCH SERVICES.

He gets out and looks around, sucking in the maddeningly delicious scent of fried onions. There is nothing interesting to see, but this is his last chance to be outdoors. He is about to give up and go inside when he notices Old Glory like a semi-inflated cock drooping halfway down the pole. Some politician's death? A day of mourning? April 22 doesn't ring any bells. Which leaves the possibility that an officer has been hurt or killed.

"Hey, Swanson," Richard calls to a scrawny man getting out of a light blue Taurus. The guy's belly, chest, and spine bow in and out in a very unhealthy curve. "TV Dinner" Swanson is the prison's dietician, and if his complexion and gaunt physique are any indication of the quality of meals he serves, Richard prefers not to try the fare. He points to the flag. "Something I ought to know?"

Swanson shakes his seahorse head. "What's the matter with you, Shapiro? That flag's been at half-mast for three days. It's that thing in Oklahoma City. I just hope the guy they nabbed in El Reno's the one that did it."

Of course. The flag had been lowered out of respect for the government employees who died in the Murrah Building. In some knee-jerk, anti-Midwestern way, Louise blames the men he works with. But most of the officers at the prison are more horrified than Louise at what that S.O.B. has done. The intended victims of that bomb were government employees. The toddlers in that preschool were government employees' kids. The officers—the *guards*, as Louise insists on referring to them—want Timothy McVeigh to fry. The bastard broke the code that prohibits a warrior from killing women and children. Never mind Matt's cockamamie theory that the FBI staged the attack to make the patriot groups look bad. Most of the guys at work figure some overzealous militia type chose the date to show contempt for the government's attacks at Ruby Ridge and Waco. And since most of the guys at work are militia types themselves, they're furious that this idiot should so pervert their cause. *Did you see that fireman carrying out that baby girl? What kind of loser thinks a baby girl might be the enemy?*

"I'm a God-fearing man," Swanson says. "But I wouldn't mind a chance to take a crowbar to that weasel."

"Makes two of us," Richard says, although he has never used a crowbar for anything except prying tiles from his mother's kitchen floor.

They reach the first entrance, a set of double glass doors designed less to keep the inmates in than keep out the morning cold. Swanson heads toward the men's room.

"You just got here and you already need to use the john?"

Swanson hitches his belt buckle, a heavy brass rectangle the size of a small book. "I drink this really strong cup of joe every a.m., it keeps me regular. I'd rather drink a cup of joe than take those laxative things, or drink that orange drink tastes like straw."

"You sound like an old Jewish mother." *My old Jewish mother* is what he means.

"Hey, those old ladies got good sense. I need advice, I go to my own mother, and nine times out of ten, she helps me out." Swanson puts his shoulder to the door. "See you this weekend?"

"Sure," Richard says. "Matt's letting me try out his Savage one-ten."

"Ah, that gun's a piece of shit. You want a good hunting rifle, you try my Remington thirty-aught-six."

"You bring it, I'll try it."

Swanson salutes and goes inside. Just as in his teens the mere mention of sex gave Richard an erection, the act of saying "Savage one-ten" gives him a hard-on now. The excitement has nothing to do with actually using a gun to kill a living creature, although he does intend to accompany Matt and Floyd on a hunting trip next fall. It's the pure hormonal satisfaction derived from lifting the gun and sighting it and watching the bullets fly. He has never trusted himself to own anything that destructive. Which is why he drives such a fucking nothing car. He always believed that if he so much as sat behind the wheel of a Miata, he would run somebody down. Well, first the gun, then the Miata.

He only wishes Swanson hadn't gone in to take a crap and left him waiting in the waiting room. Of all the areas in a prison to give a guy the creeps. There's nothing remotely frightening about the place, just a bunch of hideous green chairs and a fake-wood magazine-table with nothing on it but an ashtray, which seems a form of entrapment, given the NO SMOKING sign. Today, one of the chairs is occupied by a jovial-looking white guy with a fringe of long gray hair around his bald spot—he looks like a hippie vet you might hire to play Santa Claus at a rehab center. Across from him sits an acne-faced black woman and her adolescent son. The woman peels an orange and hands a section to the boy, who wears a T-shirt that reads VALET. The bald guy uses a stubby pencil to work a puzzle. Richard smiles at all three, and the woman offers him a section of orange. Richard waves his hand, declining. Every time he passes the waiting room, he imagines his stately white-haired father and his willowy, tastefully dressed and perfectly accessorized mother perched stiffly at the very edges of these awful green chairs.

What he likes about the relatives of the men he treats is

they don't act as if their lives are over. Even with a husband or son in jail, they can still enjoy an orange. Maybe this is only a middle-class conceit and the families are as shattered as his own parents would be if he ended up in prison. But he honestly doesn't think they are. His parents expect him to be perfect. A single mistake on Richard's part and their lives would be ruined. Maybe this philosophy is confined to German Jews who learned that the most trivial mistake might betray you to the Gestapo. But Richard doesn't think so. As a freshman at Columbia, he had been assigned a story by James Joyce—an Irish Catholic, after all—in which an adolescent boy imagines himself bearing a chalice through a crowd. Richard wasn't exactly sure what a chalice was, but he sensed he had found a metaphor for how he felt: he pictured himself carrying his mother's brittle glass kiddush-cup filled with some extremely precious liquid—the last drops of Christ's blood, or the blood of his four murdered grandparents, or maybe the cure for polio— through the boisterous halls of his crowded high school, the white-carpeted rooms of his parents' house, up and down the hills at every cross-country meet he had ever run, knowing that if he so much as spilled a drop, his parents would give up on him and he would be damned by man and God.

Well, miracle of miracles, he managed not to slosh a single drop of that precious liquid for thirty-eight years. Then he not only dropped the cup, he stepped on it and smashed it. Thirty-eight years of vigilance, ending with a suicide and a fire. But then—how could he not have known?—none of it mattered. Even if you dropped the chalice, nothing would happen. Except that you got to walk around for the rest of your life *without* the fucking cup, which was its own kind of blessing. Or someone handed you another cup and said, *Okay, this time be more careful*. But it wasn't as if that second cup mattered either. Some of his clients had been spilling blood and breaking cups their entire lives, and *they* got second chances. Even if you killed a person, there was such a thing as repenting and starting over, even if it meant repenting and starting over in jail.

Louise pities him because he has given up his private therapy practice. He no longer has the "privilege" of treating patients like Tony fucking Kaufman, who wanted to be assured he didn't deserve his employees' enmity or the hatred of his son, which in both cases he did, or Ellie Cunningham, who thought she was entitled to have an affair with her daughter's soccer coach because her husband had slept with a whore in Vietnam a decade before Ellie was even born. In the prison, Richard counts among his patients a homosexual necrophiliac whose fundamentalist parents beat the shit out of him for so much as looking at his own penis, let alone another man's, and a guy who strangled his girlfriend, chopped her up, and put the pieces in a cooler because he didn't know how to tell her that he had fallen in love with someone new. Louise sees this as a comedown. But Richard had wanted to work in a prison all his life. He *loves* working here. The only part of his day that upsets him is walking past this waiting room. What's taking Swanson so long? Richard is tempted to go ahead and leave the poor bastard. Standing here reminds him of the time he got a B+ in tenth-grade chemistry, and his parents made an appointment to see the headmaster. The three of them went inside, and Richard's parents complained that the chemistry teacher's methods of grading were unfair, at which Mr. Tomlinson overruled the grade, thereby preserving Richard's straight-A record and forcing him to carry that fragile cup yet another year.

"Excuse me?" The man with the fringe of hair holds his pencil above his puzzle. "You wouldn't happen to know the thirteenth president."

Richard lifts his hands. "Nope. Sorry. I don't."

"That's all right." The man starts filling in some blanks, bearing down hard against one knee. "I'll just say Buchanan. It's got the right amount of letters. If you keep an optimistic attitude, you can make the wrong answers work as well as the right ones."

At last Swanson emerges from the men's room.

"Another minute and I'd have called out the Marines."

Swanson wipes his hands on his shirt. "Some things you can't rush."

"I'm not going to be late to my first session of the day because you needed to take a dump."

The dietician punches Richard's arm affectionately. "Wouldn't want my regularity to interfere with Doc Shapiro's miracle talking-cures."

The two men continue toward the guard booth. Before the officer can ask to see their IDs—if you wait to be asked, you don't belong—Richard flashes his badge. The women wear their badges around their necks, but the guys keep their cards in flip-style wallets. With one authoritative flick, you flash your ID, causing the officer to hit a button and open the electronic doors, unless you're dumb or inexperienced enough to be carrying something metal, which Richard is tempted to do, if only because he likes the idea of being frisked, the rough contact of the ritual, the James Bond importance of standing spread-eagle while an officer waves that metal wand around your arms and then up between your legs, as if your very genitals might be lethal.

Once you get through the metal detectors, you're free to go through the doors. Which aren't just any doors. Despite the DO NOT MOVE WHILE DOOR IS IN MOTION warning, more than one impatient new employee has been knocked on his ass. The doors stand fifteen feet apart, heavy metal barricades that could do serious damage to a formidable farmer like Matt Banks, let alone a flimsy New York Jew like Richard. The first door swings slowly toward him. He waits, then walks through it, and as that first door swings shut behind him, the second door begins to move. He waits for *that* door to finish opening, then walks through and lets it swing shut with a sucking thud. Thhhhhh-*wunk*. Pause. Thhhhhh-*wunk*. Over and over, everywhere you go. It's the noise that haunts the lifers, and a fair share of the officers, the guys who don't like their jobs but can't earn this kind of money anywhere else.

But Richard loves the thud of those metal doors, the rhythm that allows him to make it through without breaking an arm or leg. He can't help it; he really gets off on the high-security rigmarole of his job. Maybe what he wants isn't to be a superhero but a secret agent. Napoleon Solo or Illya Kuryakin. Or even Maxwell Smart. He doesn't need his psychology degree to know that the stories he grew up hearing about his father's daring exploits in evading Nazi thugs are responsible for his own desire to perform similarly courageous acts, with few venues for such achievement other than acing his SATs, outrunning a bunch of suburban white kids at the state cross-country championships, and, in his daydreams, outsmarting Goldfinger and Dr. No.

He waits for Swanson to maneuver through the doors. Together they find their name tags on the wall and flip these from red to green so the officers will know whom to rescue if a riot breaks out. A corridor, another door—thhhhhh-*wunk*—and the two men are outside again, "outside" being a relative term, given that the courtyard is enclosed on two sides by a twenty-foot fence with a double roll of barbed wire across the top, on the third side by the building they just exited, and on the fourth side by the prison. A few inmates are down on their knees, planting flowers along the walk. Richard doesn't know the flowers' names—tulips, maybe, and the yellow ones Louise says remind her of opera singers—but their beauty is so heartfelt and unexpected it takes away his breath. The two inmates to his right don't look up, but the inmates on his left, one white and one Hispanic, lift their heads and stare like— he hates to say this—expectant dogs.

"Hey," Richard greets them, "how's it going," although only the white one, Russo, is an inmate Richard knows. He doesn't like being on his feet while other men are crawling on their knees, but he takes pleasure in the idea of criminals working off their crimes by planting flowers; it reassures him that if he ever fucks up worse than he already has fucked up, he might earn his way back into the good graces of humanity by planting bulbs and pulling weeds.

The path runs a hundred and fifty feet across the courtyard, but Richard and Swanson take their time. A robin lands not five feet from Russo. Balanced on his knees and one hand, Russo extends an arm, but the bird flaps a few yards off and starts pecking at a different mound of dirt. Maybe it's the bird, or the sally port in the fence, but Richard suddenly has an image of himself trapped in a wire cage. The sally port is hinged to open horizontally like the doors in the cages at that awful bird-lady's house. Whenever he drops off Molly, he feels an instinctual male revulsion at a witch, as if the birds are men and boys she has captured and transformed for her own nefarious ends. And God help him, after what Matt told him about what happened to Em in college, Richard can't help but think of her as tainted and corrupt in ways that make him nervous about allowing his daughter to play with her. He knows this isn't fair. Em was the victim. None of it was her fault. If Em had been his client, he would have managed to hide his gut response. But as it is, where Molly is concerned . . . Not that he and Louise have anywhere else to leave her. Not that he could betray his neighbor's trust and tell Louise what he's found out, especially since Em appears to be the only friend his wife has made since he dragged her to Stickney Springs.

"So long, Doc." Swanson salutes again, then branches off on a path that leads to the cafeteria. "You have a nice day."

Richard salutes back and sets off whistling across the remainder of the courtyard. But just before he reaches the opposite end, he senses someone behind him, and, heart scudding, he wheels around, expecting to see an inmate. But it's an officer, Barney Sipp, and Sipp's sidekick, a nonentity named Ira Rosenkrantz.

"Jesus, Sipp, you trying to get yourself killed?" If there is one thing a person who works in a prison knows, it's not to come up behind anyone else without making a lot of noise. One of the older guys, Dirk Crusoe, had been vacationing in the Bahamas when a beggar came up behind him, and Crusoe, not remembering where he was, swung around and decked the poor bastard.

"Jesus? No, I don't think Jesus has anything to do with what goes on between you and me." Sipp holds up two pudgy palms. "You *do* know that's the Lord's name and you're not meant to use it as a curse?"

The guy is taller than Richard, but only by the height of his thistly flat-top. He looks like one of the Katzenjammer kids all grown up. As for Rosenkrantz, he might have a Jewish-sounding name, but he's as Aryan as they come, so slight and fair Richard doubts he throws a shadow. A lot of guys at the prison have Jewish-sounding names. Stern. Goldhammer. Klein. There even was a Schwartz—well, all right, the guy spelled it "Swartz." But in the Midwest, the Kleins and Swartzes mostly turn out to be German Christians. Richard has heard that Rosenkrantz does a knock-out Presley imitation, but if anyone looks less like Elvis Presley than this guy, Richard hasn't met him. You could define the guy's appearance by taking Presley's features one by one and ascribing their opposites to Ira Rosenkrantz. Thin lips, transparent hair, not an ounce of soul or sensuality about his eyes, which are an iceberg-lettuce green. Every time Richard sees the guy, he wants to ask Rosenkrantz to do his Presley imitation. He can't imagine any transformation that extreme. And seeing Rosenkrantz as Presley might help Richard find something to like about the guy.

"You know, Shapiro, if I were you, I'd get my hearing checked." Sipp reaches the set of double doors leading to the prison proper. Holding open the first door ceremoniously for Richard, Sipp jerks his beefy head toward Rosenkrantz. "Either of us coulda stuck a shiv in you, you wouldn't have known what dropped you."

Rosenkrantz snorts. "You just about pissed your pants!"

In an elaborate show of courtesy, Richard holds the second door for Rosenkrantz and Sipp. He has heard that the two of them have organized a secret fraternity of white officers who take it as their duty to hassle the black and Hispanic prisoners. According to Richard's sources, some ugly shit has been going on, but it takes a much stronger base of support than Richard has developed to challenge such misbehavior. If you squeal on a bunch of renegade officers and the authorities don't deem it worthwhile to investigate and root them out, you are totally screwed. Just try to get through a day in a prison if even a few of the officers hold a grudge.

Rosenkrantz and Sipp saunter past; Richard goes in after them and shuts the door. On the bulletin board hangs a poster illustrating what to do if someone chokes, another poster detailing why it is prohibited for employees to take home office-keys, and a sign that announces the time and location of the memorial service for the victims of the bombing. Richard slows his step so Sipp and Rosenkrantz will enter the stairwell first. Sipp is already sweating through his shirt. Richard wrinkles his nose at the guy's body odor, although, to be fair, prisons make everybody sweat. Everybody except Ira Rosenkrantz. Seeing Rosenkrantz sweat would be like seeing a ghost sweat. Of all the tough guys and psychos at the prison, Rosenkrantz is the only one, even among the inmates, who truly frightens Richard. The man clearly is seething on the inside, but on the outside? Nothing, not even sweat. Richard has encountered more than his fair share of people who dislike the Jews, even a few who hold the Jews responsible for all the world's financial shenanigans and conspiracies. But he has never met anyone who hates the Jews the way Ira Rosenkrantz hates them, if only because Rosenkrantz seems to hold the Jews responsible not only for their own shenanigans and conspiracies but also for the perversion and despoliation of America by black people, whom Rosenkrantz loathes even more than he despises Jews. If not for Jewish lawyers, doctors, professors, politicians, social workers, and yes, psychologists, most black people in this country would be where they belong: behind bars. No matter what Richard says, whether at a meeting about the incidence of drug use in the prison or an informal encounter in a stairwell such as this, Richard can hear Rosenkrantz mumbling cryptic phrases such as "Yeah, sure, that's what *you* would say," or "Yeah, like you don't know whose fault *that* is," or "If you had your way, animals like that would be out on the streets." Richard would have called the schmuck out, but there is something about Rosenkrantz that he is afraid of setting off. Sipp, for all that he is a bully, is not much different from all the other bullies Richard has been outsmarting all his life. With Rosenkrantz, you could be as smart as they come and he would still find a way to get back at you.

Besides, Richard isn't the only guy who thinks Rosenkrantz is a cretin. Nobody dislikes a macho jerk worse than his fellow officers. The majority of the officers might not want to snitch on Sipp and Rosenkrantz's cadre of goons, but that doesn't mean they approve of them. "You stay away from those assholes," an officer named Eddie Zink has warned Richard. "We can't stop Sipp from saying the stupid shit he says. But he tries anything on you, he's got a bunch of us to answer to." It's almost worth having to put up with a jackass like Sipp to know the other guys would beat the crap out of him if he went too far in hassling Richard. If there ever is a riot, the officers will run in to save whoever needs saving. Richard doesn't doubt that even Barney Sipp and Ira Rosenkrantz would risk their lives to save his. But it brings a knot to his throat that so many of these men would put a little something extra in their stride running to protect him. They like that he reads about their kids in the local paper and remembers to compliment them on a daughter hitting a game-winning run or a son making the honor roll. He answers their questions about a mother with Parkinson's or a mind-numbingly confusing insurance policy or a teenage kid's recently discovered stash of pot. They consider him to be just about as smart and successful as any human being was meant to be. One of the officers ran into him at the Big Boy with Molly and Louise, and the next day this officer announced to the other guys that Richard had the best-looking wife he had ever seen off a movie screen. The other officers don't believe that Rosenkrantz's crack about Jews getting the cushiest jobs was called for. Richard got his job because he went to school and studied, unlike the rest of them, who stopped attending school the minute they were allowed to stop. In their eyes, it isn't anything to be ashamed of, being smart and working hard.

"So, Shapiro, I gotta ask." Sipp pauses before turning off at the landing. "That Japanese piece of shit break down on you yet?"

"Nope. Not yet. Any Corolla worth its salt gets two hundred thousand miles before it even needs a tune-up."

"I hope you know who pays your salary. It sure as hell ain't the fucking Japanese."

"Look," Richard says, "Corollas are made in Kentucky now, okay?"

"Yeah, well, Kentucky ain't Detroit. And the only reason Toyota built a plant in Louisville is because the fucking Nips already bought the fucking state."

"Floyd Goodman drives an Isuzu." He feels queasy using Floyd Goodman as an example of anything, but he isn't above dropping a famous name to get this gorilla off his back.

Sipp uses a fingernail to pry a particle of food from between his teeth. "Yeah, so what. Goodman's a fucking kike, too."

As Sipp and his sidekick lumber down the corridor, Richard considers how much more satisfying it is to be called a kike to your face than to sense the unspoken distaste behind your back. Growing up, he was always the only boy who showed up in class when hunting season started. Despite his teachers' grudging affirmation that he scored highest on their tests, they looked at him as if he were something moldy they had found at the back of a refrigerator. If not for a directive from the principal, the teachers would have been out hunting, too. Well, now Richard is one of the hunters. He has gone fishing with Matt and Floyd and caught a steelhead and netted a mess of smelt and bitten off the head of not one but two of the little fuckers—it wasn't all that much different from sinking your teeth into a chunk of pickled herring—and Matt and

Floyd's friends smacked him on the back and described the even greater thrill he was going to feel when he bagged his first buck, and if Barney Sipp and Ira Rosenkrantz don't like having him on the hunt, that's going to be too fucking bad.

He climbs the second flight of stairs, picks up the keys to his office, then passes the final checkpoint, flipping open his wallet to show his I.D. to the officer who sits behind a two-way mirror, so Richard appears to be flashing his badge at himself. Everything is fine until he smells the smoke seeping from the guard booth. Then he is on that mountain in Colorado, heading back along the remains of the trail he and Louise had covered at a run not fifteen hours earlier. He was supposed to show the ranger where the fire started. But the sight of all that smoldering stubble, the nitrous pall of ash, and the knowledge that this barely fathomable destruction had been his own careless fault choked his lungs and made him retch. He hadn't eaten anything but trail mix in the previous forty-eight hours, but still he had to puke, and the ranger stood shaking his head at the poor shmuck who not only couldn't light a stove without setting fire to a tree but couldn't face his punishment without heaving up his guts.

Except he isn't in Colorado now. He's in Michigan, smelling the cigarette smoke oozing from the security booth, where the officer can smoke an illegal cigarette without worrying that his superior might see him before he has a chance to put it out. Richard hurries down the hall and unlocks what passes for his office. Four bare walls the size of a closet. Any officer, including Barney Sipp, has the right to unlock the door and come in at any time. The only personal item Richard allows himself—and this he keeps hidden in a dauntingly thick copy of the DSM III diagnostic manual—is a photo of Sophie Pang. It is the photo from her obituary, the one in which she looks like a wide-eyed, unlucky boy staring up at another homer sailing for the fence. Why does he keep the photo? He doesn't feel responsible for her death. At their last session, he asked Sophie if she was depressed enough to kill herself, and Sophie told him no, and Richard believed her, because really, when he asked, she *wasn't* suicidal. She didn't become suicidal until two or three days later, when her lover informed her that she was having an affair with another member of their rugby team. No one saw it coming—not Richard, not Sophie, maybe not even Sophie's lover. And it was the lover's leaving, not Richard's incompetence as a therapist, or even Sophie's unforgiving parents, that pushed her to take those pills. Every therapist Richard knew had gone through something similar. The only difference was that he had assumed himself exempt. After all, he still was carrying that chalice. But now he knows he's no more exempt from making mistakes or suffering misfortunes than anyone else in this sorry world.

So no, he doesn't keep Sophie Pang's picture to remind himself that he is responsible for her being dead. He keeps it because he loved her. Not that he knew he loved her when Sophie was still alive. He thought he looked forward to her visits because she was funny and smart. She did killer imitations of her coworkers at the computer firm and her parents' pidgin-English denunciations of her unmarried lesbian state, and even her beloved roommate, that brutish American dyke who didn't deserve a woman as funny and smart as Sophie Pang.

He presses his lips to Sophie's face. Once, after she left his office, he allowed himself to succumb to a full-blown ten-minute fantasy, complete with masturbation, about making love to Sophie Pang. Then, after she was dead, he lay on the sofa in his living room listening to Louise tell him to stop blaming himself for Sophie's death while he was thinking the entire time about how much he had been in love with her and how much he was going to miss seeing her twice a week.

He slips the photo back in the DSM like a bookmark to a disease and heads to the lounge for a cup of coffee. In one corner of the dingy communal room, an inmate mops the floor while Richard's colleague Ron Lowenstine sits reading the paper and eating doughnuts. Richard squeezes between Lowenstine's chair and the counter and pours himself a mug of coffee.

Lowenstine licks a finger. "Hey, Richard, got a minute?"

Richard glances at the inmate with the mop. What is Lowenstine thinking, using his first name? A slip-up like that from Ron Lowenstine, of all people. Lowenstine is one of the cagiest, most abrasive guys Richard has ever met. That's the Israeli in him. Lowenstine spent his first half-dozen years in Haifa, where his father served in the Irgun, and he looks like a guy you wouldn't be happy to see behind an Uzi, at least not if you're an Arab. Richard can't help it, he loves to meet tough Jews. Lowenstine's arms are thick as hams and he has a face that looks like it got smashed by an inmate's fist. One of the administrators told Richard the secretaries think Ron Lowenstine resembles Robert DeNiro. He's been married three times, and the secretaries started a bet about whom Lowenstine would ask out next. Women were strange creatures if they couldn't keep their hands off Ron Lowenstine. He's a man's man, Richard thinks, without knowing what that means, since he doubts many men would want to be friends with Ron Lowenstine, if only because they couldn't risk introducing him to their wives. It's more that nobody messes with Lowenstine. Lowenstine once told Barney Sipp it was a good thing Christians don't circumcise their peckers. "It gives you an extra inch right where you need it most." Lowenstine wagged a finger an inch from Sipp's crotch, and miraculously, Sipp did nothing but say, "Fuck you." Lowenstine had practiced therapy in Ann Arbor before "the shit hit the fan," as he grunted when Richard asked, which leads Richard to believe that Lowenstine works at the prison because it's the only way he can keep from getting in trouble with female clients.

"So listen." Lowenstine draws a cheap ballpoint from his shirt pocket and clicks out the point. "There's this petition you need to sign."

This surprises Richard, since Lowenstine isn't the type to fight for causes. Usually, he just likes sitting at the table eating doughnuts and bitching about Yasser Arafat.

"You hear about this putz, Mike Korn? You ever listen to the shit this guy puts out?" He shakes his shaggy head, which is strong-featured as a bison's. "Most of these militia guys, they just like to get together on the weekends and spook each other with stories about black helicopters coming to round them up and eat beans from a can and fart. But this Korn, he's one dangerous sonofabitch." Lowenstine crumples the paper towel he has been using as a plate and tosses it toward the trash. The inmate with the mop bends and picks it up. "I'm no Chicken Little, but I don't like the idea of a nut like that working in an institution where my daughters spend eight hours a day. There's this minister, he's heading a drive to get Korn fired. I'm not ashamed to say it. I want that sonofabitch out of that job. If it's not my girls, it's going to be someone else's kids." He holds out the pen. "I know your little girl isn't in high school yet, but thinking ahead, you might want to put your name on the dotted line. It's gotta be even worse in Stickney Springs. You've got that crazy church, and that club where the militia guys hang out. Too bad you didn't ask me before you moved there. I could have told you it was no place for a guy named Shapiro to put down roots."

Richard looks again at the inmate. What the hell is wrong with Lowenstine? You never mention where a coworker lives, especially not after you just said the guy's name. He stares at Lowenstine with a "what gives" expression until Lowenstine throws open his hands to show he had forgotten where he is.

The inmate, an older black guy, senses what's going on. "Hey, it's cool. Even if I had a grudge against either one of you fine gentlemen, which I do not, and even if I managed to get the hell out of this joint, which is highly not likely, I wouldn't be stupid enough to show my black ass in Stickney Spring." He jams the business end of the mop in his bucket and drags it into the hall.

"See? I'm not making this up. Your wife works at the high school, right? Louise? You ask Louise about this Korn. She's on this committee. But I don't see your name on this petition."

The way Lowenstine cocks his head, you can almost see him sniffing out the weakness in Richard's marriage—that he has taken to sleeping on the couch, that out of some misguided she-needs-to-do-things-for-herself perversity he has been treating his beautiful, lonely wife like crap for too many months. Lowenstine had been present when Hildebrandt told the guys he had seen Shapiro's wife at Big Boy and damned if she didn't remind him of an actress—Meryl Streep, or that classy British chick with the thin face and straight blonde hair and the name with a mouthful of consonants you couldn't pronounce. Richard isn't about to sit here and discuss his marital woes with a sexaholic like Ron Lowenstine.

He takes the pen. "No problem. Just figured one Shapiro counted for us both."

Lowenstine folds the petition and stashes it in his shirt. He rinses his mug, runs his fingers daintily beneath the faucet, and wipes them on his moustache. "Time to spread our own special brand of love and joy to America's most wanted."

Richard picks up a stack of inmates' files and follows Lowenstine out. Their paths diverge at the consultation rooms, Lowenstine taking the gloomier room on the north while Richard unlocks the sunnier room to the south. Except for the wash of light filtering through the shoebox-sized window in Richard's room, the boxes are identical, each with a metal desk and plastic chairs—plastic, so the psychologist's head won't get dented as badly if an inmate takes umbrage at his advice. The walls in each room are decorated with the same insipid nature-posters, which Richard refuses to look at because they remind him of Colorado and because the drippy sayings make him sick.

As always, he takes the chair facing the desk, so the inmate will need to sit where the officer in the hall can keep an eye on him. Some prison shrinks wear panic buttons, but Richard hates this display of insecurity. If you pick up the phone but don't dial within ten seconds, an alarm goes off. Besides, if anything were to happen, the officer outside the door would be inside in an instant. So far, the only time Richard has felt threatened has been when the foot fetishist stretched his leg beneath the desk and used his shoe-tip to caress Richard's instep. The guy was a serial rapist who liked his victims dead. The whole thing creeped Richard out so much he told the guy if he so much as glanced at Richard's foot again, he would report him to the warden. That stopped the footsie.

He flips through the folders. At twenty minutes per session, a psychologist can go through a lot of inmates in one day. Richard is under no illusion that he can do more for most of these guys than keep them stable enough so they can survive prison life without doing too much damage to themselves or the other inmates. He's the one who gets something from most of the sessions. He has always loved cop shows, not for the puzzles they represent in figuring out who committed the crime, but for the puzzle of the criminal mind itself, the insights into why, if Richard Shapiro was so focused on being good, other human beings could be so focused on being bad. As a kid, he had read detective novels, true-crime stories, studies of aberrant behavior. And from his first semester at Columbia, he had known what he wanted to do. But his parents shook their heads. Psychiatry was fine, but why waste his time treating criminals when he could help normal, smart people lead more productive lives? Not to mention that he could charge normal, smart people a hundred dollars more an hour than he could charge some miserable government agency for his services.

When he met Louise and told her he wanted to work with criminals, she encouraged his enthusiasm. But as time wore on, she treated his wish as a childish dream. She could have said no thanks, she didn't mind staying in their two-room flat in Berkeley, she and Molly could get along just fine without a house in Marin County and all the expensive, time-consuming crap that went with it. There would have been compensations. Berkeley was the freest place on earth. Richard had wanted to live there since the sixties, not least because moving to Berkeley put a continent between his parents and himself. But like so many criminals, after he got away, he revisited his crime. He married a woman exactly like his mother, a woman who had been raised without a home, order, or stability and wanted Richard to provide all three.

Well, it's high time he does what he wants to do. No prison psychologist lasts more than a year or two treating inmates. But after Richard has earned his street creds, he hopes to move up in the system and re-institute a commitment not merely to incarceration but rehabilitation. For now, he is free to study what he always has wanted to study: the most extreme aberrations of the criminal mind.

A knock at the door, a sniffle, and in walks Manny Fitz. "Manny, how you doing."

Manny knows the drill. He takes the seat behind the desk, tips back the chair, folds his hands across his crotch, and tries to look as bored as possible.

"Hear any good voices lately?" Richard still isn't used to putting on a flip tone. But the sincere inflections he would have used with clients on the outside would be greeted by derision here. Manny focuses on his hands, which are the shade of peanut butter. Richard has never been able to figure out Manny's race. Not that the inmates' hallucinations vary much by ethnicity. "You taking your meds?" He knows from the folder that Manny has twice been caught selling his insomnia prescription. But he seems to be sticking to his Haldol. "Come on, Manny, I know you've been hearing the voices again. What've they been telling you?"

A microscopic shrug. "They say, 'How many shrinks it take to change a light bulb.'"

"Yeah? So? How many *does* it take?"

"Hell, the voices didn't tell me no punch line. They done told me a punch line, I woulda just laugh and gone back to sleep."

Richard points at the glaring fluorescent tube. "The joke goes like this. How many shrinks does it take to change a light bulb? Only one, but the light bulb has to *want* to change." Manny gives no indication he thinks the joke is funny, or even understands it. Never mind. It doesn't matter what you ask these guys as long as you have the right attitude. They're dying to open up and have a human conversation. "Or there's this one. How many paranoids does it take to change a light bulb?" Richard pauses a beat, then puts on a sour, aggressive face. "Hey, who wants to know?"

Manny jerks upright. "What's a paranoy?"

"Someone who thinks everyone is out to get him."

Manny slaps the desk. "Paranoy the only way to be in this place. You think everyone out to get you, you gonna be on your guard, make sure no one *does* get you." He leans closer. His clothes give off the same tomato-soup acidity that Swanson's clothes give off. "That's what them voices keep telling me. This one out to get you, that one out to get you. Last night, they say my own mother out to get me. I'm laying there trying not to cry. My own mother trying to kill me! But them voices won't quit." He rubs a thumb beneath each eye, as if to erase the freckles spattered across his cheeks. "But I remember you say banging my head on that wall won't make those voices stop. So I just let them go on saying what they want to say. I cried, man. My own mother? Can't trust my own mother? But I didn't fucking bang my head."

And so the day goes, except for the hour Richard spends reviewing cases with an intern and the forty-five minutes he devotes to visiting inmates in special needs, including the rapist who tried to kill himself with a spoon. (Today, the man tells Richard he received a make-up letter from his wife and is trying to be good so he can get out of prison before his daughter hits the seventh grade and needs her father to keep the boys *off*.) He uses his lunch hour to wind down in his office and commune with Sophie Pang. No meetings. No emergencies. No major fuck-ups, his own or anyone else's. Although you would need to fuck up pretty badly in a place like this for anyone to care.

At five, he joins the crowd heading out the way they came in, although with more smiles on their faces now. He flips his name tag to red, passes through the double doors and the visitors' room, empty now except for a few crumpled cups and that guy's puzzle book on a chair. He blinks at the sun and sneezes.

"Hey, Shapiro." Sipp's nasal, biting voice. Richard lifts his hand but keeps walking. "We've got a question we want to ask."

"Don't have many answers today," Richard says.

"Come on. We won't bite."

He stops and looks back. A bunch of guys stand in a circle watching Barney Sipp with the half-assed attention they might bestow on a TV show that has a stupid plot and inane dialogue but promises some action later. Something tells Richard to just grit his teeth and get it over with, so he goes back and takes a spot directly between Rosenkrantz and Sipp.

"We thought you might explain how come Jews are so smart," Sipp says.

"Yeah," Rosenkrantz says. "You think you're so smart, maybe you're smart enough to explain how you got to be so smart," giggling at his own joke.

"Jesus, would you give it a rest?" Richard wishes he hadn't taken the name of their lord in vain a second time. No matter, these guys seem able to concentrate on only one insult at a time.

"I was just saying how it seems a coincidence there wasn't a single Jew in that Murrah Building when it got blown up," Sipp says, smirking. "Hard to believe they all just happened to stay home sick that day. Some coincidence, none of their kids were at that preschool."

Richard considers explaining to Barney Sipp and Ira Rosenkrantz that very few Jews live or work in jerkwater towns like Oklahoma City, and, if they do, they don't have jobs in government. But explaining anything to morons like Sipp and Rosenkrantz is like banging your head against a wall, which, as he is trying to teach Manny Fitz, hurts you a lot more than it hurts anyone else. It's one thing to explain something to Floyd. You can almost see Floyd open the mental file drawer in which the false information has been stored, correct that information—JEWS CAME TO UNITED STATES FROM EUROPE, NOT FROM ISRAEL—reinsert the file, and close the drawer. But with guys like Sipp and Rosenkrantz, no matter what you say, the drawer stays locked. "Your point being?"

"No Jews were in that building because the Israelis tipped them off."

"Israelis? What the fuck do Israelis have to do with what happened in Oklahoma?"

Sipp crosses his eyes, pulls down his cheeks, and sticks out his tongue, as if Richard were the moron. "Duh. The fucking Israelis. Blow up a building, make it look like the Arabs did it, so the Zionists in D.C. get more evidence to use against—"

Richard doesn't wait to hear the rest of this crackpot theory. He imagines himself punching a hole in his parents' kitchen wall and connects with Sipp's head. Sipp mutters *ooof* and crumples. Richard looks around at the other guys, especially Rosenkrantz, preparing to break into the kind of run that allowed him to win the state cross-country marathon.

But no one makes a move. Richard backs away. As he slides into his Corolla, he sees Sipp getting to his feet. He is thirty-nine years old, and this is the first fistfight he has ever been in. After so many years living in fear of getting the crap knocked out of him, he has thrown a single punch and laid the bully out. He pulls carefully out of the lot and onto the road, drumming his palms along the wheel, then whoops and pumps his fist. He even punches his horn, which causes the eight-wheeler heading past him on the highway to respond with its own deep-throated roar, as if they are two moose bellowing in the woods.

He wishes he could tell Louise. But she already thinks he has turned to a life of crime, as if shooting bowling pins off a table might make a man eligible for the Outlaw Hall of Fame. He and Louise have always been so in tune. How could a suicide and a fire turn them into two people who can't understand a word the other says? Isn't a wife supposed to love her husband no matter what? Isn't there such a thing as constancy, or devotion? Taking the bad times with the good? He keeps telling her how he feels, but she doesn't seem to get it. He wants *her* to come to *him*, and not because she needs him to change a fuse or keep the Nazi bogeymen away.

He turns down Stickney Road. Everyone wants a sugar daddy. Half the inmates he treats are where they are because they couldn't find a father to take care of them on the outside. Even guys like Matt, who rail against that greatest of all sugar daddies, Uncle Sam, can't do without a smaller, more accessible sugar daddy like Floyd Goodman.

Okay, so Richard is temporarily substituting Floyd for his own father. But he knows what he's doing. He's using Floyd to teach him how to shoot a gun and how to throw a punch at a jerk like Barney Sipp. It isn't as if Matt and Floyd are Jew-haters like Sipp and Rosenkrantz.

Louise would be shocked to hear it, but he doesn't completely disagree with the stuff Matt and Floyd believe. How can a guy whose father and uncle barely escaped the Nazis consider it acceptable to let the government take away your guns? He believes in self-reliance, and, if not in the Christian God, then the Ten Commandments. He doesn't think abortion should be illegal. But he wouldn't want his wife to abort any child they might conceive. That's one of the reasons he can't bring himself to make love to her. She wants a second kid. So does he. But Louise is almost forty, and they would need to have one of those tests to see if the fetus was carrying the gene for Downs, and if the fetus did have the gene, Louise would want to abort it, and Richard doesn't think he could. But he also isn't sure he could raise a retarded child. He isn't saying he believes what Matt and Floyd believe. But he *understands* what they believe. What Louise doesn't get is that living in the midst of so many practicing Christians makes Richard feel more worthy to be a Holocaust survivor's son than living as a Jew among so many other Jews and atheists in California.

He parks behind the van. Inside the house, Molly and Louise crouch on the kitchen floor surrounded by ripped-up newspapers, bleach bottles, balloons, and a bowl of glue. He wants to call out: *Honey, I'm home. Guess who I decked with one punch?* But the story would only confirm her fears about all the right-wing maniacs lurking behind every bush.

She looks up from the floor, not suspecting that every time he sees her in that position, he remembers her crouching naked behind that rock beyond the reservoir in Ithaca, bright and glowing, hair and breasts so shockingly luminescent he thought that running in the heat had induced a mirage. Even now, after everything they have been through, his cock stirs at the sight of his wife in a sweatshirt and jeans, crouching on their kitchen floor. He wants to pull her up and lick the paste from her cheek. And he would do it, too, even in Molly's presence—let the child see some marital affection for a change—if not for his suspicion that at the first sign of love, she will ask him to mow the lawn.

He can't. He just can't. Not with the way she's looking up at him, trying to gauge the likelihood of his stepping on the papier-mâché giraffe she and Molly have created, or the likelihood of his stepping on Molly. They need help. He should ask Lowenstine for the name of a good couple's therapist in Ann Arbor. But the whole thing makes him tired, two therapists needing a third therapist to help them sort out their marriage. And there's the perverse thrill in seeing just how far he can let his marriage go. He has this image of dangling her like a yo-yo, Louise fluttering on a string, nearly to the floor, before he flicks his wrist and jerks her back. Then the panic hits, the sense that he has waited too long and already lost her.

He bends and kisses her head, then holds out his arms for Molly, who leaps up and throws her sticky hands around his neck. She smells of newsprint and glue. He buries his face against her curls. "What say I take my princess to the playground?"

Louise smiles a pinched smile. "How was your day?"

"Fine," he says. "The usual."

She looks at him as if she wants to press him for details, but Molly already has on her coat and is tugging at his hand to go.

"All right, sugarpie, up and at 'em." He carries her out the door, her pink rubber rain boots bouncing against his ribs, then he jogs her down the driveway, opens the Corolla, and tosses her in. He buckles the belt across her chest, or, more accurately, across her face. Who designs these stupid things? He flips the harness across her neck. That can't be safe, either, but the schoolyard is only a mile away.

"Dad?" Molly says. "There's something I want to tell you, but you can't laugh." She turns to him, the belt across her face. "If I jump off a chair and flap my arms really, really hard, I can stay up in the air. Because I'm so light? And I flap my arms so hard?"

If not for the fact that he's driving, he might close his eyes and weep. At Molly's age, he was certain he could fly. Like her, he jumped off high places and flapped his arms. Running full-tilt down a mountain, he had felt his body strain forward, faster than his feet, until he had achieved a few yards of airtime. Even as a grownup, he keeps dreaming he can fly—

not the effortless glide that other dreamers dream, but a joyless, draining labor to keep himself aloft. And every time, in every dream, no matter how violently he shouts and flaps, his parents refuse to look. The dreams are so real that even when he wakes he can't believe he hasn't flown.

He parks in the lot behind the school, and Molly undoes her seatbelt. "This is the school I'm going to in September," she says, then bolts from the car, runs across the park, and settles on one end of a seesaw.

Richard crosses the playground after her. A wood chip gets in his shoe, but he doesn't bother to take it out. More would get in anyway. He reaches the seesaw, throws his leg over the empty seat, and settles on it gradually.

"You've got to sit down *hard*," Molly says. "That's the whole *point* of a seesaw."

Yes, well, he knows that. But what if he bumps her off and she cracks her head or breaks her spine? He thought he had gotten over his fear. He's free now, isn't he free? Free of the anxiety that he might spill whatever liquid that fucking chalice holds. But he can't shake the dread that he might somehow hurt his daughter and so commit the one crime for which he could never forgive himself.

She jumps off the seesaw, and he hits the ground with such a thump that he bites his tongue. She is on the swings in no time, kicking her legs in an out-of-sync frenzy that won't accomplish much. He walks over to the swings and gives her a timid push.

"No! A *real* push. I want an underdog."

He puts his hands against her jacketed back and pushes harder.

"An *underdog*," she says in that petulant voice that reminds him of his mother.

"All right. Hold on. The next stop is *the moon*." Grimly, he grabs the seat and lifts her above his head, then runs forward, ducking beneath the swing and letting go.

"Look at me!" Forward she flies, then backward, her legs pumping wildly in resonance with the swing. Higher she flies, higher, until she swings so near the top, the chains are horizontal.

"No!" he calls. His stomach lurches, as if he is the one dropping backward on the swing. Then Molly is flying up again, and he fears she might accomplish every child's wish and go windmilling around the bar.

"Watch me! I can fly!"

The swing flies backward, then forward, and just as it reaches its apex, Molly lets go. He runs to the spot where he hopes he might catch her. But his creampuff of a daughter goes sailing above his head. Her boots fall off and batter him from the sky, surprising him so much he stumbles. Twisting in the dirt, he claws around to see where she might have landed.

She is lying on her back. "Molly!" She seems stunned, but both eyes are open. There are wood chips across her face. One of her arms is scraped. Her dress has flown up and her vulnerable white belly lies exposed. Despite knowing better, he pulls her into his arms.

"Did you see me? Did you see me? I *told* you I could fly."

His terror clears, only to be replaced by confusion. What if he says he did? She might be tempted to throw herself off even higher heights the next time. But if, like his parents, he explains the aerodynamic impossibility of a human being flying, she will hate him for disavowing what she knows to be true.

"Yes, ma'am, you sure went flying. I've never seen anything like it." He pushes a wad of scummy leaves from her forehead. "But flying can be dangerous, sweetheart. Human beings aren't birds. The few of us who figure out how to get *up* aren't all that good at coming *down*. It's the very rare human being who manages to fly without getting hurt. So promise me you won't fly that way again." He is so desperate he nearly shakes her. "Promise me, okay?"

"How about from halfway as high?"

"Sweetieplum, can't you just be glad you flew that one time?"

She relaxes against his chest. "I did come down kind of hard." She smiles up at him. "I promise, Daddy. As long as you saw me fly this one time, I guess I don't need to fly again."

FIVE

WHEN SHE ISN'T AT WORK, LOUISE SPENDS NEARLY ALL HER time wading through the news about Timothy McVeigh and his elusive accomplice, John Doe, or the Michigan Militia, or James or Terry Nichols, or the custodian talk-show host, Mike Korn. By now, the reporters have moved on to features about the coincidences that brought a victim to the Murrah Building on a morning he or she ordinarily wouldn't have been there, or the more reassuring coincidences that restrained some lucky devil from leaving home that day. A burly E.M.T. breaks down as he describes finding a tiny finger and some Fisher-Price toys where the preschool used to be, and Louise breaks down with him, crying for those poor children and their parents, as well as for herself. Her child is alive. Her husband hasn't been blown apart. But she can't rid herself of the sense that it's only a matter of time before her own family is reduced to ash and bone.

She takes to driving to Potawatomie even on days she isn't supposed to work. She hangs out at the AIDS Coalition, where someone, usually Howie or Jack, is working the hotline. There are always flyers that need to be mailed and letters that need to be written. But the truth is, she feels called upon to mount a one-woman campaign to protect the children of Potawatomie from psychos like Timothy McVeigh and Mike Korn. She keeps watch from her attic office, vigilant as a gargoyle. Who is that stranger loitering by the tennis court? Why is a yellow rental truck idling in the lot? Every clatter or clank in the steam pipes makes her jump.

When no appointments are on the books, she shadows Mike Korn. He seems more forlorn and blank than dangerous. No kids seem brave enough to pick on him now. "Hey, Korny," one boy starts, coming upon the custodian as he bends over a barrel of floor cleaner. "You ought to start playing music on that radio show of yours. Hip-hop, you know, or punk. You'd get a lot more listeners." The custodian looks at the boy as if he is speaking French. "Just a suggestion," the boy says quietly, making a motion as if to catch a basketball and toss it back to Korn. As the boy shambles down the hall, Korn turns and sees Louise watching. But her surveillance doesn't seem to register. Maybe his mind is too busy unraveling the complexities of some conspiracy. He strikes Louise as a sort of anti-superhero—mild-mannered custodian by day, fanatical, hate-mongering villain after hours.

She is tempted to ask the principal how he can allow Mike Korn to continue working at the school, but with his narrow high-cheeked face, pale hair, and sunken eyes, Hendrick van Dyke could pass for Timothy McVeigh's father. And she isn't about to distinguish herself as a troublemaker in the mind of the man who holds the final say over her getting hired.

Instead, she feels out her colleagues. Most of them keep their distance, as employees do when someone is among them only temporarily, but a few of the older men bring their paper bags and sit beside her in the lunchroom. When she manages to work the conversation around to Mike Korn, they make dismissive motions with their sandwich halves and assure her that he has worked at the school for eleven years without incident. As for the militia aficionados, playing commando has been a tradition for Michigan men as far back as Ernest Hemingway. Mr. Terwilliger, who teaches honors English, points out that "Old Hem" grew up near Petoskey and loved to hunt and fish and beat his chest, and, for all that, didn't pose much of a threat to anyone but himself.

As far as Louise can tell, there are no Jews on the faculty now that Janet Cohen is gone. She wants to ask the two black female teachers—Mrs. Norich, who teaches Latin, and Mrs. Goode, who teaches business and math—what they think of Korn. But they eat their lunch at a wobbly table barely big enough for two, leaning their heads together so intensely Louise is shy to join them. One afternoon, she finds herself sharing a table with Ervin Rolle, an enormous, sweet-faced black man who teaches music and leads the band. They bond over their shared admiration of Parker Rosenkrantz, but it takes Louise until dessert to feel comfortable enough to bring their talk around to Korn.

"You kidding?" Ervin says in a voice pitched so low no one else could possibly hear. "That guy scares the shit outta me. But that's all I need, to make myself more of a target. I just keep my distance from the dude." He eats a spoonful of applesauce and licks the residue from his moustache. "At least I know *he's* dangerous. Who among our compatriots holds similar views, but isn't broadcasting them on the radio? If you know the dynamite is over *there*, you try not to set it off. Otherwise, it's like crossing a minefield—you don't have any idea where the explosive's buried." He brings the fingertips of one hand together in his palm, then flicks them slowly out. "Boom," he says in the muted, exaggerated way he uses to lead his band. After that, every time he passes Louise in the hall, he makes that exploding motion and mimes the word *boom*.

One afternoon, about two weeks after the bombing, Louise is talking to Parker in her office when someone taps at the door. When she opens it, she sees Beverly Booth, her face and neck so flushed that Louise invites her in to sit and rest.

"Oh, I'm afraid I can't do that," Beverly tells her. "The building needs to be evacuated. Someone phoned in a bomb threat. I'm the one who took the call. It was like . . ." She whispers behind her hand. "Have you ever received a nasty phone call, and it takes until after you've hung up to understand what the man really said?" Louise glances back at Parker, who cocks his head to listen. Beverly stands on her toes and peeks inside. "You've done it up so nicely, with the rug and plants and all."

"Parker," Louise says, "we need to leave the building."

Like any teenage boy, Parker sees moving quickly as an infringement on his dignity. He collects his limbs as if these are the parts of a musical instrument he needs to pack carefully inside its case.

"Come on, come on!" She shepherds Parker down the stairs and out the door. Then she goes back in to make sure the other students get out safely. "Hurry, hurry." She makes sweeping motions with her arms as if she is driving livestock. But the other teachers aren't much calmer than Louise. Ena Goode and Nancy Norich jog down the stairs pressing their hands to their jouncing bosoms and murmuring pleas to God to let everyone get out alive. Larry Terwilliger stands mopping his forehead with a handkerchief and shouting at the kids to hurry and move their butts.

Louise goes back up to search for stragglers. Apparently, the school's one elevator isn't working, and she passes two teachers struggling to carry a girl in a wheelchair down the staircase. The second floor is empty. On the third floor, the sun shines in at the far end of the hall and reflects off the newly buffed tiles; squinting, she can make out Mike Korn using a master key to open each locker and peer inside. He looks up and sees Louise. She stares back at him—they might be two gunslingers squaring off for a duel. A stringy brown forelock dangles before his eyes. He uses a finger to push it up. His shiny taupe work shirt is tucked unevenly inside his pants. A grease stain blooms on one leg. Does his presence in the building prove his innocence or his guilt? Louise wants to ask why he hates so many people he has never even met. But she feels the same paralyzing fear she felt the time she and Richard surprised a bear in the high Sierras. As slow and harmless as the creature appeared to be, you didn't want to provoke it.

"I'm leaving," she says, backing down the hall. "You ought to leave, too." She turns and heads out. And the last thing she sees as she turns the corner is Mike Korn inspecting another locker, slamming it shut, and moving on.

Outside, she is shocked at how close to the school the kids are allowed to stand. All twelve hundred students are milling around the flagpole. "Let's move back," she says. Frustrated, she raises her voice. "I told you to all move back!"

Someone places a hand at her elbow. "That's enough. We don't want to panic them." Bess Moorehouse fixes her with a gaze a general might use while talking to a private who has lost his composure in battle. "Perhaps you want to go home? I'm sure the rest of us can handle this."

Louise shakes free and stands looking up at the brick and stone expanse, scanning it for anything the others might have missed. Two police cars and a fire truck arrive. Parker comes up to her and says he's heard a few of the black kids say they phoned in the threat, hoping Mike Korn would be blamed and fired. It occurs to Louise the black students must be even more scared than she is to pull such an idiotic stunt. Then Nancy Norich says the bomb squad will need an hour to arrive from Detroit, so they're sending the students home.

Louise waits until the last few ninth-graders are on the bus, then drives to Em's and picks up Molly. That night, the local news shows the students gathered around the flagpole. Hendrick van Dyke says that whoever phoned in the threat hasn't been identified. Mike Korn isn't a suspect "at this time." But the next afternoon, before she leaves her office, Louise looks in the phone book to see if she can find Korn's address. She doesn't expect it to be published. Would a man who believes himself the victim of a government conspiracy list his number? But there it is: *Korn, Michael, 1411 West Davis Avenue.*

She finds West Davis on a map and drives there. The houses are vinyl-sided ranches, larger than she expected. How can the Korns afford to live here? Then Louise remembers Em told her that Korn's wife works sorting mail in Potawatomie.

The Korns' yard is enclosed by a chain-link fence. An oversized American flag towers above the garage, along with a giant plywood cutout of a horse painted with the words: DON'T BE FOOLED! UNITED NATIONS IS A TROJAN HORSE! GET IT OUT NOW! Louise sits in the car a long time, but no one goes in or out. Eventually, she gives up her vigil.

Then, several evenings later, she accidentally catches Korn's talk show on the radio in the van. She is fiddling with the dial, tuning it past the country music stations to find *All Things Considered*, when she recognizes his voice.

"They did it themselves. It's a government building. That's where they keep their records. You bomb your own evidence—"

Someone interrupts. "Waco. Gulf War Syndrome. All the testimony. The evidence that could never be replaced—"

"Up it goes in flames, and you blame it on the only guys who see through your plan." Korn plays snippets from a staticky recording of a politician urging a crackdown on the militias, especially their right to horde automatic weapons. "Listen up," Korn tells his audience. "This is the arithmetic section of the show. I'm going to tell you guys how many feet of rope you would need to string up one politician. Then you can call in and tell me how many feet it would take to string up, say, four of these traitors. You think you got the right answer, you call it in. First caller with the correct number gets the rope as a prize."

Louise drives under an overpass, losing the signal, and on the other side hears Korn's guest spew a string of epithets whose target she missed. She heard right-wing radio broadcasts in California, but nothing this vitriolic. She can't believe the radio in her van is capable of emitting such hateful words—it's almost as upsetting as if she had overhead her daughter muttering curse words in her sleep.

Later, she tries to tell Richard how frightened she is to work in the same building with such a bigot. But he has hardened his heart against her. That's all Louise can think: *My husband has hardened his heart against me.*

"Korn is a racist idiot," Richard says. "But this is America. A man can't be fired for what he believes." He is putting away the groceries and turns to devote his attention to figuring out how to fit the steak and ice cream in the freezer. He presses the door shut, and even in her distress Louise can see that whoever opens the freezer next will get hit by an avalanche of frozen meat. "If the guys I work with got fired for thinking what Mike Korn says aloud . . ."

At some level he isn't wrong. Louise believes in the First Amendment. But Richard could have reassured her. He could have held her in his arms and reminded her what they both learned in Psych 101—that her anxieties, like most people's anxieties, largely are caused by her desire to control what cannot be controlled. He could have made clear that she can come home to him every night and voice her frustrations about working in a school where she feels so out of place. For all the sweet souls like Beverly Booth, there are tyrants like Bess Moorehouse and Hendrik van Dyke and fascists like Mike Korn. For all the appreciative students like Melody Hasbrouck and Parker Rosenkrantz, there are difficult-to-work-with kids like Lucas Beale, who was sent to see Louise because he propositioned another boy at a urinal. Faced with Louise's suggestion that there is nothing wrong with being gay as long as you confine your attention to willing partners, Lucas informed her that he has already condemned himself to an eternity of damnation by saying what he said to that other boy. He refuses to be treated by a therapist who hasn't been saved. "You think you're better than the rest of us," Lucas sneered. "Let me tell you, San Francisco is a hell pit of sinners. Whatever you learned there about being a psychiatrist—excuse me, a *social worker*—you better not try out here."

She can't blame Lucas Beale on Richard. But everything gets so mixed up in her mind—the images of those poor dead toddlers in Oklahoma, her suspicions about her neighbors, her fears for Molly's safety, her sudden and overwhelming need for sex—that, cut off from anyone whose advice might remind her who she is, Louise becomes unmoored. That's the word that keeps bobbing in her mind: *unmoored, unmoored, unmoored,* with a picture of her father's rowboats drifting far from shore.

Then the delivery boy tosses the *Potawatomie Gazette* on the porch, and when Louise rolls off the rubber band, she sees a photo of the Reverend Ames Wye urging the city council to fire Mike Korn. Before she knows what she is doing, she has brought the paper to her lips. It tastes of wood and ink. God, it's like having a crush on a rock star. When Ames calls a week later to give her the address of the next apartment they have to clean, she considers commending him on his efforts to protect her students. But she doesn't want to come off as a fawning groupie, so she merely copies the address and hangs up.

The following week, when she meets Ames in front of the second building in which the coalition rents rooms, they exchange pleasantries, and this normalcy reassures her. She even reaches out and touches his arm, the same way she once patted Rod's Rottweiler to convince herself she wasn't frightened of its bite. What she hasn't counted on is that constantly congratulating herself on not succumbing to her attraction keeps reminding her of how strong that attraction is. Nor has she predicted that seeing a minister on his knees scrubbing the toilet of a man who recently died of AIDS might make her want to kiss him.

She goes in to clean the living room. Unfortunately, the coalition member who boxed up the previous occupant's possessions missed the pornographic magazines and dildo inside the ottoman. These items do little to turn her on, but she needs Ames's help to carry them to the dumpster.

He holds the dildo to the light as if admiring a bottle of fine wine. She expects him to make a lewd joke, as Howie Drucker would have done. But Ames only remarks how sad it is that instead of being held by another person, a man should be so ill as to have no choice but to make love to a piece of rubber.

He carries the dildo and magazines to the dumpster and returns to clean the kitchen. Louise vacuums the carpet, then pops open the Hoover's chest, intending to throw away all the sad, linty accumulations of the previous tenant's life. But Ames is blocking the kitchen door, reaching up to dust the casing, and his shirt lifts to expose an inch of his sweaty back. "I can't get by," she says.

He turns to her, the furry rag pinched between his fingers. "May I kiss you?" he asks.

She nods, and the kiss, when it comes, isn't like any kiss she has ever experienced, although it is exactly the kiss she fantasized it might be.

"I don't want to disappoint you," Ames says, and Louise wonders if he means he doesn't want his lovemaking to disappoint her, or he doesn't want to raise her hopes that he might ever leave his wife.

"That kiss was the least disappointing thing that's ever happened to me," Louise says.

"I've never done this before." He presses his fingers to her temples.

"So why are you doing it now?" After all, he barely knows her. Other women must have offered.

He leans down and kisses her on her forehead. "I used to feel so enthusiastic about everything."

Yes, she thinks, *I know. You want to be enthused. You want to be possessed.* She tries to keep the tone light. "I was starting to think it was against the law for anyone in Michigan to be enthusiastic about anything except football or guns."

He undoes the buttons of her blouse, then walks behind her and helps her out of it, unbuckles her bra and lets it fall. He walks back around to her front and studies her as if she is a bureau he is supposed to move. She stands there, looking at Ames looking at her breasts. It has been a long time since anyone but Richard has seen her naked. She supposes any two people making love do the same basic things. What makes one case of lovemaking more erotic than any other are the circumstances that surround it—for instance, the fact that it has been thirteen years since anyone but your spouse has touched your belly or your thigh, or that the two people involved have never made love before and aren't supposed to be making love now, or that they are making love in someone else's apartment, or that one of the parties can't believe that the other party would consent to take part in such an activity.

Ames stands there so long, staring at her breasts, some charge seems to accumulate between them, and when he reaches toward her nipple, she expects to see a spark. He strokes that breast, then the other, then leans forward and kisses them. Then he makes a noise like the gasp of a man who has gone too long without breathing. She strokes his neck. When he looks up, his eyes are moist. He lifts off his own shirt, and Louise is startled by how pale his skin is, how hairless compared to Richard's, the overly pronounced rippling of the ribs and the concavity of his chest, as if some Puritan judge had tried to get him to confess by laying boulders on his lungs. Except that Ames's forefathers were the judges. Which excites her even more. *Stop now,* she tells herself. *Stop right this moment and run away.*

They make love on the carpet she has just finished vacuuming, the nap still herringboned with lines. He works so hard above her that sweat drips from his chin to her chest.

He bends and licks it off, then goes back to moving inside her until she has traveled halfway across the living room on her back.

Somehow, having intercourse on a food-stained rug in an empty living room that until recently held a stack of pornographic magazines and a rubber cock makes the act seem sadder and more erotic than sex has any right to be. Ames tightens his jaw and throws back his head, grunts and moans and comes with a terrible desperation, then collapses full-length on top of her. She wishes she could say she is plagued by guilt. But if she thinks anything, it's that her husband has stopped making love to her and she therefore is entitled to make love to someone else. Really, she tries not to think at all. Certainly, when Ames rouses himself from his post-orgasmic stupor and begins kissing her breasts again, and then moves lower and kisses her thighs, she thinks about nothing more than his lips and tongue.

"Jesus," she whimpers, "Jesus," hoping this doesn't offend him, although later, when their positions are reversed and Ames cries out *her* name, she feels—blasphemous thought— as talented as God.

"I haven't done that in ages," he confesses. "I feel like a teenager."

She nestles in his arms and tries to believe that she has just made love to a married minister. "I probably shouldn't ask you this," she says. "But isn't this against your religion?"

He winces so clearly she might have stabbed him. "Of course it's against my religion. It's completely against my conscience to be doing this. Unfortunately, a conscience isn't a very strong deterrent." He stares at the ceiling, which is stippled with stucco swirls like the craters of the moon. "You know how I think of Jesus? I think of him as a successful older brother. I talk to him all the time. The trouble is, if you tell your older brother you've been cheating on your wife, he isn't exactly going to strike you dead."

She presses her hand to the hot, wet skin above his heart, which still pounds with surprising force. Later, she realizes she should have paid more attention to what he said about his conscience. But she is struck by the idea that he thinks of Jesus as his brother. It's like finding out someone you love is related to a celebrity.

They talk a while. She tells him about working at the school with Mike Korn, about her sense of obligation to help kids like Melody Hasbrouck and Parker Rosenkrantz and even Lucas Beale. Ames assures her that the janitor has better sense than to pull anything on school grounds. As to Lucas Beale, Ames quotes passages from the Bible that might convince a boy that loving his fellow man isn't the sin the fundamentalists claim it is. It's an incredible relief to have someone to talk to, someone to hold her in his arms and commiserate about her fears.

Then they make love an amazing third time. They can't seem to stop. It's like finding out you've already gotten a parking ticket and might as well leave the car in the space all day. When at last they pull away and lie sweating on the floor, Louise feels so depleted yet satisfied she is reminded of the goblet at the wedding in the Bible story, refilling itself with wine.

They get dressed and finish cleaning. She moves in a dreamy daze. Ames is in the kitchen, but she still can feel his tongue between her legs.

Finally, they replace the bucket in the closet and go downstairs to Ames's car. "If you don't think we ought to do this again, I'll understand," she lies. "You have a lot more to lose than I do."

"But you have a husband. You have a daughter."

"Your job, I meant. A minister . . ."

"My wife—" He shakes his head. "Never mind about Natalie. If anyone calls this off, it won't be me."

Louise takes this as a promise. She thinks Ames has just said he won't be the one to end their affair. And since *she* won't be the one to end it, she feels safe to fall in love.

They stand on the sidewalk with the old Hoover between them like a chaperone. "I'll be in touch," Ames says, and somehow she knows he will. How can he not be in touch? How can he refrain from touching her again, or refrain from being touched? She knows it is very, very wrong that they have just made love in an apartment they were entering to clean. But it's amazing how little force the rules of decency exert once you question why they should. If you are making love to a man of God, then God must endorse your lovemaking. In this miserable, dying world, in which a man who looks like Satan can rent a truck, fill it full of shit, and blow up a bunch of kids, two basically decent people bringing each other pleasure can hardly be called a sin. The dead man whose apartment they've cleaned would approve of what they've done. She and Ames have filled the rooms with enough light and love to sustain whoever moves in next.

SIX

MOLLY NUDGES OPEN THE BACK DOOR AND STEPS OUTSIDE. In California, if she had so much as set a toe outside the house, her mother would have grabbed her. She's older now. Her father told her Michigan is safe for kids. But if you ask Molly, her parents simply have stopped paying attention. In California, her father paid attention to her mother, and her mother paid attention to Molly. In Molly's mind, her father is supposed to hold a gigantic umbrella over her mother's head, and her mother is supposed to hold a slightly smaller umbrella over Molly. That's the way it *used* to be, until that Chinese lady killed herself, and her father set fire to those trees, and the next time Molly looked up, her father's umbrella had collapsed and flown away. Then they moved to Michigan and Molly's mother became distracted and wandered off and poor Molly was left standing in the rain getting wet.

Except that today is sunny. She jumps down from the steps and her sneakers disappear in the tall, tall grass. She overheard her mother tell her aunt Imelda that Molly's father is afraid to use the lawnmower, and Molly wonders what's scary about mowing the lawn, and why, if mowing the lawn scares her father so much, her mother doesn't just mow it for him. She also wonders why, if her father is so scared of lawnmowers, he isn't more scared of guns. He's in the basement right now cleaning the gun he bought from Mr. Banks. Her father owns a gun! If her father can own a gun, anything is possible.

Her mother doesn't do much of anything anymore. Right now, she's in the kitchen waiting for the phone to ring. She keeps wiping invisible crumbs from the counter and reading the book that tells you how to use the new refrigerator. If the phone rings, she jumps up and grabs it in a skittery, too-eager way. Usually, her voice sounds disappointed, except once or twice it sounded excited in a way that made Molly think Aunt Imelda must have called, which one time she did, but the other time she didn't. Her mother is acting the way Molly would act if she ever made a friend in Michigan and was sitting around hoping that friend would call.

The problem started the night Molly and her mother ate dinner at that McDonald's and her mother started talking to the man with the empty earring-hole. The man had two daughters who were a little older than Molly but might have played with her anyway, if one of the grownups had suggested it. Molly's mother kept paying attention to the man, so Molly pretended to get stuck inside the slide. At first, her strategy worked. Her mother crawled in and got her. Molly slid down the slide on her mother's lap and they landed in a box of colored balls. That was the most fun she's had with her mother since they moved to Michigan, which isn't saying much. But by the time Molly crawled out, her mother was already talking to the man with the earring hole again. Molly climbed to the very top of the play structure, intending to make her mother scared. But she only scared herself. Standing on that fake plastic boat, she'd had the feeling she was drifting away from her mother. To make matters worse, her mother suddenly waved, which made Molly think she was in a real boat, and the boat was leaving the shore. She almost jumped overboard, except that she saw how high the boat was and climbed down instead.

Her mother's refusal to pay attention to her is even more upsetting than her father lying on the couch all day. Molly loves her dad, but his attention has never been the same kind as her mother's. If her parents get divorced, Molly knows she won't receive much sympathy from her friends in California, whose parents already have been divorced, if not one time, then lots of times. To those kids, expecting your parents to stay married is like buying a toy you've seen on TV and expecting it to do all the neat things it did in the commercial.

Luckily, Molly knows what a kid in her situation is supposed to do. Every TV show and movie she has ever seen has taught her. She is supposed to run away. If a kid runs away, her parents get worried and try to find her. Then the parents realize how much they love the kid, and this gets them back together. Running away from home is a very kid-like thing to do, but that doesn't mean it won't work. Crying is a very baby-like thing to do, but it gets the baby changed and fed and held.

She walks to the edge of her family's property. Leaving her

family's property is a very big rule to break. The few times in the past she disobeyed a rule that big, her mother forgave her. But Molly isn't sure her mother will forgive her now. She hasn't forgiven Molly's father, and it's been a very long time since he broke whatever rule he broke that made her mother mad. Burning those trees didn't hurt her mother, so why won't she forgive him?

Maybe she ought to walk to the playground at the elementary school and find some kids to play with. It would be a very long walk, but if she puts one foot in front of the other foot enough times, she'll get there. The problem is, the grownups at the playground will notice she is alone and call the police, which might result in the other kids thinking Molly and her parents are even weirder than they are. She can't go to Em's. That's the first place anyone will look. Then an idea comes to her that seems *brilliant*. Whenever she and her mother get in the van, they turn *that* way and drive past the Bankses' farm and Em's house and that noisy church, and they either get to Stickney Springs or Potawatomie. Molly will take the *other* direction. It's like when her mother showed her on the globe how Columbus sailed west instead of east. The sailors were afraid they would drop off the earth, but the world turned out to be round, which meant that if you went far enough you eventually got back home.

She turns left and starts walking. A little way down the road she sees a truck. Rod, the electric guy, is standing in front of it with binoculars. He's spying on her house! She thinks he will be angry that she's caught him. But he just keeps staring at her house. Smack the dog dashes around in the back of Rod's truck, throwing himself against the sides, but Rod doesn't seem to care. He lets down the binoculars. "Where you off to, Miss Molly?"

She doesn't say anything back.

"Off to see the world? Off on a choose-your-own adventure? Huh, Miss Molly Dolly?"

Usually, she doesn't mind when people play word games with her name, but she doesn't like it when Rod does. She doesn't like most of what Rod does. When he thinks no one is looking, he punches Smack. Once, he even kicked Smack. She would have told her mother, but her mother doesn't like Smack. Her mother thinks Smack is dangerous, which is silly, because if Smack were dangerous he wouldn't let Rod kick him. Molly has come up with many, many plans to steal Smack from Rod, but she can't figure out where she might hide him. The time she saw Rod kick the dog, she shouted, "Stop that!" But Rod just said, "That's called discipline, Molly. You can't let a dog get away with things, the way your parents let you get away with things. A big, tough dog like this, you have to show him who's boss."

Maybe Rod is right, but Molly doesn't think so. Smack is just a puppy, and he hates to be left alone, and most of the time Rod ignores him. Dogs like attention, and if you don't give it to them, they whine and pee. She once saw Smack pee in a corner, and she knew so well how it felt not to be paid attention to that she went over and pulled down her pants and peed a puddle next to his. She could do a better job of raising Smack than Rod is doing. Rod isn't even a grownup. He's so young he doesn't even know that a kid her age shouldn't be out alone.

"I'm going for a walk," she says, and stupid Rod just nods at her and grins.

"Have a good time, Miss Molly Golly." Then he goes back to watching her house with his binoculars.

"Bye," she says and walks past him, to where Smack is racing around in the back of the truck. She stands on her toes to pat his head. "Poor Smack. Do you want to come with me?" The dog licks her wrist and nips her hand. Rod looks back at them but seems too bored to care. *Stupid you,* she thinks. Once, she asked Rod what electricity was, and even though he works with electricity all the time, he couldn't tell her. Worse, she heard him say mean things to the other men about her mother. Something about her mother smelling like vanilla ice cream. Not her whole body, just some part of her. *Her pussy,* Rod had said. *Man, don't you just think her pussy smells like vanilla ice cream,* which at first confused Molly, because her family owned a rabbit not a cat. Then she figured out Rod meant some part of her mother's body. He talked about her mother's body all the time. She would have told her father, but she doesn't know how to tell him without using the same words Rod uses. Besides, she isn't sure her father would care. In California, he would have cared, but he doesn't care in Michigan. Which is the opposite of how it should be. Her mother is a lot prettier here than she was in California. The other mothers in Michigan all wear sweatsuits and heavy shoes. They look as if the string that's supposed to be tied around their waists got pulled and everything above the middle sagged down below it. Every mother in Michigan wears her hair short except Molly's mother, who is also the only mom who doesn't have dumpy legs.

Smack nips her hand harder. She thinks of taking him with her, but Rod would turn around and see, so she whispers *goodbye* and keeps walking. There aren't many cars. The sun gets hot, then hotter. There's a lilac bush, and Molly veers from the road and sniffs it. She loves how *purple* lilacs smell. A bee flies out but doesn't sting her. She looks back and sees Rod's truck, toy-size in the distance, but she can no longer make out Rod. She isn't watching where she's going and almost steps on a baby bird, which is squashed to the road like chewing gum. She wants to take the bird to Em's house, but ants are already crawling all over its pipe-cleaner legs and wings, and the sight of those ants nearly makes Molly sick. Before she moved to Michigan, she hadn't been scared of much. She'd had a pretty good sense of what was real and what wasn't. She knew there weren't any monsters, so she couldn't find any reason to be scared of the dark. But then they left California and she saw how immense the world could be. Her mother drove and drove and *drove*. They crossed mountains bigger than any mountains Molly could have dreamed of. They crossed a part of the country so flat and boring she thought she might scream.

And then she did scream. "What is it?" her mother said, annoyed, and Molly couldn't explain. It wasn't the kind of frustration a kid usually felt when a car trip took too long. It wasn't the same as asking, *Are we there yet?*

"I didn't know the world was so big," Molly said, and her parents laughed. She was terrified and they laughed! She had known the world was *big*, but she hadn't known *how* big. If it took this many days to drive halfway across the United States, how big could the country be? Or the world? About that same time, she learned about infinity. How big it was. How small *she* was. She wished her mother believed in God. She wanted to think *someone* was paying attention. But if she didn't believe in monsters, how could she believe in God?

Then again, with the world so big and no one to watch her, it was tempting to believe in things she might not otherwise have believed in. According to Em, Molly had once been an Egyptian magician in charge of embalming pharaohs. *You're an old soul,* Em had said. *That's how come you're so much wiser than other kids.* Em also believes that Molly has a third eye, and this third eye might allow her to see the future, if only Molly learns to use it, which Em is teaching her to do. Em believes in spells. It confuses Molly to meet a grownup who believes in spells. But she wants to be confused. She wants to believe she has more powers than she has. What if her parents die? What if she, Molly, gets killed? She hadn't thought a kid could get killed, but that must have been what those kids in Oklahoma thought before that bomb went off.

The sun gets even *hotter*. She is so thirsty that all she can think about is going home and asking her mother for lemonade. She sees a dead raccoon and a flat black snake and a squirrel with its red guts hanging out. The road stretches ahead of her to the sky, with those wavy lines and fake puddles that dry up as soon as you get close to them. *Mirages*, her mother calls them. Well, if mirages can exist, maybe so can witches and third eyes.

Molly walks some more, but she can't just keep walking all day and hope someone will come to find her. Then a plan comes to her. A very *smart* plan. She will cut back across the fields and circle her parents' property and wait in the Bankses' barn. She doesn't like the Bankses, but she does like their barn. She can practice swinging on the rope. Her father made her promise not to fly, but he didn't say anything about swinging on a rope.

She walks back the way she came, wondering why it takes more time to go somewhere than it does to come home. Just before she gets to Rod's truck, she cuts off through the field. A rabbit starts up ahead of her. It's hardly bigger than Matzo Ball, and she wonders about the difference between a wild rabbit and a tame one, and how did a wolf become a dog? She edges behind her parents' house and steps over the broken fence that marks the line between their property and the farm.

"Matt! Matt. Banks. Where. Are. You?"

Mrs. Banks must be around the front of the farmhouse where Molly can't see her. It isn't that Molly doesn't like Mrs.

Banks. It's that Mrs. Banks likes Molly too much. Molly can tell that Mrs. Banks wants something from her, and Molly doesn't know what that something is. Mrs. Banks talks all the time about her grandchild. But how can playing with Molly make up for her grandchild being gone? It's as if Mrs. Banks thinks all little girls are the same.

She darts among the Christmas trees, panting so hard her nose and lungs fill with the minty scent. She stops at the barn door, and Isabelle the cow makes that deep, echoey *muh? muh?* sound. "It's me, Isabelle, it's only Molly." She runs inside. Sunlight filters in through a window at the top, above the shelf where they keep the hay, and bits of dust float in the beam. The barn smells like wood and cow poop. *Cow shit*, her father calls it. People act as if cow poop has such a bad smell, but Molly doesn't think so. She doesn't mind how her own poop smells in the toilet or how the cow poop smells in the Bankses' barn. The only thing she doesn't like about the barn is the pitchfork. She's pretty sure the Devil isn't real. Then again, she hadn't thought witches were real, before she met Em. Aren't Em and Mr. Banks sort of girlfriend and boyfriend? Doesn't it make sense that the Devil would hang around with a witch? Except that Em isn't a mean witch, so maybe Mr. Banks isn't a mean devil. Except how can a devil not be mean?

There's a barbell on the ground, and Molly tries to pick it up. Something about Mr. Banks owning a pitchfork and being strong enough to lift this barbell really does scare her. He's just so *huge*. And he's always leaning in her face. He's like his mother, looking at Molly as if he wants to eat her. Once, she saw Mr. Banks eat an ice cream cone, licking the scoop with a tongue as big and sloppy as a cow's. The ice cream disappeared inside his mouth, and that's how Molly pictures him eating *her*.

She looks up at the ceiling, but there isn't any rope, so she climbs the ladder, and that's when things start to go wrong. She hears men's voices, and Mr. Banks and his friends come in. Rod is there, and Smack. *Here, Smack, good boy, get down you stupid dog, stop humping my leg, doesn't your master know he's supposed to cut off your balls?* What's funny is that the men act more like dogs than Smack does. She peeks over the edge and sees them circling around and batting each other with their paws. The noises they make sound more like growling and barking than talking.

She lies back against some bales of hay to wait. The men make their dog noises. Occasionally, Smack barks.

Kablooie! one man yells. *That'll teach those fuckers.*

She hears her father's name, *Shapiro,* and she starts up, feeling sick to her stomach, she isn't sure why, except that she doesn't like hearing any of these men say her father's name, which is also her name, and her mother's. Then Dolores yells again for Matt. Molly usually has a hard time guessing what Dolores says, but she can tell that Dolores wants Matt to fix the roof. The other men tease him. *Go on and help your mama. Go see what your mama wants.*

Molly is tired and bored and wishes the men would leave, but only Mr. Banks goes out. She falls asleep, and by the time she wakes up, the barn is quiet. The light seems less bright. She tries to find the ladder, but it's gone.

She looks down. The pile of hay is much smaller and farther from the loft than it seemed at the Easter party. Maybe, if she runs fast enough and jumps hard enough, she will make it to the hay. Especially if she can fly. Which she is pretty sure she can. Not high or far enough to get back to California. But high and far enough to reach that hay.

She backs up a few steps, then runs and flings herself off the ledge. Flailing and kicking, she soars above the fattest part of the hay, then down she goes, falling in a cannonball until she lands in a crouch, lifting her arms and jumping up the way acrobats do in the Olympics.

Outside, the sun is shadowy and soft. She runs home the back way and is surprised to see her father setting bottles along the fence. He puts some bullets in his gun. It wouldn't bother her if he had bought the gun to shoot at bottles. But she has heard him say that he wants to hunt deer with Matt Banks. She will never, ever forgive him if he goes in the woods and kills a deer.

He lifts the gun. Then he must have pulled the trigger, because one of the bottles leaps up in the air and flies apart. The noise hurts her teeth. She runs inside, where her mother is sitting in the kitchen with her chin in her hands and her eyes shut. Molly makes a noise, and her mother opens her eyes and looks at Molly as if she doesn't know who she is. And that's when Molly feels the most terrible feeling she has ever felt. She ran away from home, and her parents never missed her. She has been away the entire afternoon, and they never once realized she was gone.

SEVEN

LOUISE IS SITTING IN THE PASSENGER SEAT OF AMES'S RUSTY blue Escort, heading north to Handsome Lake. This is their third journey to the lake, but he still seems so nervous he sits with his arms straight out in front, as if to keep the wheel from collapsing to his chest. The sleeves of his blue chambray work shirt are rolled up past his elbows, and Louise can't resist reaching out to stroke the vulnerable length of his inner arm, which is the softest, whitest male skin she has ever touched. She imagines Ames and Mike Korn doing battle, Korn's callused hands clutching Ames's throat and banging his head against a locker. Then some Dionysian force surges through Ames's limbs and he—what? Preaches a sermon that convinces Mike Korn to love blacks and homosexuals? The forces of good seem hampered by their very goodness. At least, unlike Richard, Ames tries to put up a fight.

They take a back route out of town. The city drops away. Hills that barely deserve the name laze beside the road, lumpy and drab. Everyone says the farther north you go, the more picturesque Michigan gets, but Louise has never traveled farther north than Handsome Lake, and the countryside there isn't exactly charming. So what if the Upper Peninsula is as spectacular as the Alps? Just because two regions lie within the same state doesn't mean the first region deserves the glory of the second.

"The inn probably won't have any rooms," Ames mutters gloomily.

She checks her mental calendar. Memorial Day is coming. But who would be staying in a crappy motel in the middle of nowhere on a Wednesday afternoon?

"There's a NASCAR track," Ames explains. "I think there's a race this week."

"You sound as if you hope we'll have to go back home."

"Just thinking of the possibilities."

But she knows she's right. Ames has told her that the Wyes often feel prey to dramatic cycles of excess and regret. He meant this to describe his ancestors, all the way back to the Puritan judge who sentenced a woman to hang for witchcraft, then visited her in jail and fell in love and married her. Yet Ames himself seems prone to this same rotation. She has come to understand that when Ames promised he wouldn't be the one to stop their affair, he didn't mean he could never leave her. What he meant was, given his infatuation, he is powerless to stop seeing her and therefore hopes someone else will stop him. This makes her feel irresistible, but it also makes her feel doubly responsible for what they do.

Still, she could no more put a stop to their affair than she could open the car door and fling herself out. She studies his silhouette profiled against the bare brown fields, and the evanescence of their time together makes her long for his love even as she has it.

She runs a finger down his hair. She has no idea what Natalie looks like, but, given that she is Jewish, Louise can't help but picture her as dark. She imagines the two couples uncoupling, and then, in something like the exchange of chess pieces after a match, Richard and Natalie ending up together on one side of the board while she and Ames assume their rightful places on the other.

Shaking her head to clear this thought, she lets her hand drop, and for the last few miles they discuss the decision by the ACLU to defend Mike Korn's right to keep working as a janitor no matter what views he expresses off school grounds. Ames's committee voted not to buck the ACLU. But they have set up a schedule of volunteers to monitor what Korn says on his talk show and have vowed to support any parents who feel that the janitor's behavior puts their children at risk. Louise fights the urge to bask in her own high-mindedness, discussing politics with her lover while they drive to a motel.

They came upon the inn by accident. There are too few apartments for them to clean to allow them to meet as often as they would like. Besides, they don't think of themselves as people who do good deeds as a means to find an empty house to make love in. One afternoon a few weeks earlier, Louise accompanied Ames to the hospital and watched from the doorway as he slid his arms beneath the skeletal back and thighs of a man in his early thirties who was too weak to get out of bed. Ames carried the man to the toilet, then carried him back and reconnected him to his oxygen tank. He has told her several times that he wasn't born a good person but that he tries very hard to be one. Watching him that day, she thought there wasn't much difference between a bad person performing good deeds out of fear of his own bad nature and a good person performing good deeds from the force of his natural goodness.

Before they left the hospital, the man asked Ames if he could please stop by his apartment and look in on his cats. He had been delirious for weeks and only now remembered that he had left the poor creatures on their own. Louise and Ames drove to the safe house, and when they unlocked the man's door, the stink and mess were shocking. Louise had never seen Ames so upset. He found an empty cardboard box and put the two dead cats inside, then sat with the box between his legs and started crying. "I knew he was in the hospital," Ames said. "He doesn't have any friends. Who did I think was caring for his pets?"

They gave the animals a proper burial and then spent another two hours cleaning the apartment. Louise thought they might go home. But when they got in Ames's car, he started driving north. They passed a Super 8 and a Howard Johnson's, but these seemed too close to town. After an hour, they came upon a ramshackle motel on an algae-covered lake in a part of the state where Ames said no one would recognize either one of them. Louise agreed to check in, although she doubted they were safe. After all, Ames's face was so often in the papers. He had been interviewed on the radio. Surely people would remember where they had heard such a resonant New England drawl, where they had seen a face so guileless, so raw, so unlike a mask, more like what is underneath when a mask gets ripped off. Eventually, they would be caught. She has never confided this fear to Ames. Believing they won't be caught is the only way he is able to keep seeing her, while deep inside, at a level she can't admit, Louise hopes they will be discovered. The affair will blow up in their faces, and when the tremors have died, Louise and Ames will find themselves together, their children safe, their self-respect and essential goodness still intact.

The Potawatomie Inn is the sort of simple white horseshoe of a motel that was common in America before Holiday Inn took over. Louise has no idea how it stays in business. Do other duplicitous couples drive here from Potawatomie? Then she remembers about the NASCAR races and understands why so many pickups and S.U.V.s are in the lot. YOU CAN HAVE MY GUN—BULLETS FIRST reads not one but three bumper stickers. WHEN YOU ENVISION WORLD PEACE DON'T FORGET THE GUNS THAT MADE IT POSSIBLE reads another.

Heading toward the office, Louise sends up a prayer that a room will be available. The lobby smells like the coffee, orange juice, and blueberry muffins from that morning's complimentary breakfast, all of which still sit on a table to one side of a rack of brochures advertising various Michigan attractions, including the Mystery Spot, which makes Louise wonder how Parker is getting along with his father. She clears her throat and asks the clerk if he has a room, but he keeps his back toward her, thumbing deliberately through a box of index cards. The first time she ventured into the lobby to rent a room, this same clerk insisted that she fill out a form with her name and address, which panicked Louise so badly she found herself inventing an elaborate lie to explain why a woman who lived less than forty miles away would want to rent a room. She was writing a book, she said. She had four small children, whom a babysitter watched one afternoon a week so she could get away and work. She doubted he believed this story. But it made her squeamish to pay cash for a room and then hand back the key three hours later.

Now, this same clerk slides a registration form across the desk. "How's the book going?" he asks, smiling in a smarmy way.

"Oh, fine," she says. "Or it will be, after I get another afternoon to work."

He peers over the counter. "No laptop? No computer?"

"I write longhand. I wish I could afford a computer, but with four kids, and having to rent this room—"

"Sure," he says. "That'll be thirty-eight eighty-five."

She hands him two of the three twenties she withdrew from the ATM on her way to meet Ames. Later, Ames will reimburse her for his half. She has suggested that they take turns registering and paying, but Ames would rather split the cost, as if he expects each meeting to be their last.

The clerk holds out a key attached to a red plastic oval like the ovals on the keys at Imelda's family's old motel. "Room 30, around the back." He smirks. "The view might help your writing."

She walks back to the Escort, and when she leans down to tell Ames the room number, the spice of a breath mint wafts up. It touches her that he would freshen his breath before they kiss, but it also makes him seem fussy. She wants to taste his tongue without the mint.

They drive around the back. The lake is smaller than the lake on which Louise grew up. No melancholy firs, no Adirondacks in the distance. Yet the sulfurous, wormy smell strikes her as familiar. She remembers leading her high-school boyfriend into a room whose key Imelda had provided, an act of such bravado and stupidity—especially given how little she liked the boy—it makes her wonder if she is being any smarter now.

Room 30 is as ordinary as rooms 12 and 9 had been. The walls are papered in the same nubbly vinyl covering that looks as if the designer splattered them with creamed corn. The only feature that distinguishes this room from the other two is the seascape above the bed: a towering, foaming wave that threatens to flood the sheets.

Ames places his watch on the nightstand, then sits on the flowered quilt and bends to unlace his shoes. He sets the shoes parallel to each other and stands and walks toward her. If he had been as hesitant and fastidious about making love as he is about taking off his shoes, Louise would have ended the affair. But the Ames who makes love to her isn't anything like the Ames who wishes he could prevent himself from making love to her. Most men kiss as if the kisses are an appetizer to a more satisfying entrée. Ames kisses as if the kisses are the meal.

After a while, he unbuttons her blouse and pulls it off. He walks around and unhooks her brassiere, a ritual Louise loves simply because it *is* a ritual. Performing it, Ames declares his willingness to take part in the entire rite. He skims his lips down her throat, across her clavicle, and down her breast, and this floods her with a tenderness so exquisite she feels an overwhelming rush of gratitude. Nothing else matters—not the shabbiness of the room, not her husband or Ames's wife, only the tug and thrill of his mouth against her breast.

He hooks his fingers inside her panties and tugs them down. Surely Richard has done this. Hasn't he pulled down her panties and watched her step out of them? Yes, but Richard did it in the context of their being married. Ames strips the act of all associations other than the erotic. It is the sheer intentionality of what they are choosing to do, their decision to drive all this way for no other reason than to stand in the middle of a motel room so Ames can pull down her underwear and kneel before her and put his mouth to the soft, secret fold between her legs.

She throws back her head and cries out. How could any man be so hesitant about having an affair and yet, once he got down to it, so seriously absorbed in sex? He kneels before her on that mildewed green shag—it reminds her of weeds dredged up from the lake and spread wetly across the floor—and Louise thinks of him bowing not to worship her, which would have been embarrassing, but to worship life itself. His ability to worship the absolute through his love for her, the vocabulary of awe this gives her, allows her to feel the same about him.

They stand naked before the mirror so they can see their nakedness reflected back, Ames's arm around Louise's shoulder, her arm across his back, their torsos opening outward like the gorgeously illuminated pages of a book. Later, the memory of that image in the mirror will drive her crazy. In bed in Stickney Springs or driving aimlessly—*Ameslessly*—around the countryside, she will consider returning to the inn and renting Room 30, as if their image might be preserved inside that glass.

They watch their reflected selves with the voyeuristic pleasure of two people in a theater watching an erotic film. Then Ames lays her across the bed. He stretches her arms above her head and pins her wrists to the headboard, then kisses her breasts and ribs. Crouching between her knees, he does something with his tongue and fingers that drives Louise so far inside herself she can focus on nothing else, and, after she has come, she seems to require eons to find her way back. When she does, she opens her eyes and laughs.

"What are you laughing about?" Ames asks.

"I was on another planet. Then I laughed at how funny it was to come back to earth *here*." He looks hurt, as if she is blaming him for making love to her in such a cheap room. She takes his hand and kisses the palm. "The room doesn't matter. Don't you know how much I love you?"

"But *why* do you love me?"

He isn't fishing for a compliment. He believes that having an affair disqualifies him from warranting anyone's affection. Louise reminds him that his physical appearance would be enough to earn most women's love. Then there are his accomplishments—his early success as a playwright, his divinity degree from Harvard, his current standing as a minister, his intelligence, his concern for people less fortunate than he is, his willingness to fight for causes he believes in.

So yes, there are reasons. But the sum of these reasons can't account for what she feels. What makes her love him so irrationally is that they have no justification for driving to this inn other than to pleasure each other in ways they might be too impatient or self-centered to employ with their spouses. Falling in love with Richard was a rational decision. Louise had known the day they met that he would be an easy man to live with and a good father to their child. What she felt for Richard could be contained inside a house. When she pictures herself with Ames, they are dancing on a heath getting rained on in a storm.

She climbs astride his hips and kisses his nipples. From the noise he makes, you might have thought she was running a razor across his skin. She has never known a man so sensitive. She drags her tongue lower, bypassing his navel, continuing down one thigh, past the knee, along the calf, until she reaches his instep, which she kisses. She bathes his feet with her hair, all the while thinking of Christ humbling himself by washing his disciples' feet. She gets up and finds her bag and removes a bottle of oil and uses it to massage his legs. *I'm anointing my love*, she thinks. *I'm anointing him with oil.*

Then she takes him in her mouth. He gasps, then whispers, "No, please, I want to come inside you." And before Louise knows it, she is on her back again, knees to her chest, Ames laboring above her. He holds the flimsy headboard and moves diligently inside her, studying her face to see which spot creates the most sensation, timing his movements more and more to her sighs. Just as she begins to come, Ames gasps and sobs: "Louise!" His eyes roll back and he utters a noise that sounds so much like suffering that Louise wonders if, for Ames, ecstasy and suffering are inseparable.

At last they peel apart and rest that way, her head on his chest, so they can't see each other's faces, and after a while he begins to talk about his wife. Natalie has always been difficult, Ames admits. But difficult in a good way—strict about her politics, her scientific turn of mind, her refusal to fall for cant. Born to a nominally Jewish mother and an Episcopalian father, Natalie had been raised a Unitarian. She and Ames met on a weekend march on Washington and got married a few months later. Ames became a minister. They moved to Potawatomie and had the girls. Then Natalie decided she was Jewish after all and began "exploring her faith," which meant, at least to Natalie, that she gave up caring about any politics except those that involved Israel, kept an ultra-kosher kitchen, and observed the Sabbath strictly. She wouldn't attend his church, which nettled his parishioners, although he suspected they admired him for his willingness to suffer on his eccentric wife's behalf more than they would have excused him for deserting her.

He reveals nothing about their sex life, apart from Natalie's refusal to let him touch her half of every month. But something has to be missing, doesn't it? Why else would a married minister be having an affair? From the intensity of his disbelief when Louise takes him in her mouth, the violence with which he enters her, the excitement that nearly levitates them both off the bed, his inability to stop seeing her, although he clearly wishes he *could* stop, Louise suspects she loves his body in ways his wife doesn't or can't.

And then there is the pleasure Ames gives *her*. You couldn't invent a man like this, the way he kisses her and touches her, the way he moves inside her, the concentration on his face as he searches for the spot that will make her give herself up to him and moan, *Jesus, Ames, Jesus*, any more than you could invent a completely new beast. You would need to combine the best parts of other lovers, as the ancient Greeks combined an eagle's wings and a horse's body to make a Pegasus.

"The mystery is why anyone would want to do anything but this," he says, smiling a smile she has never seen him smile anywhere but in bed. And really, this does seem the essential mystery of human life, that anyone would let a marriage vow or the need to earn a living get in the way of lying in bed with the person he or she wants to lie in bed with.

She watches as he walks naked to the bathroom and returns with a tumbler of tap water, which he drinks from greedily before handing it down to her. He searches for his boxers and pulls them on, lifts his watch from the nightstand and stretches it around his wrist. Then he holds out his arms, grips Louise's hands, and pulls her up.

"'So let us melt,'" he whispers, "'and make no noise. No tear-floods, nor sigh-tempests move. T'were prophanation of our joyes to tell the layetie our love.'"

She pulls a little bit away and stands there eying him.

"John Donne," he explains, and she can see he is ashamed of showing off. "'A Valediction Forbidding Mourning.'"

She kisses him, and, remarkably for a man in his forties, his cock rises yet again.

Playfully, he slaps away her hand. "You need to get back and so do I."

But now their real lives seem their false lives. When Louise locks the room, it's as if she is locking their real selves at the inn and letting their phony selves drive back to Potawatomie. It seems truer to tell the clerk that yes, she has written a fair amount of her novel that day, than to return to Stickney

Springs and pretend that she is still married to her husband.

Neither she nor Ames has much to say until they reach the Kroger in Potawatomie, where Louise has left her van. She gathers her things and kisses Ames right there in the lot. He looks around to see if anyone is watching, and she hates him then—the coward!—although a minute later, putting her key in the ignition, she is so overcome with loss that she puts her head to the wheel and cries.

Someone taps the glass. She looks up, and Ames motions her to roll down the window. "I love you," he says. "I wish I knew what we could do to make things right." He leans in and kisses her. "Are you okay? I could stay a while longer." Louise shakes her head, then forces herself to drive away, if only to spare her lover the pain of seeing her sitting with her forehead against the wheel. Besides, it's time to pick up Molly.

Except that Molly isn't there. Em has a cousin who needed somewhere to leave her son while she went to Las Vegas to marry her third husband. Molly and the boy have taken Matzo Ball for a walk.

The whole thing seems implausible. Could she actually have spent the afternoon with her lover while her daughter took her pet rabbit for a walk with a boy Louise doesn't know? "How do you walk a rabbit?" she asks Em.

"I had some lanyard. We made a leash."

A leash for a rabbit? She tries not to think of the dangers that might befall a six-year-old girl, even if she has an escort. What if Molly and this boy wander onto the target range at the Sportsman's Club?

"What's wrong?" Em takes Louise's hand and studies the lines on her palm. "Is it Richard? Is it your marriage?"

Louise warns herself, *Don't say a word. Don't even start.* "It's nothing. Richard and I haven't been getting along, that's all."

Em's ostrich eyes grow wider. "You're in love with

someone." She lifts her face to the ceiling, as if it were a radio dish scanning for cosmic rays. "It's that minister, isn't it. The one you volunteer with."

Louise grows dizzy and hot. The birds flutter in their cages. She is a terrible liar—if Richard had asked her outright if she was having an affair, she would have confessed—and so she can't deny what Em has said quickly enough to be convincing. She isn't afraid Em will condemn her. Em isn't a moralistic witch. And there is no affection lost between Em and Richard. For some reason, Richard doesn't like Em, and Em doesn't need to be psychic to pick up how he feels. But Louise wishes Em hadn't guessed.

"Oooh," Em says. "You haven't even lived here a year and you've already snatched up the most illegible man in town."

She doesn't bother to remind her that Ames isn't eligible at all. Matters of eligibility don't matter to Em. Her world isn't governed by oughts and shoulds. In Em's cockeyed cosmology, rays of love are shooting out from everyone. She takes as her model the god of all postal workers, Cupid, whose mission it is to connect every sender to the most appropriate addressee. "You can't tell a soul. Promise me you won't tell."

Em zips her lips. "If anyone respects privacy, it's a mail carrier."

Still, for someone who respects Louise's privacy, she wants to know *absolutely everything* about how Louise and Ames met, what his wife is like, and whether Ames will ever leave Natalie. Em wiggles her fingers. "We could do a little spell. We could make something wonderful happen that would bring Natalie more happiness than being married to Ames." She looks out craftily from beneath her bangs. "Maybe she could fall in love with Richard!"

Louise wishes she had denied the whole thing. The very idea of Richard loving anyone but her! How could Em think she would find that funny? Who *is* this person? Does she really have Louise's best interests at heart? And does she really have the power to make Natalie fall in love with someone else?

Molly comes in accompanied by a delicate brown-haired boy with almond-shaped eyes and a rat-tail down his back. "Mom, this is Dylan. We took Matzo Ball for a walk." From the way Molly looks at the boy, Louise can tell she is in the first thrall of crushdom, and Louise grieves that she has lost the right to counsel her daughter about her love life. She has never once lied to Molly. But she is cheating on Molly's father. Em has said several times that most grownups will ignore an injured bird unless a child is with them. On her own, Louise wouldn't feel guilty about her infidelity; she only worries about how her actions might appear to Molly.

Molly and Dylan settle on the floor and pass the rabbit from lap to lap. Louise is furious at herself for having neglected her daughter these past few weeks. When she isn't with Ames, all she wants to do is think about him. She tries to get Molly to amuse herself. But Molly is only six. *Mom? Mom? Are you ready to play that game?* Once, Molly asked Louise to name her favorite thing to do. Molly was always asking such questions— what's your favorite food, what's your favorite book. "Hugging you," Louise wanted to say, and really, before she met Ames, that *was* her favorite thing. But now she hesitates before she answers, and she is sure Molly picks up on this.

"Dylan doesn't like hunting," Molly says.

He sets the rabbit on Louise's knee. "What I really don't like is my mother being away so much. She says I'll understand when I'm older, but I don't think I ever will."

No, Louise thinks, you won't. *Wait until you're older* is only something mothers say so their children won't figure out that their mothers are in the grip of their own intoxicating pleasures and can't bring themselves to sober up.

EIGHT

WITH HIS CYCLES OF INDULGENCE AND REPENTANCE, AMES
doesn't invite Louise to Handsome Lake more than twice a
month. She knows he is trying to keep their affair in its place
so it won't destroy his comfortable if unenthusiastic life with
Natalie. If, in the hopes of seeing him, she devotes more time
to political activities than she otherwise might have done,
who can really blame her?

Every Monday night, she drives to his church and helps
the Committee for a Fair and United Michigan fight the city's
fundamentalists. Like liberals everywhere, they spend as
much time arguing with each other as coming up with ways to

defeat their opponents, but Ames seems wonderfully talented at getting his adherents to overcome their differences and implement a plan. She never loves him more than when he is guiding this committee to draft a resolution, or, at meeting's end, when he exchanges a soul shake with Lee LeGrand, the blind, rotund minister of the A.M.E. Church—twice a year, these two ministers preach to each other's flock, a trade that benefits the Unitarians more than it rouses the members of the A.M.E.—or heartfelt hugs and back pats with Loretta Paterson and Mary Walz, who represent the Quakers, or Jack Lovecraft and Howie Drucker, who run the AIDS Coalition.

Louise especially likes Howie, with whom she has spent many happy hours at Coalition headquarters waiting for the AIDS hotline to ring. At first, Howie barraged her with gay jokes and monologues about computers, until Louise understood that he used computer-talk as a shield to prevent anyone from saying anything that might get through and pierce his heart, which, judging from his stories about growing up in rural Indiana, happened all the time. After she convinced him that she was not only harmless but sympathetic, he switched to monologues about his fear that Jack might run off with another man. Not that Jack has given Howie cause to be afraid, but Howie gets crushes on so many men, he figures Jack must get them, too. In fact, Louise is sure he harbors a crush on Ames. She hasn't told Howie that she and Ames are lovers, but she can't help but seize every opportunity to bring Ames into the conversation, and it's clear that Howie enjoys the chance to share his appreciation. After each meeting, he puts his arm around Ames and asks if he's heard the joke about the gay paratrooper, or the gay sheriff, or the gay astronaut or orthodontist, as if, should he find the right joke, Ames's straight façade might crack and he will confess to being gay.

While Ames listens to Howie's jokes and the suggestions and complaints of various hangers-on, Louise lingers to clear the coffee cups and tries to figure out what makes Ames so attractive to other people, which might solve the mystery of why he is so attractive to her. Something about the way he inclines his head and strokes his cheek makes people think he knows more about their troubles than they do. They reach out to touch his arm, then bring their fingers to their mouths, as if he were one of the Torah scrolls the rabbi carries around the synagogue to which Richard's parents belong.

When the last supplicant has gone home, Louise follows Ames to the shed behind the church where donations for the poor are stored. There, amid boxes of food and clothes, they make out like adolescents. Ames's eyes lose their focus. All his will drains out of him. Does he love her? Louise thinks he does. But she suspects he is more in thrall to his own desire, or to the seduction of being desired by someone else.

One evening, he confides that as difficult as it has become to make love to Natalie—on the rare occasions she wants to be made love to—he never could leave his wife. This astonishes and torments Louise. How can he refuse to claim the amazing prize God or Fate has offered them? In the enlightened mid-nineties, what obstacle could possibly keep two lovers apart? Certainly not the detail of a married minister refusing to leave his wife.

Except that Ames won't leave Natalie. He grew up in a broken home and won't subject his girls to the loneliness and humiliation his parents visited on him. He can't hurt his wife. What has she done to deserve abandonment? How would she survive the shock? And he can't risk his reputation. Even a Unitarian is forbidden to have an affair with a member of his congregation, which, given Louise's occasional attendance at services and her involvement in the church's politics, she technically is. She is precious to him, he says. He loves her. But he will never leave his wife.

All that makes sense. But deep inside, Louise believes that if Ames loved her as ardently as she loves him, none of this would matter. He would want to be with her all the time, as she wants to be with him. Once, sitting in traffic, or what passes for traffic in Potawatomie, she notices that the car in front of her is an Escort. Ames's Escort is blue not teal, but the mere suggestion of Ames's car reminds her of the way, when they drive to Handsome Lake, he works his fingers up her thigh, which leads her to remember what he does with his teeth and his tongue once they are in bed, and an electric jolt surges through her, so powerful she actually looks down to see if the van's battery has thrown a spark. Other times— waiting at the bank or sitting at the playground while Molly jumps off the swings—she finds herself closing her eyes and replaying her sessions with Ames, moving her mouth and hands, wondering if she is the only woman who gets off on going down on a man the way men reputedly get off on going down on women. When she finally reaches the teller, or when Molly cries or needs help, she has trouble rousing herself from her fantasies—*hallucinations* describes them better, that's how three-dimensional they seem to be.

She is achingly obsessed. The best she can do is control those impulses that might make Ames want to stop seeing her. She won't let herself drive by his house. The street is a dead end; Natalie might glance out a window and see Louise's red Voyager driving past, then see it drive by again. A minister's hours aren't regular. Ames might be in his study reading Emerson or outside mowing his lawn or jogging. If he sees her van, he won't believe her promise that she can keep their affair in its place. Capable of driving past his house, she might be capable of parking in his driveway and ringing the bell, or of standing up at services and announcing to his parishioners: *Your minister and I make love every other week at the Potawatomie Inn.*

The trouble is, she doesn't trust herself to control such urges forever. Until recently, the guiding rule in her life was: *Never hurt anyone.* Now she wishes Ames would leave the woman to whom he has been married for fifteen years and hurt his two girls, whom he loves with such a love that he would allow himself to be crucified rather than cause either one a twinge of pain. Never mind that Louise feels the same way about Molly. She has caught herself imagining deaths for Ames's wife, and even though these deaths are brought about by agents other than Louise—most commonly, the Volvo Natalie is driving gets hit by a truck, or its brakes fail—it upsets her to think she understands those murders in which someone pays a hit man to get rid of a lover's spouse. Any enterprise that leads you to wish another person's death can't possibly be moral.

Maybe Ames is right and it's the lot of most people to lead unhappy lives. You work hard. You get by. You do your best for your kids. You are grateful for whatever small moments of grace you are cunning enough to wrest from everyday survival. She is sickened by the hours she has wasted thinking of Ames, dressing for Ames, plotting ways they can be together, crying when they can't be. Nothing fascinates her so much as her fascination for Ames, and this fascination bores her. He is no handsomer than Richard. He chews his bottom lip. Sometimes, at meetings, his voice solidifies into something self-conscious and theatrical; as he delivers such lectures, he holds his hand beside his head, rocking it back and forth like a man gripping a football and preparing to throw a pass.

Yet she doesn't want to go back to a life in which her daily routine consists of fixing up the house, buying food, playing

Candyland with Molly, and nagging Richard about hiring someone to clean the chimney. She loves her work at the high school. But she is tired of always *listening*. She wants to live her own life, to accomplish something new. Or maybe what she wants is to accomplish something old. Since when did romantic love get such a bad name? Go to any movie and you see passion played for laughs. Those few times you stumble upon a film in which romantic love seems plausible, you can't believe it of yourself, only, just maybe, of Meryl Streep or Emma Thompson.

Louise wants to ask someone for advice, but Imelda's mastectomy is only two weeks off. Bad enough Louise hasn't hopped on a plane and gone to visit, she certainly can't expect her friend to listen to her complain about her life. She regrets telling Em. Why did she assume Em must be a hermit? Her coven meets once a month, and she often stops by the post office in Stickney Springs or the sorting facility in Potawatomie to catch up with her former colleagues, one of whom happens to be Mike Korn's wife. Did Louise know that Mike Korn refuses to wear underwear because it impinges on his manhood, or that his favorite beverage is chamomile tea? Did Louise have any idea how many households in Stickney Springs subscribe to the militia newsletter? If Em has so little compunction about passing along other people's business to Louise, she might be no more circumspect about passing Louise's secrets to other people. There is something loose about her, sloppy. Louise imagines her gossiping with her friends, the envelopes flying back and forth at lightning speed while bits of private information accidentally end up in the slots for other people's mail.

Besides, Louise doesn't want to confide in anyone who hasn't felt what she is feeling, and Em seems somehow virginal. None of Louise's friends in California have had affairs. At least, Louise doesn't think they have had affairs. She knows one woman who teaches at a girls' school in Palo Alto and develops a fixation on a new student every term. But this woman hasn't left her partner, nor, as far as Louise knows, laid a finger on any of those girls. Maybe her male friends have engaged in trysts, but they keep these to themselves. If any of her female friends had been gripped by emotions as powerful as these, they couldn't have kept their emotions hidden. It would have been like sneaking off to throw bloody steaks to a tiger in your closet.

Unless they conceal their tigers as well as Louise conceals hers.

Certainly, Richard doesn't suspect what rough beast his wife is harboring. Or he suspects what's going on but doesn't want his suspicions confirmed. She rarely even sees him—he spends all his free time hanging around with Matt and Floyd. Richard bought one of Matt's rifles, and Floyd is teaching him to shoot. In another few weeks, Floyd is taking Richard on a survival trip up north, and they spend as much time planning their getaway as any two adulterers.

Louise and Richard's mutual refusal to disturb each other's privacy permits them to continue living in the house they both love, caring for the daughter they both love. Psychologists, Louise thinks, haven't devoted enough attention to the role of houses in people's lives. Houses keep marriages together while their inhabitants fall apart. All that drywall and insulation act like the dome on a nuclear reactor, holding in—*containing*—a couple's wildness. And the contents of a house give a couple so much ballast that their marriage remains intact despite whatever forces might otherwise send it spinning. She and Richard bought their first house owning little more than a bed. But houses have voracious appetites. Appliances, knickknacks, books. The thought of deciding who might stay and who might move, who might get which chair and which CD, seems more overwhelming than sleeping on opposite sides of the bed. Maybe if they hold on long enough, she might rediscover why she loved him, the way a woman goes up to the attic to get some winter clothes, stumbles across an old lamp, remembers why she bought it, and carries it back downstairs.

In the meantime, Richard is still her husband, and his fortieth birthday is coming up. She can't throw a party. Other than the Bankses, whom would she invite? The best she can do is take him out for a fancy meal. Their first month in Michigan, they tried the French and Italian bistros that passed for fine dining in Potawatomie, but both restaurants were mediocre. It comes to her: the Busy Bee. They've been joking about trying the Bee since they moved to Stickney Springs. ("Do you think the Bee serves blintzes?" Richard kidded the first time they walked past the restaurant. Had that been the same Richard? Had she been the same Louise?) She makes a reservation, then thinks about a gift. She might not know exactly which item to get, but it doesn't require much mental energy to come up with the store in which to buy it.

She drives to Potawatomie and finds a space across from Hodgepodge Collectibles (Every Item One of a Kind!!!) and a store called Krzyzowski's (ESTABLISHED 1948), which, judging from the statues, holy cards, portraits of the Pope, and vestments in the window, sells religious articles, although the records by Hank Williams and Johnny Cash complicate this hypothesis. Two storefronts down stands Mossbacher's Guns Galore. When she steps inside, a bell tinkles and everyone turns to look; since several customers are holding guns, Louise feels like the little tin cutout that jolts across the stage at a shooting gallery. She seems to be the only person in the store who isn't wearing camouflage: the men wear camouflage pants and shirts; the women have on jeans and T-shirts and camouflage vests; there is even a toddler decked out in Osh-Kosh overalls in a camouflage pattern, with a matching camouflage cap.

Still, the store is soothing. The planks of the worn wood floor seem soft and gold as liquid caramel. The air is thick with the therapeutic scents of oil, kerosene, camphor, flannel, throat lozenges, and bug repellent. The stuffed grizzly towering in a corner and the deer, raccoons, and foxes perched above the merchandise give Mossbacher's the reverent feel of a museum. There is a carousel of vests and parkas, but Richard already is equipped with such basic gear. Foot warmers? A first-aid kit? A compass? A new stove? Certainly not the stove. Even the compass and first-aid kit carry accusations of incompetence.

Behind the register, beneath a huge display of venomous crossbows, stands a woman in a camouflage windbreaker; the variegated color and shape of her hair reminds Louise of a duck. She is about to ask the woman for a suggestion when one of the clerks approaches. More likely, this is Mr. Mossbacher himself, a very short Abe Lincoln with a lined, distorted face that seems to hold traces not only of his own history but of everyone else's. "May I help you?" he asks Louise.

She explains that her husband recently bought a gun and she wants to give him a gift to go with it. She is trying to convey enthusiasm but clearly fails, because Mr. Mossbacher asks her wryly, "Not much for guns yourself, I take it?"

"I'm not against guns," Louise says. "What I am is afraid of them."

He crinkles his eyebrows. "Surely you are aware that's part of their attraction?" He steps behind the case and walks along the staggering array of guns. Like a librarian before a stack of his favorite books, he studies the collection, and then takes down a rifle even Louise can tell is beautiful. "Here." He holds it toward her, and she reaches out and takes it. The gun is heavier than she expected, all dense wood and dull black metal. Her palm fits perfectly around the slide. She pumps it out and pulls it in, then lifts the stock against her shoulder and aims at a stuffed fox, lining up the orange triangle at the tip of the barrel with the metal notch before her eye. She can't bring herself to pull the trigger, not because she is ashamed of aiming at the fox, but because she knows she would be disappointed to hear a hollow click.

She lowers the barrel and stands looking at the gun. If the rifle had been a snake, this is when it would have bitten her.

She hands it back.

"Do you know the make of gun your husband bought?"

She looks dumbly at her hands.

"Was it a Winchester? A Remington?"

"A Remington, I think. Something with 'aught' in the number." Her old-maid piano teacher used to say "aught," and now her husband says it.

He shows her ammunition for the Remington, but she can't bring herself to buy it. He suggests a metal gun-case with a lock, but Richard would take this as a hint that Louise doesn't have faith in his ability to protect their daughter. Well, Mr. Mossbacher says, what about thermal underwear? Or camouflage boxer shorts? "We sell a lot of those," he confides, chuckling. But those items seem too intimate. "How about a knife?" Richard already owns a Swiss army knife, but Mr. Mossbacher shows Louise a case of glistening weapons whose mere existence makes you want to stab someone. She leans closer. *No good will come of us*, the knives seem to whisper.

"Ah, now, *these*." He lifts out a pair of binoculars. Louise raises them to her eyes, and then jerks back from the confrontation with Mr. Mossbacher's frighteningly gigantic face. Foolishly, she worries that the binoculars might enable Richard to focus on things about her that might otherwise remain obscure. As if to prove her point, she directs the lenses out the front window, and who should she see but Dolores Banks. Louise can make out the pink rawness of her neighbor's scalp, the mesh circle in her throat, and the logo of the health food store on the bundles in her arms.

"I'll take them," Louise says, thrusting her credit card across the counter. She has managed to avoid Dolores since a few days after the bombing, when she spotted Dolores creeping around the back of the house. Louise, who had been trying to replace a spark plug on the mower, ducked behind a bush and watched her neighbor peer inside the window to the mudroom. Dolores knocked, and when no one answered, she turned and scanned the yard, shaking her head and mumbling—Dolores mumbling sounded like a person humming through a comb. Then she began pounding at the door. It was a full minute before she gave up and stamped back to her own property. Louise can't imagine that Dolores means them ill, but she certainly doesn't want to face her at close range in Guns Galore. She grabs the binoculars and starts for the door, but just as she gets there the bell tinkles and in Dolores comes. Louise mutters an apology for being in such a rush and hurries out, but Dolores spins around and follows her. With the bundles in her arms, Dolores can't say a word. But as Louise is unlocking the van, Dolores puts down the bags and touches the button in her throat. "I. Need. To. Get. Something. Off. My. Chest."

At first, Louise thinks Dolores means she can't carry her bundles and needs a ride home. Then it comes to Louise that her neighbor wants to get off her chest a hideous opinion, a tumor of maliciousness, a gripe against Bill Clinton or Janet Reno, homosexuals, blacks, or Jews. And Louise can't bear to hear it. Nor does she want to hear how irresponsible she is for going off to work and leaving her daughter with a witch, or for having an affair.

"I really need to go," she says before climbing in the van and leaving her neighbor standing in the middle of Haarlem Avenue with her groceries at her feet and one hand pressed to her neck as if Louise had in fact bought a knife and stabbed her.

A week later, school ends for the summer. Louise cleans out her desk and rolls up her posters and is trying to decide what to do with Ms. Leesome's copy of the Bible when Melody Hasbrouck sashays in. Her sister has run off, and her parents have gotten back together to raise their grandchild. No one seems to care that Melody is still living with Jen.

"We decided to enlist." She lifts her long, fair hair and wraps it in a knot. "Clip, clip, clip, *clip*." She makes a gesture of tossing it away. "We figure if we stay around here, it's only a matter of time before we end up married to the jerks we didn't even want to go out with in high school." She gives Louise a hug. "Thanks for keeping me sane long enough to get the heck out of here."

Parker saunters in, ostensibly to give Louise a tape that he and his quartet recorded. He can hardly wait for graduation to make his big move. He intends to share an apartment with a black singer he met at the statewide band competition in Flint. "We've already got this basement flat in Hyde Park picked out. Grace has a job at a record store. She's trying to get some gigs. You should hear her voice." This reminds Parker why he has come. "The ice cream social is tonight. The band is giving a concert. It's not *my* band. It's the school jazz band. To be honest, it sucks. But Mr. Rolle, he's cool. He gave me this farewell solo. I thought, if you want to hear me play . . ."

The ice cream social! Yes! "We'll be there," Louise promises. "I can't wait to hear you! Good luck!"

By the end of the day, she has accumulated not only Parker's tape, but a dinosaur Beanie Baby from Beverly Booth—Louise wonders if this means Beverly believes in evolution—and a Bible from Lucas Beale, who tells Louise that if she is going to try to help people like him, she had better read this book. She places Parker's tape and Beverly's stuffed dinosaur and Lucas's Bible in a box, along with the Bible Ms. Leesome left behind, wondering, if she stays, how many Bibles she might collect. She is balancing the box on her hip and locking the door when Bess Moorehouse stops by.

"I'm so glad I caught you. I want to thank you for helping out. I've heard several positive comments from our students. It's only . . . to be fair . . . I feel obliged to let you know that we are required to advertise the position. We will consider you, of course. But we already have received inquiries from several attractive candidates." She holds the box so Louise can lock the door. "Have a good summer!" she says, then hands back the box and takes off down the hall, hips swaying, heels clattering—for such a conservative woman, she has a very sexy walk. Louise knows what that business about *other candidates* means. The district will interview everyone they can think of, and if, by the end of August, not a single candidate has proven mentally fit or competent, they might consider hiring her.

She drives to Stickney Springs, picks up Molly at Em's, and drives back to Potawatomie. By then, the booths for the ice cream social have been set up. She helps Molly hold a fishing rod and dangle her paper-clip hook in a wading pool full of rubber fish, then pays three tickets so Molly can throw wet sponges at Hendrick van Dyke, and another six tickets so Molly can get her face painted like a cat's. Molly and some other children search a sand pile for as many penny-toys as they can unearth in two minutes. Louise buys pizza for their dinner, and after Molly has licked the tomato sauce off her slice, she fills a bowl with ice cream, heaping it with an astonishing assortment of toppings and five maraschino cherries. While Molly spoons up this concoction, Louise looks around at the other families. The high school kids bend low to help the youngest customers at their booths. A fire truck runs a hose up its ladder and mists the soccer field with spray. Shrieking, the children chase each other, slipping on the grass. Molly leaves her sundae half finished and runs to join them. Soon, her shirt clings to her chest. Her socks and shoes are soaked, and the face-painted whiskers stream down her cheeks.

As the sun begins to set the grownups find seats on the makeshift bandstand, and Ervin Rolle wends his way through the crowd in a colorful dashiki. He snaps his head briskly, then lifts his baton and leads the musicians in a fight song, the alumni pumping their fists and cheering. After several marches, the brass section sits down noisily and the band shifts into a minor key, playing a jazz standard so bittersweet that Louise hugs Molly for comfort. Just when she thinks she can't be any more moved, Parker stands and plays his solo. He is wearing the same black Mystery Spot T-shirt he wore to her office the day they met, but he has put on a limp, faded tuxedo jacket over it. The light from the setting sun burnishes his sax, which he holds across his chest, lips to the mouthpiece, in a way that reminds Louise of Ames holding her across his chest and kissing her. And the notes . . . the notes Parker plays remind Louise of the way she feels when Ames makes love to her. Parker is even better than Louise guessed he would be. A flock of birds fills the sky, wheeling and turning, and listening to Parker's solo, Louise feels like flying up to join them. A beautiful black girl leans against a tree a little way off, and when Parker finishes playing, she puts two fingers to her mouth and whistles.

The sun is nearly down. Molly is shivering, so Louise wraps her in their blanket and carries her to the van.

"Do you think—" Molly's teeth are chattering. "Do you think someday I'll be one of the big kids running the booths?"

The question seems more profound than a matter of whether or not they will stay in Potawatomie long enough for Molly to be in high school. It has more to do with a person's ability to make her image of who she is now line up with her vision of who she wants to be. Once, Louise would have told Molly that a person has a great deal of this kind of power. Now, she doesn't think so. Otherwise, how could she have ended up married to a man she no longer loves and madly in love with a man who is married to a wife he will never leave?

The next day, while Richard is out with Floyd, Louise uses the binoculars she bought at Mossbacher's to spy on their neighbors. The Bankses have set up a huge red tent and Matt has staked signs along the road: COMING SOON . . . 500 YDS . . . EVERYTHING U NEED 4 . . . JULY 4 . . . U R HERE!!! When Louise focuses on the merchandise beneath the tent, she can make out patriotic kites, lawn ornaments, beach towels, balloons, and life-size cardboard replicas of Ralph Nader and Jane Fonda, bull's-eyes painted across their chests. The more explosive offerings are hidden in the barn. Not that the Bankses need to fear arrest. In the past few days, Louise has seen at least half a dozen police officers disappear inside the barn with Matt and reappear holding boxes decorated with snarling tigers and red-eyed snakes.

For the rest of that morning, she watches Dolores and

Matt mind the stand; the binoculars are so powerful she can see the hair on Matt's knuckles as he totes up the receipts. Once, Dolores shades her eyes and looks in Louise's direction. Louise draws back, the binoculars thudding like a heart attack against her chest. But Dolores turns and rearranges a stack of beach umbrellas, and Louise resumes her watch. Another time, while she is panning across the customers, a face looms up and she gasps. She has seen Mike Korn at school, but seeing him at this high a resolution is even more unsettling. Until now, she has never been sure what *the banality of evil* means. All the evil men whose photos she has seen—Hitler, Stalin, Idi Amin, Pol Pot—look like raving maniacs. But with his bland pudding of a face, Mike Korn seems the very definition of banality. Does that mean he's dangerous, or he's not?

Ames hasn't yet succeeded in getting this amateur Goebbels fired. Even after his committee agreed to accept the ACLU's decision to support Korn's right to express his views, Ames got another threat. (Louise asked what the message said, but Ames refused to tell her. "Just a lot of sound and fury, signifying nothing.") He hasn't told the cops. He doesn't want to scare Natalie or the girls. And he doesn't want Natalie to demand that he stop taking on such inflammatory causes.

Louise focuses on the loose red lips beneath the custodian's moustache, as if by staring at his mouth she can figure out if he was the one to leave the messages on Ames's machine. Korn tosses his packages on the passenger seat of his pickup and drives off. Bored, Louise turns the binoculars the wrong way around, reducing Dolores and Matt to figurines as small as the little plastic people in Molly's Playmobil sets. She can't imagine either one of them blowing up a building or associating with anyone who would. Then again, they probably don't see her as the sort of woman who would be lying with her face against the rug in a motel room, being entered from behind by a Unitarian minister.

Or maybe they do.

At the beginning of July, Ames goes out of town. He and Natalie and the girls always spend the Fourth with Natalie's parents in Rhode Island. Her father is a bassoonist with the Boston Pops, and they all drive to Cambridge to hear him play the *1812 Overture* and watch the fireworks over the Esplanade. "I have to say that I do like Natalie's parents," Ames informs Louise.

Well, actually, he *doesn't* have to say it. Liking anything about his wife seems a betrayal of her. What gives Natalie the right to have a father who is a professional musician when Louise's father sells worms and beer?

She asks if he will call while he is away.

"How can I?" he says. "I don't see how I could."

Sneak off to a phone booth. Take a roll of quarters. That way, the number won't show up on Natalie's father's bill. But if Ames can't be bothered to come up with such a scheme, why should she do it for him? He has been stuck in a cycle of regret ever since he returned from a convention of Unitarian ministers in Toronto the week before. Natalie met him at the airport, and when he saw her waiting in her car to pick him up, he felt a twinge of fondness. That's what he told Louise. *I'm still fond of her. She's my wife.* He can't seem to understand why that makes Louise cry.

Well, if Ames can be fond of Natalie, Louise can be fond of Richard. At the very least, she can make sure he has a relatively happy birthday. She wakes before dawn, intending to wrap his gift, but somehow ends up using the binoculars to spy on her neighbors one last time. Slowly, as the darkness melts, three graceful shapes step from the woods behind the

Bankses' barn. Louise can see the deer's tongues as they nibble the dewy grass. She imagines holding a rifle and squeezing the trigger. As if sensing her intentions, all three animals jerk their heads and bound back to safety.

Ashamed, she turns the binoculars down the road and focuses on Em's backyard. And who should slip into view but Matt Banks. He wears nothing but gym shorts, and his hair stands up in spikes. He unlatches the cage in which the one-legged hawk has been moping for the past few weeks. The bird lies huddled like a pile of oily rags, and Matt steps inside the cage, grabs the bird, and snaps its neck. Louise cries out and flinches, but she turns back in time to see him stuff the hawk in a sack. He rubs his hands on the grass and then dries them on his shorts.

Em comes out and joins him. Louise jumps up, thinking she might need to call the police. But Em doesn't seem startled. Matt points to the sack. Em nods, and the next thing Louise knows, she's in Matt's beefy arms. It's like seeing Bluto get Olive Oyl. Matt backs Em against the cage, presses his mouth to her neck and moves heavily against her. Louise thinks again of reaching for the phone, but there is something so obviously theatrical about the way Em pounds on his back as Matt bends and carries her into the house that even from this distance Louise can tell that if she does call the cops, she will be the one to be embarrassed.

Queasy and aroused, she sets the binoculars on the chair. She isn't sure what she has seen, but the incident strikes her as threatening, like a package someone has left on the doorstep in the middle of the night, and she isn't about to open it.

After Richard leaves, Louise proposes to Molly that instead of spending the day with Em, she spend the day with her, baking a birthday cake for her father.

"Really?" Louise can't tell if Molly is surprised that her mother wants to bake a cake for her father or that her mother wants to spend the day with her.

"Sure," Louise says. "Come on. Get dressed and you can pick out the recipe."

Spending the day with Molly distracts Louise from thinking about Ames, although it seems to her problematic to view one's daughter as a distraction. Both layers of the cake drop perfectly from their pans. Molly coos with pleasure as they swirl icing across the top. Later, Molly paints a picture of the three of them taking Matzo Ball for a walk, and Louise helps her to frame and wrap it.

"I really liked today," Molly says, which pleases Louise but makes her wonder if the damage she has inflicted can be so effortlessly undone. She can't reconcile her willingness to leave Molly with Em with the scene she spied that morning. People are entitled to their fantasies. But Em making love to a man whose politics she claims to detest and keeping her affair hidden from Louise, even though she has gotten Louise to confess her affair to *her*, leads Louise to wonder what else she doesn't know about her daughter's daycare provider.

Reluctantly, she walks Molly to Em's house so she can get ready for her birthday date with Richard.

"Oh, Molly," Em says, "I have some sad news. You know how sick Harvey the Hawk was? The poor thing died in his sleep." She puts her arms around Molly. "At least he won't be suffering."

Louise assumes Em is lying to spare Molly the image of Matt twisting the hawk's neck. So why does she feel yet another conspiracy swirling around her?

"Can we bury him?" Molly asks. She seems excited and upset. "Can I help you make—Mom, what's it called?"

"A tombstone?"

"Can I help you make a tombstone?"

Em winks at Louise over Molly's shoulder. "I think I have a box. We can decorate it with the gyroscopes the Egyptians used when they buried their mummy hawks."

Louise can only hope that Em doesn't intend to embalm the poor bird.

"Have a good time at dinner," Em says. "Tell Richard I wish him a happy birthday."

"Yeah, I'm sure you do." She kisses Molly, wondering if her daughter might be hurt by spending so much time with Em. Not if Em has a good heart, which Louise believes she does. But who knows? Who really knows anything about anyone else's heart? Or, for that matter, her own?

By the time she gets home, Richard is in the shower. Louise slips out of her frosting-stained shirt and puts on her second-best dress. Not the backless black shift she would have worn for Ames, but a perfectly acceptable purple silk. Richard comes to her in a towel, ducking shyly, as if he isn't sure how she might react. How has she managed to get through so many weeks of an affair without feeling guilty? It will catch up to her, she knows. But so far, it hasn't.

His skin is damp against her dress, and she has to remind herself that her sexual allegiance is to him and not to Ames. "We'll be late," she says. "I made a reservation. Maybe when we get back."

They drive to Stickney Springs in Richard's Corolla. He puts his hand on her knee, and even that feels adulterous. Her lover is in Rhode Island with his wife, and Louise feels disloyal taking her husband out for dinner.

The Bee is in the remodeled train station near the White Chief Breading and Flour Factory. Richard holds the door, which is quilted with the red leather padding you might find in a classy insane asylum. The hostess, a weak-chinned blonde in a puffy pink gown that might once have been a prom dress, leads them to a booth, which also is padded. A candle sputters in a globe. The waiter, a big, affable man with hair as shiny as a doll's, wears a frayed tie that looks as if some hungry customer has nibbled off the tip. He hands them menus padded in the same red leather as the door.

"We ought to bring my parents here," Richard kids. "They would really go for the venison and pork chops." He draws his finger down the offerings. "When was the last time you saw 'chilled shrimp cocktail' as an appetizer?"

"Don't be such a snob," Louise says, and she is only half joking. "Sometimes all you really want is a basket of bland white dinner rolls, an iceberg salad with Russian dressing, a hunk of bloody prime rib, and a scoop of green beans almandine."

After the waiter takes their orders, she reaches under her chair and brings out Richard's gift. He rips off the wrapping.

"Oh, Lou," he says, "they're great." He holds the binoculars to his eyes, and she needs to remind herself that from this close, all he can see of her is a blur.

"How were things at the prison today?" she asks, not expecting much of an answer, but Richard launches into a meticulous account of his session with an inmate who is about to be released.

"I love this guy," Richard says. "Every once in a while, I get to work with somebody who has a chance to make it on the outside. He doesn't hear voices. He isn't hooked on crack. He doesn't have uncontrollable urges to bite off people's heads." Absently, he pokes at the wax around the candle and swishes his finger through the flame. He has avoided every kind of fire since the accident, and here he is putting his finger in a flame! "This guy would have a great chance of going straight if he weren't ticked off at his girlfriend. 'The bitch can't wait three years? I'm only in for three years and she takes up with some other guy?'"

Louise wonders if Richard is offering her a lesson in fidelity. If this criminal expects his wife to wait three years for his release, how much longer should she be expected to grant Richard his self-imposed absence from their marriage? She looks across the table and is startled to realize the absence might be over. There sits the Richard with whom she was in love before Sophie Pang took those pills, before he set fire to those trees.

Their food comes—London broil for her and surf and turf for Richard. He cracks the lobster's thorax, extracts a gob of meat, and dips it in the butter. If she can't do him the favor of confessing her affair, she will confess someone else's. "I saw Matt and Em this morning. They didn't know I was watching. I guess I should have suspected it. But, well, it's not as if they have a lot in common."

Richard slices his beef, exposing the bloody center. "I promised Matt not to tell anyone. It's not as if either of them is married anymore. It's only, well, Em and her ex-husband . . ."

Em had a husband? In all the months she and Louise have been exchanging confidences, Em never once mentioned being married.

Richard chews a bite. "Em and her ex-husband, and Matt and his ex-wife . . . Not that I'm judgmental. If four consenting adults . . . The problem was, Matt didn't really want to do it. But his wife was bored, and he wanted to keep her happy, so, I don't know, they switched partners. It was supposed to be for fun. But Matt's wife took their kid and ran off with Em's husband. Matt was devastated, just devastated." On he goes, describing the injustice of Matt losing his wife to Em's ex-husband. But then, hadn't Em lost her husband to Matt's ex-wife? "At least they ended up with each other. There's a certain beauty in that. Too bad they still have to sneak around." Apparently, Dolores doesn't think highly of her son dating a pagan, and Matt can't afford to upset his mother because she owns the farm. Besides, he loves the old woman.

As Richard speaks, Louise wonders if Em has told Matt about her affair with Ames. For all she knows, Matt is friends with whatever lunatic left those threats on Ames's answering machine. The idea makes her so sick she needs to excuse herself and find the ladies' room. "I'll be back in a minute," she tells Richard, then stands and follows the signs downstairs, through a tunnel that stinks of vinegar, ketchup, and floral-scented air freshener. Beside a door labeled BANQUET HALL, a typed sheet of paper announces the weekly meetings of the Lions Club, the Elks, and the Potawatomie Chapter of the Michigan Militia.

Bile rises in Louise's throat. She finds the ladies' room and loses her London broil. Luckily, no one comes in. She assures herself that just because Timothy McVeigh attended a meeting of the Michigan Militia, that doesn't mean the other members are murderous fanatics, too. How dangerous can they be if they meet at the Busy Bee? She rinses her face, gulps some water, then walks back to the banquet hall. A splintery U-shaped table takes up most of the room, its surface littered with tinfoil ashtrays. An American flag stands in one corner beside a poster-board display that reads POTAWATOMIE CHAPTER OF THE MICHIGAN MILITIA—WE DO NEAT THINGS. Pasted to the board are snapshots documenting an outing where the militiamen and their families practiced lying on their bellies shooting guns, marching in formation, roasting hot dogs, and drinking beer. In one photo, a girl Molly's age stands with her legs spread to enable her to support the weight of the automatic weapon she holds sideways against her sparrow-thin chest. With their mustaches, beards, aviator glasses, and baseball caps, most of the men look alike. She doesn't see Richard in any of the photos, but a man who might or might not be Matt lurks in the background of several shots. And there, beside a Neanderthal with a crossbow, stands Matt's sweet, matronly mother, Dolores. In another photo, Dolores tends hot dogs on a grill. And here she is in a sweatshirt decorated with gingham Scottie dogs, holding a pistol in two outstretched hands and firing at an unseen target.

Louise wobbles back upstairs.

"You look terrible," Richard says. "I mean, you look lovely in that dress, but you're very pale. You're shaking."

She blames her pallor on something she must have eaten, and Richard drives her home, where she climbs into bed and pulls the covers over her head. In the distance, rockets hiss. A string of cherry bombs explodes so close to the house the windows rattle. Richard must have gone to get Molly, and Molly must have come in to say goodnight, but when Louise awakes the next morning, she remembers little of the evening before except those photos at the Bee.

They spend the day in an eerie, wordless peace. Cars keep arriving at the Bankses' farm for last-minute fireworks. Richard asks Louise if she wants to accompany him to a picnic at the Sportsman's Club. She thanks him but says she wouldn't enjoy herself and doesn't want Molly around the guns.

"Can we do sprinklers?" Molly asks, and Louise says sure, but they're called sparklers, not sprinklers, wondering if a brain injury can be catching. She climbs on a stepstool and brings down the package of sparklers she bought in Potawatomie the week before. "Can I light them?" Molly asks, and Louise nods, remembering the thrill of being allowed to stay up late and light sparklers with Imelda, the two of them racing around the lake, sparks biting their wrists, the purple-yellow-red-and-green trails of light leaving afterimages like paint on black velvet, the fireflies mixing in, the sweet saltpeter stink, the burn to her fingers when she couldn't resist touching the still-hot tips.

She follows Richard through the mudroom and down the steps to the backyard. He carries the Remington ought-whatever with the nonchalance of a man trying to demonstrate how comfortable he is with guns.

"Shit, I forgot the beer." He leans the rifle against the house. "Would you watch it? It isn't loaded, but I don't want Molly . . ."

He isn't gone a minute before Louise is holding the gun and sighting along the scope, which is more elaborate than the mechanism on the rifle Mr. Mossbacher let her hold. She sights at a bush, then at the weathervane on top of the Bankses' barn. She imagines crouching across the street from Ames's house and waiting for Natalie. Since she has no idea what Natalie looks like, she envisions a woman with a blank oval face, which, when Natalie sees Louise's gun, develops the expression of Edvard Munch's *The Scream*.

The door slams and Richard trots down the steps carrying a six-pack. Louise leans the rifle against the wall. If anything were to happen to Natalie, the cops wouldn't need a minute to figure out that she and Ames are having an affair. She wasn't serious anyway. Horrible ideas pass through a person's mind all the time. She is no more likely to shoot Natalie than Dolores is likely to shoot Bill Clinton. Just because you hold a gun and imagine shooting another person doesn't mean you actually want to kill her. All that happened when you sighted along a gun was that you saw your own heart, shining and red as an apple on a tree. And sometimes it had a wormhole. A small, malicious bruise. A spreading dark spot of decay.

NINE

LOUISE FINDS HERSELF WISHING SHE COULD SUMMON THE dignity to end her affair with Ames. She thinks of telling him that unless he leaves Natalie, she won't sleep with him again. But that seems too close to blackmail. Besides, if she offers an ultimatum, he might tell her that she's right and they ought never make love again.

The day he returns from his trip to see Natalie's parents, he calls and says how much he missed her. He thought about her the entire drive to Rhode Island. He thought about her while sitting on the Esplanade watching fireworks above the Charles. And he thought about her while he was lying in bed with Natalie, listening to her go on and on about how thoughtless he is to spend so much time on political causes that put his family's lives at risk. "She's so cold to me," he whispers. "She saves what little warmth she has for Bec and Ann. She's always been compulsive about keeping the house clean, but now she's compulsive about keeping kosher. We couldn't stop at restaurants. We had to pull over at a rest stop and eat cold chicken and hardboiled eggs from a cooler, like immigrants." His voice breaks. "I need to see you. Please, Louise. Can you get away tomorrow?"

She should tell him she can't. But she finds it difficult to believe he will live the rest of his life with a woman who refuses to sleep with him two weeks of every month and urges him to ingratiate himself with the wealthy white heterosexual members of his congregation rather than stir up trouble with the likes of Lee LeGrand or "that obnoxious Myrna Cott," whom Natalie believes gives Jews a bad name. She is pressuring Ames to apply for a position back East. "As if they need another liberal minister in New England," he scoffs to Louise.

This time they meet at Wal-Mart. It's the sort of pleasantly hot mid-summer afternoon Midwesterners live for. The cornstalks shake their tasseled heads and lift their arms like slender, tow-haired children begging to be held. Ames reaches across the seat and fondles her the way a man might pet a dog he abandoned at a summer house and then drove back to get. She should bite him for having abandoned her in the first place. But she nearly wags her tail with relief that he's come back.

"You know how you talk to yourself in your head? I used to think of that voice as my conversation with God." He takes his eyes from the road and stares at Louise so long she worries about their safety. "Now I'm telling everything to you."

His newfound ardor scares her. The stronger his outburst

now, the deeper his repentance later. Not that she is inclined to give him up. The Michigan summer sun will eventually give way to winter, but how can she not enjoy its warmth and brilliance while it shines?

The lot at the inn is full—there must be a NASCAR race that week. Sure enough, when Ames comes back outside he is crestfallen; that's the only word to describe the way his head droops to his chest, like a heraldic coat of arms dangling from a pike. "The nearest motel is in Montgomery. For all I know, that one's full, too. Besides, by the time we get there, we'll have to turn around and head home." He looks past the last row of S.U.V.s. "There's a state park not far from here. We could spend a few hours enjoying the great outdoors."

"Sure," she says. This might not be a bad thing. If she doesn't allow Ames's enthusiasm to get out of hand now, his remorse might be muted later.

At the park entrance, Ames hands the ranger three dollars and takes a tag for the dashboard, and Louise thinks how easy it would be to neglect to remind him to remove the tag before they leave. Natalie will discover the affair, and only Louise will know that she could have prevented her from finding that bit of evidence. The problem is, Louise is sane enough to know that the madness clouding her judgment might someday burn off. And that keeps her honest, for now.

They walk along a path that leads to an algae-covered pond smaller than Handsome Lake. The beach is furnished with a picnic table, a rusty trash-barrel, an ash-filled grill, and a bench with a missing slat. They have barely settled on the bench before Ames starts kissing her. They are only thirty miles from Potawatomie. The prospect of someone they know spending a sunny afternoon at the nearest state park doesn't seem that remote. How can he be kissing her in public and not plan to leave his wife?

Two children skip into the clearing. The older of the two, a boy who wears a beaded necklace and a tie-dye shirt, leads a goat on a golden rope. *Maaa?* the goat says quizzically. In the sun, its hair is a blinding white.

"Come on, Baby, jump up!" The girl thumps the table, but the goat just stands looking satisfied with its own gorgeous immobility. Louise doubts anyone could get that goat to do anything it didn't want to do. But the boy jerks the rope, and the goat leaps up and lands on the table with a hoofy clatter. *Maaa! Maaa!* There isn't a blemish on it. The animal gives off such a sheen of perfection, Louise almost expects the children to bind it and slit its throat as part of some religious sacrifice.

"Good, Baby, good goat!" The girl climbs up and kisses the goat on the nose. For the rest of her life, whenever Louise thinks back on the happiest day she's ever had, she will see that bright white goat standing on that table in the sun, shaking its head and bleating.

"It's beautiful here," she tells Ames. The sun glints off the lake. Tall purple flowers bloom furiously around the shore. She asks what the plants are called.

"That's loosestrife," he says, distracted. "It's not indigenous to Michigan. It chokes out the native plants. It's so invasive, it just takes over."

"That must be the way the locals feel about people like me," she jokes. But instead of laughing, he takes Louise's hand and pulls her up.

Maaa! The goat clatters from the table and stands bucking in the grass. The children stare at Louise and Ames as if they hadn't realized anyone else was there. Like Lot's wife, Louise forces herself to look ahead, following Ames deeper in the woods, as she once followed Richard.

They push through the undergrowth until they reach a willow whose branches hang down to create a tent. Light filters through the leaves. The air smells tangy but fresh, as if they have stepped inside a cedar chest. Ames lays her back in the spongy loam, then lifts her skirt and kisses her thighs. How in love he must be, not to care who sees them. For her part, she can't shake the fear that someone might be watching—one of Ames's parishioners, or Mike Korn, or Richard, who owns those powerful new binoculars. But Ames keeps kissing her between her legs, and she finally lets go of her fear and watches it float off above the trees. She clutches his head and tangles her fingers in his hair. She no longer cares who sees. Her only fear is that after such a tumultuous day, he will be overcome with guilt and decide they mustn't sneak off again.

Sure enough, he calls the next week and asks her to meet him at the diner near his church. Louise gets there first and orders coffee. When Ames comes in, he is disheveled and pale, with a blondish unshaven scum across his chin. His lower lip is bleeding where he must have gnawed it. They order breakfast, but Ames leaves his bacon and eggs untouched.

As often happens in Potawatomie, someone they know stops by. "Hey, Rev. Hey, Louise. Two of my favorite people." Howie doesn't seem surprised to see them. He probably thinks they are discussing the petition to get Mike Korn fired. In such a small city, the smartest way to conceal an affair is to conduct it in the open. "There was an interesting accident," Howie tells them. Louise knows that Howie's partner, Jack, likes to listen to the police scanner. According to Howie, it comforts Jack to know that beneath their straight exteriors, the citizens of Potawatomie engage in behaviors so bizarre that neither Howie nor Jack would dream of exhibiting them. "You know Arnie Malachowski, the president of the city council? Somehow, driving forty miles an hour on a straight, deserted road in broad daylight, Arnie just happens to detour off the road. Car ends up upside down in a cornfield. Of course, there turns out to be a passenger. Jeanette Robins, also a member of the council. You know her, too, right? Anyway, rumor has it that Arnie's trousers were, how shall we put this, in a state of disarray. He told the cops he was giving Jeanette a lift home, but they weren't anywhere near her house." Howie points quizzically at a slice of Ames's bacon, and Ames motions to go ahead.

Howie and Ames discuss the accident, but Louise can see that Ames is anxious for him to leave. Howie takes a bite of Ames's toast. Crumbs sift to his shirt. "Well, nice running into you." He pats Ames's back, rubbing it a little longer than a straight man might have done, then grabs Ames's last piece of toast and goes out.

Ames sits shredding his sugar packets. "Last night . . . Natalie finally wanted to make love. And I couldn't do it. I couldn't bring myself to touch her. She's my wife. You can't not make love to your wife. I think it's what is known as the alienation of one's affections."

Alienation of one's affections? It sounds as if he is accusing her of some crime.

"She kept asking me what was wrong. But I couldn't . . . I couldn't tell her." He shields his eyes. "She still loves me. She's the mother of my children. Would you want me to break her heart? I love you, Louise. But I can't leave my wife. It's the burden I have to bear." He slumps backward in the booth like a man who has given in and confessed what his interrogators wanted him to confess.

"Your cross, you mean."

He looks at her with a puzzled expression.

"You don't believe in being happy. You think we're all on this earth to suffer."

"That isn't true. And please keep your voice down."

"You never want to sleep with me again? You want to stay with a woman who—"

"What does it matter what I want? Who's ever cared what I want?"

"I do. I'm asking you what you want."

"'What I want,'" he repeats bitterly. "What I want is to be with you all the time. I want to go to sleep with you at night and wake up with you the next morning. I want to know you'll be there when I come home, or I'll be there when you get home, and I'll be happy to see you, or you'll be glad to see me. But it doesn't matter what I want, or what you want. What kind of excuse is that, wanting something? Everyone wants something. You can't just go around hurting people to get what you want."

"So you'll consign yourself to another three or four decades of suffering? You'll live a marriage that's a lie?"

"It isn't a lie. I told you, I'm still fond of Natalie."

"You're having an affair and your marriage isn't a lie?"

The waitress comes over. Her stiff platinum hair reminds Louise of the meringue on the pies the diner serves. "Is everything all right? Do you want another pot of hot water, Reverend?"

"Excuse me?" Ames says. "Oh, no. Thanks. I've had enough."

The woman touches him on the wrist. "I really just wanted to stop by and say I appreciate what you're doing about those science classes. I'm as good a Christian as anybody, but I don't want my kids growing up thinking that God made Adam out of clay. Like an art project? I want my kid to play with dinosaurs and know their names, so he can get a decent job."

Ames smiles his public smile. "I appreciate your support."

"You let me know if there's anything else you want." As long as she remains at their table, Ames keeps up his smile, but the moment she leaves, Louise can see that he is furious at her.

"If you weren't married," she asks, "would you have me? Would you marry me?"

"That's a hypothetical question. I learned a long time ago never to answer a hypothetical question."

"What kind of rule is that?" It takes all her self-restraint to keep her voice down. "What is this, the eleventh commandment: Thou shalt not answer hypothetical questions? If you weren't married, would you want to live with me? Would you drive me to some lake and make love to me in the woods?"

"I have to go," Ames says glumly, then slides from the booth and walks out, depriving her even of the self-respect that would have come of being the one who left the diner first.

Somehow, she makes it home. The only other time she has felt this sick was when she was nursing Molly and got mastitis and ran a fever of a hundred and four. That time, there was a magical antibiotic to cure the pain. This time, she climbs into bed fully clothed but can't stop shivering. She and Ames will never make love again. He will never again run his fingers along her cheek, never cry out her name in that crazy chant of happiness and sex-drenched love, *Louise, Louise, Louise*, sobbing from the sheer erotic splendor of it all. Who will give her advice about students like Lucas Beale? To whom will she complain about Mike Korn and Bess Moorehouse? How can she stand the thought that she will never again kiss the backs of Ames's knees or the lightning-bolt birthmark along his ribs, never again flick that soft stray lock of hair behind his ear, never again sit beside him in the passenger seat of his Escort stroking the velvety skin on his inner arm while they drive to Handsome Lake?

When Richard comes home, she tells him she has the flu and asks him to pick up Molly. Then she spends the rest of the night in bed, not bothering to get undressed, dozing, waking, biting the pillow to keep from screaming. The next morning, Richard asks if she wants to see a doctor. She promises she'll be up by noon but doesn't manage to leave the bed except to get a drink of water. She has never believed that a person could die of love. But it turns out you can. At least, getting your heart broken can drive you crazy. She can't stop imagining ways that Ames might be free of Natalie. Because he is right—despite everything, Louise isn't the type of woman to steal another woman's husband. Which means Natalie needs to be the one to leave Ames. Maybe their religious differences will come to loom so large that she will be driven to divorce him. Maybe she will get run over by a bus.

On her second day in bed, Louise decides that she will call Natalie and reveal the truth. The marriage will fall apart and Ames will be free to marry her. Except that he will be so angry at Louise he will never speak to her again. Better if she calls him at his church and says that if seeing her too often makes it difficult to sleep with Natalie, they will limit how often they get together. They will drive to Handsome Lake only once a month.

But she can't bring herself to beg. She hates Ames. How could he not foresee that one day he would need to choose between them? From the start, Louise has known that if she were required to choose between Richard and Ames, she would choose Ames. She would always regret hurting Richard, but didn't Richard desert her first?

On the third afternoon, the phone rings and she picks it up and Ames says he shouldn't be calling but he is miserable. "Are you all right?" he asks. "Are you getting through this? I'm so sorry," he says. "I love you. I can't bear to give you up."

No, she thinks, *I am not getting through this. I haven't left my bed in three days.* "I love you, too," she says. "But if you ever do this to me again, I'll find you and rip out your heart."

She gets out of bed, washes her hair, and dresses. In the mirror, her face seems thin and gray, but she feels energized and elated. She wobbles tentatively down the stairs and out the door. The doilies of Queen Anne's lace along the road seem vividly three-dimensional. The rolls of chicken wire in Em's backyard glitter in the sun. Ames tried to give her up, but he wasn't *able* to give her up, and that means something, doesn't it? If he can't give her up, and he can't continue deceiving his wife . . .

Louise goes in and finds Molly and Em folding rags to put in the injured birds' cages. The minute Em sees her, she sends Molly to get a fresh load from the dryer.

"He broke up with you, didn't he. The bastard." She puts water on the stove and brews Louise a cup of tea. "Maybe the spell will take hold. It's only been a few weeks."

"You weren't supposed to cast a spell."

Em flips back her braid. "Don't tell me you're not grateful."

Louise has to admit that if Em could cast a spell that would result in Natalie leaving Ames, she wouldn't try to stop her. She sips the sludgy tea.

"I could do a better job if you would give me some part of Natalie. Nail clippings. A strand of hair. A dirty Kleenex."

Stealing hair and casting spells? This has become more than a little ghoulish. Louise decides the only way to cure her compulsion to get rid of Natalie is to meet the poor woman. If the target that keeps appearing in the crosshairs of Richard's gun were to take on a human face, she would find it impossible to pull the trigger.

But she can't very well sit outside Ames's house and wait for

Natalie to emerge. She can't follow Natalie to the store. She keeps trying to think how she might arrange to meet her, but she can't come up with anything until she sees an educational supplement in the paper advertising open houses for various private schools. One small notice urges parents to find out more about All Faiths Daycare Center. Molly will no longer need daycare in the fall. But it couldn't hurt to stop by at the open house.

They find the building on Spruce Street, and Molly races up the stairs. By following the high-pitched voices and the smell of grape juice and disinfectant, they reach two cheerful rooms, one filled with cubbyholes, sleeping mats, and tiny desks, the other with milk crates, blocks, a box of stuffed puppets, heaps of dress-up clothes, and a cardboard theater for giving puppet shows. Within minutes, Molly is dressed in a doctor's coat, issuing orders to two younger girls who, at Molly's command, perform open-heart surgery on a stuffed panda whose great beery belly makes him resemble nothing more than the victim of a coronary occlusion.

Besides the four mothers, there is a pudgy brunette Louise guesses must be a teacher. A wispy older black woman introduces herself as Marley MacLean, a member of the daycare center's board of trustees. "That your little girl? My, isn't she the pretty one. Small, but a big personality."

They chat about Louise's move from California and the importance of social workers in schools while Louise keeps an eye on the door, wondering if Natalie will show up. Marley MacLean hands her an application. The other girls' mothers take them home. Reluctantly, Louise gives Molly a five-minute warning to close up the panda's incision.

"Do I have to?" she moans.

A woman walks into the room. "I'm afraid you do," the

woman tells Molly. "We can't expect Ms. Jolie here to stay overtime just because one child wants to keep playing."

If Louise's intention was to give Ames's wife a human face, that intention is thwarted by her instant and overwhelming dislike for the woman. Natalie is tall and toothpick thin, with a ginger-ale complexion otherworldly in its paleness beneath her brutally short red hair. She is striking, Louise decides. But there's something forbidding about her. As a therapist, Louise can come up with a dozen theories as to why a man with an alcoholic mother, a gambler father, and a history of forebears whose indulgence of their passions led to scandalous falls from grace might have married such a wife. But she is Ames's lover and not his therapist. That he prefers to stay with Natalie wounds Louise so deeply it's as if Natalie has been the one to shoot *her*.

"So tell me," Natalie asks, "just how observant are you?"

The question stuns Louise. How does Natalie even know that Louise is married to a Jew? And why would Louise's degree of religious devotion matter to anyone but Richard? "I've been to temple a few times," she says, "but not since we moved to Michigan."

Natalie stares at her as if Louise were demented. Then she laughs. "I meant, how many of our little grammar mistakes did you notice?" She drops her voice. "Ms. Jolie here is lovely with the children, but her command of spelling leaves a bit to be desired." Natalie points to the word *girafe* beneath a photo of a long-necked mammal, and rule number four in a list of ALL FAITHS RULES, which warns: "Do no hit other children." As she goes on calling Louise's attention to other errors, Louise feels herself shrink to the child she once was, coming to school with dilapidated shoes and unwashed hair.

"We really must lock up now," Natalie says. Marley MacLean and the ill-educated Ms. Jolie already have left. Natalie switches off the lights. "I know this will sound strange, but I was wondering if you might drop me at the garage. I was planning on walking there, but I'm afraid these shoes are new, and, well, they're absolutely *killing* me." They start down the stairs, and Natalie limps a bit to show how much her new shoes hurt. "It was the most terrifying thing. I was driving to Ann Arbor the other day and the steering mechanism on my Volvo simply locked up. The highway curved and I couldn't do a thing about it. Thank God my daughters weren't in the car. I managed to stop *this* close to a tree." She pinches her fingers to show just how close to the tree she came. "The mechanics couldn't find a thing wrong. But I am not about to get back in that car. I will drive it home from the garage, but after that, my husband can drive the Volvo and I'll drive his ratty Escort. Better embarrassed than dead, I say."

Em's spell couldn't possibly have caused the steering mechanism on Natalie's Volvo to lock up, could it? *Could it?*

"I can't explain," Louise tells Natalie, "but it's very important that I leave here right away." She grabs Molly's hand and flees, and as soon as they get back home, Louise calls the ticket counter at Northwest Airlines and makes a reservation to fly to San Francisco the following week.

TEN

LOOKING DOWN AT THE VAST TURBULENCE OF THE ROCKIES, Louise wonders why she has always given so much credit to Imelda's mother for saving her life and so much less to Imelda. Maybe what you wanted as a child was to know some grownup was in charge. But once Louise reached her twenties, it was Imelda who gave her what she needed. With her broad, round Eskimo of a face and her flyaway wavy hair, Imelda looks the part of an earthy sixties waif. But she has a mathematician's rationality. By thirteen, she had figured out the most efficient way to clean a motel room. With equal precision, she plotted the trajectory of hard work and exceptional grades that would allow her to escape Mule's Neck, New York, and the Lenape Lake Motel.

Louise doesn't really understand what Imelda does for a living, other than that she is the highest-ranked female mathematician at U. C. Berkeley. With such a demanding job and a recurrence of the cancer that already took one breast, she has more on her mind than curing Louise of her obsession with a married minister. But Louise hopes that merely basking in the orderly field of Imelda's good sense will straighten out her thinking. Why hasn't she gone back to visit Imelda before this? Not only has her affair caused her to neglect her daughter, it has led her to neglect her oldest, dearest friend.

The moment Louise realizes that the bony woman with close-cropped graying hair who approaches her at the baggage carousel is that same oldest, dearest friend—Imelda hasn't yet started chemo but has shaved her head to prevent a recurrence of the depression she felt the first time she lost her hair—her self-pity vanishes. What a lot of nerve she has to think she can control her love life when her brilliant best friend hasn't been able to control the cells in her own body. Assuming you can lead your fate around by the nose like a docile goat is as much an abomination as thinking you can destroy a tumor by visualizing a horde of anti-cancer Pac-men scurrying through your veins.

She has come for a five-day visit. When Imelda tells her that the mastectomy is scheduled for the day after she leaves, Louise offers to stay another week, but Imelda won't hear of it. What she wants is for Louise to accompany her on what used to be their favorite hike behind Louise's house in San Rafael, a hike Imelda is afraid she no longer will be able to make once the treatments start.

They exit the airport and cross the bridge. To keep the

tone light, Louise launches into a satirical description of Richard's new hobby. The idea of Richard in camouflage fatigues wandering the woods with a gun strikes Imelda as so ludicrous that she laughs herself into a coughing fit. "God, what I wouldn't give to see your husband gutting a bear!" She asks Louise to hand her a tissue so she can wipe away the tears. "So, Lulabelle." She stifles a final hiccup. "Did this minister of yours break off the affair, or are you out here because you're trying to get up the nerve to tell Richard you're leaving him?"

Louise has told Imelda next to nothing about Ames. All she mentioned is that she spends a lot of time volunteering for an AIDS organization led by a Unitarian minister. Is everyone psychic but her? Or is she so predictable that a person doesn't need a crystal ball to divine what she's hiding?

"You didn't tell me his name, so I've been thinking of him as the Reverend Arthur Dimmesdale. Remember when we read *The Scarlet Letter* in tenth grade, for Mr. Sheffley? It takes a lot of nerve to teach a novel about adultery when you're screwing the principal's wife."

Louise hasn't thought about Mr. Sheffley in years. Had *The Scarlet Letter* been required reading? Or had Mr. Sheffley chosen it because he was having an affair and could think of nothing else? In high school, the novel had made no impression on Louise. All those thee's and thou's, the cowardly minister's inability to admit that he had slept with Hester Prynne. Now she wishes she had paid more attention. By the time you recognized a book's significance in your life, you could barely recall its name. For all Louise knows, Hawthorne based the Reverend Arthur Dimmesdale on one of Ames's ancestors. She looks at Imelda, who is the only person in her life who knows who Mr. Sheffley is, and she feels a chillingly selfish fear that if Imelda were to die, the one repository of knowledge of Louise's childhood would vanish with her.

"If you don't tell me about this minister, I'm going to think you think I'm doomed." She pulls off the freeway and takes a series of turns that will lead to Louise's old neighborhood. "Hearing about my best friend making hot love in some scummy motel is the only thing I can imagine taking my mind off this fucking cancer."

They park by Louise's house, and she finds it impossible to believe that another family lives there. Maybe the members of that family keep running into spectral versions of Richard and Louise, who, in a parallel universe, never left California.

"It's only a house," Imelda says. "You can't get sentimental about houses. Or bodies. They're just, I don't know, the Tupperware of the soul."

Louise looks at her friend and sees that Imelda has indeed achieved a certain transparency, as if her body were made of the cloudy white plastic that Tupperware is made of. Then again, she always traveled light. Unlike Louise, she can get by on her ability to live inside her head. It's a relief to see her reach in her canvas bag, pull out a floppy hat and put it on, as if to shelter that precious brain.

Louise pulls on her own sun hat, which she hasn't worn since leaving California. She and Imelda slather on sunscreen, then find the path that leads around the house before joining the trail up the mountain. Her old garden, compared to the gardens in Michigan, seems deliriously overgrown. How did she stand all this heat and light? How did she get anything done when confronted by the dazzling beauty and immensity of this place?

As they climb, she tells Imelda everything, including her obsession with getting rid of Natalie and her fears about the militia nuts. She talks so fast she loses her breath; plus, all those meals in fast-food restaurants have gotten her out of shape. She feels jealous that Imelda can still climb this trail without getting winded, until she remembers that Imelda might never climb this trail again.

They reach the top and Louise collapses on a log.

"He won't ever leave her," Imelda says, swabbing her forehead with a tissue. There is something unhealthy about the way the sweat beads on her waxy skin. "People marry who they marry for a reason. Even if it's on impulse, which this marriage wasn't. If this minister of yours married a woman who's cold and judgmental, it must be because he wanted to be married to someone cold and judgmental."

Louise starts to protest that people change. Then she remembers scolding Richard for making this same claim.

Imelda draws her cupped hand along her scalp, a gesture Louise recalls from when Imelda still had hair. "It would probably terrify him to be with someone as tolerant as you. Someone who accepts his worst impulses."

Behind her sunglasses, Louise's eyes begin to water. She takes Imelda's tissue and wipes her eyes, their tears and sweat mingling. "I can't believe he'll spend the rest of his life with that woman."

Imelda pinches Louise's chin and holds her head in place so she is forced to watch her speak. "Listen up, Lulabelle. If this guy wanted to be with someone like you instead of someone like, what's her name, Natalie, he would have married a woman like you a long time ago. But then he wouldn't have been sitting around in his forties with this loser of a wife just waiting for someone terrific like you to come along and rescue him. I mean, you *are* terrific. But there are other terrific women out there. Surely in the past twenty years, if this guy had wanted to be hooked up with a terrific woman, he would have found a terrific woman to hook up with."

Louise struggles to understand the logic by which she has lost her chance to live with Ames before she even met him.

"You took a vow," Imelda says, which shocks Louise, since Imelda is the least religious person she knows. "You promised to stick by your husband until one of you is dead. Okay, he was a mess after that woman killed herself, and a worse mess after he started the fire. And now he's out in the woods with a bunch of NRA idiots and refusing to do anything around the house. That's lousy for you, and I love you, and I wish to hell you weren't going through it. But that doesn't mean you're entitled to leave. I've been a total bitch these past two years. I can't stand to look at my own chest, so I can imagine how Andrew . . . But does that give him the right to leave?"

Louise presses Imelda's hand to her cheek. "If Andrew left you, I would have to kill him. But Richard—"

"No. You and Richard took the same vow that Andrew and I took."

"Enough with this vow thing! It's like the waiver you sign when you go skiing. Everyone knows if you get hurt because the chairlift snaps or there's a pipe sticking up in the middle of the slope, you sure as hell are going to hold the resort responsible." She looks beyond Imelda to the bay, which glimmers and swells like something too magnificent for mortals like her to see. She fell in love with Ames because she wanted to share his belief that Someone is looking after her. But she refuses to accept his God if doing so requires that she honor any vow that demands she give him up.

"The fact that there's no one to enforce a vow is all the more reason you have to enforce it yourself," Imelda says. "If you find out you have skin cancer, you keep out of the sun. If this minister and his wife make you crazy, you stay away from them. You wear the emotional equivalent of sunscreen and a hat."

Louise turns and looks east. A year before, she might have seen an empty void stretching to the Atlantic; now, it's

California that doesn't seem real. Imelda in particular seems to be fading at a sickening rate. Louise reaches out and holds her. She will spend the rest of that week in California, and after Imelda's operation she will fly back to help her friend recover. But Louise's life is now in Michigan. It's as if each person carries around a portable stage, like the cardboard theater Molly and her friends played with at All Faiths Daycare. You move somewhere and set up house and unfold your stage around you. You hand around the scripts and start your drama going. And really, you can't just leave in the middle of the play. No matter how haywire the production goes, you need to stick around, finish your part, and take a bow.

She returns to Stickney Springs determined not to sleep with Ames again. Richard and Molly pick her up at the airport and drive Louise home to a dinner of barbecued chicken, corn from the Bankses' farm, biscuits, and s'mores.

"I was afraid you weren't coming back," Richard says.

Molly shrieks. "You wouldn't do that! You wouldn't leave us here and stay in California!"

She shoots him a reproving look. "No one's moving back to California. And if I ever did, sweetheart, I promise, I would be sure to take you with me." She keeps her gaze on Richard to convey that she means what she's said.

He puts the dishes in the sink. The newspaper thuds against the door. Richard goes to get it. "Isn't this your friend?" He points at a headshot of Ames on the front page of the local section. "Isn't he the one leading that petition drive Ron Lowenstine won't stop hocking me about?"

She can't look at him. "Yes. That's who it is. Do you want to come with me to the debate?"

Molly burns the roof of her mouth on a hot marshmallow,

and Richard goes to get her a glass of milk. "You go," he says while Molly drinks. "I already know where I stand on evolution."

"Yeah? And where is that?"

He assumes the accent of a backwoods preacher. "Why, *your* family might be descended from a passel of monkeys. But *my* family, yes *my* family, we know that our great-great-grandpappy was Adam hisself." He lets his jaw go slack and does a classic impression of a monkey scratching its armpit and hooting. Molly laughs madly and jumps around scratching her own armpits and hooting. Then Louise joins in, the mother monkey, hooting and scratching with them.

The next afternoon, as part of her program to be a better mother, she takes Molly to the pool in Potawatomie and stands with the other mothers up to their thighs, spreading her knees now and then to allow Molly to swim between her legs. But Ames's name keeps surfacing like a flying fish or a dolphin trapped in the little pool.

"Did you see about the debate?" asks a leggy redhead in a flowered one-piece. "My husband and I don't want some teacher telling our children that the Bible doesn't mean what it says." She grabs her son and swings him above the water. "But that Unitarian minister is so cute, if he told me the moon was made of green cheese, I just might believe him."

Another mother smiles coyly. "I give his daughter art lessons." She is a good-looking blonde carrying a baby in padded pants. It takes Louise a minute to understand she is referring to Ames's daughter Rebecca, who is something of a prodigy in art. "I'm a happily married woman." The art teacher giggles. "But I wouldn't mind giving a few lessons to the father."

It's hopeless, Louise thinks. In a town this small, even if she and Ames were to break up, she would keep hearing about him and reading about him and running into him. Women she barely knows would giddily confess their crushes on the Reverend Ames Wye. How can a person be expected to give up something other people long for, even if she already has discovered that having that thing doesn't appease her longing?

That night, she drives to the YMCA in Potawatomie to watch the debate between Ames and his opponent, who turns out to be the Reverend Solomon Stonecutter of the Joyful Noise Church. Louise sits on a folding chair and tells herself she is there to demonstrate her opposition to the teaching of creationism in the schools. But as soon as she sees Ames lope across the gym in that confident, ungainly stride, she knows she will never follow through on Imelda's advice and give him up.

It's one of those debates in which the people who come in believing a given point of view go out thinking their spokesman has made an eloquent, airtight case while the other side comes in and goes out the same way. Reverend Stonecutter is a mild man with the fuzzy round head, wide mouth, and beady eyes of a sock puppet. Reasonably, he argues that "it can't hurt a soul" if the children of Potawatomie are exposed to the possibility that God created the universe. His manner is so sincere Louise finds it doubly frightening when he starts to decry the immigration of "an increasingly numerous tribe of intolerant liberals from New York and California who want to interfere with good Christian Americans teaching their children the doctrine preached in the Bible in the schools their tax dollars pay for." The longer he speaks, the angrier she becomes. For the millionth time, she thinks of taking Molly back to California. But that would mean leaving Ames. And something bothers her about abandoning the middle of the country to the likes of the Reverend Stonecutter and his parishioners, not to mention Mike Korn and his militia. If everyone were to follow that approach, they would end up with two Americas, neither of which could tolerate, or even understand, the other.

When it is Ames's turn to speak Louise expects him to counter Stonecutter's hateful assertions. Instead, he attempts to engage the audience's sympathies by expressing his certainty that the universe hasn't come about by chance, along with his equally strong adherence to the separation of church and state. "Public schools are charged with teaching your children science. If you want them to learn religious doctrine, send them to private Christian academies," he concludes to the applause of the six or seven liberals in the audience.

Afterward, while Ames's well-wishers congratulate him on winning the debate and the Reverend Stonecutter's more numerous supporters slap him on the back for putting his opponent in his place, Ames signals Louise to wait. When the last member of his faction leaves, he gathers his papers and offers to walk her to her car.

She knows she shouldn't say yes, but how can it hurt to talk? When they are standing beside the van, moths thudding against the streetlight above their heads, he tells her that he would have had an easier time debating Stonecutter if he had managed to get some sleep in the past three weeks. "You can't believe how much I've missed you." He bats a moth from Louise's hair. "She's going away," he says, and for a moment she thinks Em's spell has worked and Natalie is divorcing him. "She's taking the girls to a Jewish retreat in Ann Arbor. I doubt you'll be able to arrange it, but this could be our only chance to spend a night together."

An eerie euphoria comes over her. Richard and Floyd will be camping up north the same night Natalie and the girls will be staying in Ann Arbor. The coincidence is stunning. She can leave Molly with Em and spend the night with Ames.

"Have you ever seen Lake Michigan?" he asks. "It won't take us long to drive up there. I know the perfect spot. We can go to the beach. Then, well, I know somewhere we can stay." He looks up and down the dark street, then leans down and kisses her. "An entire night together. We have to be grateful. He's giving us that much, at least."

But the morning of the day Louise has planned to spend with Ames, Richard says he's had a premonition that he shouldn't go on his trip with Floyd. "Why don't I tell Floyd to go by himself, and you and I can spend the day getting reacquainted?"

Louise knows she should tell him yes. The circumstances surrounding her trip with Ames are too perfect to be a coincidence. There has to be a trap, even if she can't explain who set it. "But you were so looking forward to going," she tells Richard. "There'll be plenty of time for us to get reacquainted later."

"You're sure?" he says.

Good old familiar Richard. She wants to pull him down and keep him in their bed until Molly wakes up and joins them. But a car horn honks, and Richard goes over to the window and waves. He comes back and kisses her, and Louise clings to him, as if he is the one about to betray her. Then he goes down to meet Floyd.

Louise struggles up from bed and looks out and sees Floyd with his arm draped around Richard's shoulder. She waits for Richard to toss his gear in Floyd's Isuzu, and then she remembers that the whole point of the trip is to survive without equipment. Floyd waves up at her. She ignores him and blows Richard a kiss, which he catches but doesn't blow back.

Half an hour later, Molly comes down to the kitchen, sniffling.

"My throat hurts," she whispers, so hoarse she sounds like Dolores. "My nose is all stuffed up."

Sure enough, her eyes have the heavy-lidded look any mother recognizes as the sign her child is sick. Louise presses her lips to her daughter's forehead, which feels warm but not yet hot. "You're supposed to spend the day at Em's, then have a sleepover," she says, counting on Molly's enthusiasm for spending a night with Em to overcome her desire to loll around the house and bask in her mother's sympathy.

The trick works so easily Louise wants to shoot herself out of guilt. Molly pulls off her pajamas and picks out the shirt and shorts she wants to wear that day. "Em and I are planning to set one of the kestrels free. I wouldn't want to miss that."

Louise helps Molly to pack her bag. Really, she will be no more uncomfortable at Em's house than she would be at home with her. Less, since Em and the kestrels will distract Molly from her sniffles.

Except that Em will have no way to reach Louise if Molly's cold turns worse.

Luckily, by the time Molly is eating breakfast, her eyes have regained their luster. "My throat feels okay now," she says, sipping her glass of juice. "I guess it was only dry."

Louise drops her off at Em's with her overnight bag and her burgeoning collection of Beanie Babies. She tells Em she is going to visit Janet Cohen in Ann Arbor, browse the bookstores, treat herself to dinner at a decent restaurant, and stay overnight at a nice hotel. "Yeah, well, hope you guys have a good time," Em says, and from the crooked, complicit smile, Louise knows "you guys" means "you and your married minister."

"Bye." She hugs Molly. "If Em says you behaved, I'll buy you the Beanie of your choice tomorrow."

"I always behave," Molly says, which Louise has to admit she does.

She is hurrying back to her house when Dolores comes trotting across her lawn. "There's. Something. I. Need. To. Say." She hasn't brushed her hair, and her shirt is on inside out. Louise tries to read the legend backward . . . MICHIGAN FEED AND SEED?

"Dolores," Louise says, "I'm so sorry, this isn't a good time. How about if you come over tomorrow and we'll talk then?"

Dolores puts her finger to her throat. "Tomorrow? You. Promise?"

"You come over tomorrow morning and we'll have a nice chat." Anything to go inside and get ready.

Of course, what seems like a triumph now can turn out to be a failure later. If Louise's encounter with Dolores hadn't delayed her, she might have reacted differently when she went back inside her house and found the electrician's assistant, Rod, slouched against the banister in the foyer. She might have called the cops. As it is, her only thought is how to get rid of him.

"Leave," she says. "This minute."

He wears black nylon gym pants that swish when he moves. His hair is longer than it used to be—a ponytail instead of a mullet. Louise remembers when construction workers would have beaten up a kid for wearing long hair. Now the construction workers wear ponytails. Even intolerance has its styles.

"I was in the neighborhood," Rod explains. "We're fixing the church. I didn't like the way we left things."

Left things? He seems to think they had a relationship

that ended badly. "You don't touch a woman without her permission. If you do, it's called assault, and the woman has the right to have you arrested. Which is what I plan to do if you aren't out of my house in fifteen seconds."

"I only want—" He is interrupted by a yelp. The basement door stands open, and Rod clatters down the steps. "What is it, fella?" Louise hears him say. "Did something bite you? Are you okay?" He leads his whimpering dog up the stairs, then kneels and runs his hands along Smack's belly and between his legs. "It comforts them, you know, to have their privates held." He looks up from where he crouches. "You really don't have a very high opinion of me, do you."

"Maybe if you wouldn't keep disrespecting my privacy—"

"There's privacy and there's neighborliness. There's people dropping by to make sure you didn't take offense when they overstepped the last time." He cuffs Smack on the head. "If I was you, I'd be concerned what upset my dog."

She thinks he is holding her responsible for whatever trauma the dog suffered in her basement. "Thanks. I'll look into it. And now, if you would please get out?"

He hauls the dog, nails skittering, toward the door. "I still don't see why we can't be friends," Rod says peevishly.

"Just go!" She snaps the lock behind him and races upstairs to put on makeup and a sundress. A minute later, when she hears the crunch of tires, she checks her reflection and runs downstairs and gets in Ames's Escort, and even though she suspects Dolores is watching, she leans across and kisses him.

Ordinarily, Ames might have shied away. But he appears uncharacteristically relaxed. He wears a buttery yellow shirt, jeans, and sockless loafers. "I can't believe you've never seen Lake Michigan. It's beautiful this time of year."

They pass the Bankses' farm, then Em's bungalow, and she nearly tells Ames to stop the car. She says nothing, and an hour later, when they pass the turn-off for Handsome Lake, she feels as if they are driving past the edge of the known world. She tries to think of things to say, but she can't very well reveal that Molly has come down with a cold—what kind of woman palms off a sick child on a neighbor so she can carry out a tryst with her lover? Nor is she eager to talk about her encounters with Dolores or Rod—Ames is skittish enough without giving him cause to think he has anything real to fear. Yet the silence makes her anxious. What if they get married and find nothing to say? After a while, any two people use up their best stories. Sex becomes routine. She likes to think she will always feel so lucky to be with Ames that she could never feel blasé. But what about Ames? Would he consider whatever life they might build together worth the cost?

"Why so quiet?" he says.

"I don't know. Just a little worried." It bothers her that she hasn't told him about Em's affair with Matt. Bad enough keeping secrets from her husband, but keeping secrets from her lover? "Those phone messages. Have there been any more threats?"

"A few. Why?"

"Aren't you afraid?"

He shrugs. "It's not as if those guys are really dangerous. Most of them are just . . . I don't know, lost. They think life is supposed to be lived a certain way. The husband is supposed to provide for the wife and kids. The woman looks after the children. Everyone looks up to Dad. And Dad takes his orders from . . . Well, you've got your Bible. And your Constitution. You know how to use your gun, and you've got your survival cellar stocked. And if someone comes along and tells you that the Bible is nothing but a bunch of pretty poetry, and women have as much right as men to be in charge, and it's okay for guys to ream other guys up the ass, and, oh yeah, the government has the right to come storming into your house and shoot your wife and kid, the way they did at Ruby Ridge, you get a little shaky. So you're going to hold your meetings. You're going to go out in the woods and do some drills. But that doesn't mean you're going to take pot shots at some minister."

"But a few of them . . . the Korns and the McVeighs . . ."

He shrugs again. "It wouldn't be the worst way to go."

"Don't say that." She sees herself at Ames's funeral, dissolving into grief at the back of the church while Natalie and the girls lean on relatives up front. Would she feel as stricken if Richard died? Richard is as kind a man as Ames, as valuable to the world. He is the father of her child.

"Hold on to your hat," Ames says, veering off the highway and bumping along a dirt road. He parks and they leave the car, carrying the picnic basket between them. The day is hot and clear. They reach a rise of sand that Louise has to admit rivals the dunes of Cape Cod. But how can she be so near the lake and not smell the water? And deciduous trees at the water's edge? Where are the beach plums and dune roses? Why pebbles instead of shells? It's like a description out of Molly's Mad-Libs book—the adjectives don't fit the nouns.

"Behold," Ames says, "Lake Michigan."

And truly, the lake is huge. How can this even be called a lake, if *lake* also describes the body of water on which Louise grew up? The wind whips up waves along the shore, and even though these waves are no bigger than the waves in a wave pool at an amusement park, there is something thrilling about there being waves on a lake at all.

Laughing, they race down the dune, then set up their blanket and change into bathing suits, shielding each other with a towel. They wade in the lake and Louise ducks beneath the surface. The water is warmer than the ocean in Cape Cod would be, she has to say that much for Michigan. They walk out to a deeper spot and she wraps her arms around Ames's neck. His erection presses her thigh, and she feels buoyant with happiness. He nibbles her ear. She licks the hollow in his chest, disappointed the water doesn't taste of salt.

They stumble dizzily back to shore and lay out the feast Ames has brought—roast chicken, strawberries, a wedge of Wisconsin cheddar, a bottle of chardonnay, and a bar of melting chocolate. Afterward, they stretch out and take a nap. Louise wakes first, dazed by the heat, and then lies watching Ames sleep. So what if they can't spend every day together. Why do human beings feel the need to make comparisons? Being dissatisfied with what she and Ames have is like being dissatisfied with Lake Michigan because it isn't the Atlantic Ocean.

She runs her nails down Ames's leg. His eyelashes twitch. The wind picks up. The sky turns pink. A gang of teenagers gallop down the dune rolling a beer keg.

"Come on," he says, "let's get out of here."

He hands her one end of the blanket to shake; the husks from the strawberries flutter to the sand, where they lie like tiny green crabs. Carrying the basket between them, they wade along the shore, then cross a rough wood bridge that traverses a marsh and climb a steep set of rotting steps. Above them looms a brown house with an imposing verandah. From that angle, she can't get a feel for its size, but it certainly isn't small.

"Does this belong to some friends of yours?" she asks. "What do you have, standing permission to bring your mistresses here to make out?"

When they reach the verandah, he lifts a flowerpot and removes a key.

"Whose house *is* this?" she asks again, and he holds his finger to his lips.

Inside, the house is dim and cool and smells of mice. The stairwell is lined with sepia portraits of high-busted women in front of Grecian ruins (in the shadowy light, she can't tell if the ruins are real or a studio backdrop) and mustachioed men in stiff collars standing beside roughly attired timber-crews on barges stacked with logs. Flappers in pleated dresses and handsome men in bathing costumes cavort on a beach that shows the same marsh she and Ames have just traversed. In another shot, a startled young man with glasses looks up from a picnic not much different from the one that she and Ames spread for their own lunch, except that the man in the photo is Teddy Roosevelt.

On the second floor, Ames pushes open the door to a room that holds nothing except a bed. Being in someone else's house makes the very act of touching him seem a trespass. That, and his refusal to speak. He peels off her bathing suit, but when Louise tries to pull down his trunks, he pushes away her hand. Instead, he lays her on the bed, the ticking coarse beneath her skin. He runs his finger along her breast. "You have no idea how beautiful you are." He stands looking down at her, and she sees herself as Ames must see her, splayed across that bed with her breasts rising toward him, the jutting angularity of her ribs, the blonde well-tended topiary between her thighs, the long expanse of legs.

Then he is on top of her, pushing into her as deeply as he can, not bothering to acknowledge who she is, not even bothering to kiss her. Only after he finishes does he say her name—"Louise?" Then he kneels between her legs and goes down on her, and she whimpers and comes. There is something of a wedding night about it, some sort of consummation. It is almost as if there should be a crowd of peasants cheering beneath the window, wishing them long lives, shouting for an heir.

They lie there a long while. The bed smells so strongly of mice Louise wonders if the creatures might have made their nest inside the mattress. A ship sounds its foghorn. At some point, she realizes Ames has fallen asleep. She slips out of bed, feels her way along the banister beneath the portraits of his disapproving ancestors, and goes outside on the verandah. It's later than she thought. The stars have come out and are doubled in the lake. *Two infinities added together still make one infinity.* She knew the Wyes were rich, but she hadn't guessed they once owned half the timber in the state. It seems no less dishonest for a rich person to pretend to be middle class than for a poor person to pretend to be wealthy. But how can she be angry at a man who wants so fervently to make up for what his ancestors have destroyed? Think of all the good she and Ames might do with his family's money, and how ironic it would be if poor Louise Heinz, who grew up in a dilapidated bungalow on an algae-covered lake in upstate New York, should end up in a mansion above one of the world's largest inland seas. She sees Molly and Ames's daughters playing on this beach while she and Ames sit on this verandah, watching. What more could anyone want than that?

She goes back upstairs, folds Ames in her arms, and kisses him awake. "So," she says, "the house is really yours?"

"I suppose it is," he admits groggily.

"You *suppose*?"

He seems embarrassed. "This was my grandfather's house. He lived in Chicago, but he had a summer home here and he kept a yacht in Harbor Springs. He was a very rich man, and he was a very terrible man. He's the one person in this world I try most not to be like."

"So this is *his* house?"

Ames shakes his head. "He's dead, thank God. My mother won't step foot on the grounds. There's a caretaker who looks in on the place. I come up now and then with Natalie and the girls. But no one ever stays here."

She starts to say how happy she is that he has brought her there, but Ames interrupts to confess that he can't follow through on their plan to spend the night. "It isn't you. It definitely isn't you. There are just too many ghosts."

She might argue against driving back home so late, but she isn't sure she wants to sleep in this beautiful, awful house any more than Ames does. The night is turning chilly. She is worried about her daughter.

Ames gathers their damp suits and puts these in the basket. He hasn't put on his shirt, and his belt hangs from only two loops. "My God," he says, "I love you so much. Maybe I can find a way . . ." She thinks he might lie back down with her, but instead he zips his pants, buckles his belt, and puts back on his shoes. They go downstairs and let themselves out. Ames replaces the key beneath the flowerpot.

"Careful." He helps her down the steps and across the marsh. They walk back through the woods, which are alive now with rustling and scraping. She realizes they have left the picnic basket at the house. Oh well. Let the mice make a feast of the leftover bread. Ames can pick it up the next time he drives up here.

They stop for dinner at an elegant old hotel in Petoskey, the perfume and aftershave of earlier generations of rich Detroiters and Chicagoans still so redolent she imagines she is dining with Ames's great-grandparents and the elegantly mustachioed Theodore Roosevelt. She waits for Ames to suggest they take a room upstairs. But he doesn't bring up the subject, and Louise is too tired and confused to ask.

They don't get back to Stickney Springs until well after one. As they pass the bungalow, she thinks of stopping to ask how Molly is but doesn't want to wake Em. Ames pulls over across from the Bankses' farm. "There's a light on in your house," he says. And sure enough, Louise can just make out a glow in the basement. Something must have gone wrong on the survival trip, although she can't imagine what disaster might have interrupted an outing whose purpose was to endure whatever needed to be endured. She tells Ames it's a good thing they didn't stay longer. As it is, she will need to lie to Richard about where she has been so late. She leans over to kiss Ames goodbye, but he seizes her and holds on. "I love you," he says. "I'm sorry I'm so bad at all of this. I wish to God I knew how to make things right."

She gets out and he drives away. Later, she will think that she might have covered the distance sooner if she hadn't been preoccupied with thinking up an alibi. She is nearly to the porch before she sees that the glow in the basement isn't coming from a bulb. Strands of smoke thread from beneath the door, and she is stupefied by fear that someone needs saving. But Molly is at Em's house, and Richard's Corolla isn't here. When he set that fire in Colorado, he and Louise tried to put out the flames before they understood that they weren't in control, the fire was. But the entire time they were running away, she'd had the crazy urge to lie down and give in to the forces of destruction she had been fleeing her entire life.

Later, she will find it difficult to explain why she didn't simply run next door and rouse the Bankses. But she doesn't consider any possibility except running to Em's house and assuring herself that Molly is safe. She makes it the entire way without stopping to catch her breath, then jams the doorbell again and again, dumbly reading and rereading the sign: PLEASE BRING BIRDS AROUND BACK. She bangs with both fists, and Em opens the door and stands there blinking; Matt towers behind her, a colossus of hairy flesh in tight black briefs. "My house is on fire," Louise says, and then stands there as if her only purpose in waking them was to impart this information.

"What about Matzo Ball?" Molly asks, poking her head between Matt's bulky hips and Em's muscular legs.

Louise starts to say she doesn't know, but Matt pushes Em aside and takes off down the road. "I'll call 4-1-1," Em yells as Louise races after Matt.

By now, smoke streams from beneath the front door. "Where do you keep the bunny?" Matt demands, and Louise looks at him and is so shocked by all that luminous flesh, the briefs stretched lewdly across his genitals, she can't find the presence of mind to say he mustn't even think of risking his life to save a rabbit.

"Is it in the cellar?" he asks again.

"No," she says, "in the mudroom," thinking only to save him from running down the steps to that smoke-filled basement.

Matt rushes up to the porch, throws open the door, and jerks back as if someone has flung water in his face. He takes several deep breaths, his chest swelling and deflating—he reminds Louise of the Big Bad Wolf preparing to blow down her house—then lunges inside. She screams and almost runs in after him. Why isn't she thinking more clearly? If Matt was determined to save Molly's pet, he could have run around the back and snatched the rabbit from the mudroom.

Em comes up, leading a frightened Molly.

"Where's Dad?" Molly screams. "Where's Dad?"

"He's fine, sweetheart. He isn't here." Molly's lips are blue. She looks feverish and small; Louise kneels to hold her, but Molly struggles free.

"Where's Matt?" she screams. "Where's Matzo Ball?"

Louise can't meet Em's eyes. Why didn't she stop him?

They wait for what seems an impossibly long time before Louise sees him coming around the back of the house. He must have gone straight through the front of the house to the mudroom and out the back door. He hobbles closer, coughing into one enormous fist, the rabbit hanging limp from his other hand.

So many things happen at once that later she can't separate them in her memory. The flashing lights from the fire trucks, the flames shooting up through the roof, men in yellow suits strapping tanks on their backs and tugging hoses across the lawn. A paramedic throws a blanket around Matt and makes him sit on the bumper of the ambulance with an oxygen mask around his face. Someone takes the flaccid rabbit from Matt's hand and, in a gesture that strikes Louise as idiotic beyond measure, passes it to Molly, as if Matzo Ball were a sooty beanbag toy.

The confusion is indescribable. Em is the only person with the presence of mind to find a blanket for Molly and hold her on her lap, which leads everyone to assume she must be Molly's mother. A Volkswagen Beetle drives up and—of all people—Howie Drucker and Jack Lovecraft unfold their giant, sloppy selves from the front seat. They shuffle Louise off to one side, asking how the fire started and is there anything they can do to help. She recalls that Jack's hobby is listening to the scanner.

"Come on, Lou, cheer up," Howie cajoles. "You didn't want to have to clean such a big house anyway."

"You can take the insurance," Jack points out, "and you can use it to buy a condo downtown and become urban pioneers like us."

Sparks explode through the roof as if someone were setting off fireworks in the living room. The firefighters climb a ladder to put these out.

"I hate to bring out the heavy guns," Howie says, "but have you heard the joke about the two gay firefighters who go in this house to put out a fire and get caught butt-fucking in the bedroom? The chief barges in and says . . ."

The joke doesn't strike Louise as the least bit funny. But something is so absurd about standing in her yard being told stupid gay firefighter jokes by Howie Drucker while Matt Banks sucks oxygen from an ambulance and her daughter cradles a dead rabbit named Matzo Ball that she can't help but crack up. Maybe she is in shock, but once she starts laughing, she can't stop.

"Hey," Howie says, "I should have tried that one on Ames."

By the time the fire marshal comes over, he has more than enough reason to mistrust Louise, not least of which is that he has just seen her laughing hysterically while her house burns down. "Ma'am," he says, "I was wondering if you could tell me how this happened."

He is older than she is, so the deference seems forced. He has stiff black hair swept up in a ducktail and stands tapping one white shoe as if he were the handsomest teenager at the sock hop, an impression reinforced by the flowered shirt and Bermuda shorts he wears. With his left hand, he jiggles the change in his pocket; in his right hand he holds a cigarette, thumb on the bottom and four fingers spread along the top as if he is playing the coronet. "Would you mind coming with me, ma'am? Over here?" He leads her to his car and holds open the passenger door before getting in the other side. They sit at opposite ends of the seat like teenagers on a date. "Ma'am, if you don't mind, would you tell me again how you found the house?"

She almost confesses—not to setting the fire, which it becomes increasingly clear the fire marshal believes she did, but to having an affair. If she doesn't come clean about this one detail, it will muddy everything else. But she needs to think of Ames. And the more questions the fire marshal asks—about the puzzling relationships that seem to join Matt and Em and Molly and Louise, about her husband's absence, about the two boisterous men who have shown up at the house and caused Louise to laugh, about the overheard word "insurance"—the more defensive Louise becomes. By the time he broaches the subject of Richard's previous arrest for arson—where was it, Colorado?—she feels dangerous with rage. How could the fire marshal in a jerkwater town like Stickney Springs get information about a previous arrest so quickly? How could he believe that her mild-mannered husband liked to set things on fire?

"Ma'am? Can you explain to me why your neighbor Mr. Banks there would run in a burning house and open the front and back doors the way he did? You do know the blaze might have been contained if Mr. Banks hadn't done exactly the one thing assured to feed the fire oxygen."

"But I told him not to go in." She points to Molly, who sits huddled in Em's lap with the dead rabbit in her arms. "Mr. Banks likes to see himself as a hero. He ran in to save my daughter's pet."

The fire marshal plucks the cigarette from his lips and flicks it out the window, as if one more fire can hardly matter. "That's difficult to comprehend, that a man would risk his life to save a rabbit. A dog, maybe. A lot of people run back inside to save their dogs. But I find it hard to think that Mr. Banks would do what he did to save a rabbit. As opposed to, say, a dog."

A dog. Rod's neurotic Rottweiler. It can't be a coincidence that she caught Rod lurking in her house the day it caught fire. She remembers him going down to the basement. He could have fiddled with the wiring or doused a rag with kerosene.

He could have seen Louise drive by the church, then walked back to the house and set the fire.

With the smoke and the flashing lights and her inability to distinguish which part of her fears are true and which are no more real than the conspiracy theories the militia crackpots weave, she feels as if the fire marshal's car is filling with lethal gas. She reaches for the door, afraid to find it locked. But the handle turns and she stumbles out. The acrid stench—the inspectors will tell her later that cyanide, asbestos, and other toxic fumes were released by the burning house—scratches her esophagus until she retches and vomits up the whitefish dinner she had with Ames.

"Here." The fire marshal hands her his handkerchief, which she uses to wipe her lips. She offers to give it back, but he makes a motion that she should keep it.

"I think I know who started the fire," Louise tells him.

"Someone started it?" He puts a wad of gum in his mouth and chews it with a full, open-mouthed chew. "The fire didn't start itself?"

She tries to tell him about Rod groping her on the day of the bombing and his return to her house that very day, but the fire marshal keeps interrupting to ask why she didn't call the police either time, and where she was earlier that evening, and with whom, and who might have seen her there.

"I don't want to say anything else." She walks away, daring him to arrest her.

He takes her by the arm. "I certainly understand you might not want to tell me more right now. You'll want to take your little girl somewhere warm. There will be plenty of opportunities for you and I to speak. The inspectors will be doing their work, and we'll be able to discuss what they find."

She twists from his grip. The inspectors won't find any

traces of her afternoon with Ames. And even if they do turn up evidence of arson, that can't incriminate her, can it? The investigation will no doubt show that the fire was started by a burned-out fuse or a faulty socket or the electrician's shoddy work. Even if she left on an appliance, they can't arrest her for that.

"Ma'am, I need to ask where you'll be staying. We could notify the Red Cross and see what they have available."

She looks back at the house. Most of the flames have been extinguished. The roof and walls are still intact. But the windows have all been smashed, and there is soot and water everywhere.

"Come. Home. With. Us." Dolores stands beside Em and Molly in a threadbare white nightgown. Her white hair stands up around her head, and in the weird glow from the fire, she looks like someone's dead grandmother. "We. Have. Extra. Room."

Louise can't shake the sense that she is being asked to give in to an enemy she is no longer strong enough to fight. If Em told Matt about her affair with Ames, who knows what Matt and his mother might have come up with to punish her. Otherwise, how could Matt have been stupid enough to open both doors and feed the blaze? Maybe Floyd lured Richard on the survival trip so Matt could stay home and set the fire. Em could have assured the Bankses that Molly was safe with her.

She thanks Dolores but tells her that she and Molly had better get used to staying at a hotel. There's a Comfort Inn in Potawatomie. That way, Richard can be near his job.

Then she thinks: *Richard.* She feels a crushing wave of sympathy. "Can someone please make sure my husband knows where to find us?"

The fire marshal says he will be *sure* to speak to Louise's husband. Does she see those men over there, the ones bringing in the generators to run some lights? Those are the inspectors. They will be working at the house for the rest of the night and the following day. They will certainly tell Mr. Shapiro where she is.

"Are you sure you ought to be driving?" Em asks.

"I'll be fine. It's just . . ." She points to the dead rabbit in Molly's lap.

"Sweetie," Em says, "why don't you let Em have the bunny and we'll bury him in the bird cemetery. You know, where we buried Harvey the Hawk?"

Sleepily, Molly offers up Matzo Ball. "He's dead," she murmurs, as if to explain why she is giving up her pet. Louise lifts Molly clumsily, still wrapped as she is in Em's funky quilt, and carries her to the van, making sure everyone sees she is buckling her daughter safely in her harness before she waves and drives off as carefully as a drunk who knows the cops are watching.

No one is behind the desk at the Comfort Inn, so Louise presses a buzzer, and a sleepy Indian woman in a pink sari emerges from the back. Louise rents a room at a weekly rate, wondering vaguely how many weeks it might be before they get their insurance check and are able to rebuild the house. Or before Richard finds out where she really was that day. Or before she is arrested for arson.

She lays Molly on the bed closer to the bathroom, as if to protect her from whatever danger might come hurtling through the window above the other bed, then sinks to the floor and cries. Molly could have been inside the house when the fire started. The heat and fumes might have killed her. Louise lies on the sour-smelling carpet for the rest of the night, enumerating the disasters she has just evaded, willing the sun to rise, and wondering if a person's subconscious might be strong enough to cause her to leave a stove on without remembering that she left it on. Maybe God is punishing her for being so ungrateful as to wish in a careless moment that her house might burn down. Or He is as literal-minded as Molly and actually believes that He has rewarded her by granting that thoughtless and offhand prayer.

ELEVEN

WHEN FLOYD TOLD RICHARD WHAT TO BRING ON THEIR survival trip, he said: "T-shirt. Jeans. A good pair of boots." Which certainly was a contrast to the wealth of high-tech equipment Richard and Louise used to carry when they went hiking in California. Richard feels so light he could fly. The day is sunny and warm; even if he and Floyd find little to eat or drink for the next thirty-six hours, they will suffer little worse than mild discomfort.

If anything, Richard wishes the day might be cooler. Floyd drove them north for four hours, then, once they left the highway, he took so many unmarked turns that Richard has no idea where they are. Within minutes of leaving Floyd's Isuzu, Richard is sweating copiously. Usually, mosquitoes don't attack until dusk. Today, they start drilling the moment Richard and Floyd hit the trail. Not only does Richard tend to attract more mosquitoes than anyone else, he reacts more violently to their bites. Without his usual dose of DEET, he is soon tearing away at lumps as hard and red as the sour-cherry candies his grandmother used to serve when Richard and his family came to see her.

Around noon, Floyd stops and holds up his hand. "Behold Nature's grocery store," he says theatrically, sweeping his arm to indicate a clearing that seems devoid of anything the least bit edible. It thrills Richard that Floyd knows where nutritive treasures might be found, as if Floyd might snap his fingers and a flying carpet laden with delicious food would hover into view.

Floyd points to a thicket clotted with dark red berries. "Okay, partner, start picking," he says, and, reaching to pluck his first handful, Richard gouges his arms so savagely he nearly yelps. He pops the first berries in his mouth in the hope their sweetness will make the pain worthwhile. But they are so bitter and hard, it's all he can do not to spit them in his hand. The rest of lunch consists of wild onions and the root of a yellow weed Floyd consumes with gusto but Richard finds so woody and dry he can barely choke down a bite.

Floyd swipes the dirt from his lips and says that in another few hours, they will make it to a lake where they can take a quick swim and set up camp and go shopping for a real dinner. "By which I mean meat," he says.

The entire drive north, Floyd painted an idyllic picture of the lake. According to Floyd, the water there is cool and clear, and a pure, icy spring bubbles from the ground a few feet from the shore. Floyd and a bunch of pals chipped in and bought the land, and no one, not the DNR, the EPA, or the SPCA, can tell them what to do with it. The guys go hunting in the woods, in and out of season. They hold training camps and paintball wars. They drive here to get away from their wives and girlfriends and swim buck-naked in the pond, build a fire and grill some steaks and sit around shooting the shit and drinking beer.

But when Richard and Floyd finally reach the lake, it turns out to be a scummy, dank mud-hole. The mosquitoes swarm so thickly that Richard sucks a few up his nose with every breath. Already he feels feverish from the bites.

"Would you look at that," Floyd marvels. "Haven't been here in a while. Could be the drought. Or the runoff. I read where weeds grow that way because of a chemical in detergent. Or something the farmers put in the fertilizer. The entire planet is going to end up one big stinking cesspool and no one gives a darn."

This is when Richard's opinion of Floyd begins to shift. What's to keep people from turning the planet into a cesspool if not the intervention of the very government Floyd and his friends despise? Does Floyd think the manufacturers of detergents and fertilizers will suddenly become so appalled by the damage their products are inflicting that they piously refuse to sell them? Will housewives stop using phosphates? Will farmers forgo more plentiful crops to save the country's lakes? Then again, maybe the reason he is annoyed is that Floyd promised him a refreshing swim and an icy drink, and this lake will deliver neither.

The spring turns out to be a muddy damp spot beside a rock. Richard cups his hands against the moss for minutes and gets only a few grit-filled drops. By then, it is five or six o'clock and his stomach is cramped like a fist.

"Don't worry." Floyd lays his hand on Richard's sweaty back.

"Nature's grocery store is open twenty-four seven." From one of his many pockets Floyd produces a length of rubber inner-tube. He shows Richard how to stretch the rubber across the prongs of a forked stick, fit a pebble against the band, pull it back, and shoot a squirrel. Floyd brings down five of the little beasts and Richard wounds one, which Floyd finishes off by crushing its skull beneath his boot.

"Bet your dad and uncle would have eaten the brains and guts," Floyd says respectfully, and Richard nods. He was raised on stories of his father and uncle chasing down and eating rabbits in the forests of Upper Silesia, where they were hiding from the Nazis. "And these were not the puny creatures you have here in America," his father used to remind him, words that come back to Richard every time he sees his daughter's runty pet. "These were giant Polish hares, jump fast as kangaroos." As a boy, Richard pictured his diminutive, sloe-eyed father racing after a kangaroo-sized rabbit and wrestling it to the ground. In his teens, Richard learned that most of the animals his father and uncle ate were victims of German trucks barreling down the roads that crossed the forest, but this didn't diminish his admiration, because he also found out his father and uncle had been so scared of German patrols that they ate their road kill raw. After that, every time Richard saw a dead rabbit or a raccoon lying dead beside the road, he imagined ripping off the skin and sinking his teeth into the slimy, cold flesh. After five weeks in the woods, Richard's father and uncle convinced a sympathetic Polish schoolteacher to hide them in his cloakroom. But the stories Richard heard about his father's weeks in the forest outside Pszczyna did more to shape his character than anything else. Why else had he agreed to come on this crappy camping trip with Floyd if not to prove that if the Nazis ever came to Michigan, he could survive on the raw flesh of rodents?

Louise equates Floyd with the Nazis, but whenever Richard tells Floyd about his father's trials in the Polish woods, Floyd puts himself in Richard's father's place. "That's why we've got to be on our guard," Floyd said. "You never know when your government will go bad or some Communist invaders are going to round you up. The citizens who survive are the ones who don't obey the orders to turn in their guns or report to the trains and camps."

After Floyd guts and flays the squirrels, he spears their bodies on pointed sticks. The red flesh glistens wetly. Flies pick their way delicately across the meat—to keep them off, Floyd builds a ring of stones, lays the sticks inside, and covers them with large, flat rocks. "Shopping's done," he says. "Time to put up our house."

That's the most fun Richard has, helping Floyd build their shelter. It's like building a fort with the older brother Richard never had. First, Floyd uses his knife to strip a long, thick branch; then he wedges one end in the crook of an upright oak and jams the other end in the ground. The two men strip an entire stack of thinner branches, which Floyd leans against the longer, thicker pole to form a triangular lean-to tall enough to enter standing up. If they intended to spend a longer time, Floyd says, they would daub the surface with mud and let it dry. As it is, they weave leafy branches in and out of the larger sticks. The branches would provide good camo, Floyd says, in case an enemy were in pursuit, which no enemy happens to be, but you can never be too sure. Finally, Floyd shows Richard how to lay the floor. "You sure as heck don't want to be sleeping on bare dirt. The cold and damp would seep right through you." As Richard cushions their bower with leaves, he can't help but think how good the squirrel meat will taste, hot and grilled and rubbed with salt.

"Okay, buddy," Floyd says, "now you get a lesson few other

men will be fortunate enough to get: Floyd Goodman's Life-Saving Lesson on How to Build a Fire."

Richard wonders if Floyd is making a reference to the Jack London story, in which an arrogant loner freezes to death because he overestimates his ability to light a fire in the snow, but Floyd shows no signs of self-mockery. He spends the greater part of an hour instructing Richard on how to stack the twigs and moss so the fire will burn its brightest, and then he surprises Richard by pulling out a lighter and setting the stack ablaze.

"I thought this was a survival trip," Richard says. "I thought you would, I don't know, rub two sticks together."

"This isn't the friggin' Boy Scouts," Floyd scoffs. "If worst comes to worst," he can light a fire without a match. But what self-respecting warrior takes to the woods without a lighter? The sun is going down, and Richard's sweat makes him shiver. The mosquitoes won't let up. He is hungrier than he has ever been in his life and isn't about to argue against anything that might bring him food.

But as the fire flares, Richard catches his breath. As recently as the Tax Blast, the smell of smoke kindled a foreboding so strong he cringed. Sometimes it seems he hasn't taken a single deep breath since he set his match to that stove in Colorado.

The image comes back to him, the valve open too wide, the flames jetting up too high, the sere brown needles popping into flame. The fire was his fault. He isn't glossing over that. But no one, thank God, got killed. The forest will grow new trees. Accidents happen. It's as simple as that—*accidents happen*. He arranged this trip with Floyd not as a way of overcoming his fear of starting another fire but as a test of his success in getting over the vanity that of everyone alive, only he, Richard Shapiro, isn't entitled to make mistakes.

He moves closer to the fire. Except for their missing heads, the squirrels still resemble squirrels, legs and paws extended as if Floyd had speared them up the ass while they were fleeing. But the scent of their roasting flesh is so tantalizing Richard can barely wait until Floyd hands him a stick.

"Here you go. Compliments of the chef."

Richard takes a bite and scorches his tongue. The meat is so sour and difficult to chew he could be gnawing the inner-tube from Floyd's slingshot. Worse, his mouth is so dry that clods of meat keep getting stuck in his throat. He barely can get down half of one squirrel before he quits.

"You had enough?" Floyd motions with his thick jaw at the last two sticks. "I was thinking we ought to save those two in case we don't catch any fish for breakfast."

Richard nods, though he is still edgy with hunger. A mosquito stabs his shin while a second drills the pulsing flesh below one ear.

"The little suckers are chewing you up pretty bad," Floyd says sympathetically. Then, before Richard can say anything, he disappears into the woods and returns with a handful of oily, hairy leaves he advises Richard to rub across "the afflicted areas." Richard waits for the cure to work, but he might as well have rubbed toilet paper across his skin. A mosquito gets lost in his ear, filling his head with its frenzied whine.

"What I don't get is why mosquitoes bite white people more than they bite the colored," Floyd says. "Is it the difference in body odor? Or is it something in the blood?" He flicks a mosquito from his wrist. "I thought Jews would get bit somewhere in between white people and colored people. But you're getting bit worse than I am."

The mosquito in Richard's ear escapes or dies, silencing its whine.

"Good thing you're not a homosexual," Floyd says, laughing.

"If one of these little suckers took a sip from you and then shot it into me, I'd be a goner."

Wearily, Richard explains that AIDS can't be transmitted by mosquitoes. For months, he has been enjoying his discovery that a man's man like Floyd might actually value whatever information a runty Jewish intellectual like Richard might have to share. But all he feels now is anger. He came on this trip to prove he could have survived the Holocaust by hiding in the forest. But it occurs to him that if he had been living in Upper Silesia when the Nazis came marching in, he wouldn't have bothered hiding. He would have tried to slime his way out of the concentration camps by sucking up to attractive, stupid, bigoted Aryans like Floyd Goodman.

He plucks a fern and tosses it in the fire, where it withers to a charred skeleton. "So," he says. "Floyd. You never did tell me about this Jewish ancestor of yours."

Floyd busies himself removing a cigarette from his vest. He draws a brand from the fire and lifts it to the cigarette, which, Richard sees, is thick and loosely rolled. Floyd takes a very deep drag and holds the smoke in his lungs. When he lets it out, the sweetly intoxicating odor confirms Richard's suspicion. Floyd offers him the joint, and Richard, laughing, puts it to his lips. Floyd Goodman smokes pot? Well, that makes a distorted kind of sense. Floyd doesn't want the government interfering with his basic right to smoke a blunt. Richard keeps thinking Floyd and Matt are stalwart Christians, when in point of fact they behave like teenage boys who don't want their parents telling them what to do.

He takes a hit, praying he won't cough, and is glad to discover that his lungs are as resilient now as they used to be in grad school. He hands the joint back to Floyd, who pinches it between his massive fingers, inhales another long drag, and then lets out the smoke with a satisfied hiss. "Richard, when

I said I had a Jewish ancestor, I wasn't speaking in a personal connotation. I was referring to Father Adam and Mother Eve."

Richard starts to say that Adam and Eve weren't Jews. Not until Moses received the Ten Commandments did an identifiable Jewish people emerge. But he is too lethargic and hungry and high to care. Too bad Floyd doesn't have an actual Jewish relative. It would give Richard the same bemused delight as when he read that Elvis Presley's grandmother on his mother's side was Jewish. Not that Ira Rosenkrantz had appreciated that tidbit of genealogical information. Not that Rosenkrantz hadn't threatened to smash in Richard's head if he mentioned that bullshit "fact" again.

Floyd passes the joint to Richard, who hesitates before taking another toke. He isn't sure why. He doesn't need to drive anywhere. Molly isn't about to walk in on him smoking a joint in the middle of the woods. Maybe the dope will take the edge off his misery. Then again, it might only make him hungrier. Best to keep his wits. Although Floyd is in charge, isn't he? Isn't Floyd looking out for his safety?

"As an Aryan," Floyd goes on, "I'm descended from Adam and Eve. That is, I'm descended from Abel, their son. As a Jew, you're descended from Eve's mating with Satan. You remember how the serpent seduced her? That's how Cain was born. Cain was the Devil's spawn."

Richard knows the pot has taken hold because he has to spend a ridiculously long time figuring out how Abel could have left descendants if he was dead. Oh, right, he must have produced a son or daughter *before* his brother whacked him. Or he'd had a son *and* a daughter, because how else could his descendants have had descendants? Unless one of Cain's offspring had messed around with Abel's kid.

He turns to Floyd, eager to discuss the ironies of the

human race descending from a brother having sex with his sister or a murderer's child mating with his victim's survivor, but he is stopped by the vacant expression on Floyd's genial face. Before Richard met Louise, he'd had a girlfriend named LeAnne, who was strikingly beautiful in a classic *shiksa* way. LeAnne so rarely said anything that Richard was able to persuade himself she was smarter than she was. That is, until he took her to see *Last Tango in Paris*. Looking at her sideways by the projector's light, he realized that LeAnne didn't have a clue what the movie was about. After that, he could no longer sustain the illusion that he loved her. He hadn't thought of LeAnne in years. He was only thinking about her now because he felt the same way about Floyd.

"You see, Richard." Floyd plucks a shred of pot from his bottom lip. "The Bible doesn't come right out and say it, but if you read between the lines you can see that Cain's descendants had no morals. Abel's sons and daughters were the true Israelites. Fair haired. Fair skinned. They could blush, and if someone can blush, it indicates that he or she has a sense of shame. Abel's sons and daughters became the thirteen tribes of Israel, and one of the members of one of those tribes gave birth to King David, who, after a whole lot of generations, gave birth to Jesus Christ. Christians are the true Israelites. The people we think of today as Jews are the counterfeit Israelites, spurred by jealousy to bring down the *true* chosen people, by which I mean the white Christian Aryan race."

Richard is so high he listens good-naturedly as Floyd goes on describing the complicated machinations by which Satan tried to lure the Aryan descendants of Adam and Eve into entering into carnal relations with the dark-skinned, kinky-haired descendants of Cain and the even darker, kinkier-haired children of Enosh, the race we now know as Negroes.

All this intermixing kept polluting the blood of the true Israelites, who eventually became the Europeans, except that after Europe had been thoroughly polluted by the descendants of Cain, a few representatives of each of the thirteen tribes sailed to the New Jerusalem, where each of these thirteen tribes started one of the thirteen colonies. Unfortunately, the descendants of Cain and Enosh followed the Israelites to America and resumed their fiendish tricks here.

On and on Floyd goes, mouthing all the old calumnies about the international cartel of Jewish bankers who plunged the world into a Depression and then duped Congress into setting up the Federal Reserve and passing the blatantly unconstitutional income tax, by which the government could steal billions of dollars from honest Christian taxpayers and loan the money to hardworking Midwestern farmers like Floyd's and Matt's dads, then jack up the interest rates and keep prices for commodities artificially low so they could foreclose on all those farms. Law by illegal law, the Communists and Jews were destroying the United States, primarily by legalizing the murder of innocent Christian fetuses and allowing the kinky-haired, dark-skinned sons of Enosh to intermarry with the fair-haired, blushing daughters of Eve, but also by hiring homosexuals to teach in the public schools and adopt babies who would otherwise grow up to be heterosexual Christians. In these ways and others, the children of Enosh and Cain are steadily tearing down the only Christian white republic the world has ever known.

Richard wonders if he is hallucinating. Maybe the suspicions that Louise planted in his brain have inspired him to invent Floyd's anti-Semitic rant. In any event, he feels too muddle-headed to argue. The best he can do is to take issue with one of Floyd's facts. "Uh, Floyd, there are only twelve tribes of Israel."

"What?" Floyd sucks a clumsy final hit from the roach; from where Richard sits, it looks as if Floyd is sucking on his thumb.

"You said thirteen. If there were only twelve tribes, the Israelites couldn't have founded the thirteen colonies."

"You sure? Only twelve?" The confusion on Floyd's face is almost endearing. Can it be that all it took for Floyd's moronic cosmogony to crumble was Richard pointing out one error at its base? He feels the same surge of pride he used to feel when he overtook some strapping blond runner on the last hill of a cross-country meet.

"It's bullshit, Floyd. Everything you said . . . not one word of it is true."

"Not even the part about the bankers?"

He wants to tell Floyd that until recently a Jew couldn't have gotten a job in the banking industry unless he bought the bank. There are a few big European Jewish banking-houses like the Rothschilds'. And brash young Jews like Ivan Boesky have bullied their way into the lower echelons of a financial community that shuddered at their entrance. But it's better not to give Floyd too much information. "Sorry, Floyd. All of it . . . a total crock."

Floyd flips the roach in the fire and sits staring at the sky. There are very few stars, only a pinkish smudge where someone seems to have used a dirty eraser to rub out the moon. Floyd shakes his head and looks back at Richard like a kid who bought the answers to a test, only to discover the answers don't fit the questions. "That's what Matt said. Especially the part about the spaceships."

Richard lets out a chirp of incredulity. "Spaceships? You've got to be kidding."

"No, I am *not* kidding. The way I heard the story was that the Jews fought on Lucifer's side, and Lucifer lost, and he and his minions got kicked out of Heaven, but the angels, instead of letting them fall to their deaths, pleaded with God to spare them, and God said, Oh, all right, and He let the angels furnish Lucifer with these heavenly spaceships, then sent them down to earth and gave them a second chance, which Lucifer and his cronies used to seduce poor Eve." Floyd regards Richard hopefully, as if Richard might yet give in and say sure, that sounds reasonable.

"Jews are aliens? But you said we're Satan's spawn. Or are we both? Do you want to see my horns and tail? Because Floyd, I hate to break this to you, I don't have any appendages you don't have. I'm not a devil out of Hell, and I didn't come from outer space. The only way I'm different from you is that I'm missing the tip of my dick."

Floyd gives an embarrassed shrug. "Actually, I'm missing mine, too. My mom thought it was cleaner that way."

Richard struggles to his feet. "Why did you tell me all that crap, Floyd? Didn't you think I would get upset being told I'm descended from the Devil and responsible for just about every evil deed the world has ever known?" He has never seen the top of Floyd's head and is amazed to find a bald spot the size of a silver dollar. This seems even more significant than the fact that Floyd is circumcised.

"Heck, Rich, you're not exactly an international banker, if you don't mind my saying. How could you be a banker? You work at the prison. You live next door to Matt. I mean, all bankers may be Jews, but not all Jews are bankers." Floyd smiles broadly, pleased that he has topped Richard at his own game. "Besides, no matter what a person is, he can change. If the end of the world comes, anyone who's with us is with us, is the way I look at it."

The idea hits Richard that Floyd and the other guys haven't accepted him as a Jew but have been hoping to convert him.

Maybe the point of this survival trip was to lead him deep into the woods with Floyd, get him high as a kite—*high as a kike*, he thinks, giggling—and convert him to Christianity. He looks down at Floyd, who is looking up at him like a golden lab that wants to be petted. Maybe Floyd gets a thrill in being with a Jew. Maybe he is attracted to what frightens him the most.

Maybe Richard is as well.

"I'm all done in," Floyd says, struggling to his feet. "Don't forget to put out the fire," and Richard wonders if Floyd is getting back at him by reminding him about the accident in Colorado. But the reminder sounds more like something a middle-aged housewife might say to her husband as she heads up to bed.

"Will do," Richard says. Floyd lumbers off and takes a piss—Richard can hear the brittle patter of Floyd's urine on the leaves—after which he offers Richard an evergreen twig. "Good for brushing your teeth," Floyd says, swishing a branch around his own mouth and spitting. Then he takes off his boots, sets them before the entrance to the lean-to, and wriggles in feet-first until only the top of his balding head is visible.

Richard remains beside the fire, trying to clear his mind. Getting in the lean-to with Floyd strikes him as obscene. But the air has turned clammy, and he has no desire to sleep outside. He has been headed here for months, to this small patch of nothingness in the middle of nowhere. There are no appliances to fix; no one is asking him to make an appointment with the dentist or replace the grouting in the shower. But a longing overcomes him to be back with his wife in their comfortable, warm, clean house, a longing so strong he jumps up, as if even in the dark he might find his way back. *Louise!* he nearly cries out. *Please, sweetheart, come and find me and take me home.*

From the shelter comes the murmur of Floyd's even breathing. Richard wants to put out the fire. He supposes he could find his way to the lake and dump some mucky ooze on the embers. Instead, he unzips his jeans. With as little as he has drunk all day, he doubts he has much pee in his bladder, but his cock might be a firehose, that's how plentiful the stream that bursts forth is. *Take that*, he thinks, *and that*, pissing on the remaining squirrels. Better to starve than eat leftover squirrel meat for breakfast. He doesn't bother to brush his teeth. Let Floyd get a whiff of some truly Satanic Jew-breath.

He does take off his boots before slithering in next to Floyd, who smells pleasantly of marijuana. The fact that Floyd isn't Louise makes Richard so bereft it's all he can do not to wrap his arms around the guy. Louise is having an affair. At least, Richard is fairly sure she is having an affair. He isn't sure with whom. Probably someone she met at school or that AIDS Coalition she volunteers for. Maybe Howie Drucker isn't as gay as everyone assumes he is. Or the minister isn't as holier than thou as Lowenstine seems to think. Or maybe *Lowenstine* is screwing Richard's wife, which, come to think of it, is the only possibility that makes him angry enough to consider getting even.

Well, it doesn't matter who it is. What matters is that Richard has known for months and he hasn't stopped her. Why hasn't he? So he won't need to feel like a shit for falling in love with Sophie Pang, or for making Louise move to Michigan and take care of Molly and fix the house while he gets to play James Bond? He will need to tell Louise he doesn't really blame her for screwing around. Maybe they can have that second kid. If the test shows the fetus is damaged, well, they'll need to talk things out. If she wants to move back to California, he'll agree to move back with her. Although he hopes they can stay in Michigan so he can keep working at the prison.

Wherever they end up, there will be therapy for all three of them, especially Molly. The idea makes him tired—finding three good therapists, paying for all those sessions, talking and talking. But that's the deal you make. At least, it's the deal you make if you're a liberal New York Jew. Instead of believing your problems are caused by a conspiracy of bankers in league with Satan and Trotsky and putting your trust in Smith and Wesson to set things right, you attribute your problems to a conspiracy of your parents and your unconscious and put your trust in Sigmund Freud.

When dawn comes, Richard and Floyd crawl from their shelter as grumpy as any married couple that knows their romance has long since given way to irritation. Floyd kicks the sodden kindling. "You piss on this?" He uses his boot to nudge the squirrels. "Guess you didn't like my cooking."

Richard makes a dismissive motion with his head. "Didn't exactly have any water to put it out with."

"Suit yourself." Floyd unspools a length of filament from another pocket, then extracts a metal barb and marches off toward the pond. Richard debates building a fire, but Floyd has the lighter. Besides, he barely has time to collect the wood before Floyd comes back carrying a string of whiskered catfish. If Floyd had gone to the corner store, he couldn't have brought breakfast any sooner.

Floyd skewers the fish and sets them cooking. The eyes bubble and pop; the rubbery brown skin crinkles above the flames. Richard feels delirious with the smell, but some convoluted spite prevents him from eating.

They hike back in silence. Later, when they stop for gas,

Richard makes sure to pay. Floyd has been generous enough to drive, and he doesn't want Floyd to think that Jews are cheap. After the tank is full, he and Floyd bicker about whether to stop for lunch. Floyd wants to go inside the restaurant and eat, but Richard wants to get back on the highway.

They compromise by buying take-out. Richard tries not to faint from the greasy, enticing smell of Floyd's burger or the sound of Floyd slurping his cold, sweet, milky drink. Oddly, the closer they get to home the more petulant Floyd becomes. He reminds Richard of a woman who understands that her squabbles with her lover have not only ruined their vacation but ended their affair. "What did I do wrong?" Floyd asks plaintively. "Did I say something that offended you? Or was it the pot? There's nothing in the Bible about smoking pot. But maybe I got stoned and said something I shouldn't have? I'm sorry you didn't have a good time. I'm sorry the pond dried up."

He offers everything he can think of to make amends, and his cluelessness softens Richard. "Floyd," he says, "you can't just go around telling people they're Satan's spawn and not expect them to be upset. I didn't come here on a spaceship. I'm as human as you or Matt."

"I knew it!" Floyd slaps the wheel. "It was that crud about the spaceship!"

Richard is famished and has a headache. They pass the Bankses' farm. The night before, Richard assumed from what Floyd said that Matt didn't buy his anti-Semitic bullshit. Now he wonders if Matt just disagrees with some minor points.

Then they pull up to his house. If nothing had been left but ruins, he wouldn't have needed so long to understand what must have happened. But the house is basically intact, so he is out of Floyd's truck and halfway up the walk before he has taken in that half the roof is missing. Most of the windows have been smashed or blown out. The front door hangs by a hinge. Charred rugs and singed drywall, installed a few weeks earlier, have been tossed in the yard. Gingerly, he steps inside, where the floor is covered by muddy boot-prints and a paste of damp ash. The notion that he went to the woods to overcome his fear of fire, only to return home to find his house burned down, strikes Richard as so crazy he starts to laugh. The laughter makes him lightheaded, and he puts his hands on his knees to keep from passing out.

"Your family certainly has an unusual way of reacting to a fire."

Richard looks up to see a man in Bermuda shorts and a flowered shirt smoking a cigarette. "I didn't know there was a usual way to react," Richard says.

"Let's just say most people don't laugh. They get home, they see their house has burned down, they tend to make inquiries about their loved ones."

"What are you saying?" Richard's head spins and his stomach heaves. "Are you saying my wife is hurt? What happened to my daughter?" He wobbles so badly he nearly pitches forward. The smell of smoke hits him, and the squirrel meat rises in his throat. *Molly?* he thinks *Louise?* He never acknowledged how lucky he was the first time. He hadn't stopped to think how much worse it could have been.

"Now, that's a bit more the usual reaction." The man tosses down his cigarette, right there on the floor in Richard's house. "Of course, most people don't need quite so much prompting."

The man's smirk seems intolerable. "If you don't tell me what happened to my family—"

"Whoa, whoa. Your wife and little girl are safe. They're staying at a motel. Only problem is, I don't think I quite remember the *name* of that motel." The man jingles some change in his pocket. He has the thinnest legs of any man Richard has ever seen. A man with legs that thin shouldn't be wearing shorts. "Then again, the name might come back to me. If you don't mind chatting with me a while."

They're safe. Molly and Louise are safe. So why won't this awful man tell him where they are? "Are you the police? Would you mind telling me what happened to my house?"

"It looks to me like it burned down, is what happened. The question is *how* your house burned down. Which is my job to ascertain. I'm the fire marshal. Marcus Kiss."

Floyd lumbers up the porch. Richard thinks maybe this Marcus Kiss knows Floyd, and Richard will get a few points for being Floyd's friend. But the two men have never met. Floyd introduces himself and Kiss nods and shakes Floyd's hand, but he immediately turns back to Richard. "So, where did you say you were last evening?"

Richard's knees buckle. Floyd grabs him on one side and Kiss grabs him on the other side and they support him down the steps. He bends double and tries to keep down his dinner. He notices that Louise's yellow flowers have been trampled. "Floyd and I were camping. We were . . . I don't know exactly where we were, but Floyd does."

Floyd seems reluctant to say much of anything.

"Come on, Floyd. Tell him where we were."

The fire marshal regards Floyd intently. "You with this gentleman? Camping? But you can't tell me where?"

Floyd draws his hand along his jaw. "We were camping. I prefer not to specify the location."

The fire marshal looks disgusted with them both. "I'm afraid you'll have to come up with a better alibi than that."

"Are you insinuating I had anything to do with my own house burning down?" Richard asks.

"It's my job to inquire into the nature of suspicious blazes. And you happen to fit the profile of a homeowner who might set fire to his own dwelling."

"And what profile is that?"

The man has a peculiar way of holding a cigarette. This irks Richard, as does the man's propensity for chewing gum with his mouth open—*you're chewing like a cow,* his mother would have said. The man chews and smokes, surveying Richard's house as if its smoldering remains provide a clue to the cause of its destruction. "The profile of someone who buys a house for a heck of a lot more money than it's worth, then puts in a heck of a lot more money to fix it up, then finds out he and his wife aren't happy living where they're living, except that now they can't sell the house because no one will pay what they paid for it, let alone what they want after they put in sixty or eighty grand, so the only way this guy can get back his investment is to burn the place down, collect the insurance, and move back where he came from."

Richard struggles to clear his head. Doesn't his inability to understand the crime prove he couldn't have committed it?

"And to be honest, some classifications of people have a higher incidence of arson than other classifications of people."

Richard's head begins to clear. "By which you mean?"

The man tosses down his second cigarette in what once was Louise's flowerbed. "Someone's business isn't going too well, an Italian might hire someone of his own persuasion to blow it up or burn it down."

"And Jews? Are Jews another of these arson-happy classifications?" Richard turns his face sideways and taps his nose. "Isn't this the profile you really mean?"

The fire marshal smirks and primps his ducktail. Floyd is staring at Richard's profile so openly that Richard fights the urge to punch him. But he knows Floyd won't go down as easily as Barney Sipp.

"All I'm saying is that people who already have a record

of burning down one thing might be likely to burn down something else."

Richard has spent a long time beating himself up for burning down that forest in Colorado. But it's like being stupid or fat; you can make fun of yourself, but no one else has the right. "That was an accident," he says quietly.

"Oh?" The fire marshal's eyebrows creep up. "And this wasn't?"

He looks back at the house. Where had Louise been while he and Floyd were in the woods? Where was Molly when the fire started?

The fire marshal turns to Floyd. "Mr. Goodman, was Mr. Shapiro with you last night or not? Are you able to account for his whereabouts all the time you and he were on this camping trip?"

Floyd looks like a girl to whom it has just occurred that the reason for her boyfriend's coldness is that he has been sneaking off with some other girl. "I went to bed kind of early. Rich stayed up alone." Richard can tell from Floyd's expression that he is calculating whether Richard had the time to jog twenty miles back to Floyd's Trooper, hot-wire it, drive to Stickney Springs, set fire to his house, then drive and hike back. "Uh, no," Floyd says. "He couldn't have done it."

The fire marshal acts as if Floyd has been raising his hopes only to disappoint them. "Mr. Shapiro, I'm sure you are eager to reunite with your wife and daughter. As I said, they're staying at the Comfort Inn in Potawatomie. After our inspectors analyze their data, we'll be in touch. Your insurance company will want to send their own investigators to determine the fire's cause."

All Richard wants to do is find Louise and Molly. He wants to take a shower and get some sleep. "Fine," he says, "you do that," not sure if this is an appropriate rejoinder to anything that came before. He takes one last look at Floyd, wondering if Floyd might be the clannish, conniving person Louise has taken him to be, the person Richard himself took Floyd to be the night before. But the longer he stares, the less qualified he feels to judge. He only knows that Floyd is studying him in much the same way.

TWELVE

AMES LOOKS DOWN AT THE STACK OF TWO-BY-FOURS AND thinks of all the ways he might make a clown of himself by carrying them. If he doesn't grasp the planks at their exact center of equilibrium, they will fan out like pick-up-sticks and slip from his fumbling, gloved hands. Worse, there is the Laurel and Hardy maneuver of misjudging your turning radius and whapping some bystander in the gut. Even if he makes it across the crowded yard to the sawhorses where Myrna Cott mans the electric saw, he might forget the measurements he is supposed to give her. The idea that petite, freckled Myrna has the wherewithal to operate a power saw without his own cringing fear of slicing off a finger reduces him to the awkward self-loathing he entered the ministry to avoid.

As usual, his fear of humiliation drives him to do what needs to be done. He stoops and wraps his hands around the boards and carries them across the yard.

"Hey there, your holiness." Myrna flips up her goggles and wears them like a tiara on her sleekly bobbed head. She takes the wood from Ames's arms, leaving him chastened and relieved, as he used to feel when Natalie took Ann or Bec and pressed the squalling infant to her breast. "You got the numbers on these boards?"

He is about to panic when he remembers that he hasn't trusted them to his memory. He fishes out the scrap on which Jim Blankentrip jotted in greasy pencil the dimensions to which the planks need to be cut.

"Doesn't it give you a really good feeling to see everyone work together?" Myrna asks in her warmhearted liberal lesbian way. She gestures with her goggled head at the frame of the house they are building. A dozen middle-aged men and women in T-shirts, jeans, and work boots are occupied around the site. Another five or six are readying refreshments beneath a tree. The effect is so charmingly disordered it brings tears to Ames's eyes. Myrna is right. It is a miracle that human beings have evolved to the point where they feel compelled to join their talents to dig the foundation of a house, erect a frame, add a roof, insert pipes and wire conduits to bring in electricity and whisk away the sewage, all so Donna Small and her diabetic mother and two asthmatic sons might have a decent place to live.

"Just goes to show what a bunch of like-minded individuals can accomplish," he says to Myrna. This comes out sounding like a platitude, but he does admire the way everyone is chipping in.

"Hey, Rev!"

Ames shades his eyes and looks up. Balanced on a corner of the frame stands beefy, red-faced Jim Blankentrip, whom Ames has put in charge of directing the volunteers. Like a crazed Captain Ahab, Blankentrip points down at Ames and bellows: "Quit yakking and get those boards cut! You're holding up the works."

Ames salutes to acknowledge that aye-aye, Captain, he is steaming full-speed ahead; a minister might outrank a construction worker on the Potawatomie social ladder, but on this particular ship, the Reverend Ames Wye is nothing but a swab with clumsy hands. Blankentrip is a minor tyrant, but he knows how to get things done. Thank God for Baptists. Unitarians are crackerjack at organizing interfaith cooperation. But you can't beat a Baptist for knowing how to read a blueprint or wield a nail gun.

He hands the boards to Myrna, who snaps her goggles in place and slides a two-by-four beneath the saw. Ames checks his watch. Louise was supposed to meet him here at ten and it's already a quarter past one. He hasn't talked to her since their outing to the lake. Clearly, something is wrong. After he dropped her off, he passed a sleepless night, then called Louise as early as was proper, but no one picked up. He thought of driving to Stickney Springs in the hope of catching her outside, but they had made plans to meet here and he doubted she would use her anger at him to punish poor Donna Small.

Myrna finishes sawing the boards and hands them to Ames. "There you go." She smiles a pixyish smile that makes him remind himself it's a sexist fantasy that a lesbian only needs the right man to make love to her. He settles the load between his arms and starts back to where Blankentrip is waiting. The ground is treacherous with empty pallets and trodden drinking cups. A moat twenty feet deep runs around the foundation, with a few planks as a bridge. He hadn't considered how precarious this would be, crossing a springy board with an armload of lumber. If he falls, he will find himself twenty feet down in a muddy hole with a bundle of two-by-fours avalanched on top of him. Louise thinks he's brave for standing up to the right-wing nutcases in Potawatomie, but it's the risk of looking foolish that makes him quail.

He closes his eyes and crosses the plank, then maneuvers cautiously through the crowded interior of the house until he stands before Jim Blankentrip.

"What'd you do, Rev, go out and chop the trees yourself?"

Ames leans the two-by-fours against a wall. If this weren't an act of charity, Blankentrip would have asked, "What took you the fuck so long?" But religion is the guard that Jim Blankentrip has erected against his temper. Ames long ago decided that for most people Christianity is a defense against some unpleasant aspect of their personality. He stands idly while Blankentrip consults another man and then comes back and hands Ames a second scrap of paper on which he has jotted the dimensions of the next set of boards. Ames heads back across the bridge; without the two-by-fours, the crossing isn't hard.

He hears a car drive up and turns eagerly, hoping to see Louise. But it's Howie Drucker's Beetle. Howie gets out of the car, goes over to the saw, and taps Myrna on the back; she stops the saw and looks up, then squeals and hugs Howie— she barely reaches his ribs—and hands the goggles and gloves to him. Ames picks up another load of planks and carries them to Howie, who stinks of cigarettes, which strikes Ames as odd, given that Howie doesn't smoke.

He prepares for whatever joke Howie might tell. Not that he minds. Louise thinks Howie is a pest. She has no notion of Ames's gratitude for Howie's willingness to play out the courtly formality of the joke. For the length of time it takes Howie to tell the build-up, Ames needs to do nothing but tilt his head and look at Howie with a friendly yet suspicious smile, as if he expects the joke to be terrible but doesn't care because Howie is his friend. And when Howie delivers the punch line, all Ames needs to do is groan and punch Howie on the arm (isn't that why they call it a punch line?).

The rules that govern such interactions differ little from the rules of male companionship Ames learned in seventh grade. The rejoinder to any joke is required to have something to do with sex, which in Howie's case is gay sex, but the pattern remains the same. Even a guilt-ridden boy like Ames, with a case of acne so severe his cheeks resembled the puckered rubber mats on the locker-room floor, could figure out the rules for responding to a joke. And a minister in his forties who is supposed to be adept at conversation can fall back on those same rules whenever the need arises. A person never outgrows his younger self. He only accretes older selves around it. Ames has some secondhand sense that he is attractive to women now and that other men look up to him. But he feels none of this in his bones. One of the reasons he became a minister is that the rituals of the job are so rigidly defined. He never needs to return to those terrifying days when the slightest gesture—carrying his books, swinging a hockey stick or a bat—left him queasy with uncertainty.

When all six boards are cut, Howie lays them in Ames's arms but doesn't release the load. The men stand holding the wood between them. "Ames, you know, I make these stupid jokes . . . but you and Louise . . . without people like you and Louise . . . What if she moves back to California? We can't let that happen."

Tears rise in Ames's eyes, but he doesn't have a free hand to wipe them away. "Thanks. I'll see what I can do. But really now, the wood . . ."

Howie lets go of the lumber and Ames staggers beneath the weight. He carries the boards to the house, closes his eyes, and crosses the bridge, then delivers the wood to Blankentrip and stands there numbly, awaiting his next assignment. Blankentrip consults a clipboard and nudges Ames in the direction of one of the volunteers. "Why don't you work with . . ." He squints at the woman's name, which is written on a slash of masking tape across her shirt. "Why don't you let Trudy here show you how to brace these struts."

Ames pulls off his glove, wipes his palm on his khakis, and offers his hand to Trudy. She is heavier than Louise but five or ten years younger. A Polish girl. Catholic. A member of St. Francis or Sweetest Heart.

"Trudy Wisniewski." She takes his hand and lifts it knuckles-first, the way a Catholic might greet the pope. "I can't say I'm much of an expert on bracing struts. I just have a dad who does construction, and four older brothers, so I picked up what they taught me," a generous touch to spare his pride, or whatever shred of it is left. Ames is hardly the Jimmy Carter of the Habitat for Humanity crowd. More like the Mike Dukakis. Then again, where could he have learned to brace a strut? If his mother needed a repair, she called a servant. The faculty at Exeter hardly taught shop. And he couldn't have picked up much about building techniques while living in his grandfather's penthouse on Lake Shore Drive. Earlier in the day, Blankentrip informed Ames that he was holding his hammer wrong; apparently, Ames grips the handle too close to the head and taps it instead of swinging it. What kind of man can't use a hammer properly? Thank goodness it's blonde, buxom Trudy Wisniewski teaching him to brace a strut instead of that asshole Blankentrip.

"Here, you see this, Father?"

"Reverend."

"Sure. I'm sorry. Reverend."

"Better yet, call me Ames."

She brushes a wisp of hair from her face, which is so bright and open it reminds him of the fake gold coins that come with his daughter's board games. Trudy isn't as pretty as Louise, but just imagining her without that Michigan Wolverines T-shirt leads Ames to fall a little bit in love.

"You put the two-by-four like this. So it's sort of, what's it called, horizontal? Or is it vertical I mean?"

"Diagonal, I think."

She laughs a brassy laugh, like nails falling in a can. "Sure. Diagonal. You put it diagonal to these other boards, and you stick the nail like this."

She reaches above her head to bang a nail, and that's when it happens. From Ames's position by her knees, she seems to be lassoed by her wrists to the boards behind her. And that image of Trudy Wisniewski with her head thrown back to expose her creamy throat, the bottom of her shirt rising to reveal a luxurious expanse of belly, coincides so exactly with his memory of a photo from one of his grandfather's magazines that a trap door might have opened and dropped him into that other realm in which he is a fourteen-year-old boy hunched in the hollow beneath his grandfather's desk, marveling at the image of a young blonde woman lassoed to a cross of dark wood that seemed to Ames to come directly from one of his grandfather's forests. The woman's plush round breasts seemed to rise up off the page, so unnervingly white that Ames couldn't help but cover them with his thumb. Below the narrow waist and jutting pelvis, she wore a silky slip pulled so low it exposed everything but the part Ames wanted most to see, which forced him to imagine nudging the slip-thing down her legs, which were cocked against the boards behind her in much the same way that Christ's equally feminine legs were cocked against *His* cross.

Even as a boy it had bothered Ames that his resplendently tailored and impeccably polite grandfather liked to see women suffer. The old man's power and position, coupled with the desperate poverty of not a few young women who lived in the Chicago slums and the rural expanses of northern Michigan, had given him the means to satisfy his desires, a story Ames came to learn when he was removed from his grandfather's care and returned to his mother because the old man was facing charges for doping a cleaning lady's chocolates and performing certain unmentionable acts on her nearly unconscious form.

Thankfully, Ames has inherited none of his grandfather's predilections toward seeing women suffer. But even in his youth he understood that he was destined to have a hard time curbing his desires. His vision on that bridge across the Charles revealed to him that a life in the ministry would provide fewer temptations than a life in the theater or the self-indulgent indolence that generations of Wyes before him had pursued.

And Natalie. As soon as Ames met her, he knew that Natalie would never allow herself to be one of those compliant, naked women spread across the pages of his grandfather's magazines. There was a place inside his wife that seemed tantalizingly beyond anyone's reach. In the first days of their marriage, Ames had seen Natalie plunge her arms inside a pillowcase, turn it inside out, grab the corners of the pillow, and flip the case so the pillow was inside. That's what he wanted to do with Natalie—flip her inside-out and tongue the moist, secret recesses of her heart.

And at the beginning, Natalie had wanted to be flipped inside out. She had never had an orgasm. No one had taken the time or care to make Natalie come! Ames had remedied this omission, and Natalie had seemed shaken to her core. Not that her gratitude translated into reciprocal concern for *his* orgasms. But he couldn't help but hope that someday it might. Besides, it seemed petty not to marry a woman because she wouldn't give him oral sex. He was working toward his divinity degree. Not getting a blowjob from his wife hardly seemed important. Only when Natalie grew distant and cold, and later, when she wouldn't let him touch her two weeks of every month, only then did he feel the lack. And not only the lack of sex. She used to care what he said and did. She didn't act supremely bored when he talked about his work. She had their daughters to keep her occupied, and her responsibilities directing All Faiths Daycare, and her computer business, and her religion, which, because it had so many more rules than Ames's religion, seemed more deserving of respect.

So yes, of course, he was foolish not to marry someone like Louise, who cares about the same things he cares about and likes sex as much as he likes it. The trouble is that even with Louise, after he has come, he wants to come again. Unless a person wastes his entire life in bed, he will always feel dissatisfied. What if, after hurting Natalie and the girls, Ames were to end up with an easy, companionable life with Louise, which is pretty much what he has with Natalie? Or a *worse* marriage? What if Louise isn't as enamored of him close up, day to day, as she is driving with him to Handsome Lake a few times a month? How can she be so sure that she will be any happier with him than she is with her current husband? And there's something else about Louise. She wants to be taken care of. She wants to be led. She wants Ames to be her minister as much as she wants him to be her lover.

And—what Louise doesn't understand—if he turns all his attention to her, if he achieves the satisfaction with her that he hasn't achieved with Natalie, what will be his motive for continuing to do good? He knows it doesn't make sense— nothing about religion makes sense—but his passion for doing good is in some bizarre way an equal and opposite reaction to his inclination for being bad. And he wants to keep doing good. It's difficult for a man like him, but deep in his heart, he really and truly does want to do some good on this planet.

By now he has missed the entirety of Trudy Wisniewski's demonstration of how to nail a strut, but he bravely plucks a nail from his apron, positions a two-by-four at a slant, and prepares to hammer the board in place. He hits the nail at a funny angle and it bends, which causes the two-by-four to swing out from the frame, hang for an instant, and then clatter to the floor. He jumps back and manages not to curse. Everyone turns to look.

"Happens to me all the time," Trudy says gallantly. "You can't fit the hammer in such a small space. You have to hold it upside down." She walks back to him, face shining with concern. "Why don't you finish the struts I started, and I'll do the ones that are so hard to get the nails in."

He smiles to show Trudy he doesn't take this as an insult. He accepts the easier task, hammering extra nails at the bottoms of the boards Trudy has fastened at the top. After an hour, they take a break. Ames allows Trudy to cross the moat before him, partly out of courtesy and partly so he can watch her backside shift as she places one foot before the other on the plank.

Emerging from the shade of the half-finished house, he feels the brunt of the sun. His skin reeks. His tongue is dry. At a table in the shade, he and Trudy find a stack of paper cones and fill these with lemonade. There are apples and homemade muffins.

"Tastes pretty good, huh, Rev? The reward for a good day's labor." This comes from Myrna Cott's girlfriend, Mitch, who has the sort of endearingly handsome Amelia Earhart face Ames finds irresistible.

"This is about the only honest work I've ever done," he confesses.

Mitch hitches up her tool belt. "It's a relief to see there's something you're not so good at." Her smile makes him grateful to be maladroit. He is trying to think of something clever to say—it strikes him as sweet that a lesbian who was christened Michelle should have taken the nickname Mitch—when Howie comes over and tells him another joke. Unfortunately, he is still thinking about Mitch and doesn't hear a word Howie says.

"I'd better get some new material," Howie tells Ames. "That one didn't make Louise laugh either. She's going to need a lot of cheering up. Talk about a string of bad luck."

Ames's first thought is that she has been diagnosed with cancer. He isn't sure how this could have happened in the two days since he saw her. Unless she had known all along that she was sick. "What happened to Louise?"

Howie looks at him incredulously. "Her house burned down. Didn't you know?"

"That's impossible." He says this before he realizes that a) Howie will want to know *why* it's impossible that Louise's house has burned down, and b) the house might have caught fire after he dropped her off, and c) the house might have been burning when he left her, since, like the spineless prick he is, he hadn't seen her to her door. "Did anyone . . . Where was Louise when the fire started?"

"Hey, take it easy. No one got hurt. The little girl was

sleeping at a friend's house. And Louise's husband . . . Do we even believe Louise *has* a husband? Has anybody ever glimpsed hide or hair of that guy? I'll tell you, if I were straight and Louise were my wife, I wouldn't be off in the woods with some other man."

Blankentrip yells down to them that the refreshment break is over, and the other volunteers put aside their lemonade, fill their aprons with nails, and return to whatever tasks they've been assigned. Howie saunters over to the electric saw and snaps the goggles across his glasses, which makes his eyes seem even fishier than usual. He positions a board beneath the saw, and Ames grabs his wrist—Ames has a hideous moment when he realizes he could have caused Howie's hand to swerve beneath the blade. "Do you know where she is?"

Howie shouts above the teeth-softening whine of the machine. "A hotel. In Potawatomie. I don't remember which one."

She hasn't been hurt. *Thank you, dear Jesus.* How could he have borne it, seeing Louise in pain? Or—he knows he shouldn't care—hideously deformed by scars? Where is she? He has to talk to her. There aren't many hotels in Potawatomie. Maybe he can stop by each of them to check.

That's when Louise's Voyager drives up. Howie stops his saw as Louise walks across the site and crumples against Ames's chest. Ames tells himself it's perfectly reasonable for her to be here. She signed up to work on the house—he has been looking forward for months to spending an afternoon watching her do the sorts of things with planks and nails he has seen Trudy Wisniewski do. But he remains as stiff and unyielding as the two-by-fours he has just finished nailing to the house.

He glances at the van and is puzzled to see Molly's face pressed to a window. He is wondering whether to advise Louise not to leave Molly in the hot car when she extricates herself from his embrace and takes a step back. She looks as if she hasn't slept in weeks. Her color seems dead, her hair stringy and dull, although this only makes his compassion go out to her more. She smells the way the fireplace in his grandfather's library used to smell.

"I have to talk to you," she says, and his heart goes nuts. He hates himself for caring more about his reputation than his lover's house burning down. So what if they hugged. People hug him all the time. Louise's philosophy makes sense—if a pair of lovers act as if they have nothing to hide, people won't think to search for whatever they might be hiding.

"The fire department thinks we set it. They know about Richard—that forest he set fire to. They think we set fire to our own house to collect the insurance."

A selfish relief washes over him; he has never done anything so inept as setting fire to a forest. He glances at Howie and Mitch, who are pretending not to watch. The sun beats on his head. He looks at the waxy paper cone still in his hand

"I was so shaky about telling the fire chief where I was, he started to suspect I had something to hide." She brushes an oily clump of hair from her face, then looks back at the van and motions to Molly that she won't be much longer. "Maybe it would best if you and I confess."

He closes his eyes to keep the scenery from quivering. When he opens them, she is studying his face. He wants to tell her that he will confess where they were the night of the fire and do whatever he needs to do to relieve the trouble she's in. He wants to move out of his house and live with her. Why should other men get to live with women who love and desire them while he has to keep living with a woman who recoils from his approach and finds his concerns trivial and imprudent? But if he owns up to this affair, not only will he lose his job, he will go down as yet another male Wye who has proved himself corrupt. If he confesses, the shame is certain; if he keeps quiet, it might yet be avoided.

"I wish I could," he says. She crumples a bit, as if he has just punched her in the gut. "Later, I mean. If there isn't any other way. But for now I think we should wait and see. What's the saying, you lie and I'll swear to it?"

He tries to act at ease, but the mere act of saying the word *lie* causes his head to throb. Louise says she will respect his wishes and continue telling everyone that after dropping Molly at Em's she drove to Ann Arbor for the evening. Unless the fire marshal comes up with someone who saw them at the beach, how can he disprove her claim?

"That's the best plan," Ames says. "I'm sorry I can't . . . But if you need need anything, food or clothes or furniture—"

She shakes her head. "Richard talked to the salvage company. They said they ought to be able to save some of our things. He rented us an apartment. It's a dump, but we only need to stay there until the insurance comes through."

Molly finds the horn and honks it. Louise tells Ames the name of the apartment complex where she and Richard are staying. "We don't have a phone, but if you need to tell me anything, you can stop by. I'm usually out back, watching the kids. You wouldn't believe the way some people let their children . . . Never mind, I'll tell you about it later."

As she walks across the construction site, Ames understands that the woman he loves most in the world is driving off and he will never sleep with her again. He wants to run after her and tell her that he will do whatever he can do to make her happy, but his feet won't move. He might as well have fallen in that muddy pit with the lumber piled on top of him, that's how helpless he feels to save anyone he loves, or even to save himself.

THIRTEEN

THE LAGOON OF LOST CHILDREN. THAT'S HOW LOUISE THINKS of it, a shimmering expanse of blacktop enclosed by the dispiriting tan brick façade of Meadowbrook Estates. To enter the lagoon, you turn off the main strip a half-mile past the prison and drive between the cracked plaster deer that stand to either side of buildings 1 and 6; then you try to find a space in the chaotic, unlined lot where the tenants park their cars. No one designed this blacktop as a playground. The tenants' kids were meant to play in a broken-fenced corral that looks like a pen for hogs. The enclosure must once have held sand but now contains crusted dirt, ground glass, cigarette butts, and dog shit; the equipment consists of a rusty metal slide with sharp edges, a concrete sewer-pipe tall enough for Molly to stand in, and a stack of tractor-sized tires bound to the ground with chains.

Molly and a pear-shaped, bespectacled black boy named Devone are climbing the wrong way up the slide. Hunched as inchworms, they crawl up a few feet and skid back down. A dozen other kids wander among the cars. Children as young as six mind toddlers who can barely walk. Louise so rarely sees another parent she might be living out her dream in which a nuclear explosion has orphaned Molly's friends. Maybe the other mothers occasionally glance out the rear windows of their apartments. But Louise has seen a child of seven or eight lose her temper at her younger brother and knock him to the ground; the boy sat weeping in the middle of the lot until, in desperation, his sister grabbed his feet and dragged him to the curb. Louise ought to notify Child Welfare. She is a social worker, isn't she? But she is too weary and dazed to call. Doesn't she have her own troubles? Didn't her house burn down? And she doesn't welcome the prospect of being known as the lady who sicced the cops on a bunch of single mothers doing their best to mind their kids and keep their jobs.

She narrows her attention to Molly and Devone. Molly stands at the top of the slide with Devone crouched between her legs. Louise checks to see if any adults are watching. Louise doubts anyone would object to sweet, plump Devone crouching between a white girl's legs. But what if someone does?

"Ma'am?" Devone calls out. "Would you mind holding my glasses? I'm afraid, if I go down, the glasses'll get broke and my mom'll have to pay for new ones." Louise reaches up and takes the delicate silver frames from his doughy hand. "Okay, girl," he cries to Molly, "this train is leaving the station!" and she settles in behind him, looping her arms around his shoulders and nestling her cheek against his neck, so much smaller than Devone that she resembles his backpack.

He lets go and down they slide. Devone lands face down in the dirt and Molly tumbles over his head, underpants flashing. Like kittens in a litter box, they shriek and paw at each other while Louise tries to make sure they don't roll too near the broken glass. She can't figure out why the older boys don't tease Devone for playing with a girl, unless he already has put himself so far outside the bounds of normal male life that the other boys would no more bother to beat him up than they would bother to beat up a mouse.

"Mom?" Molly calls. "Do you have those Beanie guys I gave you?"

Louise takes a stuffed unicorn and a stuffed lobster from her bag, and Molly and Devone sit in the dirt and act out a series of melodramas involving Molly's hapless animals and their rescue by Devone's action figures, which are modeled on the hulking wrestlers he loves watching on TV. The day Richard and Louise and Molly moved in, Louise got out of the van and looked around and her spirits sank even lower than they were. But Molly was ecstatic. "Look at all the kids!" she cried, and within minutes she was playing tag with a bunch of girls in the middle of the lot. Richard carried up their few belongings while Louise stayed to watch Molly. The only other parent was a young black woman in a polyester business suit who stood watching as her son sent wrestler after wrestler plummeting down the slide. Molly came racing back, red faced, panting. "They never even bothered to try to tag me," she said sorrowfully.

"Me neither," the woman's son told Molly. And that was all it took. Molly slumped in the sand beside him. He handed her a plastic wrestler whose muscled arms reminded Louise with a homesick pang of Matt Banks.

"Devone, honey, you share," the boy's mother admonished him, an injunction clearly issued for Louise's benefit, since Devone already had given Molly half his toys. "Did you just move in?" the woman asked. "Guess I'm the greeting committee." She held out her hand. "I'm LaShawnda Stevens. What brings you folks to the Nobody But Jesus Loves Me Apartments?"

"Our house burned down," Louise explained, and suddenly the extent of her loss became real. She and Richard had sold their house in California and moved to Michigan and bought another house and fixed it up, and just as the work was done, *that* house had burned down. The heat had melted Molly's baby pictures into fantastically twisted celluloid shapes. The lopsided flowerpot Imelda sculpted as a birthday gift for Louise in seventh grade lay in so many shards that the only piece worth saving was a jagged fragment on which Imelda had carved Louise's name.

LaShawnda touched her arm. "Nothing worse than your house burning down. You poor woman, losing everything."

And out it all came, everything Louise had gone through since moving to Stickney Springs, omitting only her affair with Ames. LaShawnda shook her head. "Stickney Springs!" she clucked. *She* wouldn't live in Stickney Springs for a million dollars. "Back when I was a little girl in elementary school," she told Louise, "I had the nicest teacher, a Miss Julia Davies. She invited our class to her parents' farm. It was just over the border into Stickney—you know, when you cross those tracks? Miss Davies rented a school bus to drive us out. We were walking from the bus to the farm and someone went by and yelled out something terrible about the little—" She inclined her head toward Devone and Molly. "I won't repeat the word. You know the word I mean without my having to say it."

They talked a while, and then LaShawnda called out to Devone not to touch the nasty cigarette butts. "I've been down on my luck with illness, but now that I'm back on my feet, I'm going to save up to buy a condominium. You know that nice area out by Wal-mart? They have condominiums, duplexes, big brick houses, all in the same development. I could buy a condominium and you could buy one of those big brick houses and the kids could keep playing together. Shame to separate two kids get to be such good playmates so quick."

Even if you took the fire into account, Louise and Richard and Molly were so much better off than LaShawnda and Devone that Louise felt embarrassed that LaShawnda should be comforting *her*. LaShawnda's apparent lack of bitterness and her desire that their children grow up together moved Louise to tears. After that, they saw each other often, usually as LaShawnda was dashing out, tying a scarf around her head and trying to get to the hospital in time for her shift as an admissions clerk, or racing back to the apartment after her shift was done. Because it was the summer and Devone wasn't in school, LaShawnda had to rely on a complicated system of babysitters and relatives to watch him. Louise helped her fill in the gaps, caring for Devone while LaShawnda did the laundry or ran out to pick up groceries.

"Devone, baby!" LaShawnda calls out now from the back entrance of their building—the Shapiros' apartment is on the third floor and LaShawnda's is in the basement; she pays a cheaper rent, but the windows barely let in any light, and after a heavy rain the sewage system backs up. "Dinnertime, Devone!"

Ruefully, Molly unburies the wrestlers to whom she and Devone have given a heroes' funeral. Louise hands Devone his glasses, which he settles on his nose as carefully as a professor. Then he runs off to eat.

Louise leads Molly up the stairs. The building stinks of rotted food, the same smell that used to gag Louise when she opened her parents' refrigerator as a kid, and the wallpaper in the stairwell is mottled by mold. Her guess is that no one has vacuumed these stairs since the first tenants arrived in the early sixties. She hurries Molly past the second-floor apartment; it worries her the way people show up at the occupant's door at all hours, knocking frantically and cursing, as if something terrible might happen if whoever is inside doesn't let them in.

Safe inside their own apartment, Louise locks and chains the door, and then leaves Molly to play while she starts dinner, if you can call canned tomato soup and grilled cheese sandwiches dinner. Then again, the only utensils Louise has to cook with are a frying pan and a saucepan. The kitchen is scantily equipped, every surface covered with a speckled mustardy-brown substance like Formica. Since the fire, Louise's sense of smell has become unbearably keen, and the sweet, gluey scent of roach spray permeates the kitchen. She debates whether to start grilling the sandwiches. Richard has gone to see the manager, a young man named Danté who has a gold cap on one front tooth, a falsely ingratiating manner, and no intention of making any of the repairs she and Richard have demanded he make. Danté has allowed them to move in without a lease. But that doesn't relieve him of the obligation to find a showerhead for the shower, install screens on the windows in the stairwell to keep Molly and Devone from falling through, or ferret out the cause of the fecal stink seeping from every drain. What baffles Louise is that the carpet in their living room is perpetually wet. Their apartment is on the third floor. She could understand a leak in their ceiling, but a wet spot in the middle of their living room floor?

"Maybe it's the brook," Richard suggested.

"Which brook?" Louise asked him angrily.

"The brook in the meadow. You know, Meadowbrook Estates?"

She was furious at him for kidding about their misfortune. But she was grateful that he was willing to present their demands to the manager. Not only that, he ordered Danté to find a way to prevent LaShawnda's sewage from backing up. As it turns out, Richard knows LaShawnda's uncle, who runs the laundry room at the prison. Since Meadowbrook Estates is so near the prison, several guards and their families live there. Richard waves hello to men with buzz cuts and tattoos Louise might otherwise have avoided. It amazes her how at home her husband seems to be in this awful place. Why is he being so competent and attentive *now*? If any benefit is to accrue from their house burning down, it's that she is now free to leave their marriage. Hasn't their wedding album been destroyed? What sign could be clearer than that?

"Is dinner ready yet?" Molly calls.

"It won't be long," Louise calls back, although she hasn't even started to heat the soup. She steels herself to open the cupboard. The salvage company claims their process removes the odor of smoke, but Louise can still smell it. Everything smells like smoke, which means everything smells like death. When she opens the cupboard, the odor that wafts out is the odor she imagines wafting from a crypt.

She pulls the collar of her shirt above her nose, opens the can of soup and pours it in the pan, slices the cheese and bread, and drops a pat of butter in the frying pan. The soup boils over, sizzling. She lifts off the pan and sets it on the fake-Formica counter, which melts beneath the pot. The butter in the frying pan begins to burn and Louise starts to shake so badly she can barely turn off both burners and get to the bathroom before she throws up.

"Are you okay?" Molly asks from outside the door.

Louise flushes the toilet. "I'll be out in a minute," she assures Molly, brushing her teeth with the toothbrush she sent Richard to buy since she wouldn't use the toothbrush from the house. She leaves the bathroom and lowers herself to the living room floor. "Mommy doesn't feel well," she tells Molly. "Do you think you can wait until Daddy comes back so he can cook our dinner?"

"Do you have a fever?" Molly puts her hand to Louise's cheek. "Warm," she says. "Should I get some medicine?" Louise reaches up and presses Molly's hand to her lips. Someone knocks at the door and, assuming Richard has neglected to take his key, Louise tells Molly to open it.

"Little girl," Louise hears someone say, "would you go and get your mother?" She struggles to her feet. The fire marshal stands to one side of the damp spot in the floor.

"Molly, honey," Louise says, "why don't you go in your room and play?"

Molly shakes her head. "I don't like how empty that room is."

Louise takes her by the wrist and whispers, "Please, sweetie, go in the other room."

Molly looks as if she is about to cry, but she shakes her head again and Louise doesn't have the heart to argue. Where is Richard? She wants to tell the fire marshal to wait until her husband gets back, but that would prolong his presence, and she hates to sound like a woman who can't handle business without a man.

There is nowhere for them to sit. The fire marshal is wearing a different pair of shorts and a different flowered shirt from the ones he was wearing the night of the fire. He taps his white shoe as if a jukebox is playing and only he can hear the beat. "It brings me no pleasure to say this, but we know for a fact that your fire was the result of arson. We found traces of gasoline."

She slumps heavily to the floor. Molly cries out and runs over and throws her arms around her mother. Louise expects the fire marshal to ask if she is all right, but he remains looking down at her coldly. The idea that someone hates them enough to burn down their house fills Louise with a nauseating anger. The room spins. She lies back on the harsh, synthetic carpet, which smells the way you would expect a perpetually damp synthetic carpet to smell. The fire marshal's shoe keeps tapping beside her head. The odor he gives off— tobacco mixed with bubble gum and hair oil—makes Louise so queasy she clamps her hand to her nose so all she can smell is the cheese she just sliced. Is the moisture beneath her back from the wet spot in the floor, or her own sweat? What will Richard say if the police ask him where his wife was the day their house burned down? She has told him about dropping Molly off at Em's and driving to Ann Arbor. He didn't seem suspicious. All he wanted to know was what the house looked like when she drove up and various details about running to Em's and Em calling the fire department and Matt opening the doors to rescue Matzo Ball. He even apologized for being in the woods with Floyd, which only made her feel guiltier. Why couldn't Ames confess that she spent the day with him? The police would believe a minister.

Then again, a minister confessing an affair might not strike them as a reliable source of an alibi for his mistress. What if the case goes to trial? Will Ames stand up for her in court? What if she needs to reveal his infidelity to save herself from jail—or worse, to save Richard?

The fire marshal takes a step closer, as if he intends to nudge her with his foot.

"Louise!" Richard comes in. From where she lies on the floor, he towers above her. "What did you do to her? What did you do to my wife?"

Molly begins to wail. "Are they taking you to prison?"

Louise draws her close and shushes her. "It's fine, sweetie. Everything is fine." She closes her eyes while far above her the fire marshal and Richard argue.

"You're not even going to try to find the person who did this," Richard shouts. Words swarm around the room—she can pick out "lawyer," "police," "insurance," "lie detector test," and "tomorrow will be suitable." When she opens her eyes, the fire marshal is gone and Richard is kneeling over her. "It's my fault," he says, which makes her wonder for a moment if he *did* set the fire. "If I hadn't burned down those trees, they wouldn't suspect us now." He strokes her head. "That idiot is gone. You stay there and I'll see about getting dinner."

After he has served the sandwiches and soup, all three of them end up sleeping on the cheap mattress they had delivered from Mattress World. When Louise wakes later, in the middle of the night, all she can make out is the stark white globe of a streetlight floating outside the window like an alien's head.

"Mom?" Molly says. "I can't fall back asleep."

Louise draws Molly beneath her chin. "That was pretty upsetting stuff. I'm sorry you had to hear it." She berates herself for not having been clear-headed enough to insist that Molly leave the room. "Everything is all right now."

Molly nestles quietly in her arms. Richard twitches and then rolls toward the wall. Molly is facing away from Louise, so she barely hears what her daughter asks. *Is anyone in charge?* To stall for time, Louise replies with the obvious, *In charge of what?*

314

"Well," Molly says, "let's say somebody wants to hurt somebody else. What's to stop them from doing it?"

Louise relaxes. Molly's question isn't as difficult to answer as she expected. First of all, Louise tells her, there are laws. A person can't just hurt another person and get away with it. "And Daddy and I would never let anyone hurt you."

"But if they *wanted* to hurt me? And no one was around to see them? What if someone said somebody else did some crime, but that other person *didn't* do the crime, but the first person said they *did* do it? How could the police tell which one was lying?"

Louise explains about witnesses and trials, evidence, hearsay, reasonable doubt. "Are you worried that Mom and Dad might go to jail? Because we won't. That man doesn't know what he's talking about. We didn't do anything wrong."

"I know that!" There is a heartbreaking urgency in her voice. "But no one is in charge! No one is in charge!"

Louise would give anything to be able to set Molly's mind at rest by telling her some powerful force exists that can prevent innocents from being harmed. Why can't Ames have given her that much? Doesn't *he* believe in God?

Then again, Louise doesn't *not* believe in God. "Sweetheart," she says, "I'm not *sure* if anyone is in charge. But I *think* someone is. Even if you don't *know* that God exists, you can have faith that He *might*. You can have faith everything will turn out all right in the end."

"But you can't *know* that," Molly frets. "You just said you can't *know* that."

Louise changes her tactics. "Sweetie, everyone has nights like this. Mostly, people don't have them until they're a lot older than you are. But everyone gets them. Usually, when you feel this way, the best you can hope is that someone will hold you in their arms and say they love you and help you get through the night."

Molly sighs. "I know. But it might help me if you promise to buy me another Beanie Baby."

Louise laughs. She doesn't want Molly to get in the habit of blackmailing her into buying her a toy every time she has an existential crisis. Then again, after everything Molly has been subjected to in the past year, the least Louise can do is buy her a five-dollar stuffed toy. "How about this?" she says. "If you try to have faith that everything is going to turn out okay, I'll buy you a Beanie Baby every day for a week."

"Do you mean that?" Sensing that she has gained some sort of advantage, Molly presses for one last concession. "Can we go and visit Em?"

Louise hasn't been able to bring herself to go anywhere near the house since the night of the fire, a reluctance intensified by her newly acquired knowledge that the fire was set. Still, it isn't fair to cut Molly off from Em. "Not tomorrow," she promises, "but soon."

Molly murmurs something, but Louise doesn't ask what. Instead, she puts her face to Molly's hair, which smells of sweat and oil but not of smoke, and swears yet again she will go back to being the mother she once was, even if it means no longer seeing Ames. He was right; neither of them has any business putting their happiness above the welfare of those they love.

That's when she remembers that Imelda was due to be operated on the day before. Or maybe the operation is set for tomorrow—Louise has lost all track of time. She is about to peel herself from Molly and call the hospital in California when she remembers they don't yet have a phone. She will need to wait until morning and find a pay phone in Potawatomie. Even if she can't speak with Imelda, Louise can make sure her friend has come through her operation. She can send Imelda flowers and books. She can make a reservation to fly out to keep her company while she convalesces. That is, if Louise is free to leave the state.

For now, she lies with Molly against her side. Someone has to be in charge. *Doesn't* someone? Doesn't there have to be someone who can protect Molly and Imelda in ways Louise can't seem to do? Lying with her daughter in her arms and her best friend in a hospital half a continent away, she can't decide if faith is the most moving of all human inventions, or a trick mothers use to help their children get through the first night they figure out that the universe doesn't give a damn what anyone does and that no one, not even their parents, can protect them from much of anything.

FOURTEEN

MATT ISN'T SURE WHAT WAKES HIM. THE BIRDS SEEM CALM, just the usual rustling and cooing. If anything were wrong, the birds would be making a commotion. He shakes his head. Who would have thought that he would end up living in a house that has watchbirds instead of watchdogs?

Em has thrown back the quilt and lies in a skimpy top and panties so white they glow. He props himself on an elbow and looks her up and down, which she wouldn't let him do if she was awake. *What are you staring at, Matt Banks? You make me feel like a freak. How would you like it if I stared at you all the time?* In truth, he would like that fine, Em staring at him, not being able to convince herself that after all these years Matt Banks is in her life, the way Matt marvels that he has ended up in the same bed as Sue Ellen Gratz.

Of course, if Em heard him call her Sue Ellen, she would take a swat at him. But to him, she will always be Sue Ellen. If you ask him, this "Em" stuff is part of the whole big cover-up. You changed your name and hoped your past wouldn't catch up to you, and if it did, you could cast a spell or summon some goddess to protect you. He allows his hand to hover an inch above her thigh. As a kid, he spent an awful lot of time watching Sue Ellen Gratz's legs as she ran hurdles around the field on which he, Matt Banks, was supposed to be tossing whatever heavy, awkward object the coach had set him to tossing around that week. He would see Sue Ellen kick off, her front leg shooting open and out as she catapulted over a hurdle Matt couldn't have cleared if he'd had a rocket on his back. After the men's events, he would sit with the other guys and listen to his teammates make rude comments about how Mary Hasseltine stuck her ass up so high, kneeling at the starting line, you just wanted to come up behind her and jam in your thing, or how Jaycie Bett's melons swung around so wild when she pumped her arms in the home stretch it was a wonder she didn't lose her balance and go skidding across the finish line on her face. But no one made rude remarks about Sue Ellen. She was the only kid from Stickney who had good enough grades to get into U of M, not to mention winning a free ride, seeing as she placed first in every track and field event a Michigan girl could enter. And when word got around that she'd turned down U of M and decided to go to State because the kids in Ann Arbor acted too stuck up, you would have thought she was royalty, the way the crowds parted in the halls and let her through.

Of course, some of the kids thought Sue Ellen herself

was too stuck up. She never smiled. She didn't say hello. She rarely showed up at parties or anywhere but her track meets. A rumor started that the reason she ran so fast was to get away from her older brother, who was the only guy in Stickney strong enough to hold her down, but Matt figured that was just jealousy speaking. Back then, he didn't know beans about Sue Ellen. He barely was brave enough to say, "Good race, Sue Ellen," or "Way to go, Sue Ellen" as they filed on the bus after an away-meet. All he knew was, when he saw her run, his heart pumped so hard *he* might have been the one competing. The crowds chanted and clapped—"Sue *El*-len! Sue *El*-len!"—not caring then if she smiled or went to parties; all they cared about was that Sue Ellen Gratz was showing the kids from Farmington Hills or Kalamazoo that just because Stickney Springs was a nowhere town outside a cruddy city that had nothing going for it except a prison didn't mean they weren't good at something. "Sue *El*-len!" they sang, "Sue *El*-len!," until it sounded like they were screaming "Swellin'!," which described exactly the way the blood rose and burst in Matt's own chest when she broke the tape.

Then she went off to State, and before anyone knew it, Sue Ellen was back. She never said why, but rumors got around that she'd taken to drinking too much and stopped going to classes and lost her scholarship. She got a job with the postal service in Stickney Springs, and Matt saw her nearly every day walking past his farm—jogging, it was more accurate to say, even though she was loaded down with that heavy bag. He wondered if she was training for the Olympics, although he doubted even Sue Ellen Gratz was good enough to compete in the Olympics.

When she'd saved enough to put a down payment on the piece-of-crud bungalow across the road from his farm, he thought he had a chance. He went over and helped her paint the place and tack up shingles. She started taking in those birds, and Matt offered to build some cages. He lugged around forty-pound bags of feed, although Sue Ellen wouldn't have had trouble lugging them herself. He brought over a shoebox full of dead mice from his barn, like a cat bringing trophies for his mistress.

Then Sue Ellen went and married that gangster Ed Sorenson. From the start, Matt could tell Sorenson was sorry news—something about the gunslinger walk, the missing fingers, the slitty, suspicious eyes. From his own porch, Matt could hear Sorenson ordering Sue Ellen around, accusing her of sleeping with every customer on her route. A lot of days, Sorenson followed her on his motorbike—one time, he decided Sue Ellen was taking too long getting C.O.D. from some old coot, so he storm-troopered up to the guy's porch, grabbed Sue Ellen by her braid, yanked her to the road, and smacked her around right there. Matt suspected Sorenson was the slimeball who'd run her down and brain damaged her, but the cops said the paint on Sorenson's Kawasaki didn't match the paint on the fragments scattered around Sue Ellen, so maybe that was only sour grapes, seeing as how Sorenson was responsible not only for Sue Ellen's brain damage but also for Matt losing his wife and kid.

Every time Matt thinks about those years when Sue Ellen was married to Ed Sorenson and Matt was married to Kelly Martinez, the years in which Kelly and Matt's mom went at it day and night and Sorenson screamed at Sue Ellen day and night, Matt wants to put a pillow on his head. Why didn't he tell that ass-wipe Sorenson that if he didn't treat Sue Ellen better, he would beat the stuffing out of him? Why didn't he tell his mother to let up on his wife for being Catholic and maybe having a little Mexican blood and wanting to do over the kitchen, which, as far as Matt could tell, hadn't been done over since Matt's great-grandfather built the place in the 1890s? And how on earth had he allowed himself to be bamboozled into getting involved in that stupid foursome? Great, he finally managed to climb in bed with Sue Ellen Gratz, only he was so ashamed of there being four people in the bed instead of two he couldn't bring himself to do much more than graze a nipple, and even then he'd said, "Excuse me," as if he and Sue Ellen were no more than strangers in a line at the grocery and he'd bumped into her accidentally.

He studies that nipple now—it's poking up through her tight white top like a seedling just poking from a mound of dirt—and the thought that there's nobody he needs to share that nipple with now makes him want to kiss every square inch of her. He hates that somewhere out there he has a daughter he ought to be helping to take care of, but if his ex-wife doesn't see fit to let him visit their child, let alone inform him where to send a check, what can he do?

A truck goes by, its headlights raking Em's sleeping body and Matt's own before it continues down the road, as if some glowing hand has reached in and fingered them, found them wanting and moved along. He hears a whoop and a scream, the loony high-pitched spirits of teenage kids. Tires squeal and gravel flies and spatters. Other trucks must have passed earlier; that's what woke him. He warned Rich that a half-ruined house with the front door hanging open would be an invitation to the local kids. Next thing you knew, the place would be trashed so bad you'd have to tear it down and start from scratch.

He wrestles himself into a sitting position, then forces himself to stand. He reaches inside his shorts and rearranges his dick, which got plastered to his leg with sweat and cum. Then he looks down at Em, and it's all he can do to keep from sliding back in bed. He kisses her shoulder and smells her smell—some perfume she calls patchouli, mixed with candle scent, incense, those herbs she grows for tea, and the iodine and disinfectants she rubs on her injured birds. Back when he was on the track team and got sore from hurling the javelin or throwing the discus, the trainer rubbed liniment on his arm, and that's how Em smells, like something that would make you feel better if you pressed her against your skin.

Maybe he ought to ask her to go with him to check on Rich's house. Even with her brain damage, she can put together a sentence better than he could ever do. If there are two of them, the kids might see them as parents and be readier to obey. On the other hand, he isn't about to ask a woman to do his dirty work for him. Em especially. After all she's been through. A dark house and a bunch of drunken guys. He takes a guilty pride in being the only person who knows the real reason Sue Ellen Gratz came back from Lansing. But the knowledge brings with it a heavy responsibility.

Sue Ellen can't seem to shake the notion that what happened to her was her own fault. Too much drinking. Too many frat parties where she tried to match the guys' track team shot for shot. Then she woke up with no clothes on and her private parts sore and five or six big guys taking turns holding her head and making her suck their dicks. Matt can lose hours imagining what he would have done if he had walked in on those bastards. It is such an obvious no-brainer that man was put on earth to protect and defend woman, yet there exist a few moral cretins who would take advantage of their superior strength to do weaker creatures harm. Even if Sue Ellen does have a faint memory of offering to suck that one bastard's dick, the guy had no right to take advantage of her being drunk to get his dick sucked, let alone to get his friends' dicks sucked. And then, what happened later, as if Sue Ellen has any cause to feel ashamed of not wanting to have a baby whose father could have been any of those bastards. Maybe it's just because Matt is a farmer, but it seems to him that one of the main differences between people and animals is that people don't just jump the female of the species and expect her to raise the issue of that mating, no matter what circumstances might pertain.

Matt has offered to pay for Sue Ellen to talk to someone. But she's like the guys who got home from Nam and pretended they were too tough to need a shrink. Witches, she says, do not need to talk to headshrinkers. She has undergone several highly successful pagan rituals in which she purified her past. Matt tried to ask Rich what to do, but he couldn't get out the right words. Whatever Matt said, it made Rich think he was blaming Sue Ellen for getting drunk with a bunch of frat boys. Of course, if a person does what Rich does for a living, he ought to know what someone is trying to say even if that someone can't find the right words to say it. But everybody can have an off day, even a guy like Rich. When Rich and Louise move back, Matt will try talking to them again. Rich probably knows someone in Potawatomie that Sue Ellen can talk to. There sure aren't any shrinks in Stickney Springs, and even if there were, no one in his right mind would spill his guts to a person he's likely to run into twenty times a day.

Outside, the night is sticky, shrill, and hot. The crickets set up a squeal. Things Matt can't see rumble by in the dark. Something with yellow eyes slinks across the road. Matt stops opposite his own place and stands admiring the graduated rows of the baby Christmas trees, the neatly defined silhouettes of the silo and the barn. In the dark, a person can't tell that the barn isn't full of cows and that acres of corn and soybeans don't stretch around the back. It's all Matt's fault it isn't a real farm anymore. If only he were smarter. If only he worked harder. If only he could get over his fear of applying for a loan.

No, he thinks. That's like Sue Ellen blaming herself for getting screwed over by all those guys at State. Uncle Sam is one powerful son of a gun. It's as if the government *wants* small farms to fail. The only place Matt disagrees with patriots like Tim McVeigh is that you can't go around blowing up the government just because you don't like the stupid rules Uncle Sam lays down. It's like being mad at your parents. They might make cruddy rules or ground you. But you can't just blow them up.

A light flares in the Shapiros' house, and from what Matt can make out, a bunch of pickups are parked on the lawn. Maybe he ought to stop at his mother's house and get a gun. Not that he's about to shoot a kid for breaking in a house and drinking beer. But a gun might scare the kids into leaving without a fight.

Then again, his mother has never been anyone's idea of a heavy sleeper. When Matt was a kid, if he came in a minute past curfew, she got up and tried to strop him. She sleeps even lighter now. If a person went blind, her other senses got super-sharp, so it stands to reason that his mother losing her voice has sharpened her hearing. The last thing he wants is to wake his mother and be forced to listen to yet another blubbery midnight sob-session about how those dead kids in Oklahoma City are weighing on her conscience. She can't get over the idea that she might have sat next to Tim McVeigh at a picnic. She keeps apologizing to anyone who will listen. She stands up at church and apologizes. She stops people on the street and apologizes. She keeps trying to apologize to Louise, as if Louise's being from outside Stickney Springs makes her more fit to judge.

His mother is a good woman, but she's always gotten

more than a little overwrought about her politics, a trait that drove Matt's father nuts. "For Pete sake, woman," he used to say, "doesn't it ever occur to you a person can have a different point of view and still be a good Christian?" And off they would go, arguing and slamming doors. Matt wants to say to his mother now: "As you sow, so shall you reap." But she has been punished enough without him adding fuel to her fire. If there's one thing his mother loves, it's kids, and she chased away her daughter-in-law before her only grandbaby was a year old, and now she feels responsible for a daycare center in Oklahoma City being blown up. His mother doesn't want him setting off any more bombs. As if he ever intended to blow up anything. It's just what farm kids do. They get drunk and tip cows. They steal somebody's John Deere and drive around town with their prom date on their lap. They put manure in a barrel, light the fuse, and run.

And they sneak into derelict houses and smoke dope and drink beer and make out with their girlfriends. That's what Matt himself did in the old Weyrauch place before it got torn down. He has no objections to what these kids are doing, only to where they're doing it.

No more stalling. But no gun. That's all he needs, to shoot somebody's kid. He runs his hand across his sweaty chest, savoring the taut muscles and rounded pecs. That's the advantage of working out. You don't *need* a gun. If he and his friends in high school had been getting high in somebody's burned-out house and some muscular older dude had come in and said, *Okay, fellas, time to call it a night*, they might have muttered insults, but they would have packed up their dope and left.

He trots the last few yards to the Shapiros' property. Who would have thought that he, Matt Banks, would have a neighbor named Shapiro? A smart Jewish guy like Rich. A beautiful Jewish lady like Louise. Well, no, Louise isn't a Jew. "I'm not much of anything," she told him once. But to his way of thinking, not being much of anything, and being a woman, and being married to a Jew, makes you most of a Jew yourself.

He passes one of the pickups and a dog in the back lunges and barks so nastily Matt nearly falls over backward. "It's okay, boy, I'm not trying to steal anything." It's Rod Avery's Rottweiler, Smack. From what Matt has heard, Avery paid one of his pals at the prison to steal the colored inmates' dirty uniforms, then he let the Rottweiler sniff the clothes, and he punched the dog or kicked it, so the dog came to associate the smell of colored people with getting hurt. Avery blames colored people for preventing him from getting what he wants out of life. Namely, girls to screw and glue to sniff—the only reason the kid works construction is to get access to paint thinner and glue and other chemicals you had to know would kill your brain cells, if you had any brain cells left to kill, which Matt isn't sure Rod Avery has. How could colored people be responsible for the limited supply of glue and girls in Rod Avery's life? How could colored people be responsible for anything in Stickney Springs? Matt can go a year without seeing a colored face. Of course, in the very near future, some extremely nasty business is certain to hit the fan. The cities will get hit with toxic gas or radiation, and there won't be enough food to go around, and all the colored people will come streaming out like ants, and where else will they be able to go for food and clean air except places like Stickney Springs?

Trouble is, there aren't *only* colored people in those cities. Maybe in Detroit there are only colored people. But Chicago is just as close as Detroit, and there are going to be as many starving white people in Chicago as starving colored people in Detroit. What are you going to do, train your dog to sniff the difference between city white people and country white people? When truth comes to shove, Matt doubts he would be able to shoot a hungry mother with a bunch of hungry kids, no matter what color they might be.

The Rottweiler is carrying on so bad that Matt wonders if he himself smells like a colored person. More likely, the dog has gone around the bend. You can't beat a dog all the time and not expect it to start growling and attacking everything that moves.

Matt walks up the steps, not bothering to be light footed; the kids will think he's just another guy showing up to party. Funny how nervous he is. He isn't scared of getting hurt as much as getting laughed at. He remembers standing on this porch, pulling open the door and getting blown on his butt by the backdraft. What kind of jerk would open both doors to a burning house? It makes him sick. You wait your whole life for the chance to run in a burning building and save someone, and when you finally get the chance, you can't even save a rabbit.

The thought of that poor little girl seeing him come out of the house with her dead bunny in his hand makes his eyes tear up even now. Floyd asked him if he thinks Rich set the fire, and Matt asked Floyd if he was crazy. Hadn't Rich been in the woods with him the whole time? Well, Floyd said, what about Louise? Where had *she* been? The question gave Matt some pause, and when he asked Em, she said in this voice like she was measuring bird feed: "Louise told me she spent the day in Ann Arbor." Matt asked again, and Em said it exactly the same way: "Louise told me she spent the day in Ann Arbor," which didn't exactly put Matt's suspicions to rest. All he knows is that he likes Louise, even if she doesn't much like him. Maybe he shouldn't care, but from the minute he met her, he thought of Louise as a superior person whose good opinion was worth the effort to acquire. He can't believe she would set fire to her own house. What kind of mother would set fire to a house with her daughter's pet inside? And why would she run down the road and tell Em to call the fire department if she wanted the house to burn?

He steps inside and stands sniffing the malty dope-sweet stink. The house is pretty much dark, except for a flashlight someone has propped on the steps so couples seeking privacy upstairs won't trip. The glowing tips of joints and cigarettes float around the living room like fireflies. "Okay, time to call it a night." He says this in his friendliest, most authoritative voice. It's a voice he would have listened to as a kid. His father's voice, come to think of it. "Come on, guys, this isn't your house. You don't want me to call the cops."

The kids take shape, rousing themselves from whatever stupor they have managed to get themselves into, untwining legs and arms and tongues. *Oh man, do we have to? What's going on? Who is that guy?* Matt feels as if he's picked up a log and all the slow, pale creatures are figuring out they ought to find another place to hide.

"Banks, what are you doing here? Who died and left you in charge?"

Even in the dark, he can recognize Rod Avery's voice— Avery is the kind of guy who forces his voice an octave lower so it won't come out sounding as weedy and young as he really is. "This house belongs to friends of mine," Matt explains. "You know these people. You did work for them. Doesn't that mean anything to you?" The kid is standing pretty close, weaving and wobbling. He smells sharp, like whatever solvent he's just been sniffing. He turns to talk to his girlfriend—Matt can't get a good look at her, but he thinks she's the daughter of the guy who runs the hardware store. Matt has noticed the girl weighing nails and cutting keys. Any normal guy would notice her . . . and think he shouldn't be thinking such thoughts about a girl who's still in middle school. Briefly, Matt wishes he were the kind of guy who didn't see anything wrong in getting in the pants of a fourteen-year-old. Then he thinks of Sue Ellen and her brother and those frat boys up at State, and it's all he can do not to grab the asshole by his ponytail and swing him around the room.

"Listen up, everybody. If you promise not to smoke, you can use our barn to hang out in. But no matches. We're talking a barn full of dry hay. You light a match in there, you might not get out alive."

"Can we fuck the pigs?" a voice mutters. Laughter erupts from the dark, flapping around Matt's ears like a swarm of bats.

"Never mind the pigs," calls another voice. "I want to fuck a cow!" Someone moos, and the moos take on the unmistakable frenzy of a bovine orgasm. Other animals begin having orgasms. Matt feels his face prickle with shame, and he's glad he hasn't in fact brought a gun.

"Thanks for the offer," Matt hears Rod Avery say, "but we're not so hard up we want to party in your shitty barn." Avery pulls his girlfriend out the door. "Hey, guys. The boss and I are fixing the wiring on the church down the road, and guess who has the key."

Out on the porch, Matt watches the kids climb in their pickups. He shouldn't let them get high and make out in a church, but he doesn't want to press his luck. Besides, he's never had much use for Stonecutter. Matt has nothing against raising your voice in the Lord's praise, but only if your choir can keep a tune. And Stonecutter had the nerve to knock on Em's door and ask her to take down the five-pointed star she has hanging as a wind chime. That's the Devil's sign, Stonecutter said, and his congregation didn't appreciate seeing it on their way to services. Em told the guy she was a witch and if he didn't get off her property she would turn him into a little bald toad, and Stonecutter let the matter rest, but the incident doesn't give Matt much incentive to tell the kids they can't drink beer in the minister's church.

He waits until the last kids have driven off and then goes back in to see what sort of a mess they have left. The flashlight is gone and he can't make out much. What he really wants to do is to get back to Em. Next morning, he will return and clean up the beer cans and cigarette butts. On his way out, he slips in a puddle of what, from the stench of it, must be vomit. Fine, he will bring a bucket and a mop and swab that up, too.

FIFTEEN

THE MORNING AFTER THE FIRE MARSHAL INFORMS HER that gasoline has been discovered in what remains of their house, Louise waits until it is late enough to call the West Coast, then puts Molly in the van and drives to a pharmacy in Potawatomie that sells Beanie Babies and has a phone. Her sense of smell has become so sensitive she might as well be pregnant. Shenk's Drugs smells of vitamin pills, herbal shampoo, the testers for lavender perfume, the sour powdery grape and lemon candies that are popular with kids that year, and the glue and canvas of the binders stacked in the back-to-school display.

"I'm going to call Aunt Imelda," she says to Molly. "She's had another operation. While I'm talking to her on the phone, you can pick out a new Beanie."

Molly gravely bobbles her head like one of the ceramic puppies on the shelf behind her. "Okay," she says. "Tell her I hope she gets better soon."

Louise studies her daughter to detect the insincerity of a child who knows that uttering a pious wish will earn her the gift she wants, but she sees nothing except concern. Whatever Louise has lost, she still has both breasts and the best daughter anyone could ever want.

The phone booth is at the back, a wood-and-glass antique with a rotary phone attached by a steel cord. With all the numbers she has to dial, her finger gets a cramp. A nurse in the I.C.U. tells her Imelda is awake but groggy and "in a fair amount of discomfort," a term Louise knows from Imelda's first mastectomy is the euphemism for the sort of pain you might expect if someone cut off your breast. The nurse says Imelda's husband has gone down to get some coffee, but she offers to hold the phone so Louise and Imelda can talk.

"Imelda?" Louise says. "Are you there? I'm sorry I didn't call you before." She isn't about to go into the details of the fire. "You just get your strength back. I'll fly out to see you very soon. I love you. Molly sends her love, too."

She hears Imelda wet her lips and clear her throat. "Drugs," she croaks.

"I know. You're on a lot of painkillers."

"Not worth it. Remember what I said."

"Of course it's worth it. I know you feel miserable now, but you're going to be all right. You have years and years ahead of you." The nurse gets back on and tells Louise her friend needs to get some rest. "Bye!" Louise calls. "I love you!" But after she hangs up, it comes to her that Imelda might have been reminding her that her affair isn't worth the misery it might cause. Knowing Imelda, even in intensive care she would be thinking of Louise's future rather than her own.

At that, she slumps on the wooden seat inside the booth and sobs so bitterly she hopes the glass is soundproof. Her best friend has just had her second breast removed. Everything Louise has ever owned has been destroyed. Someone hates her, or hates Richard—or who knows, maybe Molly—so badly that he—or she—would burn them out, and Louise and Richard are suspected of having set the fire. She hasn't seen Ames in five days, not since she visited the construction site and asked him to confess where they were when the fire started.

She finds a quarter and calls his church. His secretary says that Reverend Wye hasn't come in yet. Louise has called him at home only once—she got Natalie and hung up—but she dials his number now, praying he will answer.

"Hello. Wye residence."

"Ames."

"Louise?"

He wouldn't have said her name if Natalie was in the room. "The fire," she says. "They found evidence of arson. They're blaming us. Richard and me. We're living in this horrible place and the insurance won't pay our claim. They're going to want to know where I was. We can't keep lying. You and me, I mean. What am I supposed to do?"

She hears him draw a long, painful breath. "They found evidence?" He puts his hand over the receiver and calls to someone in the next room. Then he gets back on the line. "We've had another threat. Maybe Natalie is right, I shouldn't be putting the girls at risk. If someone set fire to your house . . ." He excuses himself and calls a barely audible, "Just a minute!" When he gets back on, he tells Louise that he and Natalie are leaving town.

"Leaving town?" She has the impression he has just come up with this idea, in response to her call.

"I'm taking Natalie and the girls to see my mother at her summer place in Maine. I hate to leave you at a time like this, but I'm afraid for the girls. And my mother has started drinking again. She was on the wagon for eleven years, but her new boyfriend is an alcoholic and . . . Never mind. I figure we can stay a week or so and give all this a chance to blow over."

Does he mean her? Louise asks. Does he mean that his going away will give their affair the chance to blow over?

"How could you think that? The messages. The threats. Your fire. I can't—" He calls in an angry voice for another minute to finish the conversation. "I'll call you as soon as we get back."

She wants to ask the exact day he will be coming home, but Ames calls something to whoever is in the other room and hangs up.

She tries to pull herself together. The booth seems to be filling with water, and the people walking past pretend not to notice that the woman inside is drowning. She wipes her eyes, blows her nose, then goes to check on Molly.

She must look awful, because immediately Molly asks, "Did Aunt Imelda die? You're crying. She died, didn't she! Aunt Imelda died!"

Louise gets down on her knees. "Of course she didn't die. She'll be okay. I promise. I'm just a little sad." She forces herself to brighten. "Which Beanie did you pick out?"

Going through the motions of paying for the toy helps to calm them both. But when Louise is biting off the tag, someone says: "Don't do that!" She looks up, still biting the plastic tag that describes the stuffed whale's origins and date of birth, and sees Beverly Booth above them, clearly abashed at her outburst.

"If you take off the tags," she explains sheepishly, "the Beanies aren't worth anything to a collector."

"But the tags are scratchy," Molly says.

Beverly's face undergoes a series of embarrassed contortions. "Of course they're scratchy, dear. What I meant is that people who collect Beanies as an investment always leave on the tags. But little girls who buy them to love are free to do as they like."

Louise thinks of all those photos above Beverly's desk, students who have moved on without a thought to how much she might miss them, the brother she has lost to California, the dozens of carefully arranged stuffed animals, each with a tag clipped to its ear. Like any collector, Beverly tries to hold on to what she loves, but that's clearly a losing battle.

"I feel very fortunate running into you like this," she says, seemingly relieved to change the subject. "I've been calling you, but no one ever seems at home."

Louise explains about the fire, omitting the part about the authorities suspecting that she and Richard set it.

"Not after all the work you put in! You must be devastated. Is there anything I can do? Where are you staying?" She offers to take up a collection at her church to buy furniture and clothes, but Louise won't hear of it. She assures Beverly they'll be getting a settlement from their insurance company any day, although the company's representatives have just started their investigation. "What did you call me about?" she thinks to ask.

"Call you? Oh, yes. I wanted to see if you could come in and meet the new director of special ed."

Everything that went on the previous spring seems so distant to her now, it's all Louise can do to ask what happened to Mrs. Moorehouse.

Beverly lowers her voice. "She had her fourth miscarriage.

Her husband thinks it's the stress of the job, so she's going to stay home and see if that helps." She smiles a conspiratorial little smile. "Her replacement is a lovely older woman whose husband was transferred here from Chicago. Her name is Rena Goldstein. She asked me why we were interviewing for the social worker position when we already had someone carrying out those responsibilities. She asked, 'Did Mrs. Shapiro prove unsatisfactory in any way?' And I said, 'Quite the contrary, the students liked her very much.' So she asked me to ask you to come in and have a talk about your becoming permanent."

"That's wonderful news," Louise says politely. She tells Beverly she will need time to get back on her feet, but once everything has settled down she will come in and meet the new director, keeping to herself that she might be in jail by then.

Every day that week, she drives Molly to the drug store to buy a new stuffed toy and call Imelda. Then, to avoid returning to the Lagoon of Lost Children, she takes Molly on an excursion. Usually, Devone comes along. On nice days, Louise takes them to the pool. When the weather isn't fine, she searches surrounding towns for attractions the kids might like—a petting zoo, a Bible theme park, a putt-putt golf course. One morning, they travel to the cereal museum in Battle Creek and spend a fascinating time learning how cornflakes are made. Most days, she lets the children choose where they want to eat, which means Molly lets Devone decide whether he prefers a Whopper or a Big Mac, although one time Louise packs a picnic and takes them to a park where a man happens to be giving pony rides. For a dollar apiece, Molly and Devone get to ride an arthritic, disheveled Shetland around a parched baseball diamond; the pony reminds Louise of an aging Babe

Ruth shambling around the bases, head down, to allow the photographers and fans one last chance to honor him.

Molly has never seemed happier. She has Devone to play with. And her father is paying her more attention than he has paid her in a long time. In the evenings, he often takes Molly bowling. Louise can't imagine her daughter lifting the ball, but Richard has told her that Molly puts it on the ground between her legs and shoves it down the center of the alley with uncanny precision. Sometimes the ball stops halfway and needs to be retrieved. But if it makes it to the pins, it starts a slow-motion reaction that often results in a strike or spare. Richard has entered them in a parent-child competition. "Maybe she'll end up the women's worldwide bowling champ," he kids Louise. "If we hadn't moved to the Midwest, we never would have discovered our daughter's greatest gift."

She can tell he's trying to make amends for the past year and a half. He has met repeatedly with a lawyer to figure out how they might defend themselves against a possible charge of arson. After giving up on Danté, he went out and bought a showerhead and screwed it in himself. He nailed plywood over the windows in the stairwell and laid a plastic mat over the wet spot in the living room. "This isn't going to keep the ceiling below us from caving in," he said, "but that isn't our valise."

She is glad for his ministrations, but equally glad that Molly insists on sleeping on the mattress between them. Richard says that after they have gotten the insurance sorted out, he wants all three of them to see a therapist. Louise has promised she will go. How can she not be angry at Ames for his refusal to tell the truth about where they were when the fire started? But she still believes he will. It makes sense that he would delay his confession as long as possible. No one would be eager to destroy his marriage and career. But eventually he will tell the truth. At which Natalie will leave him, and Louise will use their visits to the therapist to tell Richard that she is leaving *him*.

Then, in the middle of August, Devone's mother takes him to visit relatives in Kentucky, and Molly is so despondent Louise ferries her out to see Em. They haven't been back to Stickney Springs since the fire. As they pass the Joyful Noise Church, Louise slows to make sure the electrician's van isn't there; the weedy grass is strewn with beer cans, but the church door is padlocked and no cars are in the lot.

When they get to Em's bungalow, Louise takes only shallow breaths, in case any last molecules of smoke are hovering in the air. She glances at the Bankses' porch and for the first time doesn't see a flag there. She ought to go over and thank Matt for keeping an eye on their house—Richard said something about Matt kicking out a bunch of kids who were using the house to drink in—but she isn't up to talking about the fire. And she doesn't want to see Dolores.

"Em!" Molly races across the lawn and hurls herself into Em's arms. They hold hands and dance in a circle. Then they run inside. Louise trails after them, listening to Em warble about the progress of various birds and feeling selfish for having kept Molly away so long.

Em sets Molly the task of putting fresh water in the animals' dishes and makes Louise some tea. "I didn't tell anyone," she informs Louise quietly.

Louise sets down the cup.

"They asked me where you were, and all I said was that you said you were in Ann Arbor."

Louise can tell that Em is waiting for an expression of thanks, or the assurance that Louise really did go where she said she went, but Louise isn't sure what to say. Em is better off the less she knows. "Thanks for calling the fire department. And for being so good to Molly."

Em seems abashed but pleased. "Why don't you leave her with me a while? You look like you could use some time to yourself." She raises her voice so Molly can hear. "What about it, Molly? You want your old job back? Or are you just going to lie around collecting unemployment checks for the rest of your life?"

And that's how the new routine gets started. Every day that week, after buying Molly a new Beanie Baby at the drug store, Louise drives her out to Em's, which gives Louise four or five hours to do whatever she wants. Unfortunately, with Ames out of town, she has nowhere to go. The apartment is too depressing, and there are only so many hours a person can spend shopping in Potawatomie. She thinks of stopping by Coalition headquarters to see if Howie or Jack is there. But the sight of either man would remind her of the fire, and she is afraid she might confess everything about Ames to Howie, if only because she wants to compare notes about how much they both miss him. So she runs a few errands, stopping by K-Mart to pick up replacements for the towels and aspirin she and Richard lost in the fire, and somehow, in searching for ways to fill the time, she finds herself making a daily tour of the landmarks of her affair.

The first stop is Ames's church. Ever since he left town, the billboard by the door has displayed a quote by Emerson— "Life consists of what a man is thinking of all day"—a message Louise interprets as a love note meant for her. After that, she drives to the McDonald's where she and Ames met. Some days, she merely sits in the van and looks. Other days, she goes inside, orders a sandwich, and takes it to the table where she and Molly were sitting when Ames and his girls came in.

The playground is usually empty—beneath the August sun, the glass-enclosed extension gets steamy as a hothouse—but sometimes a few mothers loll languidly at other tables reading the tabloids while their children climb the ropes or crawl through the tubes.

From McDonald's, she drives past the apartments she and Ames cleaned for the coalition. Once, she sees Myrna Cott lugging a vacuum up the steps, but Louise feels too compelled to finish her routine to get out and help. After that, she drives to Handsome Lake, checking the lot as if Ames's Escort might be there, parked in front of Room 30, or as if Ames himself might be coming out of the room with another woman.

Eventually, she drives back to Potawatomie for the final stop on the tour. The first time she drives past Ames's house, it's to convince herself he hasn't simply been avoiding her. But the lights are off, the Venetian blinds in the living room and kitchen are open, which allows Louise to see that no one is in either room, and Ames's Escort isn't in the driveway. Someone has tossed a Dairy Queen cup on the lawn, and when she drives by a day later, no one has removed it. The next day, a copy of the weekly advertiser is lying on the porch. The day after that, the advertiser is still there.

The question then becomes: When will Ames get home? He said he would be gone a week. Isn't that what he said? Didn't he promise they would get together as soon as he got back? Five days go by, then six. On the seventh day, Louise gets up thinking: *Maybe he'll be home today.* She has no memory of how she makes it through the next nine or ten hours, but at long last she finds herself in the van with the clock on the dashboard flashing 4:30. In another few minutes, she will need to pick up Molly. For now, she maneuvers the van down Hoover, down Oak, then Grand. As she passes the ivied Odd Fellows nursing home just before Ames's street, she can't help but think that someday she will be a wizened old hag rocking on some nursing home porch, wrinkled, bald, and blind, still dreaming of a minister lifting off his shirt and unhooking her brassiere.

She takes a left onto Ames's street and allows the van to coast along the serpentine curb. The plush lawns, sheltering trees, and weathered brick façades give off the sort of peace that men and women in their fifties radiate if they have become content with who they are. Thick, rich, gold light drips like honey from the leaves. Three girls on fat-tired bikes wobble along the curb, ribbons streaming from their handlebars. A woman in a stretchy beige pantsuit kneels before a flowerbed combing the plants for insects, which she crushes between her fingers. The van slithers around the next curve and Ames's house appears, the last house on the right before the street dead-ends in a circular expanse like the bulb on a thermometer. His lawn sprawls downhill, the garage tucked around the back like a stubby tail. Unlike the other houses on the street, most of which are made of brick, Ames's house is made of stone. The roof is greenish slate. The house reminds her of a turtle in the mud, and she wants to crack the shell and shake it, except she knows that if she were to destroy his house, Ames wouldn't be grateful. In cartoons, turtles unzipped their shells and stepped out of them. In real life, a turtle's shell is an extension of its skeleton. Pry a turtle from its shell and you don't get a naked turtle. You get a turtle with a hunk of raw flesh ripped from its bloody back.

The man who lives across from Ames is mowing his lawn. Despite the heat, he wears trousers and a long-sleeve shirt. *Air Force*, Louise thinks, probably because his flat, close-cropped hair reminds her of a landing deck. He pushes one of those high-tech manual mowers, ramming it at the grass with brusque thrusts, the blades revolving like a weapon. The van passes Ames's house, and Louise is startled to observe that the kitchen blinds are drawn. Does this mean Natalie and Ames are home? Then why is the sodden Dixie cup still on the lawn and the advertiser still on the porch?

The van hits the curb, and Louise bites her tongue and tastes blood. Glancing back, she sees that Ames's neighbor is staring at the van, no doubt because its front tires are on the curb. She ought to drive away. But who shut those blinds? A parishioner? A friend taking in the mail? The van's skewed position allows her a glimpse of Ames's backyard, and she sees that the playhouse is lying on its side and the rear door of Ames's house is hanging open.

Go, she thinks. *Don't go.*

She leaves the van and walks back up the street to Ames's driveway. The playhouse has been tipped over to expose a child-size table arrayed with plastic food. And yes, the rear door of Ames's real house is hanging open. The glass panel has been cracked. She will need to call the cops after all.

On the other hand, if she does call the police, she might be required to explain who she is and how she knows something is wrong. She needn't confess to being Ames's lover. But anyone might guess. And Ames himself will know that she has been driving by his house. Natalie might be suspicious. Louise might concoct some lie. She already has lied to Richard. But lying to the cops? It comes to her that no matter what she might or might not say, she won't be believed. She is suspected of committing arson. Who knows what other crime an arsonist might commit?

Just as the solution occurs to her—she will drive to the nearest pay phone and call the police anonymously—she hears a muted clamor and Ames's neighbor appears, pushing that infernal mower. He stops, the silence more threatening than the clatter of the blades had been.

"I was looking after it," she explains, motioning toward the house. "My friend is out of town. And there were threats. That's why I was watching it."

"Threats?" The man lifts a watch so elaborate she expects him to speak into it and launch an attack. "What sort of threats would anyone make against a minister?"

She points to the broken door. "Even if it was just a regular burglar, you would need to call the police. Could you go, please, and call them?"

He seems uncertain what to do. Finally, he lays the handle of the mower on the lawn and returns to his own house. Louise knows she should make her getaway, but she can't bring herself to go. Someone in the neighborhood is dribbling a basketball, and the *thud thud thud* of the ball echoes her heart. When the player takes a shot, the beat stops, then rebounds in a frenzied patter.

Ames's neighbor rejoins her. "I called them. They asked what the problem was, and I wasn't sure what to say. Intruders, I said. What sort of intruders? I couldn't tell them. But they said they would come."

He pushes the mower around to the front of the house. Louise would prefer to stay where she is, but she knows she ought to follow him. Ames's lawn is unkempt—there has been a lot of rain that week—and the neighbor, who appears to have trouble standing idle, begins trimming a swatch of grass, releasing a scent so sweet it seems an affront, like air-freshener at a morgue.

That's when the police car sidles up and parks the wrong way in front of Ames's house. Two officers climb out heavily. Both are women, which strikes Louise as odd—she somehow assumed a female cop must be partnered with a man. Then again, these women look as if they can take care of themselves. They are squat and bulky in the way of most female officers, unless this is only an effect of the unflattering uniforms and all that dangling equipment. One of the cops has short brown hair; the other has short blonde hair. Louise is sure they will guess she is Ames's lover, but whether they will guess this faster than a team of male cops she can't predict.

While the blonde officer ambles around the back, the officer with brown hair asks Louise her name and phone number. Her first impulse is to make up a name, but the neighbor would describe her to Ames and he would know who it was. Besides, she is fantastically curious to see the inside of his house. "Louise Shapiro," she tells the cop. "I live in Stickney Springs. At least, I used to live there. We had a fire. For now, my husband and I are staying at Meadowbrook Estates." The officer records this information and Louise's heart goes arrhythmic again. Now the cop will ask her to define her relation to the owner and what made her suspect a break-in.

But the question never comes. The cop jams the stubby pencil through the binding on her notebook. "Wait here," she says. "Don't go in. And don't go home." She climbs the porch, fingertips caressing the dimpled handle of her gun, then steps over the advertiser and tries the door. When the handle won't budge, she joins her partner around the back. Louise stands watching the neighbor's mower shred the Dairy Queen cup. Then the cop with brown hair reappears. "Mrs. Shapiro? Would you come with me?" The neighbor stops mowing and stares at Louise as if she has been revealed to be the criminal he thought she was all along. She feels like sticking out her tongue but follows the cop around the back, holding up her head as if she has been granted backstage access to a concert or some theatrical event.

The officer leads her past the playhouse. Louise pauses at the threshold of Ames's back door, then steps inside and sees two transparent umbrellas his daughters must have left to dry before they went to Maine. The basement is very neat—a few board games, a carton of dress-up clothes, a refrigerator box painted like a castle. Crayons and drawings lie carefully aligned on a school desk. One drawing shows a stick-figure man surrounded by blobs wearing scarves: DADDY AND THE PENGWINS is printed childishly across the top. A more sophisticated sketch—Louise remembers the art teacher at the pool—shows a woman lighting candles. Rays of glitter emanate not only from the candles but also the woman's head. The policewoman has gone upstairs, and before she knows what she is about to do, Louise has grabbed the drawing and crumpled it in her fist. Horrified, she jams the wadded paper in the pocket of her shorts and follows the cop to the first floor of Ames's house.

The living room is commanded by a stone fireplace, the mantle bare except for an elegant black-and-white vase. There are no family photos, which spares Louise the sight of Natalie and Ames on their wedding day. Still, she feels ill, seeing where her lover leads his other life. If the furnishings had been in bad taste, she could have dismissed the house as something Natalie constructed for him. But the furnishings are made of wood—Shaker, she suspects, and she has always loved Shaker furniture, always dreamed of a house with braided rugs, although it turns out that braided rugs cost hundreds of dollars, unless they are synthetic, which these rugs clearly aren't. Ames and Natalie must have bought these rugs before braided rugs were chic. Or the rugs came down through Ames's family.

"Nice place," the cop comments. "Didn't think ministers got paid so well."

They pass the master bedroom, and Louise can't help but look inside. The room is spare and light, with a spindled headboard she tries not to imagine Natalie's fingers gripping the way Louise's own hands have gripped the headboard at the motel on Handsome Lake. She wants to find a bathroom and give herself over to her grief—for the life she will never have with Ames, for the shattered consolation of thinking herself a decent, honest person, for the peace she has lost with Richard. Her husband is an intelligent, well-meaning man. She used to be content with the life they had built together, and she will never be content again.

She steals a Kleenex from the nightstand, blows her nose, stuffs the tissue in her pocket along with the drawing, and then tracks the cops' voices to the kitchen. Just before she steps inside, she imagines throwing open the cupboards and calling the cops' attention to the two sets of dishes, the two sets of silverware, the two sets of everything, one for dairy and one for meat. *Evidence*, she thinks. The dishes will serve as evidence that Natalie is an unsuitable wife for Ames.

Then she notices the broken drinking glasses on the floor, the uprooted ferns, the shattered jars of sauerkraut and pickles Natalie must have canned, and the red bull's-eye painted on the closed slats of the Venetian blinds, a mockery of the smiley faces Molly likes to paint, and she is revolted by the knowledge that this violence could have been done to her. Or worse—how can she admit this?—that she could have done something like this to Natalie.

The blonde officer steps forward, dangling a paperback book from her latex-gloved hand. The cover is black and white, nothing a commercial publisher would produce. At this point, Louise hasn't yet heard of *The Turner Diaries*, but days later, wandering Handsome Lake to avoid returning to the empty apartment at Meadowbrook Estates, she will find copies at a store that sells bait, beef jerky, guns, and flags for all occasions. She will buy and read the *Diaries* to convince herself that Ames truly had been in danger. And yes, she will see, he was. Apparently, there are evil men and women so perverted by their cause that they will destroy anyone or anything they perceive to be a threat. The book is so hateful that every few minutes Louise will need to put it down and pace around the lake to dispel the nausea in her gut.

But now, in Ames's kitchen, she is baffled by the cops' insistence that she read the passages someone has highlighted in yellow marker:

> *The Jewish takeover of the Christian churches and corruption of the ministry are now virtually complete. The pulpit prostitutes preach the System's party line to their flocks every Sunday, and they collect their 30 pieces of silver in the form of government "study" grants, "brotherhood" awards, fees for speaking engagements, and a good press. . . .*

And, nearer the end:

> *Today has been the Day of the Rope—a grim and bloody day, but an unavoidable one. Tonight, for the first time in weeks, it is quiet and totally peaceful. . . . But the night is filled with silent horrors; from tens of thousands of lampposts, power poles, and trees throughout this vast metropolitan area the grisly forms hang.*

The book had been propped against the sugar bowl. The policewomen show Louise the flyleaf, on which someone has inscribed WE KNOW WHERE YOU LIVE. Is this the sort of book the minister would read? they ask. Does she know anyone who might have broken in and left it? Louise stares at the inscription. With the writer's crazy loops, the *I* in LIVE might be an *O*. The cops ask what caused her to drive by the house, what aroused her suspicion. And even as she is gathering the words to justify her surveillance, she tries to imagine what might have happened if she hadn't called the cops.

Nothing. Not a thing. Ames would have gotten home and discovered the wrecked kitchen. He would have been furious at this violation of his privacy. He would have been frightened for his girls. But that couldn't have been worse than what actually *does* happen—namely, Ames driving up with Natalie and finding a police car parked backward by his curb, his neighbor mowing his lawn, and two officers in his kitchen interrogating his lover as to why she has driven by his house so many times in one week.

What breaks Louise's heart is seeing Ames reach instinctively for Natalie. "Why *me*?" Natalie keeps demanding. "How could anyone hate me this much?" She won't stop berating him. "No matter what I tell you, you keep pursuing activities that put me and the girls at risk." She upbraids the policewomen for not having kept an eye on the house while she and Ames were out of town. Worse, she manages to scare her daughters, who, when they first came in, regarded the break-in as exciting. "They did this because we're Jews," she tells the girls, waving a shard of china.

And Ames. Louise could swear that he considers, if only for an instant, taking those first few steps across the shattered china and glass to hold her. The vision is so real she can almost see him split in two, one version remaining with his wife, the other crossing the floor to her. Then he looks at her as if she has fallen off a boat and there is nothing he can do to save her. "Honey," he says to Natalie, "I'm sorry. You were right. It wasn't fair that I exposed you and the girls to this." He puts his arm around his wife and ushers her from the room, motioning for Bec and Ann to follow, and Louise is left in the kitchen with the police officers, too shaken and distraught to cry. Ames's decision to remain with Natalie seems as incomprehensible as the fundamentalists' belief that God created the universe in six days, or their hatred of people with AIDS, or their preparations for a time when the government will send black helicopters to round them up. But none of that matters. People believe what they want to believe, and there is surprisingly little you can do to dissuade them. No matter how right you are, you are never allowed to invade another person's house and make the sort of mess Louise is standing in right now.

SIXTEEN

AS IT TURNS OUT, NO ONE IS EVER CHARGED WITH BREAKING into the Wyes' house and vandalizing their kitchen. The police dust but find no fingerprints, walk door to door but turn up no one who has seen anything amiss. They question Mike Korn and Solomon Stonecutter, but neither man admits knowing about the crime. Nor do Ames and Natalie stay in Potawatomie long enough to exert pressure on the police to make an arrest.

Apparently, after Louise left the house, Ames confessed everything. Natalie chose not to divorce him, but she used the affair as leverage to persuade him to accept a job in Rhode

Island, which he had been offered the week before, when he and Natalie and the girls stopped there for an interview on the family trip to Maine.

Louise hears most of this from Howie. A few days after the break-in, he asks her to meet him at the diner. She would beg off, but he drops enough hints about the purpose of his invitation that she finally gives in and goes. There is a thunderstorm alert; the air is dense and gray, and the lights in the diner flicker ominously. It's the middle of the afternoon, and the place reeks of self-pity. Louise has never paid much attention to the other customers, but today she notices a couple she could swear are illicit lovers and a few solitary stragglers whose abstracted expressions and seeming lack of hunger mark them as midday misfits in the world of work or love.

Howie stuffs himself into the opposite side of the booth, and she can tell from his sympathetic look that he has guessed about her and Ames, or maybe Ames told him. The waitress pours them coffee—she is the same waitress who often served Louise and Ames, but if she thinks anything about Louise being there with Howie instead, she doesn't betray a sign. She wears a Velcro brace around her wrist, and Louise wonders if she injured herself waiting tables, or, like so many women in this town, works a second job packing onion rings at the factory.

"Can I get you folks anything else?"

Louise thinks Howie might order lunch, but he shakes his head. "Thanks," Louise tells the waitress, "just coffee."

The woman nods, then comes back with a mishmash of pie fragments. "These would all just go to waste. You two look like you need something to cheer you up."

After she leaves, Howie says, "He asked me to give you this," and hands Louise an envelope. She knows she should wait until she gets home to read it, but she can't stop herself from opening it then and there.

"Dearest Louise," the letter starts, "I will never forget any of what happened between us." She could set it down right then and know everything she needs to know. But there is something hypnotic about hearing a lover describe his version of your affair—in this case, a version in which Louise loved Ames not for himself but because she needed a savior, and he kept meeting her at the inn for reasons he couldn't control. "It's better like this," he goes on, a remark Louise finds puzzling. Better that they have been forced to stop seeing each other? Better that he and Natalie have decided to move back east? "I have no right to let my weaknesses hurt anyone else. And, to be honest, your intensity these past few months scared me. Obsession isn't passion. It isn't even love."

The truth—and nontruth—of what he has written wound Louise so deeply she finally stops reading. She knows if she keeps the letter, she will study it microscopically, again and again, to see if it might reveal anything between the lines— for instance, why she has lost her marriage and Ames has kept his. She folds the letter in half, rips the halves in strips, and rips these strips in smaller bits, which she stuffs in her half-filled coffee cup. She pours in cream, squirts in mustard and ketchup, then spoons in the remnants of a rhubarb-cherry pie.

Howie coughs. "At least you got to do more than tell him a bunch of stupid jokes."

She doesn't want to insult Howie's sense of loss, but she certainly doesn't *feel* luckier. Is it better to be allowed to start swimming across a lake if you aren't going to be permitted to reach the other side? "You're going to miss him, too, I know." Howie nods and wipes his face with a napkin. They don't say much more about Ames right then, but in the months and years that follow, whenever she and Howie meet at the Starbucks that eventually opens in Potawatomie to talk about their lives and plan activities for the coalition, they will have this between them, that they each have loved the same man.

The last time she drives by Ames's house, a few weeks after the break-in, a sign announces that it's for sale. The neighbor across the street is rigging up a sprinkler. He watches as Louise drives past, but she no longer cares who sees her. After this, she will take detours to avoid driving anywhere near this street.

Too bad the one place she wants most to avoid is the place she can't escape. The evening after the break-in, she went straight back to Meadowbrook Estates and called Em and asked her to keep Molly for the night. When Richard got home, she told him everything. They sat on the damp carpet in the middle of the living room and cried and raged and accused each other of indefensible betrayals, then apologized and cried again. Richard claimed he had known all along that she had been having an affair. He said most of the fault was his. But when Louise told him who it was, he shook his head in disbelief.

"A Unitarian?" he said. "A minister? But I thought . . . I thought you wanted . . . That guy couldn't change a fucking light bulb without asking his congregation to do it for him!" But then a mental light bulb seemed to switch on in Richard's brain. "Oh," he said, "I get it. If an ordinary, fallible human being wouldn't do the trick, you wanted to have an affair with God."

"Did it ever occur to you that I might want an ordinary, fallible human being to make love to me now and then?"

On and on it went, until Richard said he would forgive her if she promised to see a counselor, and Louise said things had gone too far for that, she wasn't sure she still loved him. "I need time to think," she said, and Richard said, "You need time to think? About what? About what do you need time to think?" He got up and went to their bedroom and threw the few items of clothing he still owned in a plastic bag. "If *you* need time to think, *I* need time to think." He said he would be staying with Ron Lowenstine and left her lying in a stunned heap on the floor of their apartment.

If she hadn't been afraid that Molly would be upset if Louise left her too long at Em's—or that Richard might pick up Molly first and not let Louise see her again—she might never have gotten up and driven to Stickney Springs to bring her home. If she hadn't felt the need to feed and bathe Molly and watch over her while she played with Devone, she might not have cared if she lived or died. If it hadn't been for Molly, when someone knocked at the door a few evenings after Richard's departure, she wouldn't have bothered to get up off the floor and find out who it was.

The fire marshal stood at the threshold, ducking his head and chomping on his gum. Well, she thought, he had finally come to arrest her. Not that she cared. If he had told her that he was marching her to her execution, she wouldn't have put up a fuss. All she cared about now was Molly. She would need to find the slip on which Richard had jotted Ron Lowenstine's number and ask him to come and pick up their daughter. Unless the police were arresting Richard, too.

"Ma'am," the fire marshal said, "the investigators from your insurance company have issued their report." He stood facing her as if he might ask her for a dance. Molly, who had been playing with a bunch of Devone's wrestlers, jumped up and squinted at him with a menacing expression. "According to the report, what started your fire was a case of canine micturation."

All Louise could do was to try to think whether "micturation" meant chewing or peeing. Was he saying that a dog chewing on a wire had caused their house to burn?

"As I recall," he said, "you don't own a dog. Your neighbor, Mr. Banks, risked his life to save a pet rabbit, but you don't own a dog." With the perpetual adolescent's disdain for a younger child's feelings, he said this in front of Molly, reminding her of her dead pet, and Louise had had quite enough of his disregard for her daughter's well-being.

"As you might *recall*," she said, "the young man who assaulted me and trespassed in my house the morning of the fire *does* own a dog, and he repeatedly brought that dog on our premises. Now, if you would tell me what the investigators—"

"In the basement? Did he, to your knowledge, bring the dog in the basement?"

"I told you he did! I told you he was in our basement!" She remembered Smack's anguished yelp and Rod's ominous advice that if she knew what was good for her, she would figure out what had hurt his dog. "Would you please tell me what the report said?"

He spit out his gum and wadded it in the wrapper. "You might or might not know that when an animal micturates on an electric outlet, the salt in the urine can short out the circuit. The stream of urine makes a connection between the animal and the source of the electricity, the electricity travels upstream, so to speak, and the animal gets zapped. The smaller the dog, the greater its chances for electrocution."

She imagined a bolt of electricity traveling from an outlet to the Rottweiler's genitals. Poor Smack! If he hadn't been so big, he might not be alive.

"The investigators found tell-tale deposits of salt on an outlet in your basement. They concluded that the deposits caused the fire." He looked at her sideways. "Unless you're accusing your electrician friend of purposely goading his dog to micturate on the outlet with the purpose of burning down your house."

"Is this about Smack?" Molly said. "Is Smack in some kind of trouble?"

Louise smoothed her hair. "Smack is fine. He peed on something and it started the fire in our house."

"Smack started the fire? But pee is water. How could pee start a fire?"

She promised she would explain everything to Molly later. Then she asked the fire marshal, "What about the gasoline? You said that your own inspectors found traces of gasoline."

He fished around in his pockets and drew out a pack of Marlboros. He prepared to strike a match.

"Don't you dare smoke in this apartment! Just tell me, what did the investigators say about the gasoline?"

He stood with the unlit cigarette dangling from his lip. "It seems the gasoline was from our own generators." He twisted his mouth in a wry grin, causing the cigarette to do a little dance. "If you recall, your electrical system wasn't working. To have any light to work by, we needed to bring in generators, and those generators run on gasoline."

"You sloshed the gasoline on our floors, then you found your own gasoline and accused us of setting fire to our house?"

He put his fingers to his cigarette in that odd way he had, with four fingers along the top, removed it from his mouth and held it at a tilt as if he had just finished a trumpet solo. "I don't recall anyone accusing anyone of setting fire to their own house."

"You said we fit the profile!"

He shrugged. "You wouldn't have wanted us not to investigate every possibility."

Her fury was limited only by her relief that no one hated them enough to splash gasoline on their house and toss a match. They needn't go to court. The insurance company would issue them a check and they could—what? Rebuild the house? Sell the land and divide the profit? How much better was it, really, to have the officials who ran your town accuse you of burning down your house as opposed to having other people set the fire? She wasn't clear-headed enough to consider any of this. All she knew was that she wanted this despicable man to leave.

She shooed him to the door. "If you have anything further to say to my husband or to me, please say it to our lawyer."

But the man refused to go. "Look," he said, "this might not be the best time, but . . . my boy? My son, Buddy?" He looked older, more vulnerable, as if his ducktail had lost its starch. "Someone told me you work at the high school. Buddy, he's getting to be a handful. Last year, they put him on suspension. Twice. Big kid, on the football team, thinks he can get away with murder." His expression implied both fatherly concern and backhanded approval of his son's behavior. "I thought you might be able to talk some sense into him. His mother and me . . . You know how it is. Kids will listen to anyone but their parents."

She was about to tell him to go to hell. How dare he ask for help when not three weeks earlier he had accused her of arson, a mistake for which he showed no inclination to apologize? But her heart went out to any child unfortunate enough to have this asshole for a father. "Tell him to stop by my office. If he doesn't, I'll try to remember to look him up."

"Really?" he said. "That's awfully nice of you." Or maybe: "That's awfully white of you." Louise couldn't tell, she already was pushing him out the door.

The first thing she did was call Richard. She almost asked him to come over right then and celebrate. She would have enjoyed laughing with him about the verdict of canine micturation and the fire marshal's chutzpah in asking her to help his son. But she wasn't sure that when the celebration ended, she would want him to stay.

Instead, she told him she had decided to take Molly to California. When they got back, he could have Molly for a few nights, if there was room for her in Ron Lowenstine's condo. The check from the insurance company would have come by then, and they could figure out what to do about the house.

And so, a week later, Molly and Louise get on a plane and fly to Oakland. They rent a car and drive to Imelda and Andrew's duplex. Although Imelda looks skeletal and drained, she is well enough to be sitting up in bed working on a paper on some aspect of topology Louise can't begin to understand.

"Look, Mom!" Molly points to the diagrams Imelda has drawn. "Don't they remind you of the tunnels and slides at McDonald's?"

Andrew takes Molly to the farmer's market, where she stuffs herself on the peaches she has missed in Michigan. Meanwhile, Louise is able to fill in Imelda on the fire and its aftermath.

"I'm not even going to try to resist an I-told-you-so," Imelda says, although when Louise starts to cry—she can't help it, she misses Ames so pathetically—she lets Louise rest her head on her bandaged chest.

By the time Molly and Louise drive their rental car back to the airport, they are surly with their mutual reluctance to leave. Louise is able to convince herself to board the plane only because she has so much unfinished business in Michigan, while Molly has her father to return to, and her best friend, Devone, and the fact that she is starting first grade in a few days. Louise stows their peaches in the overhead compartment and settles in for the flight. They do a few Mad-Libs and then fall asleep on each other's shoulders. Muzzy and out of sorts, Louise ushers Molly through the baggage claim and is surprised at how glad she is to see Richard waiting at the curb in his Corolla. *I'm still fond of him*, she thinks, surprised that mere fondness can seem so sweet.

"Welcome home," he says. She touches his leg and thanks him for coming to pick them up. "Hey!" he calls to Molly in the back seat. "You smell like peaches! I could eat you up in one bite, that's how delicious you smell!" Molly giggles and hands her father a peach, which he eats right then and there, juice dripping on his pants. "You do know that one of the things Michigan is famous for is its peaches," he tells Louise. "You could have gotten her peaches this nice at any market in Potawatomie."

On the drive back, Molly fills him in on the names of the puppies her friend Melissa's mutt, Smedley, has given birth to (poor Molly, thinking she has any chance to get a dog when her mother will forever see even the cutest puppy as a potential canine micturator). When Richard pulls up to the apartment to let Louise out, she almost refuses to leave the car. How absurd that he and Molly should be going out for dinner without her, or that he should take Molly back to Ron Lowenstine's condo to sleep. But given that the best Louise can muster for her husband is fondness, and given that she has judged Ames's fondness for Natalie an insufficient cause for him to stay married to her, she knows she would be a hypocrite to remain married to Richard. There is always the chance she might fall back in love with him. But she doesn't want to spend her remaining forty years married to someone she only feels fond of.

From then on, the apartment strikes her as intolerable. The night she and Molly get back from California, she wanders from room to room, trying to get some sleep. The air conditioner does little to make the stuffy rooms habitable. She moves from the mattress in her room to the mattress in Molly's room to the dusty, stained couch that someone donated to the church and Howie and Jack shlepped up to her apartment. Finally, she goes down to the basement and taps at LaShawnda's door until LaShawnda, hair tucked beneath a cap, peeks out and lets her in. Although LaShawnda's apartment still smells faintly of the sewage that backed up the week before, it's cooler than Louise's, and the presence of LaShawnda and Devone asleep in their rooms lessens her loneliness to the point where she manages to doze for an hour or two before LaShawnda gets up to go to work.

School isn't scheduled to start until the following week, but Louise decides to set up her office. The rug and posters she used to decorate the room the previous spring were destroyed in the fire. Purchasing replacements takes her half the afternoon, after which she wanders the school, stopping to say hello to any teachers who are setting up their rooms. She is surprised at how many of them have heard about her house burning down. The new librarian, a tall, thickset woman with a vowelly Swedish name, tells Louise she owns a cabin up north and Louise and Molly can use it to get away on weekends.

Buoyed by all this good will, Louise drives the short distance back to Meadowbrook Estates. Not only can she take Molly to the librarian's cabin, they can visit Louise's parents in Mule's Neck. Her father's seventy-fifth birthday is coming up. After all these years, it seems ridiculous to expect either of her parents to take much care of her. It's her turn to take care of them. She might choose to hold a grudge. Or she might choose to forgive them. Either way, it seems petty to base that decision on whether or not they cared for her. Being someone's child, like being someone's parent or spouse, isn't a matter of tit-for-tat. It's like giving to a charity—you don't decide to do it on the basis of what the charity has given you.

For now, she faces another evening alone, and she decides that after she freshens up and takes a nap, she will invite LaShawnda and Devone to a restaurant to eat a meal. She climbs the stairs to the third floor, wondering where LaShawnda might enjoy eating, and is startled to see a man sitting on the landing. Maybe Danté has finally gotten around to sending a repairman to fix the wet spot in the floor. Will she be pressing her luck if she asks him to fix the air conditioner as well?

"Are you Mrs. Shapiro?" The man gets to his feet. He isn't a particularly threatening person—an inch or two taller than Louise, hair as colorless as an albino's, lips so thin and white they deny his face whatever chance for color it otherwise might have had. He wears a black shirt and black jeans, which seem to float in space like the clothing worn by an invisible man.

"Yes," she says. "I'm Louise Shapiro."

"Are you a counselor at the high school?"

"A social worker. Yes."

"Do you want to tell me where you get off thinking you

know how to raise a boy better than his father? Do you want to tell me what gives you the right to get between a father and his son?" He lifts his hands, and she can see he is wearing a plain brown Timex, and it seems impossible that a man wearing such an ordinary watch could be anything but harmless. But he pushes her against the door. "Do you mind telling me what gives you the right to tell my son he should disobey his father and move to Chicago and live with a nigger whore and play nigger music at a nightclub?" Every time she lifts a shoulder, he presses it against the door. His face seems shuttered and expressionless. His eyes are green, like Ames's eyes, but colder and duller. There is a patch of hair above his lip, but she can't tell if it's a moustache or a spot he missed shaving.

"You're Parker's father," she says, surprised because he is so very much shorter than Parker. She hadn't been able to persuade Parker to tell her what about his father scared him, but she sees now it's the ugliness of his hate. Even after graduation, Parker couldn't bring himself to leave home. He told Louise that he and Grace were spending the summer working so they could afford to move come fall, but Louise wondered at the time if Parker would ever find the courage to break loose of his father, and she is even less certain now. "I'm sorry," she says. "I can see how upset you are. I would like for us to talk. Why don't we find somewhere—"

"Shut up!" He cups a hand against her throat, and the pressure makes her cough. She can feel her pulse throb against his fingers. His teeth are straight and white. A movie star's teeth. A singer's. Louise is terrified. What woman wouldn't be terrified by a man pinning her to a door? She can barely breathe, and she is afraid she will lose control of her bladder. But this isn't the first time she has come between a parent and a child. It's a dangerous place to stand, but as long as she is here, bearing his father's rage, Parker might make his getaway.

His father snaps her head against the door, and Louise instinctively jerks up one knee, but he lifts his own knee in time and pushes aside her leg. He is so close she can't tell whose heart she feels beating, but he doesn't smell of anything. Not aftershave, not sweat, not smoke. This makes him seem inhuman. Doesn't everyone smell of *something*?

"You worthless . . . Do you know how easy it would be for any of us to kill you?"

Yes, she thinks, she does know. He wouldn't even need to rely on whomever that icy "us" implies. All on his own, this colorless, odorless little man could crush the life out of her. Her knees buckle, and the only thing holding her up is his hand against her throat.

"Hey! Rosenkrantz! What the fuck?"

Someone yanks away the hand. And then, from where Louise sits crumpled against the door, she can see that it is Richard holding Parker's father by the collar, as a farmer might hold a barn cat by the scruff. Richard is barely the taller man, but he holds Parker's father with surprisingly little strain. He glances toward the window, and Louise guesses that if he hadn't boarded it up with plywood, he would have pitched Parker's father through.

"Take Molly outside!" he yells down the stairs, and Louise hears a voice she assumes belongs to Ron Lowenstine yell back: "Don't!" But Richard does. He pitches Parker's father down the stairs. Over and over the man somersaults, a clumsy burlesque pratfall, bones and joints bending in ways that bones and joints are not supposed to bend. Louise runs to the stairs just in time to see Lowenstine snatch up Molly and run with her down the remaining stairs. Richard seems to jump down the entire flight, where he lands astride Parker's father with one knee on his back, twisting his wrists behind his shoulders.

"You crazy, mean fuck!" Richard shouts. "Don't you dare touch my wife! Don't you ever touch anybody! You and fucking Elvis Presley! Elvis was a Jew! Elvis's grandmother was a Jew, and his mother was a Jew, and that makes Elvis a Jew! Elvis was a fucking white-trash Jew who sang black people music, and you had damn well better get used to it, you cocksucker Nazi piece of shit!" Richard calls up the stairs to ask if Louise is all right, and when she tells him that she is, he yells at her to go in and call the cops.

She stands there rubbing her throat. The door to the second-floor apartment opens and a man in a doo-rag peeks out, then slams the door. Louise fumbles with her key and runs inside, then runs to the window and looks down to make sure Molly is safe, which she seems to be, cradled in Ron Lowenstine's thick arms as he stands beside the dumpster with LaShawnda and Devone, so she finally calls the police, then runs back out to tell Richard they're on their way. He is still twisting Parker's father's arm behind his back and yelling crazy obscenities about Elvis and the Nazis. But when he looks up to ask Louise how long it will be before they get there, Parker's father throws him off.

Cursing, Richard runs after him, and Louise runs after Richard. If Ron Lowenstine hadn't been holding Molly, he might have tackled Parker's father. But as it is, Parker's father speeds off in his Jeep—it's small, and white, with no real roof or doors—and he only narrowly avoids crashing through a circle of teenage boys who are tossing a Nerf football around the lot.

When Richard comes back, red faced, panting for breath and dripping with sweat, Louise tries to put her arms around him.

"Isn't this what you wanted?" he shouts. "Isn't it? *Isn't it?*"

At first, she doesn't understand. How could he think she might have wanted a deranged person like Parker's father to attack her? Then she understands: he means she wanted her husband to prove he could beat someone up. It seems ridiculous that she might ever have wanted such a thing. But she has to admit she did.

The entire population of Meadowbrook Estates has gathered by then, and the crowd barely disperses to let the police cars through. Louise wonders if any of the cops will turn out to be the female officers who investigated the break-in at Ames's house, but all four cops are men. With an efficiency that impresses her, they take information from Richard, then from Louise, and then from Ron Lowenstine and those among the bystanders who saw Parker's father drive off. At the time, Louise thinks they are lucky they know who committed the assault. But considering what happens next, she wishes no one had known a thing.

What happens—they learn this later—is that Ira Rosenkrantz becomes terrified that if he ends up in jail, he might be tortured and abused by the same black and Hispanic prisoners he and his fellow guards have been harassing. He decides to flee to Canada, but he isn't about to leave behind his son, who will seize this opportunity to move to Chicago with his nigger whore. Parker's father stops at their house to pick up a few belongings and orders Parker to get in the Jeep. No one will ever know why Parker doesn't just ignore the man. He is too big to be overpowered, and his father doesn't have a gun. But Parker might not have known that.

In any event, Parker is in the Jeep when the police come screeching up. What follows is a high-speed chase, which lasts much longer than it otherwise would have lasted if

Parker hadn't been in the car. The cops don't want to cause a crash, although that's exactly what happens. Parker's father takes a turn too fast, and the Jeep flies off the road and hits a tree. Somehow, Parker's father is thrown clear, but Parker isn't. He doesn't die, not then. The police are right behind the Jeep, and they get Parker to the hospital. The doctors do everything they can to save him, but the damage to his brain is too severe.

Louise tries not to blame herself for Parker's death, but of course she can't help it. He wanted to move to Chicago, and she counseled him not to go. That was probably good advice. But if she had bothered to dig deeper and get a better sense of just how hateful his father was, she might have advised him differently. She talks it out with Richard, who claims the fault is his for not taking Rosenkrantz's actions at the prison more seriously, and with the therapist she eventually finds in Ann Arbor. She even discusses it with Parker, whom she often finds waiting for her in her office, even though he's dead. But logic doesn't matter. If one of your clients dies, you can always find ways to blame yourself.

Richard takes her to the funeral and keeps her from breaking down entirely. The casket is buried in the Rosenkrantz family plot in a derelict cemetery adjacent to what once was the family farm. That the day is sunny and warm makes the death of such a beautiful, talented young man even harder to bear. Parker's father is so diminished by grief and guilt that Louise worries he might slip through his manacles and escape, except that he seems too dispirited to run away. The two officers who have brought him to the cemetery seem more aware of the nature of the event than does the prisoner. They stand on either side of him, remove their hats, cross their hands before their belts, and bow their heads. One of them wipes away a tear.

Parker's girlfriend, Grace, is there with her mother and her aunt. The poor girl is crying so feverishly she has to be led away, although not before she slumps against her aunt and crumples to the ground. The funeral director hurries over and revives her, produces water for her to drink and a handkerchief to wipe her brow. Her mother and aunt support her between them and escort her back to the grave. The minister says a brief prayer. A flock of black birds wheels in formation above their heads, which reminds Louise of Parker's solo at the ice cream social, and she imagines him lying inside the casket in his thrift-shop tuxedo jacket and black Mystery Spot T-shirt, the question mark in white above his heart, and she sinks to her knees in the stubbly, untended grass and sobs. Rather than lift her up, Richard kneels beside her and holds her to his chest while she cries and cries and cries.

Everyone turns out for the memorial service at the school. Bess Moorehouse is there, and Beverly Booth, Ervin Rolle, and all of Parker's teachers. Louise doesn't see Mike Korn, but Matt and Dolores come, along with Floyd Goodman, who says he wants to demonstrate how much he deplores the kind of violence Ira Rosenkrantz represents. Parker's classmates come—Melody Hasbrouck, her friend Jen, even Lucas Beale. And Grace, of course. She still is so distraught Louise doesn't try talk to her—not that Louise is in any shape to talk to anyone, either—but she makes it her business to seek out the girl a few weeks later, calling Grace at her parents' house and asking if they might talk.

"Yes," Grace says, "I would like that." They meet at the diner, and after some initial awkwardness, they cry some more and talk. At one point, Grace reaches across the table and takes Louise's hand. "Parker appreciated everything you did for him," she says, and Louise nods, although what had she done but listen? In her own way, Grace holds herself responsible. She had insisted on stopping by Parker's house one afternoon to see where he lived, and his father caught them together, and even though Parker lied and said their relationship wasn't serious, Grace suspects she was a large part of the reason for Parker's father's rage.

After that, she and Louise have little more to say—or maybe they have so much more to say that they need to leave the diner right then or remain forever in each other's lives—so Louise pays the check and they stand to go.

"Oh, wait." Grace reaches in the pocket of her sweater. "I meant to give you this." She hands Louise a small flute, more like a recorder or a pipe, which someone has carved by hand. It has only two finger holes, and the opening at the bottom has yet to be rounded off. "Parker was making this for your little girl. He would have wanted you to have it." They hold each other, with the other customers looking on. "You're doing God's work," Grace whispers, "bless you," before she hurries out.

The case never comes to trial. Ira Rosenkrantz accepts whatever deal the District Attorney offers and reveals the names of his co-conspirators at the prison and the location of their stash of weapons, which turns out to be considerable, although it never is clear to Louise—or to the conspirators, Richard surmises—what they intended to do with all those guns. There is a shakeup at the prison, and some of the guards are fired, although Richard says nothing much really changes.

Louise is not one to find a silver lining in every tragedy. But because of Parker's death, as well as the subsequent revelations about the white supremacist cell at the prison and the connection between the bombing in Oklahoma and right-wing groups in Michigan, many of the militia units in the state disband or go underground. The radio station that allowed Mike Korn to broadcast his racist vitriol cancels his show; he continues working as a custodian at the high school but keeps his propaganda to himself. Louise supposes you could say her fears about the militia have proven to be unwarranted. On the other hand, her assault and Parker's death prove those fears were real. In many ways, it's worse not to know whether the dangers you face are justified or imagined. Each side suspects the other. Mutual paranoia can be the deadliest risk of all.

For a while after Parker's death, Louise considers moving back to California. The most dangerous of the extremists may have gone underground, but all that hatred still is out there, and eventually the madness will strike someone else's child. As careless as she has been taking care of Molly, she becomes that vigilant now. And what about the other kids like Parker? Shouldn't she do for them what she didn't manage to do for him?

The reporters come to town. If Potawatomie achieved a certain notoriety following the bombing in Oklahoma and the revelations about Timothy McVeigh's involvement with the militia, Ira Rosenkrantz's attack on Louise and the high-speed chase that killed his son bring the city a reputation for right-wing violence its officials can't ignore. The mayor and city council, as well as Potawatomie's more forward-thinking clergy, speak about "the need to cultivate religious and ethnic tolerance," and even though conditions don't improve overnight, they promise to change enough that Louise wants to stick around to see those changes through.

On Molly's first day of first grade, Louise and Richard drive her to the elementary school in Potawatomie and watch her skip to the entrance, turn and wave and struggle to open the heavy door and slip inside. LaShawnda drives up with Devone, who tries to squirm from her grasp as she tucks in his shirt. She whispers something in his ear. "Don't call me that!" Devone says. "I told you not to call me that anymore!" and Louise guesses that she called him his nickname, Pooh, and yes, it really is high time she gives up calling him that childish name.

The three of them walk back to their cars, then LaShawnda drives to her shift at the hospital and Richard and Louise head out to Stickney Springs. Richard has been back to the house twice since the fire, once to inspect the damage and once to show the premises to their insurance agent, but Louise hasn't been back at all. After so much recent suffering, does she need to be reminded of that earlier trauma?

Yes, she thinks, she does. She can't bear to stay at Meadowbrook Estates a day longer than necessary. The place stinks of mildew, the air conditioner *still* doesn't work, and every time she climbs those stairs, she braces herself to find some strange man outside her door.

As they drive past the Joyful Noise Church, then past Em's house, then past the Bankses' farm, Louise's lungs grow tight, as if they are again filling with the noxious odors of melting plastic and burning insulation. They pull up in front of the ruined house and Richard gets out, then leans on the van as if he, too, needs support. The fire trucks, the hoses, and all those boots have churned their lawn to mud. Shards of colored glass catch the sun and glint ominously. Louise tries to imagine coming back here to live. But she can't, not when her memories of Rod's dog peeing in the basement and Rod mauling her in the attic and the fire marshal asking her where she was on the day of the fire and her long hours of dreaming about Ames and crying about Ames would be as pervasive as the stink of smoke embedded in every square inch of the walls and floors.

She can't live without passion. But living *with* passion has exhausted her. She wants to rebuild her life. But she is afraid this craziness might flare again. Trying to live the way she has been living since she fell in love with Ames would be like living in that town in Pennsylvania where the coal mines caught fire and burned for years beneath the streets. The residents who chose to stay went about their business knowing that at any moment the ground might open beneath their feet and flames burst up from below. Does she feel passion for the man beside her? No. But she feels very fond of him. She probably even loves him. And right at that moment, it seems there are far worse possibilities than falling back in love with the father of her child.

Dolores and Matt walk up. Matt wears a T-shirt stained with what Louise thinks is blood until she remembers the signs for BANKS PICK UR OWN RASPBERRIES. Dolores carries a cardboard box. This is the first time Louise has seen her without an appliqué or a slogan across her shirt, and this makes Dolores seem oddly mute.

"Hey," Matt says. "We were wondering if you'd be coming back." He shakes his head. "Dog pee. Who'd ever think dog pee could start a fire?"

Dolores hands the box to Louise, then pushes the button in her throat. "For. Molly. To. Replace. The. Dumpling." Louise nudges aside the lid and sees not the rabbit she has been expecting but a silky brown puppy with ears bigger than the rest of it, eyes shut, mewling, pawing at its nose. She thinks of telling Dolores they can't keep a dog in their apartment, but Dolores would offer to keep it at the farm until they move into a house. And really, it seems foolish not to let Molly have a dog on the unlikely chance it might start a fire. Later, when Richard finds out that the puppy is a guilt offering from Floyd Goodman, he will wish they hadn't accepted it, but by then Molly will have become so attached to their bloodhound, Blooper, there won't be any chance of giving him back to Floyd.

"I'm. Sorry." Dolores says. "He. Was. Here. Right. Here. Among. Us. A. Murderer. A. Child. Murderer."

"Now, Mother." Matt takes her hand in his as if she were a little girl asking the neighbors for something it isn't polite to ask for. "We have been through this time and time again. At most, you might have served Tim McVeigh a beer. That isn't something you need to apologize for."

"I. Might. Have. Stopped. Him." She starts to cry. It has been five months since the bombing, and Dolores is crying about having given Timothy McVeigh a beer. "All. Those. Little. Ones." She removes a Kleenex from her sleeve. "Forgive. Me. Please. Forgive. Me."

"What Ma means is," Matt translates, "we hope you're coming back."

Louise looks at the house, trying to imagine it rebuilt. Even if Dolores and Matt did share a few beers with Timothy McVeigh, she has nothing to fear from either one. Em has been a better friend to her than Louise has been to Em. If she and Richard move back, Molly can continue caring for the birds. Louise can always take her to Potawatomie to play with Devone.

But that's what stops her. The idea that even if she were to take Molly to Meadowbrook Estates to play with Devone, LaShawnda would never feel comfortable bringing Devone here to Stickney Springs to play with Molly. If she and Richard have a second child, as Richard has said they might, they would be raising that child in a town where everyone

373

is Christian, white, and straight. Men like Timothy McVeigh and Ira Rosencrantz might be rare even in this part of America, but Louise can no longer be sure she is as familiar with the country in which she lives as she once might have claimed. For one thing, America is a lot more countries than she thought it was. And even within those countries, there are other, smaller countries, some of which are so tiny and isolated they appear to be inhabited by only one or two citizens, although those few citizens are so heavily armed as to pose a threat to the larger countries that surround them. Some of those countries Louise knows a lot about. Others she feels comfortable visiting. But there are countries about which she knows absolutely nothing, except, barely, that they exist. Maybe everything will work out in the end, and all these countries will figure out how to get along. For now, Potawatomie is the most daring outpost in which Louise is prepared to settle.

"We'll come back to visit," Richard assures the Bankses. "It's pretty close to Halloween—Molly will want to pick out a pumpkin. After that, we'll be back to get a turkey and one of Dolores's cranberry-apple pies."

Matt looks disappointed, but he holds out his hand for Richard to shake, and then thumps him on the back. "You two take care of each other. You hear me? You take care of him, Louise. And Rich, you take care of her."

It's possible that Matt has just said something as trite and offhand as "Have a nice day." But to Louise, he has just put into words a truth whose essence has been eluding her for years. "We *will*," she says—so forcefully that Richard turns to look. "Won't we?" She squeezes his arm. "Won't we take good care of each other?"

Tears come to Richard's eyes. He lifts Louise off the ground, and the force of his embrace brings back the panic she experienced when Parker's father pushed her against the door. To quiet this fear, she puts her nose to her husband's neck, hoping to inhale his deodorant and cologne, the soap they both use, the brown sugar oatmeal he and Molly ate for breakfast. The thick perfume of charred wood still hangs heavily in the air. But it comforts Louise to pretend that, like the bloodhound in the box, she can distinguish among the scents of her enemies and her friends, of safety and disaster, of passion, hate, and love.

ACKNOWLEDGMENTS

Although the characters in this book are fictitious, many of the events are based in fact. My deepest thanks to the following people for providing me with the information I needed to write this novel: Tony Alvarez, Eva Cameron, Jessica Carroll, Jeremiah Chamberlin, Marlene Higby, Marian Krzyzowski, Mark Levine, Tamara Lyn, Jerry Miller, Elwood Reid, Frank Siloski, Fritz Swanson, and—above all—Lisa Levine and Ed Rudder. I am also indebted to Daniel Levitas for his important book *The Terrorist Next Door*.

As usual, I could not have completed this novel without editorial advice from my generous readers: Charles Baxter, Suzanne Berne, Nicolas Delbanco, Susan Hildebrandt, Laura Kasischke, Elizabeth Kostova, Vesna Neskow, Maxine Rodburg, Adam Schwartz, Therese Stanton, Lynn Stern, and Joan Pollack Warren. Finally, I would like to thank my agent, Maria Massie, for all her good counsel, encouragement, and support; my son, Noah, for always giving me a reason to keep going; and everyone at Four Way Books for all their hard work, wisdom, and dedication.

ABOUT THE AUTHOR

Eileen Pollack is the author of a collection of short fiction, *The Rabbi in the Attic*, named in 1997 by the *Washington Post's Book World* as one of the editors' "favorite books of the past 25 years"; a novel, *Paradise, New York*; and a work of creative nonfiction, *Woman Walking Ahead: In Search of Catherine Weldon and Sitting Bull*. *In the Mouth*, her second collection of short fiction (Four Way Books, 2008), received the Edward Lewis Wallant Award, was short-listed for the Paterson Fiction Award and the Sophie Brody Medal, and received a silver medal in *ForeWord Magazine*'s 2008 Book of the Year Awards.

Eileen has received fellowships from the Massachusetts Arts Council, the Michener Foundation, the National Endowment for the Arts, and the Rona Jaffe Foundation. Her stories have appeared in *AGNI, Literary Review, Michigan Quarterly Review, New England Review, Ploughshares, Prairie Schooner*, and *SubTropics*. Her novella "The Bris" was chosen to appear in the *Best American Short Stories 2007*, edited by Stephen King, and was later made into a short movie. Her stories have been recognized with two Pushcart Prizes, the Cohen Award for best fiction of the year from *Ploughshares*, and similar awards from *Literary Review* and *MQR*. She lives in Ann Arbor and is the Zell Director of the MFA Program in Creative Writing at the University of Michigan.